McFALL

Other Books by Scott Nicholson

The Red Church
Drummer Boy
After: First Light
After: The Shock
The Home
The Skull Ring
The Harvest
Liquid Fear
Chronic Fear
Kiss Me or Die
Disintegration
October Girls
Creative Spirit
Speed Dating with the Dead
Solom: The Scarecrow
The Gorge
Cursed (with J.R. Rain)
Meat Camp (with J.T. Warren)

Children's Books

If I Were Your Monster
Too Many Witches
Duncan the Punkin
Ida Claire

McFALL

SCOTT NICHOLSON

PUBLISHED BY

47N●RTH

Text copyright © 2013 Scott Nicholson
Originally published as a Kindle Serial, September 2013

Published by 47North Seattle

www.apub.com

Amazon, the Amazon logo, and 47North are trademarks of Amazon.com, Inc., or its affiliates.

ISBN-13: 9781477849231
ISBN-10: 1477849238

Cover design by Inkd Inc
Author photo by Marie Freeman

Library of Congress Control Number: 2013943972

Printed in the United States of America

Grateful thanks to Angela Polidoro, David Pomerico,
Lexie Danner, and Death Cab for Cutie.

McFALL

EPISODE ONE

CHAPTER ONE

"Double dawg dare ya."

"Stuff it." Ronnie Day squatted on the top rail of the bridge, cupping his hands under the weathered plank to steady himself. The river twenty-five feet below was slow and black, as if it had just recently oozed out of a crack in the primordial past. It was early May, the first day of the year with even a hint of spring, and the water would be so cold that he'd chatter his teeth into little Chiclets of enamel. Assuming he made it to shore.

How do I get myself into these situations?

Easy. Dex McAllister was pretty much the Hitler of Pickett High School, and even the guys who didn't like him ended up living by his rules. The worst part was that Ronnie's best friend, Bobby, *did* like Dex. So while Dex taunted Ronnie with various slang terms for the female anatomy, Bobby just leaned against the bridge railing and chuckled, occasionally skipping a hunk of gravel across the current.

"You going to jump or just squat there like you're taking a dump?" Dex said.

"I'll take a dump on your head," Ronnie said. "Might improve your looks."

"I figured a Day wouldn't have the stones to go first," Dex said.

"What's that supposed to mean?"

"Exactly what it sounds like."

Ronnie glared at Dex, who took a drag on a Camel and made an exaggerated purse of his lips as smoke streamed out of his lungs and whisked toward the mountains. Dex was wearing a windbreaker with a McAllister's Bowling Alley logo stitched over the left breast, corded gym shorts, and pointy-toed cowboy boots. Bobby had baseball practice later that afternoon, even though it was Saturday, so he was wearing gray sweatpants, a stained Nirvana T-shirt, and a red baseball cap featuring the high school's highly unoriginal "P" logo.

Ronnie wore only a pair of nylon swim shorts. Suddenly he realized the other boys had never intended to go swimming—this was all a test of Ronnie's manhood. Part of Dex's little power trip was that everybody in his circle had to impress him by enduring rites of passage. Dex owned a Jeep, an ATV, three hunting rifles, and about six girlfriends who were dumb enough to be impressed by his dad's bowling alley. Ronnie got social cred only from stories about his up-close-and-personal experiences with the local ghosts, but he mostly kept those to himself. As everyone knew, the line between fringe cool and outcast wacko was way too thin. He wasn't eager to cross it.

"You guys don't seem to be in any big hurry to get wet," Ronnie said. The brisk wind off the water caused his skin to tighten and his nipples to harden into little dark points. He hoped Dex didn't notice, or he'd be sure to make a comment.

4

"I was first last year," Bobby said, like a guy who had nothing to prove and could care less about what Dex thought. Of course, Bobby could afford that attitude. He was a star pitcher for the baseball team and the drummer in the heavy-metal garage band that he and Dex had started.

"I'm growing a beard here," Dex said. "Hell, I'll probably get lung cancer before you make a move."

Bobby pushed up the brim of his cap and flashed his charming grin, the one he could use to steal away any of Dex's six girlfriends if he weren't so busy chasing Melanie Ward. "Come on, Ronnie. You know what they say. What doesn't kill you makes you stronger."

"Except for what paralyzes you," Ronnie said, buying time.

He wasn't all that afraid of the jump. The bridge was a popular summer hangout, even after the state had posted a diamond-shaped, yellow sign that said "No Swimming Jumping Fishing From Bridge." The lack of punctuation was bad enough, but what made the sign particularly offensive was that it was there because of the lobbying of the residents of Riverview, a nearby gated community. The high-end houses were populated by a bunch of wealthy imports who wanted to govern the Blue Ridge Mountains of North Carolina now that they had fouled Florida and New York beyond all salvation. The local kids had refused to surrender their turf to some measly piece of metal, but the sheriff occasionally drove over the bridge to uphold the new rules.

Ronnie had made the leap at least fifty times, and he'd never so much as skinned his knees on the submerged rocks. Even at its lowest in the heat of August, the diving hole offered a deep well of water. While upstream the riffle and rapids caused a persistent swishing whisper, the current here at the bridge was sluggish enough that even a beginning swimmer could handle it.

No, Ronnie wasn't afraid of the act of diving itself, although he always jumped feet first rather than imitating Bobby's athletic jackknife or Dex's boisterous cannonball. He was more afraid of what might be under the water.

Or *who* might be under the water.

"You going to jump, or am I going to have to push you?" Dex said.

"We should have brought our fishing poles," Bobby said. "Bet there's some fat trout down there."

Ronnie didn't want to think about a hook trolling the depths, snagging on to whatever might be roiling just out of sight. Ever since he'd watched Archer McFall disappear into the river—along with a whole graveyard full of dead folks—Ronnie had never gone into the water alone. If Dex and Bobby had been there that night, they wouldn't be any more eager to jump first than he was.

Ronnie took one tentative step away from the railing, tucking his bare foot into the notch of a wooden support beam. Dex wheezed a smoker's laugh and flung his cigarette off the bridge. "You're built out of backdown, Ronnie Day," he said.

"Hell with it," Bobby said. "We ought to go into town and cruise The Depot."

"A coffee shop?" Dex mimed looking at a wristwatch and yawned. "It's almost happy hour. I can sneak us a pitcher of PBR out back at the bowling alley."

"I can't get drunk. I got ball practice."

"And Ronnie can't drink because he's a fuzzy little cooter," Dex said.

"Not all of us are staying in Pickett County forever," Ronnie said, wishing he had a shirt. His towel was in Dex's Jeep, which was parked in the weeds at a little turnoff popular with the local fishermen. "Some of us need to preserve our brain cells so we can get into college."

"Ooh la la, listen to the man with a plan," Dex said. "Tell you what. After you get your square black hat with the cute little tassel and spend six months looking for a job, just come on down to the alley and I can get you a gig running the floor buffer up and down the lanes."

Ronnie looked past Dex to Bobby, whose face was expressionless, as if he wasn't paying attention to the conversation. Ronnie's dad was a carpenter, Bobby's a plumber. Besides owning the bowling alley, Dex's dad served as a county commissioner and was a big shot in the Chamber of Commerce. Dex was already getting his hand in various commercial interests around Barkersville and Titusville. His father was also one of the Riverview investors, and he'd plied the county planning board so that the project had gotten a free pass on a number of costly zoning ordinances. In Pickett County, one good-old-boy hand still washed the other.

As Dex had gleefully pointed out, "Your dads got paid once for that job, but my dad gets paid for the rest of his life."

Ronnie felt like throwing Dex off the bridge. That would do wonders for the guy's bowling jacket, which looked goofy with his cowboy boots and white tank top. But Dex had fifteen pounds on him, and Ronnie couldn't count on Bobby's help. His friend was staring off at the hazy gray peak of Mulatto Mountain. A boy had disappeared there a few years ago, but that was another thing nobody liked to talk about in these parts. Ronnie hadn't known the kid, but apparently Bobby was still bothered by it.

"I'm over this," Ronnie said, confirming what they all knew. "Why should I get soaked and freeze my ass off while you guys stand up here and—"

7

A car approached from the wooded road to the east. Bobby had enough time to get off the bridge before the car reached it, but Ronnie and Dex were stuck. Ronnie only hoped it wasn't the cops. Dex would be able to sweet talk their way out of trouble, but then Ronnie would be even more indebted to him. The longer Ronnie lived in this Southern Appalachian backwater, the further he was drawn into Dex's web.

The car was a black Lexus with tinted windows, way too fine for a patrol cruiser, even for the FBI or Secret Service. Ronnie felt naked despite his shorts, his embarrassment heightened because he couldn't see who was inside. What if it was some young babe ogling his scrawny white ribs and hairless chest? Since Bobby was safely by the side of the road, he ignored the car, but Dex leaned his back against the bridge railing and gave a cool flip of a salute. The Lexus slowed as it reached them and the driver's-side window descended.

Ronnie assumed it was some rich jerkwad from Riverview ready to ream them out for breaking the law. No surprise, Dex leaned toward the window to field whatever the driver had to say. Ronnie didn't hear the words issued from the interior of the Lexus, but Dex gave a nod and a grin. "Yes, sir!" he said cheerfully.

Dex waved Ronnie over to the idling car. Ronnie crossed his arms and slunk over to the window. Bobby paid no attention to the car or his friends, still staring off at the mountain.

"He wants to meet you, dude," Dex said, as confident as a stock broker.

Why would somebody driving some sweet wheels like this want to meet me? Ronnie felt more vulnerable than ever. At least it was a "he" instead of a woman or, God forbid, a hot co-ed from Westridge University.

Ronnie stood just behind Dex, as if anticipating gunfire. The man behind the wheel was healthy-looking and handsome, with one of those strong jaws that inspired confidence and made people want to hand over their money. His gaze was dark and impenetrable, but not cold. The man smiled, his eyes glinting with cheer. He looked vaguely familiar, but Ronnie decided it was just because he had the stereotypical look of success: a close shave, tan skin, hair trimmed close to the collar.

"You boys brave enough to go for a swim today?" the man said, his voice mellow and kind.

"Thinking about it," Ronnie said.

"I used to jump off this bridge, a long time ago."

"Really?" Dex said, already easing into brown-nose mode. "Couldn't have been too long ago. You're not that old."

The man gave an easy laugh. "Depends on who you ask. They've refurbished the bridge since then, put up some new rails and filled the potholes. But the river is just the same."

"No, it's not," Ronnie said, having no idea from where his sudden courage had come.

The man's smile froze in place and Dex scrunched his eyebrows into a glare as if to say, *"This dude is a mover and shaker, so give him respect. Haven't you learned anything about getting ahead?"*

"What do you mean by that?" the man asked Ronnie. "It says 'Blackburn River' right there on that sign, the one right below the sign telling you not to have fun on the bridge. The river's name is the same, but the other sign wasn't there when I was a kid."

"The river's different every second," Ronnie said. "It squeezes out from the rocks up there in the mountains and trickles down here, over and over. Every drop is new, and the river never repeats itself."

Dex gave an uncomfortable laugh. "Don't mind him, mister. He's just been studying too much poetry in English class. It's rotted his brain."

The man ignored Dex, keeping his dark, appraising gaze fixed on Ronnie. "An interesting observation. Not only scientifically accurate, but emotionally resonant as well."

Ronnie's belief that the past was far downstream was the only way he managed to hang on to his sanity. He was comforted by the notion that the ghosts in the river had long since been washed away to a new place, never to return. Of course, he had never told anybody the whole story about what he'd seen. Only, in his deepest sleepless prayers, God.

And even though he clung to the notion that the river had scrubbed itself clean of all unwholesome things, he was still worried about entering its cool depths. There were no guarantees in the realm of the dead. Unless you believed that death was the end. Ronnie sure didn't.

Dex eagerly changed the subject, not used to people saying "resonant" in his presence. "My name's Dexter McAllister. My dad's a county commissioner."

The man kept his eyes focused on Ronnie, who shivered from more than just the brisk May air. "So, are you jumping or not?"

"Not today," Ronnie said.

"He's chicken," Dex said, desperate to insert himself into the conversation. Bobby had ambled over from the bridge's abutment but was staying away from the Lexus.

"Don't blame you," the man said, smiling again and still speaking to Ronnie. "The river's new every single second, so you don't know what it will be like this time, right?"

Ronnie had that sinking feeling of déjà-vu. He was sure he'd never seen the man before, but something about him was so familiar . . . something about his eyes, maybe.

"You don't know what's in the river," the man said. And then his eyes glinted red in the sun.

Ronnie gasped and backpedaled, but there was nowhere for him to go except over the rail. He tumbled into space, away from the man and his red eyes and the past that should have long since been washed away. The moment of freedom was sweet and brief. His senses took in the trees whirring by, the saturated stones rimming the riverbank, the silvery sparkles of the sun off the surface.

And then he was in the water, the river sheathing him in its numbing frigidity, the bubbles against his ears like laughter, the current tickling his skin, all while gravity pulled him down down down ....

Where the dead things are.

Suddenly he was certain they hadn't moved on or been swept away. They had been down here waiting for him all these years. Now they *had* him.

Ronnie kicked and clawed and slapped, but he couldn't get any purchase. He couldn't tell up from down, although he was pretty sure he'd landed feet-first, because the soles of his feet stung with an electric intensity. On previous dives, he'd barely been able to touch the bottom and give himself a nudge upward off the smooth, slick stones below.

Of course, the river constantly shifted—*different every second*—and that was part of the dare, too. What if this was the year that the winter floods had tumbled a boulder into the diving hole? What if a jump resulted in a shattered spine? Would Melanie Ward go to the dance with some loser in a wheelchair?

What if ....

And then, almost miraculously, gravity freed him and other laws of physics took over, the oxygen in his lungs and stomach and bloodstream tugging him toward the glittering surface. He broke through with a whoop of exhilaration, both from surviving and escaping, while Dex and Bobby hooted and applauded from

11

high above. As Ronnie rolled over into a backstroke, he could see his two friends dangling over the railing, Bobby shaking a triumphant fist in the air. The Lexus was gone.

Easy breezy. Now Dex will keep his yap shut for at least a week. But that man . . . .

Ronnie didn't want to think about him. Probably some rich jerkwad from the development, that was all—a middle-aged guy who longed for a little of the youth and joy he'd traded in for a Lexus loaded with all the options. For him, jumping into the river was just another memory that had been swept along on the currents of time.

His shoulder slid against an algae-skinned rock. He was nearing shore. He rolled to paddle the last few feet, and came face to face with a bloated, bug-eyed corpse.

He screamed.

Death wasn't the end.

CHAPTER TWO

It was a horrible day for a funeral.

Winter had held on a little too long in the Blue Ridge Mountains that year, and the late frost had given way to a cold week of rain that swelled the creeks and churned everyone's hopes for spring into mud. The maples and poplars that had sent out tentative buds now seemed to be having second thoughts, shivering against the gray slopes. The rainfall drummed a weary rhythm against the canvas awning that covered a hole on the slight rise of meadow. The mourners crowded together more out of a desire to stay dry than shared sorrow.

Sheriff Frank Littlefield knew most of the assembled. The guest of honor, Darnell Absher, had been a clawhammer banjo player, and most of the county had sat down with him at one time or another to pick a tune. While some folks drew hard lines between bluegrass and traditional mountain music, Darnell always said he just plucked the notes out of the air and didn't care where they come from.

SCOTT NICHOLSON

Addie Mae Absher, the deceased's estranged wife, claimed those notes came straight from the devil's jack-in-the-box. But such sentiments hadn't kept her away from his funeral and whatever inheritance she stood to collect. She was only a minor suspect in his death, after all. In her knit cap and matching cardigan sweater, she looked far too frail to have inflicted damage on anyone, let alone a full-grown man.

"We offer Darnell up to the angels," Preacher Staymore said in his querulous voice, hunched under the awning like a question mark in his black suit. "He's got a bigger part to play now. Although he leaves sadness behind him on Earth, he's bound for eternal joy above."

"Amen," murmured a few of the two dozen mourners, barely audible above the steady rain.

Littlefield scanned the crowd. Even after thirty years in law enforcement, more than half of them in his current position as sheriff, he wasn't able to divine the guilty face of a murderer. He wasn't even sure Darnell Absher *had* been murdered. But this was Pickett County, and it never hurt to assume the worst.

Darnell's corpse had been found beneath a bridge that spanned the Blackburn River, his body half in the water. His skull had suffered enough contusions and lacerations for it to leak out what few brains he had left after four decades of imbibing bottom-shelf bourbon. The medical examiner, Perry Hoyle, said it looked like a clear case of Darnell falling off the bridge while suffering from his usual near-toxic level of intoxication.

Nobody really stood to gain from Darnell's death. He lived in a rented camper trailer out back of an automotive garage, and aside from his musical instruments, he had little worth stealing. His wallet was missing, but Littlefield suspected that had been scavenged by the teenage boys who'd discovered the body. What

14

worried Littlefield the most was where the body had been found: barely half a mile from the McFall property. Legends had swirled around the McFall family for generations, and they were blamed for every mystery and mishap imaginable. The last deaths on their land had happened years ago, and—with no one around to act as a reminder—the family had mostly been forgotten except for whispers around Halloween campfires. But since Littlefield had lost both a younger brother and a deputy to the McFall property, it still haunted him deep inside where he stored all his bad memories.

Preacher Staymore was winding down his eulogy, keeping it on the short side. The brevity was more a testament to his advanced age and the lousy weather than an inability to spin gold from sorry thread. Like most Baptist preachers in the South, Staymore saw funerals as a marketing opportunity, a chance to bring folks into the flock before they suffered their own terrible demise and subsequent descent into the lake of fire.

After the last "Amen" and just before old Stony Hampton tossed away his cigarette and started the diesel engine of his backhoe, Littlefield lowered the brim of his hat and braced himself for the fifty-yard walk down the gravel path to his Isuzu Trooper.

"Sheriff?" someone called from behind him.

He turned, annoyed by the water sprinkling down the back of his neck. But he managed a grim smile for Linda Day, whose chapped face peered out from the yellow hood of a rain slicker.

"Hello, Linda," he said. "How is the family?"

Littlefield really meant *How is Ronnie?*

Being the town's sheriff meant maintaining a professional distance while still being polite. Littlefield had learned that even the most innocent socializing could end up revealing useful information. He didn't have to worry about votes anymore, having already announced he was retiring when his term was up in December.

He wondered if he'd made the decision eight years too late. Still, he was already looking forward to the transition from collecting facts to forgetting them, especially in Pickett County, where most of those facts doubled as impossibilities.

"The boys are fine," Linda said, squinting against the rain, accenting wrinkles she'd earned the hard way. "Work's a little slow for David, but you know how things go in this economy."

"Ronnie said anything else about . . . ?" Littlefield nodded toward the muddy brown rectangle that held Darnell Absher's casket.

"No, and I wouldn't bring it up. The boy's got enough on his mind."

A little distance away, under the massive gnarled tree that gave the cemetery its name, Oak Rest, the Absher family was receiving condolences. A well-dressed man shook the hand of the Absher matriarch, Miriam, giving her elbow a squeeze like a professional in the aftercare industry. The man looked familiar enough that the sheriff was disturbed not to have a name for him. "You know him?"

Linda didn't speak, didn't even seem to hear him. She was too busy watching the newcomer, her mouth parted in a vacant reverie, a drop of water collecting on the tip of her nose.

Littlefield gave the man a mental rundown, as if cataloging him for the write-up of a suspect's description. *Caucasian, mid-forties, six-three, dark-brown hair, hazel eyes, tanned complexion. Last seen wearing a charcoal-gray suit with a powder-blue tie.*

The tan was noteworthy because it marked the man as an outsider. People in Pickett County didn't have tans in May, not after fighting six months of winter. Despite the hysteria over global warming, the early months of the year had seemed to grow more bitter and gray over the last decade, although Littlefield allowed that it might be his own personal perspective. He'd never had what

16

they called a "sunny disposition," but positivity didn't get you a tan, and no local man would withstand the ridicule of renting a tanning bed down at Betty's Brite Styles.

The man gave Miriam Absher a final kind word and moved on, followed by an attractive, petite blonde woman carrying a black umbrella. She was dressed in funeral fashion, as if she'd shopped especially for the occasion. Her pleated black dress extended respectfully below the knee while still showing off graceful calves sheathed by dark hose. She managed a regal balance in her high heels despite the mushy, muddy ground. Like the man Littlefield assumed was her husband, she'd marked herself as an outsider—in her case, with her poorly chosen footwear.

"It can't be him," Linda whispered.

"Can't be who?" Littlefield said, watching the couple hold hands as they walked down the gravel road to the cars parked along the highway at the cemetery's entrance.

"Archer McFall."

Littlefield frowned. That was a name that was no longer mentioned in Pickett County, by silent and mutual agreement. But Littlefield had noticed the family resemblance, too. "He's gone for good."

Archer McFall was a preacher who'd revived services at the little red church his predecessors had built by the river. Several deaths and disappearances had followed in short order. Littlefield had good reason to know Archer was dead, but that wasn't exactly the right word for the man, not in a place where the dead didn't always stay that way. Officially, he was listed as a missing person, and everyone was eager to assume he had drowned. The McFall property that stretched for two hundred acres along the river was held in trust for dozens of McFall heirs scattered around the country. Littlefield had been all too happy to see the family abandon the area.

17

But he didn't like the coincidence now staring him in the face: A stranger shows up in Pickett County just after a local man meets a violent end.

"When Ronnie settles down a little, I'd like to talk to him again," he said to Linda. She bit her lip and nodded, still staring at the man.

The sheriff headed down the hill, pausing under the tree to shake Miriam Absher's trembling hand. "Sorry for your loss, ma'am."

"The worst thing is he never changed his papers," she said. "That means *she* gets it all."

The old woman's eyes glittered with fury around her cataracts as she glared at her former daughter-in-law, who was still under the awning with a couple of Darnell's musician friends. Addie Mae Absher was in mighty fine spirits, considering the weather.

"I was under the impression that Darnell didn't have much," the sheriff said cautiously. He didn't want to insult the deceased's mother by implying that she'd bred and raised a shiftless, no-account weasel.

"Don't matter," Miriam Absher said. "She don't deserve none of it, even if it's nothing."

Littlefield gave her what he hoped was a respectful smile as he bowed. He hurried on, Miriam already venting her vexation to the next person in line. He wanted to learn more about the stranger, maybe even have a word with him. By the time he reached the edge of the cemetery service road, the rain had slacked off to a heavy drizzle.

Two Buchanan men leaning against the hood of a Ford pickup stopped talking as the sheriff walked past. The odor of alcohol around them was strong, but Littlefield had no interest in disrupting the ceremony for a misdemeanor arrest. His quarry opened the passenger door of a new Lexus and helped his wife inside.

Littlefield didn't quite break into a jog, but he accelerated to draw up alongside the man as he circled the front of the Lexus.

The sheriff tipped his hat. "Sorry for your loss, sir."

The man appeared surprised by the greeting. He met the sheriff's gaze, the insignia on Littlefield's hat provoking no reaction from him. "Thank you, but it wasn't my loss."

"My apologies. A friend of mine thought you were a relative."

The man chuckled. "If I was an Absher, I certainly wouldn't claim it, would you?"

The ancient Romans had a saying: *Speak nothing but good of the dead.* Back in high school, Littlefield had known it in Latin, a language which itself was dead. Even though the phrase was outdated, the sentiment was sound. After all, Preacher Staymore's eulogy had made Darnell Absher out to be one of the finest examples of Christian living that had ever walked the hills, despite all evidence to the contrary.

"All the old families are related in one way or another," Littlefield said. "I believe I have some Abshers for fifth cousins on my momma's side."

"If that's your circumspect way of finding out my name, I'll save you the trouble," the man said, extending his hand. "I'm Larkin McFall."

Littlefield forced his face to remain blank. *Linda was close to right.* As they shook hands, he shoved down the lid on the Pandora's box of memories that threatened to burst open inside him. Larkin McFall's grip was strong, firm, and cool, but it didn't stray into the masculine competitiveness that some people displayed with a bigger man.

"Did you know the deceased?" the sheriff asked.

Larkin gave an easy laugh. "'Deceased'? Are you asking as a sheriff or as a family member?"

Littlefield shook his head. "This is my community. I don't like to lose anybody."

"Even a bum like Darnell Absher?"

"You must have heard a different sermon than I did."

"A man hears what he wants to hear. But that doesn't change the truth of things."

"Do you always come to funerals of people you don't know?"

"Like you said, all the old families are related in one way or another."

A plaintive voice came from inside the Lexus. "Come on, honey, I want to change out of these wet clothes."

Larkin opened the driver's-side door and gave a last glance up at the hill, where the heap of grave dirt ran with brown rivulets. The sheriff looked past him to the woman inside the car, who had the sun visor down and was fussing with her ringlets of blonde hair in the mirror. She was pretty in an ordinary way, lean almost to the point of being gaunt, her eyes made larger with make-up. She was the kind of woman who was expected to ride shotgun in a high-class car—the kind you couldn't afford if you had to ask the price.

"A pleasure meeting you, Sheriff," Larkin McFall said as he slid into the driver's seat.

"Have a safe trip home."

Larkin grinned as if he were two moves ahead in a game of invisible chess. "I'm already home."

The door closed and Littlefield hunched down into the collar of his jacket. The Lexus started with a powerful but sedate rumble, and the vehicle pulled off the grass and onto the highway. The speed limit was thirty-five on the stretch along the cemetery, and the Lexus maintained what Littlefield judged to be a perfectly lawful speed.

Too perfect.

Perfect car, perfect wife, perfect handshake.

And a perfect little rectangle of a hole left in the rearview mirror, soon to be filled.

The voice came from so close behind him that he nearly jumped. "The McFalls are back," Linda said.

"Not for long," the sheriff said. "Not if I can help it."

"Maybe they never left."

As Linda headed to her ragged Dodge van, pulling her slicker tight around her shoulders, the sheriff called after her. "Bring Ronnie down to see me."

CHAPTER THREE

"I don't want you in no trouble with the cops," Elmer Eldreth said from his well-worn spot on the sofa. The Braves game was on, which meant there would be a row of empty Bud Light bottles on the coffee table. Of course, that was true of just about any show Bobby's dad watched, from "Dancing with the Stars" to The Weather Channel.

"I didn't get in trouble," Bobby said, pouring a glass of milk. The milk was on the edge of sour. "Don't you listen to anything I say?"

"Sure, I listen. And it's mostly bitching and moaning. You don't know how good you got it. Why, when I was in high school—"

Bobby tuned out the rant about how Ronald Reagan just about put western civilization in the poorhouse, a speech so well rehearsed that even his dad barely listened to it. Then the crack of a bat sounded from the television, followed by the roar of the crowd. Elmer forgot all about the important life lesson he'd been imparting.

He sat forward, squeaking a fart against the vinyl, and began yelling at the television instead of Bobby.

Bobby carried his milk through the mobile home to his bedroom. Ordinarily he would have watched the game with his dad—it was one of their few common interests—but ever since Ronnie had found the body at the bridge, Bobby had kept to himself even more than usual.

He pulled a wrinkled comic book from a stack on his desk. After six pages of *Spiderman*, he pushed it aside. Masked superheroes had been cool at one time, when the world seemed limitless, Vernon Ray was still around, and good always delivered the KO to evil, but now the whole idea just seemed silly.

There was a knock at the door, Mom's gentle tapping. Dad didn't knock, he banged or kicked. Or just shoved the door open, even when it was locked.

"Come on in," Bobby said, cracking his U.S. history textbook to make it look like he cared about his upcoming finals.

Vernell Eldreth entered, smelling of the bleach and lemon soap she used in her housekeeping job. She had not aged well. Her reddish-brown curls had been long and flowing in her youth, and that, combined with cute freckles and flashing green eyes, had turned the heads of every boy in Titusville. Most of the boys knew not to get too serious. It wouldn't do to get a girl pregnant when her folks were two missed paychecks away from food stamps, but Elmer had persevered and eventually won the prize. He'd been bitching and moaning about it ever since.

Vernell stood by the door, respecting her son's space. "How are you, honey?"

"Fine."

"You don't look fine."

I could say the same about you. She'd had a cardiac scare that had turned out to be a thyroid problem, and now she was on some expensive medicine to keep the engine running steady. Her girlish freckles had bloated into big, brown blotches on her face, and wrinkles creased the corners of her mouth and eyes. Her blunt-tipped fingers were chapped from years of scrubbing.

"I'm studying," he said, staring at the book as if he truly gave a damn about the Monroe Doctrine.

"It's a shocking thing, to find a dead body like that."

"I didn't really find it. I was just there."

"It came at a bad time, though. You got tests, the dance, and the conference playoffs. You don't need any distractions."

"A man got killed. I'd say *he's* the one that got distracted."

"It's harder on you because of what happened to the Davis boy all those years ago."

Bobby bit back his rage. If he acted like the pain was still fresh, Mom would "be concerned." His friend Vernon Ray Davis had vanished in a cave that had collapsed on Mulatto Mountain, and his body was never found. Bobby knew the cave was haunted, and he hadn't gone back there in years for fear that he might see Vernon Ray's ghost. Everybody else, including his dad, had developed a case of collective amnesia about the whole thing. Even the sheriff's report still officially listed his friend as missing, as if Vernon Ray had simply hopped a Greyhound to Kokomo or something.

From what Ronnie had told him about the McFalls and the red church, Bobby had decided Pickett County was some sort of Twilight Zone where you were better off not thinking too much.

"Mom, all I have to do is finish the school year, and I'm outta here. None of this will matter anymore."

SCOTT NICHOLSON

"Not then, but it does now. I'm old, but not so old that I've forgotten what it's like. Everything's just *bigger* now for you, more important. High school is life and death."

Bobby was uncomfortable with this chat, because it was turning his mother into a human being with memories, hopes, and fears instead of the stranger who made sure he had clean blue jeans for school. "If I don't pass this history test, it's going to be death, because you're going to kill me."

"All you need is a C. No pressure."

Elmer appeared behind his wife, smelling of beer, sweat, and hair oil. "He don't need good grades. He's getting drafted next month."

Bobby couldn't help glancing over at his baseball glove on the dresser. The leather had been carefully treated with Murphy's Oil Soap until it gleamed. A baseball was tucked into the webbing, the seams of the white orb showing. When he played ball, the glove was like a sentient part of his body. He was a superhero on the diamond, and like Spiderman taking off his mask and becoming plain old Peter Parker, Bobby out of uniform was just another kid from the trailer park.

"Coach Harnett said that's a long shot," Bobby said.

"The Braves sent scouts to see you. So did the Marlins."

"We were playing East Wilkes. They were scouting Hernandez, not me."

"Honey, be happy he has a scholarship," his mother said to his dad.

Bobby had inked a letter of intent to play at Appalachian State University, contingent upon qualifying academically. That was one reason finals were important. He wasn't even sure he wanted to go to college, even though App State was only an hour away. But he wanted to make his mom proud and shut up his dad, so he figured he'd put in a year and see what happened.

If nothing else, it would get him out of Titusville and away from all the ghosts and memories.

"Bobby's picked up four miles per hour on his fastball this season," Elmer said. "Once the scouts lock the radar gun on him, he's in. Even late-round picks are getting decent signing bonuses."

"If he signs, he won't be able to attend college," Vernell said. "And he might never make it out of the minors."

Bobby slammed both fists down on his desk, standing so suddenly that Vernell drew in an audible gasp. "I'm not a meal ticket," he said. "In two weeks, I'm graduating, and I get to decide what happens to me. The least you two can do is to stop talking about it like I'm not here."

Elmer's face reddened with alcoholic anger. "Listen here, boy. I've wriggled under houses in raw sewer to put food on this table. And as long as you're under my roof, I've got a say."

"Some roof," Bobby said. "A shitty stretch of tin that leaks in a hard drizzle."

"Goddamn it, don't you cuss in front of your momma."

Vernell tried to shrink back into the hall and disappear, but Elmer blocked her retreat. Yet Elmer didn't push her around any either. Bobby was five inches taller than Elmer, and although Elmer had the edge in weight, his was all hanging over his belt buckle, while Bobby's was bound in muscle around his chest and shoulders.

Bobby closed his textbook and shoved it into his backpack. He shouldered his way out the door, Elmer grudgingly giving ground. "You forgot your glove," his dad said.

"I'm not throwing tonight," Bobby said. "I'm studying."

Elmer tried a familiar guilt trip. "I was rolling a ball back and forth to you when you was in diapers. I played catch with you even when my back was knotted up from work. I tossed you batting practice until dark. I *made* you what you are."

Bobby was disgusted by his father's chronic beer breath and the faint smell of sickness that hung about him, as if his organs were rotting inside his abdomen. "You have no idea what I am."

"Please, Bobby," Vernell said as he passed her, patting him on the shoulder. But she didn't articulate what her plea was for. She'd always failed to stand up to Elmer beyond a token resistance, and her weakness depressed Bobby. Long after he was paroled from this cramped metal prison, she'd be trapped here in a life sentence with a man who didn't respect her at all.

As Bobby fled through the living room, the broadcaster droned about a player's batting average against left-handed pitchers. He wished he had a baseball bat. He'd shatter the screen and scream, "Foul tip!" just to watch Elmer's face turn purple.

He walked out into the cool May evening. The rain had diminished but the moisture clung to the new blossoms of spring, filling the air with a lush, sweet smell. He tossed the backpack into the passenger seat of his Toyota pickup, started it up, and drove away. He thought about popping the clutch and spinning gravel against the trailer, but Jeff Davis, the trailer park owner, would issue one of his prissy little warnings in the mail.

On Highway 321, Bobby immediately felt better. He plugged his iPod into the sound system and tapped the wheel in time to the Black Keys. He'd learned to play the drums on straight-up, four-beat rock-n-roll, and even though his chosen genre was now an endangered species, a garage rock band was much easier to form than a string quartet or a hip-hop ensemble.

Bobby had no intention of studying history. He could probably coast to a C just on memory, and even if he flunked, he didn't mind going to summer school. That beat hell out of working for Elmer's plumbing business. By the time Bobby wheeled the pick-up onto Taylor Lake Road, the tension had drained from his body.

When he pulled into the McAllister's driveway, the reality of his station in life slapped him in the face. Parked beside Dex's new Jeep was a Lincoln Town Car, a Mercedes, and a 30-foot bass boat. A dozen Eldreth-sized mobile homes could fit inside the family's two-story Tudor-style house. The windows were all brightly lit, even though most of the rooms were unoccupied.

Hell with it. I'm here to rock.

But as he dug into his backpack for his drumsticks, he couldn't help fantasize about signing a big, fat contract to play for the Atlanta Braves. First thing he'd buy would be a Jeep with even bigger mud grips than Dex's, and then he'd buy his mom a nice, classy ride. Dad could walk to hell and back for all Bobby cared.

The door opened before he knocked. Even though the McAllister home had a two-car garage, the band gear was set up in the basement. Mac McAllister had said he didn't want any vomit stains on his nice concrete floor, and besides, he'd added with a wink, "The closer to the devil you get, the better the music, right?"

"Yo," Dex said from the doorway. "You're early."

"Never too early to jam. Besides, if we're going to play 'Stairway to Heaven' at the dance, I've got to hone my chops."

Dex emitted a Robert Plant screech in the high registers, a sound like a possessed banshee mating with the wrong end of a rhinoceros. "I hear you, man. Let's rock."

He slapped Dex on the back and led him into the basement. Besides some weights and other workout gear, a widescreen TV, and a ping pong table, much of the space was occupied by Bobby's drum kit and stacks of amplifiers. All the money he had earned helping his dad had gone into expanding the kit. The drum kit wasn't quite on the level of the legendary John Bonham's of Led Zeppelin, but Bobby was more proud of it than of the no-hitter he'd tossed last month against Covington High.

Dex, as owner of the jam space, was the self-appointed lead singer of The Diggers, although his unappealing vocal combination of shrieking and growling had been compared to a full-moon midnight at the animal shelter. "Been working on a new tune," Dex said.

"Cool." Bobby sat on the stool and thumped the bass drum, rolling the sticks lightly around the drumheads to test their tightness. Soon he was lost in the rattle and thud, a world where the Braves and Dad and Melanie Ward and U.S. history were kept at bay by a sheer wall of sound.

Floyd Frady, the bass player, couldn't practice tonight because he had to babysit his little sister. Their lead guitarist, Jimmy Dale Massingale, was ten times the picker that Dex was, but he didn't have an original bone in his body. So Dex used the five chords he knew to craft a cacophony with a predictable rhythm that made it easy for the other band members to follow along. Dex had written several songs so far, most of them variations on "Gonna Do Ya," including the unforgettable "Gotta Digg It"—Dex made a big deal of spelling it "D-I-G-G" even though a listener would never know the difference—and "Whole Lot of Loving," which was a direct rip-off of a Led Zeppelin rip-off of the black blues masters. Bobby had suggested they spell "whole" H-O-L-E, since the band was called "The Diggers," but Dex said that was stupid.

Dex plugged in his Fender Telecaster and strummed a chord. A couple of the notes were out of tune, but he didn't seem to mind. He punched a phase pedal, ramping up the distortion so much that tuning no longer mattered, then stepped up to the mike in front of the drum kit. "Ya ready?" Dex bellowed, assuming an arrogant thrusting of his hip as he strummed.

"What's the tempo?" Bobby said, easing off until he was vamping the snare drum along with a splashy accent of the high hat.

"Four-beat, hard *rock*," Dex said with a sneer, as if there were no other time signatures or timbres. "Huh-ONE two three *FAWWWW.*"

Bobby fell into the rhythm as Dex strummed madly for a few strokes and then dipped his mouth to the microphone. Dex's dad had bought them a killer sound system, so Dex's vocals were clear even above their combined racket: "Once had a friend name o' Vernon *Raaaay*...."

Bobby filled in the back of the line as Dex cha-chunked and tore into the next line: "Can't say for sure but I think he was gaaay...."

Bobby faltered, his foot slipping on the bass drum pedal, but Dex didn't notice, caught up in his own joyful superstar fantasies. He strummed and sang again. "Got lost in a hole and never came back...."

Bobby stopped in mid-bar, the ride cymbal still ringing along with Dex's electric guitar. Dex barely even noticed the absence of the drums as he completed the stanza. "Some kinda monster pulled him into the black."

Bobby shoved away from the drum kit, knocking the high hat over. It fell against the snare and tumbled to the floor with a shivery crash. Bobby headed for the door, cheeks burning.

"Hey, man," Dex shouted. He stopped strumming but feedback squealed from his amplifier. "That last line needs some work, but it's got a solid beat."

Bobby turned, his fists clenched. "You can't sing about Vernon Ray."

Dex, seeing the serious set of Bobby's jaw, flipped off his amp and let the guitar dangle limply from its strap. "You're the one who said our songs were too much like jock-rock. I was trying to draw from personal experience. Do something real."

"Well, it's shitty. He's dead, and you're *still* picking on him."

31

Dex held his arms apart in mock indignation. "It's been five years, Bobby. The statute of limitations must have run out on your guilt trip."

The door opened behind Bobby and Jimmy Dale sauntered in, flipping his long, greasy hair out of his eyes. He was carrying a guitar case and a six-pack of Pabst Blue Ribbon, like a hipster redneck on holiday. "Yo, dawgs, what's the haps?" he said, and then picked up on the tension. "Bummer. Don't tell me the band broke up while I was out stealing some brews."

"We're just having what you might call 'creative differences,'" Dex said. "You don't reach the top without a little give and take. The Lennon-McCartney thing."

"Dex has another stupid song," Bobby said to Jimmy Dale.

"Just four lines," Dex said. "I need some help on the bridge."

"You need help on everything," Bobby said.

Jimmy Dale set down his guitar case and gave Bobby an exaggerated hug. "My man's in a mood. How about we smoke a joint?"

"Can't," Bobby said. "I got a history test coming up and I'm pitching in the playoffs next week."

"Aw, don't tell me you're choosing reality over rock-n-roll?" Dex taunted. "When do you really feel alive? When you're in *their* world, or when you're kicking out the jams?"

Bobby looked over at the drum kit. He'd actually started playing because of Vernon Ray, who had longed to be a drummer boy in the local Civil War re-enactments. In a way, Bobby was pounding the skins for V-Ray as much as for himself.

"To hell with it," he said, grinning at Jimmy Dale. "Fire it up."

CHAPTER FOUR

Barkersville was the nearest incorporated town to the McFall property and the red church, but Titusville was the county seat. Larkin McFall had decided he'd best start out big and get bigger instead of starting small and working his way up like so many McFalls had tried before him. He was a man who learned from the mistakes of others.

Bernard Gunter and Logan Extine were the county's biggest property attorneys, the first to learn about foreclosed property and short sales. They'd done pretty well for themselves when the housing bubble burst and now were taking advantage of historically low interest rates to add even more land to their empires. By Gunter's reckoning, they owned nearly twenty percent of the county between them, although most of the purchases were by dummy corporations with Charlotte addresses so that they could still play the part of small-town neighbors interested in the community good. Larkin loved working with men like them, even if it meant he had to forego the pleasure of subtly corrupting his subjects.

We all must make our little sacrifices to serve the greater good.

Larkin had selected 24/7 Waffle for their Sunday afternoon meeting. He didn't want to sneak around and make people suspicious. No, he wanted the town to open its arms to him. They were partners, after all—Larkin couldn't fulfill his mission here alone.

The crowd was a mix of after-church families in their polyester JC Penney finery, hungover youths, and retirees who seemed to be turning to dust even as their crablike fingers snapped at packets of sugar and artificial creamer. The waffle house served up the usual greasy spoon specials but also offered some healthier alternatives like yogurt fruit salad and whole-grain bagels. While Gunter and Extine went for the Trucker's Platter, Larkin contented himself with coffee and an order of hash browns, with plenty of ketchup.

"The McFall property's been up for sale for nearly five years," Gunter said, mopping at his perpetually sweating bald head with a white silk handkerchief. "Archer McFall was listed as the property's legal owner, which made things a little tricky."

"I understand he disappeared," Larkin said. "According to legend and the official police report."

"Yeah," Extine said, talking around a mouthful of scrambled eggs. His face was like a magpie's, his large nose making his eyes seem tiny. "We had to get a friendly judge to vacate Archer's claims to the property. Even though the other heirs couldn't legally have him declared dead, they found an obscure statute that waived his rights of interest."

"That's good," Larkin said. "I don't want anything to come back and bite us."

Larkin was aware that Gunter had fabricated bills of sale for at least seven of the twelve remaining heirs. Those seven were scattered across the country, and in one case, across the Pacific Ocean, and probably weren't even aware they were due a cut. No doubt they would have gladly sold out for less than the few thousand that Extine had listed on the contracts.

"You're in the clear," Gunter said. "All told, after the deed tax, you'll get all two hundred acres for half a mil."

Extine grinned, a bit of bacon stuck between his two front teeth. "During the boom, it would have gone for two and a half, easy."

"Times change," Larkin said. "A man has to change with them."

"I'll drink to that," Gunter said, hoisting a mock toast with his coffee cup.

The waitress came over, a pretty brunette who looked to be either a high school student or a college freshman. Barely legal, in other words, according to the arbitrary moral standards of the state of North Carolina.

"Refill?" she said to Larkin, holding out a brown plastic urn.

"No, thank you, but can I ask you a favor?"

She frowned, probably used to enduring the flirting of middle-aged men for tips. "I can't give away any recipes."

Larkin laughed. She had good, strong shoulders. So many teens slumped, but posture in a young lady projected confidence. "I'd never ask for secrets."

The young woman glanced around at the tables she was serving. "I only have a minute."

"I'd like to invest in this area for the long haul, but I want to make sure the young people have a reason to stay. Are your friends happy here, or are they all eager to escape to the big city?"

"It's okay here," she said, picking a safe answer. "Not many jobs."

"What about you? What are your hopes for the future?"

Gunter and Extine's eyes crawled all over her shapely figure as if they wanted their partnership to extend into the perverse instead of the merely corrupt. Larkin wanted to slam their faces into the puddles of syrup on their plates, but he stayed calm. He even smiled. Such weaknesses could be exploited if necessary.

"I hadn't thought about it," she said. "I guess I'll keep working here after graduation and maybe take some classes at the community college."

"You're a good waitress," Larkin said, hoping he didn't sound condescending. "I'm sure you'll do fine."

She took that as permission to go check on her other customers. "Holler if you need anything."

Gunter's eyes shone as if he needed *plenty*. Larkin spoke to him to yank his attention from the girl's swaying hips. "Any other obstacles on the development?"

"Things pop up," Gunter said. "But we're in pretty good shape. We pulled in Bill Willard, who developed Mulatto Mountain. And Logan tapped Mac McAllister, a local business owner and county commissioner. They carry a lot of water with the planning commission, so that will get us around some of the more expensive subdivision requirements."

Extine beamed at their cunning. "The bank pretty much gave us an unlimited line of credit, too. Everybody's on board."

"Think there will be any blowback?" Larkin switched from coffee to ice water, so he wouldn't be too wired for the day ahead. There was much to do. "Environmentalists, competition, or a snooping local media?"

"Not around here," Gunter said. "You get some university hippies from time to time, but they're busy with Wall Street these days. They don't get hits on their blogs about ridge-top destruction unless they're taking on the coal companies or global warming."

Larkin saw Extine's gaze shift out the bleary window, to the commercial strip that was as soulless and corporate as any in America. "Mr. Extine? Are you holding something back?"

"Well, we do have a squeaky wheel on the commission. Heather Fowler. Some tree-hugging dyke from the university who's against any kind of development."

"I don't think she's a lesbian," Gunter said. "She just hangs around with women because men are scared of her." He turned to Larkin. "Don't worry, we can handle her. She's pretty easy to marginalize, and if it gets right down to it, she's just one vote against four."

Larkin hid his amusement. "Anything else?"

Extine's tiny eyes somehow became even smaller, two black pinpricks beneath a hooded brow. "Your connection to Archer McFall may lead to some talk."

Larkin had wondered if they'd get around to that. One thing he'd learned was that people rarely wanted to talk about the most important thing, tiptoeing around the elephant in the room so it would sleep longer. Larkin adopted an expression that was a mixture of curiosity and concern. "What do they say about Archer?"

Gunter and Extine exchanged a weighted glance, as if neither wanted to speak of it. Finally Gunter, his plump lips shining with bacon grease, spoke in a lowered voice that was barely audible over the surrounding chatter and the clink of silverware.

"It wouldn't have been so bad if he hadn't been a preacher," Gunter said. "Reviving that old church and building a little congregation. You're from Texas, so you don't know what it's like in these parts. Mostly Baptist and Methodist, with a little Episcopalian mission work left over from the 1800s. But Archer was a fringe preacher, and people whispered that he was starting a cult."

Extine dipped his beakish nose lower and cut in. "A couple of bodies turned up on the property. The medical examiner said they were killed in animal attacks, and the sheriff went along with that story. But...."

Larkin gave the appropriate frown of dismay. Archer had made a mistake by using religion. While faith was a good weapon in anyone's arsenal, it ignited too many base emotions and aroused too much controversy. Religion was absolute—either you bought into it or you believed it was the root cause of all evil, suffering, and exploitation in the world. That might have been all well and good for the Catholic Church of a thousand years ago—and few had wielded the whip and the cross in such perfect tandem—but this was the Modern Age, a New Enlightenment.

Spiritual persuasion was no longer effective. The best conquests were performed through voluntary and eager participation. The buy-in.

It was so much cheaper to just purchase people's souls than to foreclose upon them.

"But what?" Larkin McFall said in response to Extine's unfinished sentence.

Again, both men seemed reluctant to speak. The waitress came by with the coffee pot and Larkin allowed her to pour him a refill. Neither Gunter nor Extine tried to look down her blouse when she bent over. This was a serious subject, apparently.

"Well," Extine continued. "Given the McFall history...you know how people gossip."

"The ghost stories," Larkin said. "Even my branch of the family has heard them. So you're saying we should back off these potential millions because of the Boogie Man?"

Gunter and Extine both sat up in alarm. Gunter was practically ebullient, pressing his ample waist against the table as he lurched forward, his paisley neck tie curling as Larkin's coffee slopped around the rim of his cup. "No, no, no," he gushed. "That's all in the past. People will talk, sure, but then they'll go back to their beer, their football, and their bills. Nobody has the energy to worry about old family grudges."

Larkin nodded. "Okay, then. Let's roll."

He flagged down the waitress for the check. When she ripped it from her pad, he looked it over and said, "Good handwriting. It's encouraging to see a person your age who values clear communication. What's your name?"

The young woman had obviously been trained that the customer was always right, even hundred-year-old grab-assers who sat at the counter all day working a ninety-five-cent cup of coffee. Her face was flushed from the oily heat of the kitchen, and Larkin hoped she would make her escape from this rural purgatory. Not that he had a personal stake in it or anything.

"Melanie," she said.

Gunter made a big display of reaching for the check. Larkin knew the man's playbook from front to back—he always researched his potential partners so he would know how to play them. Gunter was always there at the United Way campaigns, the mission-trip fundraisers, and the community education summits, but his tax returns revealed that charitable contributions constituted barely half a percent of his income. He was only generous when it offered deep dividends.

"Thank you for the excellent service, Melanie," Larkin said. "I'm Larkin McFall. I'll probably be coming here more often."

Her pretty gray eyes widened slightly at the "McFall," but she gave her on-duty smile and said. "I hope ya'll enjoyed your food."

Larkin left her a twenty-dollar tip. Cheaper to buy than foreclose.

CHAPTER FIVE

Sheriff Frank Littlefield sat down at his desk and looked around at all the junk he'd soon have to start packing.

Most of the piles of paper would stay for his successor—thank God—and the department memorabilia could probably stay as well, although undoubtedly most of it would end up in a county auction as soon as he was out the door. He'd take his Officer of the Year Award, which had been bestowed on him by the North Carolina Sheriff's Association in 2001, but he could care less about the collection of confiscated bongs. In his early years in the office, a drug bust had been a big deal, but then the murders and disappearances had started piling up, and skater kids smoking a stinky green weed had stopped seeming like such a priority.

Yes, he would soon leave this job, but he was pretty sure it would never leave him.

Officer Perriotte stuck his head in the open door. "Heading out on patrol, Sheriff," he said.

"You on the west end of the county tonight?"

"Yes, sir." The "sir" wasn't necessary, but Perriotte hoped to ride the transition with a newly elected sheriff, and since no one was sure who the candidates would be, he was working every angle. "Got my fishing pole and camping tent just in case the weather's nice," he joked.

"Can you do me a favor and cover Little Church Road? Check on the Day place while you're out there?"

Perriotte's cheerful expression froze. "The McFall property, you mean?"

All the officers knew that Littlefield's younger brother had died at the red church decades ago, and it had only been a few years since Littlefield and a female deputy had driven a vehicle off Little Church Road and into the river. The deputy had drowned. Her death had been the third fatality during what Littlefield referred to as "six weeks of hell." But the sheriff didn't want sympathy, and he certainly didn't like the look he saw on his officer's face.

"A McFall is back in town and we've got a violent death on our hands," Littlefield said. "It's probably just coincidence, but Darnell Absher wasn't found all that far from the McFall property."

"You mean this Larkin McFall guy? If you don't mind my saying so, he's too much of a sissy to get his hands red with murder. And what would his motive have been?"

"If you believe the legends, McFalls don't need a motive," the sheriff said, well aware he was in danger of sounding like he was suffering from early-onset dementia. Although he supposed it wouldn't be all that early. Christ, he felt a hundred and ten already.

"Okay, Sheriff, I'll give it a look. Do you want me to stop in on the Days?"

The sheriff waved a tired hand. "No, no, just do a drive-by. Make sure nothing's out of the ordinary."

"You've got it." Perriotte hurried off before he had a chance to gather more reasons for questioning Littlefield's competency.

Littlefield picked up the phone and dialed Hoyle's number at home. The balding little medical examiner had been threatening to give up the post for decades, even though he still worked part-time as a pediatric doctor. A county ME received a modest stipend that was nowhere near fair compensation for being on call around the clock. But Littlefield suspected Hoyle liked grumbling almost as much as he loved a good medical mystery.

"Sheriff, are you still up?" Hoyle said, having apparently seen the departmental number on caller ID. "I figured you'd be done with your milk and cookies and all tucked in by now."

"I couldn't find my teeth, so I couldn't eat my snack," he joked back. "And I forgot which pillow was mine."

"Sleeping alone is hell, isn't it?"

"At any age," Littlefield said. He didn't sleep alone every night, but he didn't need to tell Hoyle that.

"Just hope you don't get an enlarged prostate. Getting up and whizzing every two hours is for the birds."

"I can hardly wait," Littlefield said, hoping Hoyle didn't break into a marketing pitch for adult diapers. "Got anything new on Absher?"

"Just what I already told you. Multiple contusions consistent with a fall of more than twenty feet onto a hard surface—or in this case, multiple surfaces called 'rocks.' Cause of death is subdural hematoma. He was likely unconscious and the blood vessels in his brain didn't clot fast enough to give him a chance. Of course, if he'd been found sooner—"

"You don't think he died instantly?"

"The only thing that bothers me is that it almost looks like *too many* contusions. A couple of the skull fractures were on different sides of his head. I suppose he might have bounced off a big rock and struck a smaller rock, but it's almost like he injured himself and then climbed up the bank and dropped off a second time."

"Except he would have been unconscious after the first fall."

"Theoretically. Brain trauma is a tricky thing. At an ME convention, one doc told me about this man who accidentally drove the blade of a hatchet into his forehead. The blade lodged perfectly between the two hemispheres of his brain. He not only survived, he drove himself to the emergency room like that, the hatchet handle dangling between his eyes."

Littlefield rubbed his brow and wondered if his looming headache was psychosomatic. "If he was high on something, he might not have had a normal perception of pain."

"Still waiting on the toxicology report from the state. Everyone in town knows he had a history of alcoholism, but from what I can tell his blood-alcohol level was normal at the time of death. Of course, for Darnell, that meant about two-and-a-half times the legal limit."

"Well, I still don't know how he got there, but he sure didn't drive."

"That's your job, Sheriff—figuring out the stuff nobody can explain."

Yeah, and that's why I'm retiring. "Okay, fax me over the tox report as soon as you get it."

"Fax? Nobody faxes anymore. You really are an old coot, aren't you?"

Littlefield smiled and rang off with a "'night."

The phone had barely hit the cradle when Sherry, the departmental secretary and communications coordinator, buzzed him on the intercom. "Someone to see you, Sheriff."

Littlefield sighed. He'd always worked well beyond his posted office hours, mostly because he didn't want to sit alone in his small house looking for something to do. But he usually handled public calls and personal meetings during the day—a fact Sherry well knew, because she handled his schedule. This must be someone special.

Littlefield pushed the response button on the intercom. "Send him in."

"*Her*, sheriff. Her."

Damn.

He made a big show of staring at the clock on the wall as Cindy Baumhower came in, but he couldn't help glancing at her. A tendril of her flowing auburn hair was stuck in one corner of her mouth, looking fetchingly cute. But her brown eyes were serious. "You were supposed to call."

"Got a dead man on my desk, in case you hadn't noticed."

She pressed her palms on his desk and felt around. "Must be the Invisible Man because I don't see anybody."

"Come on, Cindy. You know about Darnell Absher. You wrote a story about him."

"And I did you a favor. Played it like an accidental death. Better be glad I'm on your side."

"Sleeping with the editor of the local paper sure has advantages."

"I don't recall us doing much sleeping." Cindy came around the desk and Littlefield stood to meet her. She puckered her lips and bent forward.

The sheriff drew back. "Not in the office," he said. "You know what a blabbermouth Sherry is."

"We're just about the worst-kept secret in Pickett County."

"Since I'm still on duty, you have to ask official questions from a safe distance." Littlefield had maintained firm boundaries during the first stages of their relationship, but lately he'd come around to an attitude of "to hell with it."

Cindy pulled from a pocket the spiral-bound notebook she habitually carried. She flipped through scribbles to a clean page and plucked a pen from a coffee cup full of them on the desk. "Any developments in the Absher death?"

"No, ma'am. We're still officially calling it an accident while we await the toxicologist's report."

"Any reason to suspect foul play?"

"Not at this point."

"Anything to say about the fact that he died near the McFall property and the red church, where half a dozen people have died violently under mysterious circumstances over the past fifty years?"

Littlefield swallowed. Cindy was an excellent researcher, but she also took a deep interest in the paranormal. Or at least she had back when ghost stories were more about folklore than idiots on reality TV shows yelling "Boo!" in the dark.

"We have no reason to connect this incident with any other incidents which may or may not have occurred," he said.

"You're saying 'we,' Sheriff. That's a distancing mechanism. Aren't you accepting full responsibility for this investigation?"

"As long as I'm the sheriff, the buck stops here."

Cindy made a big flourish of writing the quote in her pad. "Clichés are another distancing mechanism. One last question. Didn't the victim die near where Detective Sheila Storie's body was found after that crash five years ago?"

Littlefield clenched his jaw and muttered through tight lips. "Goddamn it, Cindy. That's not fair."

"All's fair in love and journalism."

"I wouldn't push the 'love' angle if I were you. That one has a way of vanishing faster than McFalls around these parts."

Cindy slapped the notebook closed. "Off the record?"

Littlefield sighed, feeling weariness sink deep into his bones. "Yeah."

"This McFall guy who came back to town. You know anything about him?"

"I ran a background check on him. Nothing turned up."

"I think we need to join forces on this one," Cindy said, with an enthusiasm that made him cringe inwardly. "I heard a rumor that he rented a condo for the summer and joined the Chamber of Commerce."

Littlefield didn't like the sound of that. "Staying a while?"

"I saw him walking out of the Gunter & Extine law offices, and they mostly handle property cases."

"As far as I can tell, he doesn't have any claim on the McFall property, although a couple of hundred acres are just sitting there waiting for someone to make a move. Wouldn't take much to buy off the other heirs. There are a lot of them, but they'd fold cheap . . . the land's worthless to them while the ownership is divided up. Besides, who'd want to live there after . . . after everything that never happened?"

"If this Larkin McFall is a developer, he picked a good time to hit the High Country," Cindy said. "The banks are practically giving away money, at least to rich people, and land prices are rock bottom."

"Do some digging for me," Littlefield said.

"I'm not on the county payroll."

He grinned. "Maybe I can slip you some contraband in trade."

Cindy puckered again and leaned her face close. She smelled of spring flowers, all ripe and faintly sweet. Littlefield glanced at the door to make sure no one was looking, and then gave her a kiss. She wrapped her arms around his neck and pulled him tighter, and he let himself sink into her inviting breasts. After half a minute, he came up for air. "Payment enough?"

"For now," she said.

"I'm off duty in exactly two minutes. Why don't you meet me out front?"

"You want to do it in the street?"

His grin swelled into a smile. She had a way of knocking back some of the years, making him feel young again. And not completely hopeless. "I thought we'd go for a ride. Out near where the body was found. I sent a deputy to patrol the area but this is a job I'd best handle myself."

"Ooh, Sheriff, you're so romantic."

"Just don't bring up Detective Storie anymore. It's not like I've forgotten."

Cindy must have sensed there was more to Storie's death than even she'd been able to dig up. Littlefield hadn't exactly taken a romantic interest in his late deputy, but she hadn't been like a kid sister, either. Their relationship had been one of an uneasy mutual respect. In that way, Cindy was like Storie—they were both more than willing to call Littlefield on his bullshit.

And they had to do it way too often.

But Cindy was on the periphery of the strange events that plagued Pickett County. Littlefield was in the heart of it. From his high school days, when his brother had died at the red church during a prank, all the way up to Absher's death, he seemed to be around whenever tragedy struck. He could fool himself into believing it was just a function of his job, but the Littlefields had been mountain lore for generations, right along with the Potters, Abshers, Mathesons, Aldridges, and McFalls. The "old families" had seen their share of horrors and suffered plenty of ills. In Littlefield's long experience in law enforcement, he'd come to believe that the simplest explanation was often the right one.

And his explanation was one name: *McFall*.

"We'll take my car," Cindy said. "I can bill for travel mileage and you won't get in trouble for having a civilian in your patrol vehicle."

"Go on, then. And don't smile too big if Sherry asks how the interview went."

"I'll tell her she can read about it in the paper like everybody else."

"Heck, she always knows more than me anyway."

After Cindy had left, Littlefield put on his hat and called Perriotte on the radio. His deputy reported that the Days were home and Little Church Road was quiet.

"Deader than a mule's balls out here," in Perriotte's words.

"Okay. Head on over to Green Valley, then. We've had a couple of break-ins lately and a show of force will boost civilian morale."

"Ten-four, Sheriff."

Littlefield got past Sherry without any teasing, and then drove his Isuzu Trooper around the block, followed by Cindy in her Toyota Prius. He parked in the employee lot behind the county courthouse and climbed into the passenger seat of her car. He was amazed at the quiet ride of the hybrid engine when it switched from gasoline to electrical power. He'd accused Cindy of being a "save-the-world sucker" when she'd purchased the car, but she was getting nearly fifty miles to the gallon while Littlefield seemed to drive from station to station.

As they cruised down the streets of Titusville, Littlefield was struck anew by how hard the recession had hit the town. A third of the storefronts were dark, a couple of them boarded up. The Chamber of Commerce had blamed the Wal-Mart built out on the commercial strip near the interstate for the decline in local businesses, but a general malaise had settled over the national economy and only bankers seemed immune. Everybody was biding their time until an opportunity came along, but no one wanted to make the first move.

"Starting to look like Deadsville," Littlefield said.

"Ad sales are way down," Cindy said. "We may have to let one of our reporters go."

"You've only got three, and I know you can't drop local sports. That's half your readership."

"I'll just have to work longer hours."

"You're practically married to the *Times* as it is."

"Nobody else is asking me to the altar," Cindy said, without taking her eyes from the street ahead.

Littlefield let that one pass. "If Larkin McFall is planning to invest here, he'd get a warm reception."

"People will look past his family name to his money."

"That's what I'd like you to check out for me. If he's got as much money as everyone is assuming—including me—then there has to be a track record somewhere. Business dealings, deed stamps, articles of incorporation."

"Good thing he's not a preacher. You can never penetrate those non-profit and privacy walls."

"Good thing he's not a preacher for other reasons, too."

Several of the McFalls *had* been preachers, and this had led to the legend of the red church. Ezekiel McFall had been a horseback missionary preacher in the early 1800s, and people still claimed to hear hoofbeats in the dead of night. His grandson, the Reverend Wendell McFall, lived on in ghostly legend following a scandal during the Civil War. He had hanged himself with the bell rope from the ugly, monstrous dogwood at the edge of the graveyard. In the years since, there had been several sightings of his ghost dangling there in the mist, and though the bell rope had never been replaced, a soft clanging sometimes resonated across the valley on Sunday mornings. The church had stood abandoned for decades until a local man started using it as a storage barn. He painted it red, a color that conveyed far too much symbolism.

When Preacher Archer McFall had returned to the area five years ago, he began holding services at the church, drawing all the old families into his congregation with an undeniable charisma that scarcely veiled his malevolence. His sinister revival had coincided with the "six weeks of hell," which Littlefield knew to be no coincidence at all. As a "missing person," Archer had never officially been linked to foul play. Never mind that Littlefield himself had watched as the man's resurrected body led a flock of ghostly followers from the cemetery into the river on a misty autumn night.

Not that he'd ever testify to such a thing, even if he were standing before the throne of the Almighty. Small chance of that happening—he'd sloughed off a thin skin of faith long ago, as the body count mounted with no sign of divine intervention.

As they left the outskirts of Titusville and exited onto the river road, Littlefield realized the past had come full circle: He was once again riding shotgun into the unknown.

CHAPTER SIX

"**Y**ou okay, Ronnie?"

Ronnie turned away from the dark window. His brother Tim was a straight-A student in the eighth grade at Barkersville Elementary, but he was pretty stupid about a lot of things. Ronnie couldn't be too hard on him, though. At that age, his own head was a whirlwind, tackling stuff like God and Jesus and Melanie Ward and algebra all at the same time.

Life was a little simpler now at eighteen. All he had to worry about was Melanie.

And the dead guy he'd found under the bridge.

"I'm fine," he answered.

"Want to talk about it?"

"Jeez, you're starting to sound like Mom."

"You can tell me. I understand better than anybody...about what you're looking for out there." Tim almost seemed to be taunting him, blue eyes bright behind his wire-rimmed glasses.

"I'm not looking for anything."

"You're looking for *ghosts*."

Ronnie didn't try to laugh it off by claiming ghosts weren't real. They both knew better. They'd been believers since their mother tried to lure them into Archer McFall's congregation. Archer had changed into some kind of monster in front of their eyes, and somebody had shot him right outside the red church … but it was like Archer had wanted it to happen, like he'd come back to Pickett County to fulfill some sick messiah complex. Creepiest of all, he *had* risen from the dead, taking his ghostly congregation with him. Sure, Sheriff Littlefield had covered it all up by claiming the church members had been suffering from drug-induced hallucinations, but Ronnie's memories were still horribly fresh, like a shovelful of dirt turned on an old grave.

"No," Ronnie said. "They're all gone. They washed away in the river, just like the legend says."

"But ghosts can't just be *gone*. That doesn't make any sense."

"Forget it." Ronnie moved from the window to where Tim sat at the desk in their bedroom, doodling on a sheet of lined notebook paper. He was drawing a vampire-zombie mash-up, with a fanged, bloody mouth and a balloon caption saying, "Smile! God loves you."

"And I thought I was the morbid one in the family," Ronnie said.

"No, you just happen to find all the dead bodies."

"This was an accident. Darnell Absher doesn't have anything to do with the past."

"Come on, Ronnie. I'm not a little kid anymore," Tim said, capping off his drawing by putting sunglasses on the creature. "You don't have to bullshit me."

"You're still too much of a kid to say 'bullshit.' Mom will blister your hind end for that."

"I'm too big to get spanked."

"Oh, yeah? I dare you to say that to Dad."

Dad was working late again and hadn't been around much. The hard winter had shut down construction, and now he needed to make up for lost time. Which doubly sucked, because Dad had started an addition to the house so Ronnie could finally have his own bedroom. The project was a few years behind schedule, but better late than never, especially since Ronnie would be living at home for his freshman year at Westridge University.

"I wish Dad would let us move," Tim said. "I don't want to waste my life out here in the sticks."

"We can barely afford to live here. Dad would be real lucky to sell this place even if he wanted. Besides, nobody's building houses anywhere. He'd never find another job."

"Well, first chance I get, I'm headed where the land is flat and the sun shines once in a while."

It was a corny move, but Ronnie reached out and fluffed Tim's hair. The dirty-blond strands stood up in feathery spikes. His brother shook his head in dismay and rubbed his hand over his scalp to smooth it down. Then he glanced at his reflection in the window. He froze, mouth agape.

"What?" Ronnie asked. He wasn't going to fall for that one.

"Don't you see it?"

"Yeah, right. A whole crowd of ghosts drifting across the garden. Or is it the Hung Preacher, climbing out of his noose to punish the sinners?"

Tim's voice fell to a whisper. "I don't know."

If the dork was acting, he was giving an Academy Award-worthy performance. His face actually went paler, which was difficult to fake since he'd hardly seen any sun since October. Ronnie moved over to the window again, blocking Tim's view.

On the rise beyond the barn, where the pasture gave way to forest, a series of lights bobbed among the dark trees. In the middle of summer, fireflies illuminated the woods by the thousands, but the weather was too cold for them now. Plus these lights moved in a concentrated pattern, drifting slowly across the ridge. Ronnie could only imagine them as torches, and in his mind they were carried by stooped things in sodden gray robes, faces hidden by heavy hoods.

"It's nothing," he said out loud. "Probably just headlights coming up the road on the other side of the hill."

"Those don't look like any headlights I've ever seen," Tim said.

Ronnie drew the curtains and turned away from the window, keeping his movements casual. "I don't care. You need to brush your teeth and get ready for bed."

"What if the ghosts are back?"

"Answer me this, genius. Why would ghosts need to carry a light? Can't they see in the dark?"

"Because they're scared of something," Tim said.

"Let it go."

"You can't treat me like a baby anymore. You don't have to protect me." His defiance hinted at the young adult he was on the verge of becoming. Ronnie wasn't ready for Tim to grow up. This was Dingle Dork, the Runt, the kid whose glasses fell off every time he jumped the garden fence.

"I don't have to protect you from things that don't exist." Ronnie swooped down and yanked Tim's cartoon from the desk. "Most boys your age have outgrown vampires and zombies."

"Give that back." Tim snatched for the paper but Ronnie held it higher, out of reach. Ronnie was only slightly above average height, but Tim hadn't yet hit his growth spurt. He was still a runt.

Tim rose from his chair with sudden fury, catching Ronnie off-guard. The backs of his knees knocked against the railing of

Tim's bed and he lost his balance. He landed on his back, his skull banging lightly against the wall. Tim clawed on top of him, reaching for the drawing.

"Okay, okay, demonspawn," Ronnie said, relenting. "Here."

Tim snatched the notebook paper away and clutched it to his chest as if it were a treasure map. He retreated to the foot of the bed, huffing in anger. All Ronnie had wanted to do was distract Tim from his obsession with old legends, and on that count he'd succeeded. But the little runt had scratched his cheek with a fingernail, and the wound stung something fierce.

Ronnie rubbed at his face. "You drew blood."

Tim calmed down just a little and managed a joke. "McFall needed a sacrifice."

"Be glad I'm in a good mood, or I'd pin you down and give you an Eskimo sunburn. Now go brush your teeth before Mom gets home."

Tim opened the middle drawer on the desk and slid the now-rumpled page onto a stack of similar pieces of artwork. They shared the desk, and Ronnie got the top drawer because he was oldest, but he didn't leave anything in it but schoolwork. He didn't trust Tim with his private stuff. Anything really important, he either hid in a dried-up old paint can in the tool shed or left in his locker at school.

The noise of a rusty muffler rumbled up the driveway. "Mom," Tim said, without emotion, and headed to the bathroom.

When the door closed down the hall, Ronnie eased open the middle drawer. He turned over the drawing of the monster cartoon and saw the name "Brandi Matheson." He grinned. That explained a lot. Not only was the runt getting those weird hormones raging through his system, he was sweet on a girl. Ronnie understood. He'd done the same thing with Melanie Ward, slipping her jokes and drawings and poetry before finally summoning the nerve to ask her out. He returned the drawing and went down the hall into the kitchen.

Linda Day was unpacking a paper bag of groceries, store brands of basics like potatoes, macaroni and cheese, tuna fish, and milk. Ronnie couldn't wait until he started his summer job, mowing lawns for Mac McAllister's rental properties. He needed to save for college, but since he'd be staying at home for at least one more year, he felt a responsibility to take on some of the bills.

"Hi, Mom," he said, grabbing the cardboard suitcase of beer she'd brought for Dad and sticking it in the refrigerator.

She didn't bother with a greeting. "The sheriff asked about you."

"What did you tell him?" Ronnie turned his back on her, stacking cans of pinto beans in the cupboard.

"That you didn't have anything else to say."

"They've been saying that Darnell fell off the bridge."

"The sheriff probably thinks it's weird that you found another body." Linda popped a Diet Sprite, a drink she wouldn't let her sons have because it was too unhealthy.

"It's not like I did it on purpose," Ronnie said. "I was just out at the bridge with the guys. It could have been any of us."

"Bobby Eldreth told the sheriff that a man in a car drove up just before you jumped."

Ronnie didn't want to think about the driver's burning red eyes. Just his imagination, that's all...or so he'd been telling himself. The last thing Ronnie needed was to believe in another impossible thing. He still had faith in Jesus, even though he had to hide it—he was already considered pretty weird by his classmates, and anything else that pushed him to the fringe was best kept a secret. "Just some rich guy from the Riverview development. He drove off. It didn't have anything to do with the body."

"Well, you know how the sheriff is. He likes to turn everything into a big conspiracy. Those Littlefields have been kooky since way back. A man like that should never have been put in a position of authority."

Ronnie didn't want to remind her that the sheriff had saved them all from Archer McFall years ago. Linda only remembered that Archer had tried to raise a congregation for the little wooden church around the bend, and that he'd skipped town over some controversy or other. The McFalls always seemed to be leaving under a dark cloud. "Well, I'm not afraid to talk to him, but I don't know anything else."

"What's it like?" His mother's brown eyes took on an unwholesome, hungry gleam.

"What's what like?"

"To touch a dead body."

Weird. His mom had touched plenty of dead bodies, especially given the Southern Baptist penchant for open-casket funerals. The mourners were expected to line up and walk past the deceased before giving the family their condolences, all while marveling over the fine condition of the dearly departed, who was "just sleeping."

He thought of Tim's bloody cartoon caption: *Smile! God loves you.*

"It was kind of squishy but rubbery," he said. "I guess he'd been dead long enough to bloat a little bit. I didn't look too close. Once I saw what it was, I just screamed my head off until Bobby and Dex ran down the bank."

They both heard Dad's big Ford pickup crunching up the road and shared a look. The conversation was over. David Day didn't put up with foolishness, and talk of dead bodies, ghosts, and old mountain legends never sat well with him. Linda pretended to be a normal mom, asking, "Have you and Tim already eaten?"

59

"We had some SpaghettiOs."

"I'll make your dad a ham sandwich, then."

The door opened with a squeak. The jamb was out of square, and the corner of the door rubbed each time it was opened or closed. "Going to have to fix that," David Day said for the hundredth time, almost to himself. "Hey, honey. Ronnie."

He put his thermos and metal lunch box on the counter and kissed Linda. He smelled of pine sawdust, metallic sweat, old coffee, and new beer.

"You're later than usual," Linda said to him.

"Got invited out for a cold one after work."

"Just one?"

Ronnie headed out of the kitchen, hoping to be gone before the Linda & David Show really got rolling. But his dad stopped him. "You'll want to hear this, Ronnie, since it affects you, too."

Ronnie braced himself. This could mean anything from Dad demanding a divorce to Linda being pregnant. But Dad was smiling, so it was likely neither of those things. "Got a real good job lined up. It's going to keep us busy past Thanksgiving, easy. No more piecing together a renovation here and a roof patch there. This is new construction from the ground up."

Even Linda managed a smile. "That's great, honey."

Ronnie felt some weight fall off his shoulders. That meant he'd be able to take a full load of semester hours and work maybe ten hours a week on the side instead of fitting classes around a full-time job. Life around the Day home would be a little less stressful, and Ronnie might even be able to save up for his own car instead of sharing one with Mom. His social life was enough of a hardship without the handicap of bumming rides. No wonder Melanie went out with Bobby more than she went out with him.

"That's really cool, Dad," Ronnie said. "What's the deal? I thought the housing market was dead."

"Well, every rainbow has a pot of crap at the end of it. I'll be working for a McFall." David's face tightened as he studied Linda's eyes for any reaction. Ronnie's breath turned to stone in his lungs.

"The one who just moved to town?" Linda asked.

David smiled again, but this time it was tight, a cruel jester's expression. "Didn't take you long to meet him, huh?"

"I just saw him at the funeral is all. I'd never heard of him."

"Larkin McFall," David said. "I asked him if he was kin to the Mama Bet branch, and he said he was a distant cousin. But somehow he ended up with the family place."

"And the church?" Ronnie couldn't help asking, although the abandoned church was now legally part of the two hundred acres of McFall property.

"All of it," David said. "That's one of the projects. He wants to put up a housing development there."

"But we're ten miles from town. Who would want to live way out here if they can afford a new house?"

"I don't care," David said. "I hate to see the community get crowded, but it's paid work. Bill Willard, Mac McAllister, and the usual gang are silent investors, apparently. That's good, because it'll keep the building inspectors from getting too picky."

Ronnie's throat was tight and he barely trusted himself to speak. "They'll have to leave the graveyard alone, right?"

David opened the refrigerator and tore open the carton of Budweiser, fishing out two cans. "All graveyards have a permanent easement on them. So the dead are guaranteed their rest." He popped one of the cans with a *whoosh* of spray. "Even the ones at the red church."

"I hope they tear that church down," Linda said.

"It's about to fall over on its own," David said. "A hundred and fifty years will do that."

Ronnie hated that goddamned church. It sat there on the hill just above the road, the mottled and mossy tombstones jutting from the ground around it like the crooked teeth of some sleeping monster. They had to pass it every day, and most of the time Ronnie could avoid looking, but whenever he couldn't resist, he usually saw a ripple in the old glass, a shadow darker and larger than geometry could justify, or the flapping of a loose shingle when there was no wind. Sure, it had been used as a barn for years before Archer McFall had revived it for services, and it had stood empty since, but it was still a sinister storehouse of unwholesome darkness.

Ronnie's faith had matured since those days, so he couldn't reduce anything to a simple battle of Good versus Evil. There were too many shades of gray, where one of those sides masqueraded as the other. But if Evil had fortified secret strongholds across the globe, the red church was certainly one of them.

David had already finished his first beer. He crushed the can and tossed it at the recycling bin in the corner of the kitchen, spattering wet stains across the vinyl flooring. Linda threw a dish towel at him. "Clean it up," she said.

David opened the second beer. "Got to get my strength up first."

"If you keep guzzling like that, you won't be able to work tomorrow."

Ronnie had endured enough. "I better check on Tim," he said. Neither of his parents paid any attention to him, already squaring off for the night's verbal brawl.

The bathroom door was open, and the living room was dark. In the bedroom, the overhead light was off but the desk lamp sent a cone of yellow onto the floor. Tim must have gone straight to bed. Ronnie's bed was on a raised platform that harbored bookshelves and a dresser beneath it. He kicked off his shoes, but when he pulled his shirt over his head, the breeze gave his bare chest a brisk scrubbing.

"Did you open the window, Runt?" Ronnie turned to see the curtains billowing. Tim's bed was empty.

No way. No way would he be that stupid.

Through the window he saw a flashlight beam bobbing across the pasture.

Tim was heading up the hill toward the flickering torches. The red church waited on the other side.

He recalled his earlier words to his brother: *"I don't have to protect you from things that don't exist."*

But it was the things that *did* exist that had him worried.

He put his shoes back on.

McFALL

EPISODE TWO

CHAPTER SEVEN

The church stood in silhouette on the hill, as if it had siphoned the color out of the surrounding dusk, congealing it into the deep, rich shade of old blood.

As the car rounded the curb, Sheriff Frank Littlefield was consumed by a fear that was almost childlike in its intensity. Perhaps "fear" wasn't the right word. What he felt was sheer terror.

"Looks like that church is about to fall over," Cindy Baumhower said from behind the wheel of the Prius.

"Slow down," Littlefield said, wary of the treacherous traction of the gravel road that wound beneath the base of the hill and into the valley.

"Is this where the car went off? The night your detective drowned?"

"Somewhere over there." Littlefield waved vaguely to the left, where the dark river wound somewhere below them. He couldn't pinpoint the exact location. Too many saplings had grown up, and the weeds were lush from recent rain. But he would never forget the sight of his little brother, Samuel, standing in the road that night, more than twenty years after he'd died. *That* memory was unchanged, the details as crisp as if they'd been recorded in high-definition digital video and imprinted in his DNA.

"You don't believe the church is still haunted, do you?"

"No." He'd told her about seeing his brother's ghost, and she had taken him seriously. So seriously she'd assembled a regional group of paranormal investigators to conduct a fruitless hunt. The team hadn't received permission from the McFall heirs, but Littlefield had let that slide. To him, the whole thing had just been a big carnival of technology. Did anyone really believe ghosts would leave a convenient trail of evidentiary breadcrumbs?

No, ghosts were like faith—you couldn't prove they existed, but you knew it when you experienced them. Strangely, they were part of the reason he no longer had faith in much of anything.

Picking up on his mood, Cindy slowed the vehicle. Littlefield forced his gaze to the summit of the hill. The sun was still clinging to the backside of the world, throwing a purple halo across the rim of the mountains. The forest came down to the edge of the cemetery, and the grave markers were nearly invisible in the river mist that hung across the weed-choked grounds.

Besides the additional years of weathering, the church had changed little since his last visit. The wooden cross atop the steeple had broken, leaving only a sliver of bare wood angling toward the heavens. The belfry was cloaked in shadow, but the old-fashioned windows, capped with stained-glass triangles, caught glints of the dying light. It was easy to envision them as the eyes of watching creatures—bats and rats and slithering reptiles.

Then Littlefield realized that *light* was glinting from around the church. Orange reflections flickered against the glass.

He'd intended to roll right on past the church and stop in on the Days. But he couldn't ignore suspicious activity, even while off duty. And Darnell Absher had died barely half a mile away just ten days ago.

"Pull in," he said to Cindy, inadvertently reverting to his "sheriff voice."

"Aye-aye, sir," Cindy said, veering into the church's rutted driveway. A steel cable was stretched between two stone pillars, from which swayed a scarred metal sign that read "PRIVATE PROPERTY." Because of the ghost stories, the church had become an occasional destination for bored teens who dared each other to go up and knock on the door. But the place was so foreboding that no one came back a second time, and the teens had found livelier places to drink beer, smoke weed, and fool around.

"Thought I saw something." Littlefield got out of the car, not waiting for Cindy, which caused her to yell in protest.

"Don't you think you need a ghost hunter if you're going up there?"

"You're not a ghost hunter," Littlefield said, although he waited for her to catch up. "You're an occasional paranormal enthusiast."

Littlefield had left his revolver in his Isuzu Trooper back at the courthouse, and now he felt naked and vulnerable. He didn't even have a flashlight. What had possessed him to come out here? Had he wanted to stare down the past because he no longer had much of a future to worry about?

"What did you see?" Cindy said. "The legendary Hung Preacher dangling from a tree?"

"I cut that tree down five years ago."

"Doesn't matter. If there are ghost people, there can be ghost *trees*, right?"

The church was about fifty yards up the barricaded driveway. The spring mist settled around Littlefield like damp gauze, chilling him in his taut gut. Frogs croaked from the mud of the riverbanks, and even the distant lights of the farmhouses set among the forest did little to quell the foreboding sense of isolation.

It was as if the church grounds and the entire ridge that comprised the McFall property had its own rules of geology and physics. Gravity was stronger here, night was blacker, and all the attendant forces inexorably tugged at anyone who was audacious or insane enough to approach the church doors.

The church's red color was almost a mockery of its original virginal white. In the night, it was the color of burnt motor oil. Littlefield fought an urge to grab Cindy's hand for comfort. He was the sheriff, and protecting this church was his responsibility. He didn't get to pick and choose his duties. Enforcing the law was all or nothing.

Unless that was just another of those lies he had told himself to give his life importance and meaning.

"What's that?" Cindy said, and Littlefield instinctively looked up at the belfry, bracing for a winged slice of darkness to tear from its roost and swoop down for blood.

But Cindy was pointing toward the trees at the edge of the black forest. Light flickered in a coruscation of yellow and orange among the trunks.

Littlefield lowered his voice. "That's what I saw from the road."

"Trespassers?"

"Those are either flashlights or torches. Or maybe Coleman gas lanterns."

"Looks like more than one person."

"You better wait in the car."

"Sorry. You're off duty, and we're on a date. So you don't get to boss me around."

"This might turn into a 'situation.'"

"Good. It'll give me something to run in Wednesday's edition of the paper."

"Sometimes I think you're only dating me for the scoops."

Cindy squeezed his arm. "I date you for the crazy monkey sex. The scoops are a fringe benefit."

She always gets her way. I'm getting to be a damn pushover in my old age.

He sighed. "Okay, but if things get dicey, stay behind me. If I get a civilian hurt while I'm out on unofficial police business, you'd have your headline and the county commission would have my ass."

And maybe you'd score an extra obituary.

The lights glimmered brighter and more frequently as the figures who carried them approached the church, picking their way through the trees. Another light, removed from the rest by thirty yards, bobbed down the steepest part of the ridge from the north.

Littlefield veered well clear of the church, passing between the old tombstones and worn gray markers. His trouser cuffs were soaked with dew. Cindy was close behind him. She uttered a sharp hiss of breath that trailed into a "*Sheee*-it."

"You okay?" Littlefield whispered.

"Stubbed my toe on a rock."

"Might have been a skull."

"Ha ha."

He took her arm to help support her. "If you'd waited in the car—"

"Hush. Hanging with you, I'm used to pain."

The lights had almost reached the edge of the forest now, and Littlefield thought he saw dark silhouettes moving in tandem with them. The lights pulsed with an uneven intensity. The lone, steadier light to the north was also closer, sweeping back and forth through the scrubby vegetation. Littlefield worked his way to the side of the church so that he was between the building and the forest.

The first figure emerged from the trees and held a torch aloft. It was made from a blunt branch topped with rags, and it gave off smoke that smelled of diesel fumes. The man holding it was dressed in tan coveralls and a broad-brimmed hat that threw most of his face in shadows. Another figure emerged, then another.

"Creepy," Cindy whispered.

Because of the mist and settling darkness, the three men didn't see the sheriff and Cindy. One of them grunted with effort, his torch swaying with motion, and then something hard clattered off the wooden side of the church.

Throwing rocks?

A second man drew back and hurled a rock, and this time glass shattered. "Hell, yeah," one of the men whooped.

Littlefield decided it was time to move. "Hold it right there," he called, his voice firm and calm.

He expected the men to flee, but the nearest just raised his torch higher. The movement revealed his face. Littlefield instantly recognized Stepford Matheson, a stonemason who'd done some work on the courthouse steps.

"Who's there?" Stepford called.

"Sheriff Littlefield. You gentlemen are trespassing on private property."

Not to mention that if the woods weren't wet from mist and recent rains, you probably would have set the whole mountain on fire.

"Since when did you want to protect this old church?" Stepford said.

"Yeah," said the second man, whom Littlefield recognized as Sonny Absher, Darnell's older brother. "Your brother got killed here, just like mine. Enough people done died because of this place."

"I'm sorry for your loss, Sonny, but your brother's death was an accident." The sheriff took several strides forward, assuming a position of authority. Now he could make out the third man in the group, too: Cole Buchanan, a scrawny scarecrow of a man who had recently served six months for breaking and entering.

"Just like Samuel Littlefield's death was an accident," Sonny Absher said. "Sure seems to be lots of 'accidents' round these parts."

Cindy, in defiance of Littlefield's orders, moved to his side so that she also stood between the men and the church. Littlefield hoped they would think she was a deputy. He didn't want any more gossip about him to make the rounds, although at this point in his career, probably no one gave a damn. Still, he had taken a stand and now he had to follow through.

"What are you fellows doing with those torches?" Littlefield asked.

"Came to do what should have been done years ago," Stepford said. "Burn the damn place down."

"There won't be any vandalism or arson on my watch."

"Then why don't you get gone?" Sonny said. "This isn't your fight. We got old scores to settle."

"We live by the rule of law here in Pickett County. Throw those torches down in the grass." Littlefield tried to imply that he had a gun, but he didn't want to look foolish if they challenged him. His only weapons were his brains and his mouth, and neither was as reliable as it once had been.

"We heard a McFall came back to town," Cole Buchanan said.

"He doesn't have anything to do with what happened before," Littlefield said. "He didn't even grow up around here. He's a McFall in name only."

"But as soon as he comes to town people start dying," Sonny said. "Sounds like a McFall to me."

"What are you doing in these parts, anyway?" Stepford asked, but Littlefield wouldn't allow him to turn the conversation.

"Drop the torches and go on home, and we'll forget about the trespassing and property damage."

"That church needs to burn in hell, along with all the McFalls," Cole said.

Cindy could keep quiet no longer. "Is it worth more jail time?"

"Who are you, Robin the Boy Wonder?" Cole said, snickering as he looked at something beyond the sheriff.

Littlefield was so focused on the showdown that he'd forgotten the extra light coming from the woods until it pinned him in its blinding circle. *My damned reflexes are giving out. I hope none of these guys have a gun, or I'm screwed.*

"Who's there?" Littlefield said, squinting.

"What's going on?" said a boy.

"Just a brat," Cole said. "The whole damn county's popping up out of nowhere tonight."

Sonny slammed his torch against the ground, snuffing it out in the damp weeds. He slung the wooden hilt toward the church, and it landed with a bang against the siding. "Hell with it," he said. "Let more people die, Sheriff. See if I give a shit."

Stepford doused his torch, too. Cole took two steps toward the building, and Littlefield braced to tackle him. The church was all pine, maple, and cobwebs—if the man's torch made contact, the whole thing would be ash within an hour.

Then Cole turned and flung his torch into the graveyard, where it tumbled end over end three times like some circus trick before bouncing off a granite marker and going dark. As the three men seeped back into the shadows of the forest, Littlefield turned to the boy who was holding the flashlight.

"Tim Day," he said, finally recognizing the hidden silhouette. "What are you doing out here?"

"I saw the torches. Thought it might be some creepy cult meeting or something."

You're one weird kid. But you live next to the red church. That would warp anybody's mind after a while.

"Don't tell anybody what happened, okay?" Cindy said to the boy. "These men were grief-stricken. People do crazy things under stress, and we should try to have compassion for them."

Footsteps pounded in the dark, accompanied by the sounds of wet grass slapping at cloth and hard breathing. "Tim!"

Tim's flashlight swung around to spotlight Ronnie Day. The sheriff glanced at the church belfry. *Just like old times.*

"Jesus, Sheriff, did Tim do anything stupid?" Ronnie said.

"No," the sheriff said, "but he seems to have appointed himself to the community watch."

"You dork," Ronnie said to his brother. "I scratched myself to pieces running through the woods in the dark."

"You didn't believe me," Tim said. "They were here, weren't they, Sheriff? I knew those lights weren't from ghosts."

"No, they weren't ghosts," Littlefield responded. He almost added the automatic "Ghosts aren't real," but that was pointless. These two kids knew the whole truth—they'd seen what had happened at the red church.

"We can give you a ride home," Cindy said. "We're headed that way anyway."

Ronnie snatched the flashlight from Tim's hand. "Sure, thanks. But drop us off at the road so we can sneak back into the house. Mom and Dad would kill this little runt if they knew he was sneaking out to the church in the middle of the night."

Littlefield wondered if Ronnie had caught the irony of his own words. The kids' mother had put them in danger *because* of the church. Because of a McFall. He hoped to hell things weren't coming full circle.

As they negotiated the tombstones to return to Cindy's car, Ronnie paused once more to play the light along the church steeple.

Making sure that the ghosts and monsters haven't come out to play.

Littlefield declined to look. If you didn't see it, it didn't exist. That was another type of faith. One that even he could get behind.

CHAPTER EIGHT

Larkin McFall burned the church on a fine Thursday afternoon.

The Barkersville Volunteer Fire Department had been invited to use the structure for a controlled burn, and it was a grand affair. The chief, Fred Smoot, started the fire in the belfry so the department could employ its new $800,000 ladder truck. Larkin found it amusing that a rural fire department had a five-story ladder, but it made for a good show and, besides, the taxpayers had funded it. He wrote out a check for a $10,000 departmental donation anyway, and Smoot, in full hazard gear, posed with him for the obligatory grip-and-grin photograph that would appear in the next edition of *The Titusville Times*.

The *Times* editor, Cindy Baumhower, introduced herself before taking the photograph with her digital camera. Larkin could read all the questions in her eyes, but Smoot pulled her away to snap some shots for the department's newsletter before she had a chance to ask any of them.

As the church continued to blaze, the hired help was serving up the catered barbecue that had been supplied by Larkin. A few dozen neighbors had stopped by the side of the road to gawk, so he waved them over to join the festivities.

"Just be sure to keep a safe distance, okay?" he said as he welcomed them. "Wouldn't want my insurance rates to skyrocket."

That drew a hearty laugh from Gunter, Larkin's property attorney, who was on his second helping of roasted pig. Mac McAllister was there too, taking advantage of the opportunity to distribute coupons for ten percent off the rental price of bowling shoes. County attorney Baldemar Francisco was the only person in attendance wearing a jacket and tie.

Cindy, now finished with Smoot, made a direct line for Larkin across the graveyard. Most of the guests had steered clear of the headstones, even though the last corpse had been interred decades ago. Larkin was impressed by the journalist's refusal to observe proper boundaries.

"Do you have time for a brief interview?" she asked him.

Larkin looked at the church, which was nothing more than a blackened skeleton of joists and timbers around a boiling sea of orange. Steam rose as the firefighters used their hoses to confine the blaze to the church's stone foundation.

"Anything to serve the community and the Fourth Estate," Larkin said.

"We're not an estate anymore," Cindy said. "We sold out to the highest bidder."

Larkin liked her. There wasn't a bit of backdown in her. He'd enjoy her as either an ally or an enemy. "I wish more people were passionate about being informed," Larkin said. "Great evils are perpetrated when no one cares."

"Really, Mr. McFall, this is a controlled burn, not the rise of a New World Order."

Larkin laughed. "So true, ma'am."

"Call me Cindy."

"Only if you'll call me Larkin."

"Only when I'm off the clock, Mr. McFall. Otherwise, it might be seen as chummy favoritism. A newspaper's only as credible as its reputation."

"Fine. I understand there will be some natural curiosity about a newcomer planning an expensive development here."

Cindy's tone became cooler and less casual as she removed a notepad from her blouse pocket. "Why did you decide to develop on this site?"

"As you probably know, it's a family estate that has been passed down for generations. But the local McFalls are gone, and I'd like them to be remembered."

"You're aware of controversy surrounding your family?"

Larkin nodded. A lesser man—a lesser character—might have downplayed her question by evading it with humor or hinting that only crackpots who babbled about Bigfoot and aliens taking over the White House believed in ghosts. Instead, he said, "I realize my family has a bit of a colorful history. But that's true of all of the old settler families in the Appalachian Mountains. Instead of burying the past, we should honor and recognize it, even as we move firmly into the future."

"So you see your development of the traditional family property as a progressive act?" Cindy's brown eyes sparkled just a little, and Larkin realized she was enjoying their intellectual joust.

"I don't want to get caught up in labels," he answered. "I'd just like for this beautiful mountain to be a home to as many fine and deserving families as possible. That's the best legacy the McFalls can leave."

"Aren't you taking a big financial risk, given the economy and the state of the local housing market?"

"Offer people something of worth, and they'll be willing to pay a fair price," Larkin said. "Money isn't the only currency."

"There she goes!" someone shouted, and a murmur went through the crowd. The flaming framework of the church gave a great shudder and collapsed, sending a volcanic geyser of smoke and sparks into the air. The firefighters, displaying their skill, tracked down any stray sparks that threatened to ignite the grass, then returned to hosing the perimeter.

Larkin looked down at the mouth of the driveway, where Sheriff Frank Littlefield leaned against one of the stone pillars, watching the proceedings from behind dark sunglasses, arms folded across his chest.

"Thank you for your time, Mr. McFall," Cindy said.

"Make me sound good, okay?" He winked.

"I can only write down what you say. It's not my place to judge."

She walked past the tables of food and the vehicles lining the driveway, heading toward the sheriff. Larkin wondered whether she would give him a full report or make him wait until the next edition hit the street. Right now, he had other...interests.

Larkin walked over to the table where Melanie Ward was serving up platters of barbecue, with slaw, baked beans, and seven choices of soda. He'd hired her for the evening, along with several of the cooks from 24/7 Waffle. A male teenager was helping her by stacking napkins and pulling canned sodas from cartons and putting them in an ice cooler.

Ah, the things we do for love. How endearing.

Larkin recognized the kid from the bridge, but he'd always known him. Always.

"Would you like anything, Mr. McFall?" Melanie asked him.

"No, thank you. I just wanted to say hello to your helper here."

Ronnie Day glared at him, and then flicked his eyes to the crumbling remains of the church. "Howdy," he said brusquely.

"Oh, do ya'll know each other?" Melanie asked.

"We've met," Larkin said. To Ronnie, he added, "I wish I had stayed around when you dove off the bridge. If I had known—"

"Gosh," Melanie said. "That was terrible. Ronnie's had the worst luck with things like that. It's almost like he's cursed."

The kid pressed his lips together in annoyed embarrassment, then turned to Larkin. "Like you said, you didn't know."

"Must be strange to see the church go down," Larkin said. "Growing up right next to it all these years."

"I'm glad it's gone," Ronnie said. "It was creepy and ugly."

Melanie gaped at him in mild shock. "It was a cute little country church, Ronnie. If they had painted it white again . . . ."

"I considered giving it to the local historical society for preservation, but I fear it would have placed a tremendous financial burden on them," Larkin said. "It was falling down and was a safety hazard. Many, many parishioners found peace and comfort here over the years, but as the Good Book says, 'All things must pass.'"

"No," Ronnie said. "That was George Harrison. The Bible says 'For all these things must come to pass, for the end is not yet.'"

Larkin was impressed. Perhaps Archer's use of religion as a weapon hadn't been foolhardy after all. He was reminded that he couldn't be consumed by hubris—each McFall had his own special gifts and talents.

"Well, we'll still be neighbors, Ronnie," Larkin said. "I'm thinking of building a house right on top of the ridge for me and my wife. Near the old Mama Bet homestead. The view up there is spectacular."

And I'll be able to look down on your valley, and all the valleys. I'll look down on the Days, Abshers, Buchanans, Potters, Mathesons, Greggs. All of the old families.

Mac McAllister came to the table, dumped his soggy paper plate into the trash, and asked Melanie for another barbecue sandwich. "Mighty fine party you threw here, Larkin."

"I'm pleased with the county's support of this project, Mac. I appreciate your personal help, too."

Mac beamed with pride. "What's good for business is good for the people of Pickett County."

A faint breeze arose, sending damp smoke across Larkin's face. Ronnie coughed and Melanie turned away. The fire department started packing up its gear. The church was now a heap of gray ash and black embers.

"I hate to see history go, but property values will improve now that the old church has been cleared away," Mac said, taking a sandwich from Melanie. "Once you get your white fence around the graveyard, pavement on the driveway, and a little bit of landscaping around the entrance, why, you'll be selling lots left and right."

"I don't want to get ahead of myself, but I'm eyeing some more property around these parts," Larkin said. "I would hate to compete with places like Riverview, though. I know many of our local leaders have a partnership there."

"We're always looking for new partners. Doesn't matter how many ways you slice it when there's plenty of pie to go around." Mac grinned at Melanie and gave Ronnie a friendly punch on the arm. "Ain't that right, Ronnie-O?"

"What's Dex up to tonight?" Ronnie asked, rubbing his bicep.

"Left him in charge of the bowling alley. Good to get some management skills at his age. You're still planning to work for us this summer, right? Mowing grass?"

"Sure," Ronnie said. "At my age, it's important to develop those kinds of skills."

Not realizing he'd been served a sarcastic remark, Mac said, "Yeah, I hope Dex doesn't waste too much time with that rock band. Fun is fun, but a point comes when you just have to grow up."

"I like their band," Melanie said. "They're good."

"You like Bobby, you mean. Don't blame you. Sometimes I wish he was *my* kid. Good-looking, a hell of a jock, a guy who's going places. If I were you, I'd nail him down before he heads off to college and all those co-eds get their hands on him."

Both teens reacted to that statement, Larkin noticed—while Melanie was blushing, Ronnie was trembling with suppressed anger. He filed that information away. He didn't have to be Archer McFall in order to exploit each of the seven deadly sins. Why stick to just greed when other opportunities were ripe for the harvest?

After all, like he'd said to the journalist, money wasn't the only currency.

Mac seemed to recognize someone in the group of people gathered around the heap of ashes. He mumbled an "Excuse me" and took a bite of his sandwich as he walked away. The firefighters were preparing to roll the department's ladder and pumper trucks off the premises. Sheriff Littlefield began directing traffic and waving drivers to the side of the road to clear a path.

Then someone screamed. A woman standing near the blackened stone foundation of the church pointed into the heap of smoldering embers.

Littlefield broke into a sprint, followed by several firefighters, who were slowed by their bulky turnout gear. A young boy pointed into the heap of smoking ruins as well, his eyes wide, and the people who had been dispersing suddenly formed a crowd, surging forward with single-minded purpose.

Larkin fell in behind Littlefield, his leather oxford shoes slipping in the drenched grass. Bits of words became audible from the murmuring crowd.

"What is it?"

"A *hand*?"

"Oh my sweet Jesus."

By the time Larkin reached the scene, Sheriff Littlefield had yanked a shovel from one of the firefighters and was digging in the steaming gray pile. He levered the handle against a pile of river rocks and up popped a black length of gristle with ivory-colored bones showing through here and there.

"Get back," Littlefield yelled. "Get them kids out of here. Fred, radio for an ambulance."

Larkin found himself standing beside Mac, who was cussing under his breath. When he noticed Larkin, he said, "Looks like this might set you back some. Just pure bad luck is all."

Littlefield let the charred human arm drop back into the ruins. No heroic measures could save this one.

Ronnie ran up, coming dangerously close to the still-intense heat before one of the firefighters caught him and held him back. The boy struggled in his grip, shouting. "Tim! Tim!"

Larkin was touched by the show of brotherly love. Ronnie had no way of knowing that it wasn't Tim who had died in fire.

Cindy Baumhower was busy taking pictures of the presumed crime scene until Littlefield shooed her away. The merriment of moments ago gave way to grim silence and whispered speculation.

"Nothing good ever come of that church," said a woman Larkin recognized as Lena Gregg. She was in her forties and had undoubtedly missed the church's heyday. But she was eager to dispense judgment nonetheless. "It's no surprise that church didn't go down without taking somebody with it."

"But we checked a dozen times," a firefighter said to Fred Smoot. "Inside and out, even under the floor."

"Must have missed him," came the solemn reply.

"Or it could be suicide. Maybe he snuck in after we torched it."

"The person could already have been dead," Mac offered, obviously eager for the simplest and least controversial explanation. "Some vagrant that crawled in there and died of a heart attack."

"You people stay back," the sheriff said, waving the crowd to the edge of the graveyard. All earlier respect had been abandoned, and people stomped over long-dead McFalls and Abshers with abandon.

Cindy made her way to Larkin, notepad in hand, camera dangling from a strap around her neck. "Mr. McFall, do you have any comment on the apparent death that occurred on your property?"

Larkin cleared his throat and hoped he was appropriately pale. "I'm shocked and . . . shocked and appalled. Let's just hope there's a simple explanation."

"When was the last time you were in the church?"

"I've *never* been in the church. I peeked in it once, and it was so unstable that I didn't dare step on those rotten old floorboards."

"How will this affect the future of your housing development?"

"You're grilling me like a police officer, Miss Baumhower. Perhaps you've been spending too much time with the sheriff."

"What if someone who knew about the controlled burn used it as an opportunity to get rid of a victim?"

"I'm afraid I can't answer any more questions until I speak to my attorney," Larkin said.

As if on cue, Baldemar Francisco stepped between him and the reporter. "My client has no comment."

Larkin had not actually retained the tall, curly-haired Hispanic, but he liked the man's suit. Sometimes, in a court of human law, that was all you needed.

CHAPTER NINE

"What's eating you, Ronnie?"

Bobby pulled his Toyota pickup into the parking lot at Pickett High, down near the football field where the grandstand partially hid the students from view of the main building. It was the last week of school, but graduation had been pushed back because of all the snow cancellations during winter. The sun barely broke through the tops of the tall white pines.

In the passenger seat, Ronnie crinkled his brown paper lunch bag. "This freaking peanut butter. Third time this week."

"I didn't ask what *you* were eating," Bobby said.

"What do you think? Every time I turn around, a dead guy turns up."

Bobby gave a morbid laugh. "Yeah, Melanie says you're cursed."

"Oh, yeah? Well, at least I'm not a frigging vampire."

"Too bad. You'd get all the squeeze you wanted." Bobby reached under the seat and pulled out a brown pint of whiskey he'd taken from the back of his dad's truck. "Here. You could use some of this."

"No way. I got a math test."

Bobby twisted the cap and the smell of the sweet, heady spirits filled the cab. Old Crow. His old man sure was a connoisseur of the finest bottom-shelf rotgut. "Well, you're twice as smart when you're seeing double." Bobby took a generous swig, gargling obscenely before swallowing. "Beats the hell out of Listerine."

Ronnie looked around, wary. Students streamed past them on the way to school, and the first bell was only five minutes away. "Don't you have baseball practice today?"

"I'll sober up by then." Bobby burped and made a sour expression. He jerked his head toward the window. "Hey, check out Amy Extine. Some sweet stuff, ain't it?"

"Not bad," Ronnie said.

Bobby actually thought Amy was a bitch. In ninth grade, she had poured Coke on Stephen Reynolds's frog dissection, causing the organs to turn black. Stephen, one of the smartest boys in the class, had gotten a D because of it.

But she was pure candy in her knee-high vinyl boots and tight sweater. She walked like she was well aware of it, flanked by a couple of her sisterly sycophants as she swished her honey-blonde hair from side to side. One of Amy's oft-stated rules was to always be friends with fat chicks so that you looked better by comparison.

"Maybe I'll ask her to the dance," Bobby said, gauging Ronnie's reaction. He knew Ronnie liked—well, was in *love* with—Melanie. Bobby didn't like to rub their occasional dates in his face. Senior year was tough enough already, especially for guys like Ronnie who were under academic pressure.

"You can't ask her to the dance," Ronnie said. "Your band's playing."

Bobby hit the pint of Old Crow again and tucked it back under the front seat. "I'm not asking her to the *dance*, you idiot. I'm asking her . . . ."

Ronnie looked at him as if he had no idea what came next.

Poor guy. No wonder Melanie is worried about crushing his heart.

"Yeah, well, I guess I'll be pretty busy," Bobby said. "But once the dance is over, the real dance begins."

"Five more days," Ronnie said, gazing up the hill at the ugly brick building with its institutional glass. "If we can hang on that long. Then good-bye, Pickett High, where brain cells go to die."

"What really happened, Ronnie?"

Ronnie gave him that confused look. "When?"

"When you were younger. You know, in that old church."

"Nothing," Ronnie said, in a way that meant *plenty*.

"Melanie said you saw ghosts there." Bobby's eyes stung from the alcohol and his head already throbbed a little. Whatever pleasant effects it had imparted had now congealed into an acidic fireball in his stomach.

"I don't want to talk about any stupid old ghosts." Ronnie's hand tightened around his lunch bag. "I have *real* problems. Come on. I heard the bell."

"Maybe you *are* cursed, Ronnie. Think about it. How many bodies have you found?"

Ronnie looked up at the school. "Four."

"Don't you think that's a little weird?"

Ronnie turned, exploding with a ferocity that fogged the truck's windshield. "Of *course* it's goddamned weird. But you were there when we found Darnell. Half the town was there when they found that guy cooked in the church fire. It's not like I'm murdering these people or anything."

Bobby gripped the wheel as if he were driving to nowhere. "But if you connect the dots, you're the common denominator."

"Not the only one."

"What do you mean?"

"McFall. Every single time, there's been a McFall around."

"You mean that slick asshole who drove off while we were on the bridge? The one Dex was practically slobbering over?"

"You can be tardy if you want." Ronnie opened the passenger door. "You've already secured your scholarship. Me, I've got to finish strong."

"Nice try, Mr. Smooth." Bobby wanted another drink bad, but damned if he wanted to end up drunk by noon like his old man. Besides, he really did have practice, and Coach Harnett had been busting his balls as they advanced deeper into the playoffs.

Ronnie sighed. "I think the McFall family is behind all this."

"You think he cooked that body they found in the church?"

Ronnie shook his head. "I don't know. I used to think the first one—Archer McFall—wanted me. Like as a disciple or something. My mom got all brainwashed by their little cult, and she tried to drag me and Tim into it."

Bobby gave in and pulled out the Old Crow. This time it didn't burn as it went down. When he held out the pint to Ronnie again, his friend grabbed it this time and took a dainty swallow. Ronnie coughed and stuck out his tongue. "Where did you get this snake oil?"

"Stole it."

"Maybe God will overlook your sin this one time. If it's for a good cause."

"If it keeps me from murdering old geezer Stribling in English, I'd say a higher purpose has been served," Bobby said.

"The rising seniors might think differently."

Bobby grew solemn. "You get into the religious stuff after that Archer McFall thing?"

"Maybe," Ronnie said. "I just didn't like being alone. With God, I know there's always somebody on my side."

"I'm on your side, man."

"Not all the time. You can't be there like God can."

Bobby looked at the polished leather baseball glove lying in the seat between them. He had a won-lost record of 13-2 as a starting pitcher for the Pickett High Pioneers, and he'd never once asked God for help with an inside fastball. Hell, maybe he could have gone 15-0. Maybe a little praying would have added fifty points to his batting average.

He giggled. Old Crow felt like battery acid going down, but it did the job. So why did he feel like crying?

Somebody banged on the driver's-side window. Bobby turned to see Dex McAllister's distorted face pressed against the glass. He was wiggling his eyebrows like a maniac, and the tip of his nose was smeared with mucus. Bobby rolled down the window.

"You guys making out in here?" Dex said. "The windows are all fogged up."

"Thinking about skipping out," Bobby said. "What about you?"

Dex yanked his newest addition to his roster of girlfriends, Louise Weyerhouse, close to the truck so he could wrap an arm around her. She smiled shyly, not used to being with the popular kids. "Nah," Dex said. "I need to pass algebra or I'll be sitting in summer school. Dad says I can't manage the alley if I fail."

"Need any help studying?" Ronnie asked, leaning across the front seat.

Dex grinned. "Louise helped me study last night." He gave her a kiss on the cheek as she blushed.

The second bell rang, and Bobby said, "Sweet. Another tardy on the record."

Ronnie climbed out of the truck. "Thanks for the ride. See you in History." He hurried up the hill, his backpack banging against his thighs.

Bobby thought about offering Dex some whiskey, but then he'd have to take another drink himself, and there was a long day ahead.

"Come on," Louise said, tugging on Dex's arm, clearly anxious about being late. She was in that shadowy group known as the "good girls," the ones who did their homework, weren't in Homecoming Court or on the cheerleading squad, and went to Meredith College or the University of North Carolina, where they married well and were never heard from again. Bobby had no idea why she was hanging around with Dex, a notorious bad boy and player.

Maybe it was true that girls always went for the bad boys. A Beatles fan he'd dated had told him that all the birds went out to dinner with Paul but ended up going home with John. Not that it was any of his business. He couldn't even manage his own relationships, much less solve other people's problems.

"You going to skip or not?" Dex said, looking around the rows of silent cars.

"Haven't decided."

"Got a quiz in first period, so I'd better roll," Dex said. "See you at band practice."

Bobby nodded. As they walked away, Dex doing something to cause Louise to squeal in protest, Bobby got out of the truck and stretched. He popped a TicTac to hide his booze-breath, locked the truck, and stooped to look under the engine compartment to check on his latest leak. A black circle of oil had already collected, and a fat drop hung from the oil pan. There went another hundred bucks.

Bobby started around the grandstand, where a paved path led to a set of concrete stairs. Nobody but the nerds and teachers used the stairs. A dirt path offered a more direct but steeper route to the main building from the parking lot. The gymnasium was set partially into the side of the hill, and beyond that was the baseball diamond. While the football stadium held crowds of thousands, the metal bleachers behind the backstop might play host to two hundred on a sunny day.

Bobby passed the stairs and continued to the baseball field. He'd played all the major sports—linebacker on the football team, small forward in hoops—but he was most at home on the diamond, and it showed. It was where he'd earned his athletic scholarship, after all. The outfield grass was cropped close, greener than the rest of the school's lawns, dew glinting in the dawn. The foul lines were freshly chalked and as precise as anything in Mrs. Matheson's geometry class. A grid was scratched in the dirt around home plate, which Coach Harnett obsessively raked.

Bobby sat down on the bottom bleacher, just behind the backstop. He imagined a scout sitting here watching him pitch and wondered how he would grade out on mechanics, ball movement, and those obscure "intangibles" that ranged from the way he glared at the batter to the subtle way he worked the umpire.

"Beautiful field, isn't it?" came a voice from the dugout.

The low sun cast the concrete-block dugout in severe shadows, making it hard to see. Bobby thought he was busted, that Principal Gladstone had sent out the Goon Squad to bring in stragglers. But the voice continued. "But it's the game within the game that matters."

Bobby walked to the edge of the dugout to see who it was. As he got closer, he realized it was the McFall guy, the one from the bridge. The man was sitting on the wooden bench, wearing a jacket and tie, legs crossed as if he had all the time in the world.

What's he doing here on a school morning? If Gladstone finds him without that cute little visitor badge, he'll call the cops.

"You're Bobby Eldreth," McFall said. "The plumber's son."

"Yeah. You were at the bridge that morning."

"I've read your clippings. You threw a two-hitter in the first round of the playoffs."

"Just got lucky, I guess."

"I know, I know, it's the jock thing to say you couldn't have done it without the help of your teammates, the support of the fans, blah blah blah," McFall said. "But when you're out there on the mound, with a full count and the other team's star slugger digging in against you, where's the crowd then? You don't even know anyone else is there, do you?"

Bobby swallowed. The whiskey headache hit him hard in the temples. "I . . . I guess I never thought about it."

"You have a special talent, Bobby. You're in luck, because it happens to be one that the world values. I hear your dad is a skilled plumber, but do they televise his toilet installations or when he roto-roots a sewer line? Does anybody care if he has to wade through a mile of shit for a paycheck?"

Bobby wasn't sure whether McFall was praising him or shooting down his dad. He didn't trust himself to speak.

"Sit down." McFall patted the bench beside him and Bobby wondered if the guy was some kind of pervert.

"I'm supposed to be in class."

"Me, too," McFall said, smiling. If he was a pervert, he sure broke all the stereotypes. He had a smile that must have cost ten grand and a fat golden wedding ring. "But the best education is found outside the lines, don't you think?"

"Guess so."

"Big game coming up tomorrow, right?"

Bobby nodded and looked back at the mound. He couldn't even count the number of times he had banged his cleats against the pitching rubber to clear the mud. McFall was right. Out there, the rest of the world didn't exist. It was a zone where he dwelled alone, him and the batter. In a way, even the opponent didn't matter, because ultimately it was Bobby against his own limitations.

"What if I could guarantee you a shutout win? Pickett would advance to the state playoffs, you'd headline the sports section in the local papers, and I'm sure Amy Extine would go to the dance with you."

Bobby's fists balled involuntarily. "How do you know about Amy?"

"Relax. I'm friends with her dad. She's mentioned your name and . . . well, believe it or not, I was young once, too."

"What do mean by 'guarantee'?" The guy was obviously loaded. Was he going to bribe the umps or something? Nobody took bets on high-school baseball games, and he'd never heard of Pickett County having bookies.

"Let's just say it's a philosophical question. You've spent a lot of your life practicing, and you know success takes sacrifice. I believe your coach employs the highly unoriginal motto of 'No pain, no gain.'"

"I play mostly because it's fun." Bobby's eyes burned from the liquor. McFall appeared to be studying him.

"Don't bullshit me, Bobby. When you're holding the ball and everyone's watching, you're the lead singer. You're the rock star. You like the high and you like the power and you like the acclaim. You wouldn't be human if you didn't."

"I don't care if we win or lose," Bobby said. "If we lose, the season will be over. No more pressure."

"Sure, you've already got your scholarship either way." McFall stood and dusted his hands, like a baseball manager getting ready to call in a relief pitcher. "Okay, so you don't care about the game within the game. But what if I could make your band a success?"

The dim mists instantly evaporated from Bobby's brain. "How did you find out about The Diggers?"

McFall laughed and held up a palm. "No conspiracy theories. I know Dex's dad, too. It's a small town."

If the guy has money, maybe he wants to get in on the glory. Just like with baseball—the only time Dad gives a damn about me is when his fat ass is parked in the bleachers and the other dads are patting him on the back.

Bobby thought about what Ronnie had said—weird things happened when McFalls were around.

"What, are you going to try and get us a record deal or something?" he said. "We're not that good."

"Just like with baseball, Bobby. Practice. No pain, no gain."

"The band is not just me. I'd have to talk to the others before making any decisions."

"You do that." McFall eased past him, his faint cologne overwhelming the scent of cut grass. He walked across the diamond, choosing a path—deliberately, it seemed—that left scuffed footprints in Coach Harnett's anal-retentive rake work.

Bobby started toward the school building. He took his time and was twenty minutes late for first period.

All the while his brain was buzzing with McFall's words: *It's the game within the game that matters.*

CHAPTER TEN

"It's Cole Buchanan, all right," said Perry Hoyle.

The medical examiner planned to ship the charred body to the state office for more tests, but the dental records were plenty enough evidence for positive identification. Two of Cole's upper teeth had been knocked out in a prison fight, and he'd never bothered to replace them. The man's only dental records were from the prison system, since he'd apparently never sat in a dentist's chair before or after his incarceration, but the X-rays and impressions from his taxpayer-funded medical treatment confirmed Littlefield's suspicions.

They were in the morgue, an unadorned room in the basement of the county hospital. The walls were finished with light-green tiles, and the whole room was redolent of formaldehyde and the stench of decay. Hoyle's desk was a battered metal relic, military surplus from the pre-Vietnam era. Buchanan's body—what was left of it—lay on a stainless-steel table. The dead man looked like he was poised to punch someone or defend himself from attack, which suggested a struggle at the moment of death.

Much of the water in his blood cells had been boiled away, and his organs were swollen and cooked. A yellowed rope of intestine bulged from a gap in his side. Littlefield was pretty sure he'd lost his taste for spare ribs.

"I know you don't have much to work with, but does your prelim suggest any sign of violence?" the sheriff asked.

"He looks like he's fighting, but that's what they call 'pugilistic attitude,'" Hoyle said. "It's the natural result of intense heat on muscle protein. The tendons dry and shrink."

Unlike the MEs on television shows, Perry Hoyle didn't eat while he worked nor did he have much gallows humor. Death seemed to annoy him, and his brusque manner suggested that it was downright rude of anyone to die suspiciously when he could have been fly fishing instead.

"This stippling here," Hoyle said, waving a latex-encased hand over a raw section of flaked skin. "That was made by the force of the fire hoses, peeling away—"

"What else?" Littlefield asked, not wanting the gruesome details.

"No sign of blunt trauma or any entrance or exit wounds made by a projectile," Hoyle said. "No large foreign objects embedded in the flesh."

Littlefield glanced around the room, which only had eight refrigerated chambers. Two were occupied. Darnell Absher had already been buried, so the other current tenants must have died of natural causes. Littlefield wondered how long it would be before the morgue was at capacity. "Was he alive during the fire?"

"The skin doesn't have the red lividity you'd expect if he inhaled carbon monoxide before getting cooked. That would have suggested he died of smoke inhalation. There's no soot in his windpipe, either, so he wasn't breathing in a bunch of embers in his last moments."

"Any way to tell how long he'd been dead?"

Hoyle peered at something in the seared skin around the dissected throat. "You say you saw him three days before the body was found?"

"Yeah. And a couple of witnesses said he was driving around the day before the fire," Littlefield said. "He was drinking, but that wasn't unusual."

"Could be he got drunk and decided to make a statement by going down with the church. I know he didn't like the McFalls much."

"Cole Buchanan wasn't the type to martyr himself for a higher cause," Littlefield said. "Maybe he just got drunk and broke into the church to sleep it off. Had a heart attack or something."

"But that still bugs me," Hoyle said. "Why wouldn't the firefighters have seen his body?"

"Hell, maybe he was a zombie. Could be he hid from them and then crawled up to the altar to deliver a sermon to his brethren."

Hoyle cocked an eyebrow and didn't smile. "That would be funny if it weren't so close to being true."

Littlefield shucked his latex gloves and cloth mask, and then collected his hat from Hoyle's barren metal desk. "How long until you hear anything on Darnell Absher?"

"The state office is backed up, and they haven't gotten to the samples yet. These damned budget cuts, I swear. I'm hearing at least three weeks, maybe four. Apparently they're stacking bodies up like cordwood down in Chapel Hill."

"I hope we don't start doing that here," Littlefield said.

"Let's call it coincidence," Hoyle said. "Just because there's a McFall in town, and that family's been linked to mysterious deaths for a century and half—well, no need to run with rumors and conspiracy theories."

"It's only a theory until it becomes a fact," Littlefield said, and with that final word, he left the sterile room and headed out into the welcoming afternoon sunshine.

After checking with Sherry for any calls, he drove to the *Times* office, located in an industrial park just beyond the Titusville city limits. The newspaper had once been headquartered in the heart of downtown, back when the paper was the primary form of local information, along with an AM radio station that had since been replaced by syndicated talk shows scheduled by computer. The *Times* had been bought by a regional corporation, and its offices had been moved to save on rent. The newspaper was now produced in a corrugated metal building that more closely resembled a welding shop than it did a bustling center of intellectual enterprise.

Littlefield parked behind the building, where empty ink barrels and cardboard spools were piled around mangled newspaper racks. The front entrance was nicely landscaped to welcome the customers who came in to place classified ads, but in the Internet Age, the newspaper's audience skewed ever older and more conservative. Cindy Baumhower predicted the newspaper would limp along for another decade, giving her time to retire before she had to look for another occupation.

She hopes to be married before then, pardner.

Littlefield pushed that thought aside. He entered through the back door, walking past the clanging presses that rolled out huge sheets of paper. Dwayne Potter, a swarthy man with a mullet who kept the machinery running with duct tape, baling wire, and alternating prayers or curses, depending on the situation, waved a greasy rag at him. Littlefield saluted back, wondering how much of the man's hearing had been sacrificed to the constant cacophony.

Cindy's office was the closest to the back door. As she liked to say, if a disgruntled story subject kicked in the front door with guns blazing, she wanted plenty of targets between her and the maniac. But Littlefield suspected that should such a scenario unfold, Cindy would go down typing, writing about the event as it unfolded, even if it ended in her obituary.

He tapped on the glass that separated her office from the series of cubicles where the reporters and ad staff toiled. She looked up from her monitor and waved him in. The office was cluttered with stacks of newspapers on the floor, a bookshelf packed with reference guides, and a dry-erase board mounted on the wall and covered with uneven squiggles of Cindy's handwriting. A recycling bin full of dented Dr. Pepper cans served as a testament to her deadline addiction.

"I hope I'm not interrupting anything," he said. He didn't know a darn thing about flowers, but he believed she smelled like lilacs—a heady, haunting fragrance that was a subtle reprieve after the horror of the morgue.

"Nothing too serious," Cindy said. "Just exposing the Illuminati and transposing an exclusive interview with Bigfoot."

"I wanted to thank you for being discreet about the fire victim."

The *Times* had duly reported the death, running twenty column inches along with a photograph of a firefighter spraying a hose into the flaming church. Cindy had not speculated on the cause of death, ending with the standard "Sheriff Frank Littlefield said no other information will be released until the victim is identified and the next of kin are notified. The incident remains under investigation."

"Oh, it's not buried. I'm just waiting on more information," she said. "I can't let the *Charlotte Observer* or television news scoop me on this one. Especially since I'm sleeping with my primary source. People would lose all respect for me. So, tell me, was it Cole?"

"It was him, all right. But I need to notify the family before you run with it. Don't worry—I'll put off the other reporters for a little while. How about this? 'I can't comment at this time because the investigation is ongoing.'"

"Great way to say nothing," Cindy said. "I still think you ought to run for higher office after your term's up."

"Sure, except I might accidentally get elected, and then I'd have to spend half the year in Raleigh with a bunch of idiots who think they can solve the very problems they created in the first place."

"A wise man. Must be why I love you."

"I thought it was the scoops. Or the monkey sex."

"Whatever. Anything new on Larkin McFall?"

"I'm not willing to link McFall to either of these deaths. Even off the record."

Cindy's cheeks crinkled in a wry smile. "We've already gone down that road. So don't get coy. It doesn't suit you."

"Okay. I did a deeper background check, including Texas records. Division of Motor Vehicles, Department of Revenue, and Texas State Police. Nothing on McFall. So I drilled down to El Paso, the city he said he was from. No deeds, no business licenses, nothing on file with the city or county."

"So you think he made it all up?"

"Or else he just walked out of a time machine a couple of weeks ago," Littlefield said. "In my experience, people don't lie unless they have something to hide."

"I agree. I searched the LexisNexis database of news articles for him and came up with nothing. If he's really such a successful businessman, there's no way he could have avoided dozens of Chamber of Commerce award ceremonies and ribbon-cutting events."

"Maybe we're attacking this from the wrong angle. All we're doing is searching for him by name. But what if he's using an alias?"

"That would be incredibly overdramatic. Posing as a distant relative in order to make an apparently legal purchase of a family property that no one really wants?"

"Maybe he's some kook," Littlefield said, finally sitting in the uncomfortable little interview chair across from Cindy. Her cell phone rang to the tune of the David Bowie and Queen song "Under Pressure." She looked at the screen, shook her head, and let the call go to voicemail.

"A kook?"

"Yeah," Littlefield said. "Maybe he read about a haunted church in the mountains on some ghost-hunter website or something. Decided to play an extended practical joke on the locals...."

Cindy gaped at him.

"Yeah. Pretty farfetched." Littlefield looked down at the scuffed floor for a moment. Then he asked, "Your ghost-hunting buddies didn't post anything about the church, did they?"

"Sheriff."

She only called him by his official title when she was exasperated. Littlefield knew the feeling. "Okay. So we need to drill deeper. That means fingerprints or DNA."

"Don't you need a warrant for that? No judge in the land would grant you one based on supernatural legends and a hunch, not even your bowling buddy Erwin."

"He's not my buddy. We're just both Republicans."

"Anyway, nobody is going to take you seriously on this one."

"What I need is a legitimate reason to dig into his past without making it a formal criminal investigation. Maybe he'll apply for a concealed-carry permit."

"He doesn't strike me as the gun-owning type," Cindy said.

"If I can get his fingerprints, I can run it through as a background check."

"You're planning to forge an application in his name?"

Littlefield rubbed his palms on the sides of his trousers. "Don't look at me like that."

"Just because you think it serves a higher purpose doesn't make it right. And as the government wiretappers found out, a little bit illegal is still illegal."

"I'm not the type of officer who would ever contrive evidence to get a conviction," Littlefield said. "But I've sworn to protect the public, and two of my constituents are dead."

"So, what're you going to do? Are you planning to invite him down to the courthouse to get printed?"

"What's funny is that I think he'd voluntarily comply, smiling all the while. But then he'd know I'm checking up on him."

"I'm sure he knows that already," Cindy said. "He retained Francisco to represent him, and there's no way a lawyer will let him just walk into your clutches."

Littlefield stood and paced. "I just get a feeling he's playing all of us. He looks at me like he can see right inside my skull, like he's rooting around in all my memories and failures. I don't know what his game is, but it's pissing me off."

"What if he's nothing more than what he appears to be? A well-off guy returning to his ancestral home to invest in the community."

Cindy's occupation required her to give people the benefit of the doubt, but Littlefield's had taught him to assume guilt until innocence was the final possible alternative. "He's a McFall."

"Unless he's lying. You said it."

"Fingerprints," Littlefield said. "Will you help me? You can do it without arousing suspicion. Just get him to sign something, let him borrow a pen, anything."

"You're asking me to break the law?"

"We're in this together." Littlefield realized the statement conveyed a number of meanings, all of them frightening. He gave her a boyish grin that hid his anxiety, and she softened a little and sighed.

"Okay. Now get out of here. Some of us have to work for a living."

CHAPTER ELEVEN

At least the *mountain* was the same.

Heather Fowler had only lived in Barkersville a dozen years, nowhere near long enough to be considered a local, but in that time she had witnessed a number of unsettling changes. The Baptist Church bore a flashing neon sign out front that looked better suited to advertising Las Vegas showgirls than inviting people to salvation. At first the only chain business on the main commercial strip had been Wendy's. Now Wal-Mart, Ruby Tuesday, Staples, three grocery stores, and a number of other national chains had sprung up in defiance of the area's declining socioeconomic status. The chain businesses had siphoned vitality from downtown. Drugstores and clinics now clustered all around the county hospital, leading to its nickname, "Death Corner."

Heather had settled in the area for the whitewater rafting, the rock climbing, the hiking, and other activities that were best enjoyed far from a dense population. So she was less than pleased when the ugly sprawl spread through and around the town, driven by outside investors and fueled by local power brokers. Ironically, the horror she felt had brought her into the circle of power as well, although only at the very fringes.

"Keep up," said Susan Barinowski, her friend and hiking partner.

The words broke Heather from her reverie. She'd been so introspective that she had fallen behind by a good fifty feet and was totally missing out on the natural beauty that was the reason they were out here. Well, that and the exercise.

"Okay, okay," Heather said. "When did you turn into Robojock, anyway?"

She increased her pace on the leaf-covered trail, the surrounding forest glowing greenly in the sunlight filtering through the overhead canopy. The delicate, fleshy stalks of pennywort and trillium penetrated the dark loam, and the air was ripe with the twin odors of new growth and decay. Here and there, large, time-worn boulders protruded from the slopes, spotted with gray lichen and moss. The climb was exhilarating, both because of the untamed environment and the steepness of the trail.

"At my age, you need to kick up the cardio," Susan said, which was only half sarcasm. Like Heather, Susan was in her late thirties, and neither were the type to sit in front of a television parroting "Buns of Steel" videos. But Susan was doing pretty well with her shape, a trim one hundred and twenty pounds with firm thighs, high breasts, and strong shoulders.

Heather was more into leisurely recreation than hardcore outdoor adventuring, but she always pushed her limits on outings with Susan. She wasn't ready to surrender to middle-age sag. Although she considered herself a feminist, she was also aware of her ticking biological clock, and she didn't have a life partner yet. Her life was full and rewarding at present, but she didn't want to wake up one day thirty years from now to find only one pillow on her bed.

"Race you to the top," Heather said.

"Ha," Susan said. "I could take a nap and still win."

The incline was too demanding for Heather to break into a sprint, but she managed a steady jog. Mud flew from her sneakers, and she shucked her zippered sweatshirt, wrapping the sleeves around her waist. The sports bra dug into the skin beneath her armpits, but she was pleased with the fullness inside the fabric. While big boobs were inconvenient at times, she'd had enough men—and women—admire them that she accepted them as a blessing. As her mother had always said, "Life is tough, so use whatever you've got."

That didn't help her win this race, though. Susan easily ascended the final stretch of the trail, scooting gracefully between a cleft of boulders to emerge on the peak of the ridge, where a stony, fern-covered glen opened into vast space. Huffing and puffing, Heather caught up, bending over and catching her breath before she took in the view.

"Never gets old," Susan said, barely panting despite the exertion.

"To think this mountain has been here for half a billion years," Heather said. "I guess we should just be glad we're not on it during its volcanic period."

"I'm just glad I'm not on *my* period."

"You take all the fun out of science." Heather squinted out across the valley. The view wasn't fully panoramic; there were a number of taller ridges and peaks around them, including Grandfather Mountain to the northwest and Mulatto Mountain to the south, towering over the lines and squares that marked the town of Titusville at its base. But from this vantage point, Heather was simultaneously overwhelmed by a sense of insignificance and a soaring urgency to help protect and preserve the region's natural resources.

Susan shaded her eyes and pointed to the thin ribbon of highway that connected Titusville and Barkersville. "What's that patch of raw dirt down there?"

Heather groaned. "They're breaking ground for an AutoZone."

"Doesn't Titusville already have two parts stores?"

"I guess not all spark plugs are created equal."

"You sound annoyed. Queen Heather not getting her way?"

"If I had my way, it would be off with *all* their heads."

Susan had started the "Queen Heather" bit when Heather had been elected to the Pickett County Board of Commissioners two years ago. She had never sought out a political life and still considered herself a one-issue candidate. The Titusville Town Council had proposed a new water intake system well outside its borders, and Heather had viewed it as such a moral affront—stark proof of not being able to live within one's means and resources, whether environmental or economic—that she had led the successful fight to block the necessary state permits.

At the urging of other environmentalists, she had run on the Democratic ticket during one of those rare times when the conservative mountains were in a wild mood swing, and now she was the outsider on a board composed of native Good Old Boys.

"I don't know why the lady doth protest so much," Susan said, mangling a Shakespeare quote. Like Heather, Susan was a professor at Westridge University. They often carpooled for the half-hour commute. Heather taught anthropology, and Susan was a chemistry instructor; this led to many debates about hard versus soft sciences.

"I would just hate to see all this ruined in the course of a single generation," Heather said.

"It's being changed, not ruined. Trust me, once we wipe ourselves out with global warming, this view will restore itself in the blink of an eye. Of course, no human will be around to see it, but maybe that's the point."

"I hope I never get as a cynical as you."

"They say if you scratch a cynic, you'll find a frustrated idealist, so you're halfway there." Susan began high-stepping in place so her legs wouldn't cramp. Her snug gray leggings rippled against her calf muscles. She bent from side to side like a ballerina to keep her back loose.

"I'm going to fight for as long as I can," Heather said, swiveling her hips to work out the stiffness that was already starting to settle there. "The voters will probably kick me off the board in the next election, so I only have a couple of years to make a difference."

Susan stopped her stretching. "What the heck is *that*?"

Heather turned in the direction her friend was pointing. The forest flattened out to a stretch of meadow below them, and from where they were standing, she could make out a driveway, an old cemetery, and a rectangular heap of gray and black. "Oh, you didn't hear about that? The fire department burned down that old church, and they found a body inside. Big mystery."

"Pretty creepy."

"No foul play is suspected. But it's just another sad sign of change. The property owner is going to develop that whole side of the mountain."

"Sad?" The male voice startled both of them. Although the trail was a fairly popular destination, they'd never encountered anyone else on the ridge.

Heather turned to see a man sitting on a boulder behind them, dressed in athletic wear bearing the Picket High Pioneers logo. He was flushed and sweating, but he appeared to be in good shape, as if he'd hiked with a brisk pace while reserving a little fuel in the tank. She was surprised they hadn't heard his approach. This far from civilization, the primary sounds were bird calls, the occasional jet plane, and the muted tinkle of water that squeezed out between the rocks to form springs.

"Change is sad," Heather said. "Nobody will pray in that church anymore. Some rich person will buy the lot from the owner, since it overlooks the river and has road frontage. Probably an outsider."

"We're all tourists," the man said. He smiled, revealing white, evenly spaced teeth.

It suddenly occurred to Heather that they were a mile from civilization, and if this man was some sort of creep or molester, they had no way to call for help. Neither she nor Susan had packed a cell phone, pepper spray, or any of the usual modern precautions. The forest was so peaceful that it seemed impossible for human violence to enter into its dominion.

Susan edged away from the man. While she was in some ways a thrill seeker, this brand of potential danger held no appeal. But Heather detected no threat from the newcomer. He seemed relaxed, a fellow reveler in the fresh air and sunshine.

The stereotype of the handsome, charming serial killer was way overblown anyway. Most of them were uneducated drifters with a degree of brain damage, not cunning masterminds who seduced victims and outfoxed the cops. They usually avoided arrest through a combination of luck, jurisdictional battles among law enforcement agencies, and the sheer random nature of their impulsive crimes.

"Some say tourists are good for the mountains," Heather ventured. "They drive by and drop their money out the window, then turn around and go home."

"What do *you* think?" The man challenged her, but his tone was friendly. He brushed his brown hair from his forehead, and it stood up in a sweaty, boyish sweep that put her at ease. She couldn't stop her eyes from flicking to the golden wedding band on his left hand and was annoyed at herself for noticing.

"I support the promotion of outdoor activities and recreation," she said. "We can turn Pickett County into one of the most desirable outdoor-adventure destinations on the East Coast. We have trails, camping, bicycle routes, fishing, rafting, rock climbing, and—"

The man chuckled and held up his hand. "I'm sold. I'm already a satisfied customer."

"You're a tourist? I mean...a visitor?"

"Well, if you take the long view, we're all just passing through. But my family is native to the area, if indeed a Scottish tourist from two centuries ago can be considered a native. I'd imagine the Catawba and Cherokee tribes would have a different interpretation."

"We'd better get going," Susan said to Heather. "Alan's meeting me at the bottom of the trail. If I'm late, he'll shoot off flares and send in the rescue teams. You know how he gets."

Susan folded her arms across her chest, and Heather remembered she was wearing only a sports bra above the waist. She was probably revealing a lot of her own female attributes, but it would just draw attention to that fact if she slid into her sweatshirt. She decided to brave it out without revealing any sign of intimidation or self-consciousness.

"A local family, huh?" Heather said to the man. "I'm an import. I'm Heather Fowler and this is Susan Barinowski."

The man's eyebrows lifted. "Heather Fowler? Aren't you a county commissioner?"

Heather couldn't help but feel a rush of pride. "First term."

His eyes narrowed and his tone grew serious. "So imports should move in and decide what's best for people who have lived here for generations?"

"Come *on*," Susan said, tugging Heather's arm. "Unless you want to be the one to calm Alan down."

Susan was so edgy that she was full-on lying. She had dated an accountant named Alan, but she'd dropped him after he was charged with tax evasion. She was invoking the image of an over-protective psycho boyfriend to scare off the stranger. Nice ploy, but the man didn't seem the least bit worried about Alan, fiction or fact.

Heather put her hands on her hips and couldn't help thrusting out her chest in defiance, remembering Mother's advice to exploit all her assets. "I was elected by the people of this county, so they must be okay with it."

His expression subtly shifted and he laughed. "Just kidding. I'm sure you do a great job. If I'm still here next time you run, you have my vote."

The tension drained from her just a little. A certain segment of the population held her in deep contempt, so she was always happy to find a supporter, even in the most unlikely of settings.

"Thank you, Mister...."

His smile became even warmer—it seemed to mirror the sun peeking through the bright May clouds. "McFall. Larkin McFall."

"You...you're the one who owns that land where the church was," Heather said. "I read about that in the paper. How awful."

"Shocking, to be sure," McFall said, nonplussed. "My lawyer advises me not to comment, but the authorities think he was a vagrant who died there before the fire."

"Are you still going to develop it all?" Heather said.

He nodded. "All the way to the top. All the way to *here*."

Both Heather's and Susan's jaws dropped. "Wait," Heather said. "I thought this was national forest. There's a sign down by the road—"

"Only a narrow strip is publicly owned," McFall said. "The rest of it is family land. And it belongs to me now."

Heather looked down at the black dirt beneath her running shoes. She'd been trespassing all these years. As had so many others.

We're all tourists.

"Come *on*," Susan said, hurrying down the trail. Heather followed, pausing once to gaze back at Larkin McFall, who sat perched on the boulder like the king of all he surveyed.

And he was surveying everything, including her.

Especially her.

CHAPTER TWELVE

"**W**hat a crappy shift," Melanie said. "Another minute and I would have turned into a greasy strip of fatback."

"Slippery," Ronnie said. "I like it."

Melanie swatted him with her tiny beaded purse. "Pervert."

"No, just a guy with a pulse."

"Same thing."

Downtown Titusville was dead for a Saturday afternoon, and they took the sidewalk side by side. Ronnie wanted to hold her hand, but that felt like such a grade-school move. Dex would have just slapped her butt and wriggled his hips against her. That wouldn't work on a girl like Melanie, though. Bobby would know how to play it just right. He'd do something cool like toss an arm over her shoulder and fall right into groove.

Brilliant. Everything you do seems to be driving you deeper and deeper into the Friend Zone, even offering her a ride home.

"Good day for tips," Melanie said, stopping in front of a boutique clothing store that neither of them had ever entered. "Another forty dollars. Maybe I'll be able to buy a car this summer."

"I thought you were saving for college."

"Look at that. Eighty dollars for that cute little crochet hat? If I wanted to be Taylor Swift, I'd just go the easy route and break up with movie stars."

"This is serious," Ronnie said, feeling stupid, because Bobby would never be serious in a situation like this one. *No wonder she likes him better than me.*

He studied Melanie's reflection in the storefront glass. She'd dyed bronze highlights into her auburn hair. Subtle enough not to offend the conservative crowd at 24/7 Waffle, they were still a tangible sign that she was breaking away, getting ready for whatever the next phase of her life had to offer. Even coated with sweat and grease from her shift, her skin was bright and healthy, and her white button-up shirt gave her a strangely classy look. Her eyes could shift from sky blue to glacial gray depending on her mood, sometimes in a single blink. Of course, she *did* smell like bacon, and Ronnie wondered why some enterprising celebrity hadn't bottled the scent into a perfume. Perhaps that all-American buffoon Larry the Cable Guy was tinkering with a formula in a woodshop somewhere at this very moment.

"Don't worry. I'll probably go to college," Melanie said. "But that's months away. Right now I'm just looking forward to finishing high school."

"But you need to plan *now*."

She turned away from the window, waved to someone she recognized down the street, and said, "Community college isn't like Westridge. All I have to do is show up at the door with a check and I'm in."

"If you skip a year, it gets way harder to go back. Look what happened to your mom."

"She got pregnant at eighteen by choice. I wasn't an accident."

Ronnie wasn't so sure, but he kept his trap shut. If God truly did have a plan for everything and everyone, why bother trying to convince Melanie to go college?

After everything that had happened, though—the red church, the dead people, his mom freaking out—Ronnie couldn't fully believe in predestination. He was pretty sure God had an absurd sense of humor and was making things up as He went along, and they were all discovering it together, God included.

He had a hunch, though, that in the end God always had the last laugh.

"Your grades are good," Ronnie said. "It would be a waste if you were stuck waiting tables the rest of your life."

Her nostrils pinched in a sneer. "Thanks for the lecture, Mr. Gladstone. Jeez."

Bad move.

"Okay, forget it."

Ronnie ushered her down to the record store, which had once sold records and CDs before the digital revolution. Pickett County had been among the last holdouts—it still had a mom-and-pop video rental store, Lights, Camera, Action—but the future had finally arrived, and the record store had gone out of business. In an ironic twist, a new owner had opened the shop as a nostalgia center, selling vinyl albums, paperbacks, a few kitschy newtiques, and oddball collectables like sports cards, magazines, and Matchbox cars.

"Do you ever wish we could go back?" Melanie asked, studying a copy of a Jimi Hendrix album with scuffed corners and psyche-delic art.

"I don't know," Ronnie said. "People talk about 'the good old days' and 'simpler times,' but I wonder when that was, exactly. Back when your biggest worry was starving to death or catching the bubonic plague? Getting eaten by a saber-tooth tiger? Or life before antibiotics? Or maybe back when mannequins had heads?"

Melanie shook her head wistfully, and Ronnie knew he'd blown it again. Why did he have to say whatever popped into his skull? The thoughts bubbled up from some stinky wizard's cauldron of nonsense that was probably simmering away even when he wasn't paying attention. What a freaking dork.

"I meant back when we were kids," Melanie said. "When Willard's Drugs was right down there and you could go in and order an ice cream."

Ronnie thought it was corny how the drugstore had tried to cash in on '50s nostalgia, much like this place. But he kept his mouth shut, instead saying something Bobby would say. "Yeah. I'd like to buy you an ice cream right now, because you're so hot."

She shook her head again, but smiled a little. Actually, that was more like something Dex would say. Why did this have to be so hard?

"I'd better be getting home," Melanie said. "I need to shower off this layer of scuzz."

Ronnie passed up the chance to make another naughty remark, because he wasn't sure whether Bobby or Dex would come out of his mouth. "Okay. I'd better get home and start studying anyway."

Ronnie was embarrassed by the grungy Dodge van, but at least he'd been able to borrow it from his mom. As Melanie climbed in and pushed aside the green plastic soda bottles and magazines on the floor, Ronnie found himself worrying the engine wouldn't start. It whined a little like it needed fluid of some kind, but it rumbled to life and he carefully backed out into the street. He was grateful that traffic was light, because he wasn't a very experienced driver, and he didn't need to look any lamer than he already did.

"Got any tunes?" Melanie asked as they hit the town limits.

Ronnie, his attention fixed on the road, said, "All we have is a radio. This car rolled off the lot back when Detroit was covered in dinosaur dookie."

Melanie fiddled with the dials, but the only thing coming in was the local AM station. Thirty seconds of static-filled Barry Manilow was enough for her to opt for silence.

"See?" Ronnie said. "We're already back in simpler times."

Melanie laughed, and Ronnie beamed with inner joy. *Bobby* was usually the one who made her laugh. Maybe he just needed to work on his material.

He wondered what it would be like if she asked him to pull down one of the side roads that led to old barns, algae-choked ponds, and knee-high hayfields. There was room in the back of the van to lie down. They could . . . .

He thought of that old song the AM station played once in a while when it wanted to be racy. He could almost hear the crusty old deejay introducing it now: "The song that *Rolling Stone* magazine called *the* song of the Seventies, 'Chevy Vannnnnnn . . .'" When he'd first heard it, he'd thought it was romantic. Then he'd figured out that the characters ended up doing it. After that, every time he heard it, he found himself wondering if the strangers had practiced safe sex. A beautiful woman hitchhiking around the country doing every guy who picked her up was a little reckless, even before the AIDS epidemic.

And he also knew that thinking stuff like that was exactly why *he* never got any. Besides, he was driving a Dodge, not a Chevy. He tried to think of another joke to tell Melanie while they wound along Highway 321, which followed the undulating curves of the river.

He realized they were coming up on the bridge where he'd found Darnell Absher's body. His pulse was erratic.

Melanie broke the silence by saying, "Pull over."

At first he wasn't sure he'd heard her correctly, but when he looked at her, she had a "pull over" face, and his heart accelerated so that it was pounding as fast as the pistons in the six-cylinder engine block. He almost slammed on the brakes, but that would have totally blown whatever mood was developing.

"Here?" he asked, his tongue thick. He looked around for an exit, a dirt road maybe. All he saw was the Riverview development dotting the hill. Maybe if he went through the gate and . . .

"By the bridge," she said.

God, how could she do this? She KNEW he couldn't handle that.

Maybe it was a test. She constantly teased him about being cursed, and a couple of times she'd even called him "Deathboy." He had to admit, finding bodies had brought him some notoriety and attention. It was the only thing that separated him from the herd.

He eased the Dodge into the same gravel turnout where Dex had parked, hoping Larkin McFall wouldn't cruise by in his Lexus. He turned to Melanie. Were they going to kiss? What should he do? Why were his hands numb?

"Tell me about it," she said.

"Huh?"

"Finding Darnell Absher."

"It was . . . ."

What? Gross? Thrilling? Interesting?

What would Bobby say?

"It was weird," he managed.

"Weird?"

"I was just swimming and sort of bumped into him. I mean, it's not like I was splashing around looking for dead people."

Melanie peered out at the water, which ran low and clear. The current cut soft ripples in the reflected sunlight, and rounded stones glistened along the riverbanks. Upstream, a man in green hip waders was casting a fly rod. A lawn mower chewed grass in the distance with a hungry grumble.

"You were there when they found that burned body in the church," she said, not looking at him.

"So were you. And a lot of other people."

"You called out your brother's name. Why did you think it was his body?"

Ronnie swallowed. "I didn't mean to . . . it just came out."

She suddenly directed a smile at him. It was like the sun had blazed into the van in an explosion of heat and light. "You're protective of him. That's so sweet."

Damn. I don't know a whole lot about all this, but I'm pretty sure "sweet" guys stay virgins until they're married.

Forget about Bobby. The way this was going, he might as well act like Dex. "I meant what I said the other day. I'm glad that goddamned church burned down. I hated seeing it there, looking like a middle finger giving God the bird. Too many people have died because of it."

Melanie was shocked by his outburst. "Chill out, Ronnie."

"People think I'm this freak, just because I live near a haunted church and I believe in Jesus. Well, I didn't ask to be born here. It's not my fault that the Days have land next to the McFalls or that this Larkin McFall guy chose to move to Pickett County. It's not like—"

Melanie's cell phone rang and Ronnie realized he'd been yelling. He gripped the steering wheel and forced himself to breathe.

Melanie answered her phone. "Yeah ... okay ... be there in five minutes." She clicked off and said to Ronnie. "Mom. Gotta go."

Ronnie started the van and rolled across the bridge, mulling the great weight of water below them, which carried everything to the sea, where it would churn in the tide and evaporate and fall again from the sky and seep up from beneath the deep cracks below the earth's mantle.

God, why do you make me think of stuff like that?

He forced himself not to cry, because that would be worse than "sweet." That would be "sensitive." Such guys *died* virgins.

When he pulled up to the Ward double-wide, Melanie's dog, Frizzell, came bounding across the yard. The yellow Labrador retriever's tongue lolled half a foot out of its mouth. Ronnie opened his door so the he could pet the dog.

Melanie said, "I'd invite you in, but ...."

"Yeah," Ronnie said.

"Thanks for the ride."

Before he could answer, she leaned across the parking-brake handle and planted her lips on his cheek. They were as dry and soft and light as a butterfly, and then she was out of the van, bounding up the metal steps and into the rundown trailer, Frizzell at her heels.

Ronnie started the van again and drove home.

She'd kissed him on the cheek.

Sweet.

CHAPTER THIRTEEN

Stepford Matheson had grown up hunting these mountains.

At the age of seven, he'd shot his first squirrel with a .22 rifle. Two years later, he'd bagged his first buck, an eight-pointer whose rack still hung on the wall of his cabin. He'd taken a few trips out west to hunt elk, but the peaks out there were too harsh and bleak. Stepford liked the Southern Appalachians for its diverse range of critters, there for the shooting.

Even though deer season had long since passed, Stepford had a good excuse for carrying a loaded .30-30 Winchester through the woods. Two of his hound dogs had been torn to shreds, and he knew it was the goddamned coyotes. Those furry bastards were all over the place out west, but the Pickett County Cooperative Extension Service agent had told him the varmints had migrated to the Blue Ridge Mountains to fill the void left when the panthers and wolves had died out. "Nature abhors a vacuum," the egghead had told him. Stepford wasn't quite sure what that meant, but he took it as proof that coyotes didn't belong here.

That made them invaders, outsiders, and no creature was going to mess with Stepford's property while he had anything to say about it. And he was happy to let his Winchester do his talking for him.

He followed paw prints that led away from where he'd found the ravaged dog carcasses and up a little creek that tumbled down from the shaded rocks high above. At one point, the tracks sank deep into the mud, a sure sign that the predators had stopped to drink from a little pool. The tracks were only half filled with seepage, so that meant they weren't far away. Coyotes mated for life, the extension agent had said, and they ferociously defended their territory if they had spring pups.

The agent had assured Stepford that coyotes posed no threat to humans. They were opportunistic, just as content with roadkill, spilled garbage, or fruit as with fresh meat from rodents or geese. They would attack dogs only if cornered, or if they were suffering from rabies. The agent had grown up in Raleigh and had two college degrees, but he didn't know a damn thing about the way the real world worked. Coyotes couldn't read, so they didn't know they weren't supposed to kill dogs.

And these coyotes had killed the wrong man's dogs.

Stepford moved with more urgency, staying low. Dusk, when coyotes were most active, was setting in, so he had a small window in which to shoot them. Even if he got only one, he'd be happy, but he wasn't sure he wanted to walk back home in the dark. Not when one of them might be rabid.

He climbed over a sagging barbed-wire fence the McFalls had built sometime in the 1980s, when they'd rented out pasture land to his uncle Lester. Stepford was damned sure they had overshot

McFALL ✲ EPISODE TWO

the property line by a good fifty yards, but he wasn't going to pay a surveyor and then fight with the crooks and lawyers that hung around the county courthouse like vultures. No, he'd ignore it. People tended to steer clear of the McFalls—those who didn't often ended up on the wrong side of the grave, like Cole Buchanan.

Stepford would bet his gun collection that the sheriff was going to let Cole's murder slide right on by, like he always did. But at least the church was gone. A man could sleep easier just on that.

Once the coyotes were cleared out.

In a laurel thicket, the two sets of tracks split and veered off in opposite directions. That was weird. Coyotes were pack animals.

Well, I'll just get one, and come back later for the other.

Stepford followed the set of prints to the right because the terrain was more level and the undergrowth sparser, although shadows were stretching longer and the canopy overhead shifted into a deeper shade of sunset red. He'd only walked for about two minutes before the tracks ended.

What the hell? Did the mangy varmint step into a hot-air balloon?

Stepford knew it was stupid, but he peered up into the branches of the surrounding buckeye and poplar. A panther or bobcat could climb, but he'd never heard of a coyote doing so.

He sensed a slight movement behind him before he heard the low growling.

He tucked his finger gently across the Winchester's trigger before he turned. With the weapon held high, across his chest, he'd have to make several coordinated motions to bring it into firing position.

Got you outfoxed....

He spun, slipping the rifle butt into the crook of his shoulder, raising the barrel. No time to use the scope—he'd just have to eyeball the sight and let fly.

The coyote crouched low, almost bellying the ground, its broad face and pointed nose projecting a menacing intelligence. Its fur was like Joseph's coat of many colors, which Stepford only knew about from the Dolly Parton song, not the Bible—patches of red, gray, black, and gold.

Stepford aimed for the center of the forehead and—

"Stepford!"

Stepford jerked as he fired, like some sort of stupid weekend warrior, and the bullet sailed high, clipping branches as the percussive *crack* echoed off the rocks and trees.

Forgetting the coyote, Stepford turned toward the voice. It was coming from the direction he'd been tracking the set of prints. That devious son-of-a-bitch Larkin McFall stood on a flat protrusion of granite, a grayer silhouette against the blackening forest. He was dressed in athletic wear, like some damned banker who had to have a special outfit before he could let himself sweat. Beside him, the second coyote squatted like a loyal pet.

Stepford peered at the tracks again. *No goddamned way the coyote could have jumped that far. And where are McFall's footprints?*

"You're trespassing." McFall's voice was hollow, and that city-slicker smile turned in and swallowed itself. "That's not very neighborly."

"The . . . them coyotes ate my dogs."

"No," McFall said. "That was me. *They* are still hungry."

The first coyote slammed into Stepford's back, covering the gap in half a breath. The impact knocked him to his knees. The Winchester flew from his hands and slid across the damp leaves. The moist, stinking doggie breath was at his ear, and the slobbering almost sounded like a whisper.

Except the whisper was in McFall's voice: "*You're mine, bitch.*"

The extension agent had assured Stepford Matheson that coyotes never attacked humans, not even in cases of extreme hunger or entrapment. Stepford swore to God that he'd never trust a goddamned Raleigh egghead again.

It was one promise he was able to keep.

The teeth closed on his neck as McFall laughed.

McFALL

EPISODE THREE

CHAPTER FOURTEEN

Bobby Eldreth tucked the baseball behind his back, squeezing it between his fingers as he leaned forward. The catcher flashed him the sign for a curveball, but Bobby shook it off. His curveball hadn't been breaking today, and the whole game was riding on this play. He wanted to go with his best bet.

The Pickett High Pioneers were ahead 2-1 in the bottom of the seventh. Under the convoluted rules of the conference play-offs, Vance High was considered the home team and was batting last, even though the game was being played at Pickett. Bobby had pitched well, giving up only three hits, but one of them had just come with two outs and a man on base. There were runners on first and third, so he needed to go for the kill, and that meant a fastball.

Normally, Bobby was in the zone while on the mound, and although he remained aware of the entire game situation in case the ball was batted back to him or a runner tried to steal, his main focus was on the opponent standing in the batter's box.

The *enemy.*

But he had lost his focus. His first mistake was letting his gaze roam over the bleachers, which on a typical day might have held fifty or sixty people. Since Pickett was in the conference finals, though, more than three hundred spectators had shown up. Bobby could handle the crowd, as long as he let them melt into a giant, roaring blob. The problem was that too many individual faces were surfacing in the mass of cheering people.

There was Elmer, in his usual seat right behind the backstop where he could dispute every call made by the home-plate umpire. He was relatively sober, since the game had started at 3:00 p.m., but his face was still bright red from beer. "Wipe 'im out, Bobby!" his dad bellowed. "He ain't got no stick."

The batter with "no stick" was Ramon Stinson, Vance County's best slugger, a well-developed guy with a full goatee who looked to be about twenty-five. Bobby had faced him four times during the season, striking him out three times but also giving up a home run—one of only three he had ever allowed. Stinson had homered on a hanging curve ball, yet another reason Bobby wanted to go for a fastball.

Bobby glanced over at Coach Harnett in the dugout. Wearing his school windbreaker despite the heat, Coach had his arms folded over his chest. He dropped one hand and flashed his fingers in a signal to the catcher, who then relayed the call to Bobby.

A slider? I can't throw a slider. What's he thinking?

Bobby shook off that signal as well. He was going to throw a fastball come hell or high water. Because there was a scout in the stands, and he had a radar gun. Bobby had seen Harnett talking to the scout, who was dressed in ratty gym clothes and looked like someone out of an old sci-fi movie, with his brushy mustache and wild gray Einstein hair. Coach hadn't mentioned anything about it to Bobby, but he was one of those old-school assholes who believed kids couldn't handle pressure and what they didn't know couldn't hurt them.

Elmer, on the other hand, had spotted the radar gun right off, and had sidled up to the dugout after warm-ups to tell Bobby a scout from the Braves was in the stands. The guy was almost certainly not from the Braves, but whoever he was, he'd want to know the speed of Bobby's fastball. Vance's pitcher threw mostly knuckleballs and curves, so the gun definitely wasn't for him. No, that scout was here to measure Bobby's heat—and his future.

Stinson, tired of waiting for the pitch, stepped out of the batter's box, and the tension in the crowd eased just a bit. Bobby almost grinned. He remembered what Larkin McFall had said, about him being a rock star while on the mound. The whole crowd—the whole conference championship—was waiting for him.

But that was another face in the crowd that bothered him. McFall was sitting in the third row behind Elmer, his pretty blonde wife by his side. McFall clapped calmly, and although he didn't shout, his voice was distinct among the whistles, cheers, and chatter. "Come on, Bobby. It's your game."

Stinson stepped into the batter's box, did the obligatory crotch-grab to adjust his jock strap, and dug in for the pitch. Bobby intended to throw a high, inside fastball out of the strike zone, hoping that Stinson would lunge for it. By throwing high, he'd be able to reach eighty-five miles per hour, which was pretty smoking for a teenager.

Bobby adjusted his grip so his fingers lay across the seams. That would give the ball a little more hop, so that it would rise in the air as it neared the plate. The scout would be impressed both with his velocity and with his wily baiting of the slugger. A game-ending strikeout to clinch the championship would look pretty good on the scouting report.

But you don't want to play baseball, do you? You don't want to go to the minor leagues and ride buses between small towns for years based on the slim hope of someday reaching the Big Time. That's a stupid dream for a kid from the trailer park.

Bobby's breath caught and he swallowed hard. He stepped off the pitching rubber to buy himself a little more time, pretending to stare down the runner on third base. Instead, he glanced past the runner to the home-side bleachers, where Melanie and Ronnie sat in the crowd. Melanie was yelling something, but he couldn't make it out. His ears were roaring.

You don't want to play baseball.

If he got a nice signing bonus from the pros, maybe he would ask Melanie to marry him. She probably would. It was a ticket out of Titusville, and a cheap one at that.

Bobby stepped back on the mound, realizing that only five seconds had passed since Stinson had re-entered the batter's box. Time was fat and slow, like when he was a kid and had broken a tooth and got dosed with nitrous oxide by the dentist. This moment was crammed full of details—the stink of chili from concession-stand hot dogs, Melanie's hair swaying in the breeze like some sexy shampoo commercial, Harnett spitting a wet brown rope of tobacco juice onto the dirt, Stinson wiggling his bat up and down, a slight scuff on the baseball's surface where it had skipped across the infield earlier. This moment was wide and opulent.

This moment was *big*.

And through it all came McFall's voice again, clear, calm, and somehow rising above everything. "Remember what I told you, Bobby."

The game within the game.

Maybe McFall really *had* bribed the ump. It sure did seem like Bobby had gotten the benefit of the doubt on several called strikes, ones that might have painted the corner of the strike zone but were probably an inch outside. Maybe Bobby just needed to cork something up near the plate and let the ump call Stinson out. Game over. The ump was a doughy, nondescript guy who looked like he'd roll over for a little cash.

No, that wasn't what McFall was trying to tell him right now. What he meant was that Bobby could do it if he wanted. He could have it all. The championship, the signing bonus, the girl. *Everything.*

Bobby didn't know the how or why of it, but he knew it as surely as he knew the pitcher's mound was sixty feet, six inches from home plate. It was a fact. If he wanted it badly enough, McFall would make it happen.

You don't want to play baseball. You'd rather play drums. Even if you never get anywhere, even if it's shuttling between gigs in a crappy van instead of between stadiums in an air-conditioned bus, you'd STILL take the drums. Baseball is a sport, but music is life.

He looked around, checking the two runners, glancing up at the cheering Melanie and the expressionless Ronnie, then at McFall, placidly smiling next to his wife, then at the scout who had the radar aimed over home plate to record his arm speed. Just before Bobby went into his wind-up, he made the mistake of looking at Elmer.

His old man looked like he was on the verge of a stroke, his cheeks purple, a thick blue vein throbbing in his temple, a strand of drool hanging from his gaping mouth. "C'mon, Bobby, just like I taught you!"

Shit. Bobby's dad was a loser. A nobody. But maybe he owed him just this much. One good pitch. One championship.

As he unfolded his body and leaned into the throw, whipping his right arm forward, he felt like the ball was going to top a hundred miles an hour, up in Nolan Ryan territory. Yes, McFall could make that happen. McFall could make the radar gun jump in the scout's hands, he could make Stinson's bat shatter into a thousand splinters, he could make Bobby Eldreth live on as a local legend, the Pickett High superstar who made it to the World Series.

Hell, YES. The game within the game.

Now Bobby understood. All you had to do was want it, and McFall would give it to you.

The pitch sailed, just as Bobby had planned. Stinson's eyes widened, and Bobby was sure the batter would wait it out, take it for ball two—unless the ump had been bought off, in which case, it would be game over. Then it looked like Stinson was about to make an off-balance lunge, just as Bobby had planned. But the guy didn't lose his balance—he'd merely been hanging back, waiting for the ball to rise, as if he'd cottoned to Bobby's plan even before the pitch.

The crack of the bat was like a thunderclap in an arid desert. It surprised everyone but Stinson, and the Vance base-runners jolted into action. Bobby's mouth fell open in disbelief, and time stretched again, allowing him to take in too much information— Elmer snarling, the scout giving a disappointed shake of his head, McFall nodding in approval, the chili still stinking. Bobby didn't even have to turn around to know the game was over, because the winning run was already galloping around third. He slammed his glove against the gritty red clay of the pitcher's mound and stared at his cleats.

The small group of Vance supporters went wild, rewarded for making the two-hour trip. The home crowd let out a mutual groan when the runner stomped on home plate to seal the defeat of Pickett—and its star player.

Bobby slouched toward the dugout, where Coach Harnett was doling out passive-aggressive applause. Just as the coach believed kids couldn't handle pressure, he embraced the old-school clichés of sportsmanship and dignity in defeat. Bobby felt like kicking him in the shins. Harnett slapped him on the back. "Good effort, Bobby. We just got beat by a better team today."

Under the crappy unwritten rules of sports, Bobby had to endure shaking hands with all the opposing players and coaches, muttering "Good game." All the while, he was thinking, *I lost the game. AND the game within the game.* He couldn't be sure, but he thought Stinson smirked at him when they low-fived. Stinson leaned in close and whispered, "McFall was right."

Then Stinson had moved past him, and Bobby tried to work back through the line to ask him what the hell he was talking about, but his teammates were annoyed, tired, bitter, and ready to go home, so they shoved him forward until the mock ritual was mercifully complete.

Elmer met Bobby by the dugout. His eyes blazed with anger and his lips puckered with resentment. "You blew it. How could you be so goddamned dumb that you threw him a high fastball?"

"I had him," Bobby said. "Anyway, it doesn't matter. All scouts care about is arm speed."

Elmer looked around, but the scout had vanished along with two-thirds of the crowd. "You weren't even reaching eighty. Granny El can throw harder than that."

"I've still got my scholarship."

"You won't never get drafted out of college. This was your—"

"Excuse me," a man said, and Elmer turned to face Larkin McFall. Casually dressed in a polo shirt and khaki trousers, McFall made Elmer look even more like a backwoods hillbilly than usual in his blue-jean overalls. The guy might be creepy, but Bobby wondered why he couldn't have had a dad like McFall, a guy who had his act together, instead of a mumble-mouthed, drunken loser.

Elmer immediately became deferential, even goofy. "Mr. McFall! Sorry, I didn't see you in the crowd, or I'd'a said howdy. Didn't know you were a fan."

"I'm a student of the game within the game," McFall said, looking squarely at Bobby.

"I'll get those estimates to you in a few days," Elmer blubbered. "That's a lot of pipe. A big project like that is harder to figure than this nickel-and-dime stuff I usually—"

"No hurry," McFall said. Then, to Bobby, "That was a tough loss, son. But you gave it your best shot."

"No," Bobby said. "It wasn't my best. I should have thrown him a fastball low and outside."

Elmer's mouth gaped in shock, flashing the dark rectangle of a missing canine. "I thought you said—"

"You can second-guess yourself until the end of time, but the pitch you threw is the pitch you threw," McFall said, an irritating counterpart to Harnett's gold standard of useless clichés, "It is what it is."

"Well, I won't throw it next time," Bobby said.

"But next time, it might *be* the right pitch," McFall responded. "You won't know until you throw it."

Bobby was unsettled by McFall's philosophical curveballs. Probably, he was just imagining the whole thing about the man having supernatural powers. God knows, people in Pickett County believed in that kind of nonsense. Still, he couldn't help but wonder if McFall would let him be a successful drummer now, since he'd somehow conspired to take away Bobby's baseball career. That was the deal, wasn't it? You had to want it to get it.

Damn. That's as bad as "It is what it is."

"See you at home," Bobby said to his dad. "Don't tell Mom about the scout. She's got enough to worry about."

Larkin McFall stood aside and for the first time Bobby noticed that his wife had been standing behind him the whole time, almost like a shadow. Her face was cool and placid, like a porcelain mask adorned with sunglasses. Although attractive, there was something vaguely...*unfinished*...about her. McFall put an arm around her, and the corners of her lips turned up in a rote smile that held neither cheer nor warmth.

Bobby made his way to his Toyota pickup in the parking lot, dragging his feet across the grass. The scoreboard on the hill reminded him of the 3-2 final tally, and the *Times* would remind him again tomorrow, and Elmer would remind him for about thirty years or until his ticker blew out, whichever came first.

Melanie and Ronnie were waiting for him by the truck. "Sucks," Ronnie said. "He just got lucky."

Melanie gave him a hug and it felt good, and then it felt *great*. Her gray eyes were a little moist—they could go from a stormy sea to a spring sky in seconds—but she managed a smile of sympathy. "You were a rock star," she said.

Bobby hoped *she* hadn't been talking to McFall, too. It seemed like everybody was talking to the stranger these days. "Yeah, well, this was my last game in high school, so the show's over," he said. "Wanna lift?"

She glanced down and Ronnie looked out across the baseball field. "Ronnie's already promised me a ride," she said.

"Cool. See you guys later."

"Call me," Melanie said, and he couldn't tell if it was a question or a command. He didn't care either way. He was dead tired.

He was no longer sure what he wanted, or how badly he wanted it. As he started the pickup, Stinson's words echoed inside his head: "*McFall was right.*"

CHAPTER FIFTEEN

"On behalf of the Pickett County Friends of the Library, we'd like to thank you for your generous donation," Nancy Holloway said. The librarian spoke slowly so that Cindy Baumhower could transcribe her dull quote word for word. "This gift will go a long way toward expanding our local history section and ensuring that the past remains alive for future generations of county residents."

Larkin McFall posed with Nancy in front of a bookshelf, inhaling her scent of old pulpwood, dust, and a cheap perfume from a pint bottle she'd likely been using since her long-ago youth. He smiled not just for the photo but because he would be appearing in *The Titusville Times* for the third week in a row.

"Okay, everyone," Nancy said to the four retirees who made up the Friends' board of directors. "Punch and cookies are set up in the conference room to celebrate."

As the small group disbursed, Cindy pulled Larkin aside, as he'd known she would. After all, she was the reason he'd dreamed up the $5,000 donation. The library was practically empty this morning, with just three people using the public computers, a young woman pushing a baby stroller through the children's section, and a filthy-looking man obsessively fingering titles in the mystery section. The man irked Larkin, because his unkempt appearance seemed out of place among the neat and orderly rows of books.

"Can I have a word with you?" Cindy asked, wresting his attention from the roustabout. "Nancy never lets anyone else get a word in edgewise."

"Sure, as long as you don't ask me about Cole Buchanan's death. The matter is still under investigation, and my attorney advised me not to comment. And, please, not so many questions that I miss out on the cookies."

"Yeah, you don't want to miss Nancy's cookies," Cindy scoffed. "They're the best that Wal-Mart has to offer at half price." Pressing her pen to her notepad, she put on a pretty good appearance of interest. "Why do you feel local history is worth supporting?"

"We should always remember where we came from," Larkin said. "Especially people in a rural community like Pickett County, where our family trees are so intertwined. Of course, local history also includes the native peoples who lived here long before Daniel Boone hunted these lands." He winked. "Is that politically correct enough, or should I also mention that the white settlers of the area never held slaves?"

"This is a puff piece, Mr. McFall. We don't have room for deeper social issues."

"I'd like to add one more thing. It's a travesty that the county commissioners have cut the library's budget by ten percent in the next fiscal year. Our local leaders should invest in building better citizens instead of playing shell games to keep taxes low."

"That's also a little beyond the scope of this particular article," Cindy said, although her nostrils flared, her pupils grew larger, and she leaned slightly toward him. She'd recently written an editorial decrying the proposed budget cuts and was obviously flattered that he shared her opinion. "And don't you think that statement would get you in trouble with your friends on the commission?"

"They know my principles," Larkin said. "True friends always let you speak your mind."

Cindy let her guard down a little, apparently seeing him as an ally in idealism. "You should read some of the letters to the editor I get. The ones I can't publish."

"You're not a good journalist unless people on both sides of an issue hate you."

She grinned at that, and it wasn't forced. Cindy Baumhower was clearly someone who thought she'd conquered her vanity merely by acknowledging its existence. But Larkin knew better.

"Is that enough for your article?" Larkin said. "I would prefer for the focus to be on the good work the library does, and its need for support, not me."

Larkin, for one, knew how to make people like him. *Keep your friends close and your enemies closer.*

"Just a couple more questions for deep background," she said. "We're going to start a Chamber of Commerce business series in a few weeks and I may as well get some basics while I have you, since you seem to be rapidly becoming one of our leading citizens."

"You can have me anytime, Miss Baumhower."

Her nostrils flared again, the only sign that his *double entendre* had any effect on her. "I'm too busy to chase you down," she said. "And we're trimming our staff, so I'll be writing the series myself."

"Okay, then," he said with a dramatic sigh, giving a forlorn look at the conference-room door. "The cookies will have to wait. Fire away."

"I believe I heard somewhere that you were from El Paso, Texas. I did a quick Google check and couldn't find any business listed there in your name."

"I was a silent investor in multiple projects. As I said, I like the focus to be on others. What satisfies me most is...enabling. Yes, enabling success. Bringing out the best of what's inside people."

Larkin was pleased to see her write the quote down. "Any names?" she asked. "Any specific developments I can mention?"

"I'll have my wife email you a full list. Although, again, I don't want it to come off like I'm bragging. I might not have grown up here, but I'm a McFall. I'm one of you."

"Oh, I'm an import," she said. "I've barely been in town for a decade."

"I tend to think we're all tourists, Miss Baumhower. Some of us just pass through a little faster than others."

The greasy-haired man passed them on his way to the circulation desk, a stack of books in his grubby hands. He walked with a jerky gait, making a guttural noise in his throat, and he nearly bumped into Cindy, his perception apparently limited in the manner of a schizophrenic or borderline autistic. Cindy stepped closer to Larkin to allow the man room to pass. He jerked to avoid contact, even though he was five feet away, and one of his books slid to the floor. As he stooped to pick it up, his eyes met Larkin's.

The man immediately dropped the rest of his books, a couple of them bouncing across Cindy's feet. "You!" the man croaked, loudly enough to draw the attention of the desk clerk.

"Do I know you?" Larkin said, instinctively putting a protective arm between the man and Cindy.

"No, but I...but I...nuh-nuh-know *you*," the man said. "I've always known you."

Larkin studied the man's spade-shaped face and dark eyes. He had the look of a Buchanan, unshaven and surly, and Larkin wondered if this was one of Cole Buchanan's brothers. Larkin would have gleefully gouged out the man's eyes and jammed them down his throat, but then he'd have to kill Cindy and all the other witnesses in the library. And he was beginning to rather like Cindy. He had plans for her, and her premature death would take much of the fun out of the summer ahead.

"I'm afraid we've never met," Larkin said, bending to retrieve the fallen books. He held them out to the man.

The grungy stranger backed away, shaking his head. "I don't want nuh-nuh-nothing you've touched."

Cindy took the books from Larkin and tried to follow the man, but he hurried out of the library's sliding doors, muttering to himself. "That was weird," Cindy said to Larkin.

"Schizophrenia is not pretty," Larkin said. "Just another area where budget cuts have hurt the disenfranchised."

Cindy looked at the books. "James Lee Burke. At least he's got good taste."

I may soon find out all about his taste. Larkin picked up the remaining books. "I'm sorry for the interruption. Is there anything else you needed to ask me?"

Cindy seemed to have forgotten the purpose of her interview. "No, not as long as I can get that list of your former business ventures."

Larkin fished inside his jacket and pulled out a business card. "Just email us and I'll have it sent over."

Cindy accepted the card with her index finger and thumb clamping the edges and closed it inside her notepad. "Enjoy your cookies," she said. "I'd better get back to the office."

"In that case, let me handle the books." Larkin collected them from her, said good-bye, and carried the stack to the circulation desk, where the pinch-faced staff member—the brass name tag on his chest read "Robert" and, in smaller letters below that, "Multimedia Specialist"—frowned at the extra work.

"I'm glad he didn't check these out," Robert said. "He never returns them on time. And pages are usually missing."

"Do you know him?"

"Sweeney Buchanan. He used to be in the psych ward at Broughton before the last overhaul of the mental health system dumped him back out on the streets. He's the brother of that guy who was found dead in the church fire."

"A shame," Larkin said. "I hope he's not a danger to himself or others."

"Oh, he's harmless. Except for a little property damage here and there."

"We all carry our damage with us." Larkin reflected on the man's words: *I've always known you.*

Maybe Sweeney Buchanan was more than just a schizophrenic. Maybe he was a visionary, like those Old Testament recluses who saw God in fire and smoke. His peculiar brand of madness might allow him to see beneath the surface. As McFall well knew, all prophets were madmen until their madness infected enough people.

Unlike everyone else in Pickett County, Sweeney might recognize Larkin for what he was instead of taking him at face value. In many ways, only saints and madmen made his work worthwhile. He gave Robert a little salute as he headed toward the conference room to flatter some of the well-intentioned but self-righteous do-gooders who made his work—his *return*—necessary.

148

CHAPTER SIXTEEN

Sheriff Frank Littlefield knocked on the door of Stepford Matheson's little cabin.

The yard was a tribute to laziness, with knee-high weeds going to seed while the path between the dirt driveway and the front door was nothing but a narrow stretch of mud. Cinder blocks and masonry stones were piled all around a dismantled cement mixer. A rusted engine block sat in what might once have been a flower bed, and busted cardboard boxes overflowing with beer cans were stacked under the sagging wooden steps. Stepford's spot-primed Plymouth Duster was parked under a tin roof supported by skinned locust posts.

The Duster was a legendary accomplice in three speeding tickets, one Driving Under the Influence, one Driving While License Revoked, and a charge of Assault with a Deadly Weapon that was dropped when the accuser ended up marrying—and soon divorcing—Stepford. The Duster—Stepford's prized possession—was in a constant state of upgrade. The newest additions, Littlefield noticed, were silver exhaust pipes that extended from the rear like machine guns.

Because Stepford had missed his Wednesday night poker game, the only ritual in which he'd ever regularly and willfully engaged, his buddy Freddy Gaithers had called the sheriff's office to report him missing. The Duster was here at Stepford's house, and not much of anything was within walking distance of the property, so it seemed likely that Stepford might have taken a ride with someone. Given the mysterious deaths of his buddies Cole Buchanan and Darnell Absher, no one could really blame him for skipping town.

Or he could be lying dead behind the front door. Littlefield hoped against hope that he'd just gone off somewhere, and that he'd stay away for a while. It would help things settle back to normal if one more hot-blooded Matheson was out of the picture.

Who the hell are you kidding? There's no such thing as "normal" in Pickett County. Just days spent bouncing between the extremes of abnormal and paranormal.

Besides, Stepford would never abandon his Duster, not with relatives and other assorted thieves hanging around. According to Freddy, nobody had heard from Stepford in three days. If the man's corpse had been trapped inside the stuffy cabin that long, in the rising heat of May, Littlefield would have been able to smell it from here on the steps.

Littlefield knocked and called again, and then tried the door handle. It was locked. Stepford didn't seem like the door-locking type, even considering the loose company he kept. Circling to the side of the house, Littlefield climbed onto a corroded oil barrel to peek in a window. Through a gap beneath the towel that hung as a curtain, all the sheriff could see was a stretch of plywood flooring and an empty couch. All the lights were off.

Littlefield considered driving back to the courthouse to secure a warrant, but that would kill half the morning, easy. What if Stepford was inside suffering from a heart attack or stroke, barely clinging to life?

Glancing around, Littlefield found an empty dog-food bag in the weeds. He folded it into a sodden square, climbed back on the barrel, and used the pad to protect his elbow. He was about to smash the glass when he realized what was missing, and why the silence was so unnerving.

Dogs.

Every time I've been out to issue a summons for child-support payments, those ugly old fleabags moan and howl like firecrackers are tied to their tails.

Even though it wasn't deer season, Stepford might have gone out for a good old coon hunt and camping trip. Coon hunters did it for the fun, not the meat—or, more likely, as an excuse to get away from it all. That made sense, although he wondered why Freddy wouldn't have been invited. Littlefield relaxed a little, eager to accept a logical explanation based on the flimsiest of circumstantial evidence.

He stooped to climb down from the barrel, a tinge of arthritis flaring in one knee. But a smoldering ember of fear pulsed in his chest, stopping him in his tracks. He knew he was so eager to accept the easy answer because he was afraid of the truth. If this returning McFall was bringing all the past malevolence back with him, Littlefield was the only one who could stop him.

Because Littlefield knew more about the McFalls than anyone alive.

To hell with it.

Littlefield flung the makeshift pad away and drove his fist into the window, large shards of glass tinkling to the floor. He picked a couple of slivers from his knuckles, licked the minor puncture wounds clean, and then knocked out the larger wedges of remaining glass before hoisting himself inside.

He scrambled over the kitchen counter, plunging one foot into a sink full of sour dishwater. Stepford apparently did as little cleaning inside as out. Littlefield pushed aside a skillet that featured a mysterious mound of fuzzy green mold. The stench didn't disguise the fact that the air inside the little cabin was stuffy, suggesting that doors and windows hadn't been opened for days.

After turning on the lights, he performed a perfunctory search of the living room, although there was nothing to indicate a struggle. The bedroom door, which bore a peeling bumper sticker that read "Don't Tread On Me," was closed. Littlefield gave it a knock before trying the handle. Bracing himself for anything, he entered.

"Hey, sheriff," came a drowsy voice from the bundle of blankets piled on a mattress on the floor.

Littlefield flipped the light switch and the bundle twitched, then a thin pale foot emerged from the blankets. "Who's there?" Littlefield boomed in his law-enforcement voice.

Stepford sat up, the blankets sliding from his shoulders to expose his bony frame. His chest was crisscrossed with old scars. He appeared to be naked beneath the covers, and Littlefield hoped the man didn't suffer a sudden urge to use the bathroom or get dressed. "Did I do something bad again?"

"Nuh-no, we just had a report that you were missing," the sheriff said, feeling foolish now.

Stepford cleared his throat and spat into a Coke can beside the mattress. He missed, and a dirty stream of saliva streaked across the lettering. Littlefield could have sworn there was blood in the drool, but maybe Stepford had some kind of gum disease. "Good to know I still got friends."

"I broke your window," the sheriff said. "I'll get Lloyd from maintenance to come out and replace it."

Stepford gave a wave of dismissal. "Hell with it. It's getting to be the time of year when a man needs some fresh air anyway."

"I apologize for barging in on you like this," Littlefield said, hoping he wouldn't be asked for a warrant. "I knocked and hollered first."

Stepford was groggy, but it seemed to be from sleep rather than booze or drugs. "Sounds like you were just doing your job."

Damn. Is Stepford being conciliatory? This is something new. He usually pisses and moans when I deliver a legitimate warrant, and here I am without a leg to stand on, and he's acting like I dropped in for a beer.

"You okay?" Littlefield asked, anxious to be out of the room, which smelled like beer farts, old socks, and a mildewed decay, as well as a sweeter kind of rot that underpinned the room's fetid concerto of odors.

"Yeah, sure. Just slept a while. What time is it?"

Littlefield checked his cell phone. "1:30."

"Day or night?"

The dark towel thumbtacked over the window admitted little light, but the sun was clearly out. Now Littlefield wasn't sure about the drug use, but he didn't want to rummage through the surrounding piles of clothes to test his suspicions. "It's afternoon. Well, Stepford, since you're okay, I'd best be getting on with my work. Call my office about that window repair when you're ready."

Stepford rubbed a hand over his scalp and then stared down into it as if surprised he still had hair. "Sure thing, Sheriff."

"Say, what happened to your dogs?"

"The varmints run off. I tell you, ain't nobody got any gratitude any more, not even 'man's best friend.'"

"While I'm out here, do you mind if I look around the woods a little? I'm still working on the Cole Buchanan case and...."

Littlefield expected Stepford's rage to boil over at the mention of his dead friend, but he merely scratched at his hairless, scarred chest and nodded. "I'm all eat up inside over it, but you got to let these things pass."

"I'm not saying there was anything suspicious," the sheriff said. "I just haven't gotten a look at the backside of the McFall property yet. Since the two of you were at the church that night with torches... well, it just seemed awful odd when he was found dead in that fire."

Littlefield was uncomfortable even having this conversation. Stepford either seemed to have forgotten the incident entirely or he'd already resigned himself to a new reality—one in which the rich folks with their attorneys made all the rules of the world while Stepford's kind hid in their bedrooms and kept their mouths shut. But Stepford was barely interested, much less angry. He didn't seem to have a thing in common with the man Littlefield had been arresting for thirty years.

"Do what you got to do, Sheriff," Stepford said. "I'm just going to sleep a little bit more. Lock the front door on the way out, will ya?"

"Be glad to," Littlefield said. "I'll put out word that you're okay."

Stepford collapsed back on the mattress as if he'd expended all his energy on the conversation. "G'night," he mumbled, followed by something else Littlefield couldn't make out.

Back outside in the inviting fresh air, Littlefield checked the dog pen. Wire mesh was nailed to narrow hardwood planks extending eight feet into the air. Even the most determined dog wouldn't have been able to jump or scramble out, and the gate had three hasps to keep it secure. Checking the latches, Littlefield saw old brown spatters on the wood that might have been blood, along with small swatches of fur.

I'm staying away from conjecture. I don't need to feed my paranoia. Maybe it's just a coincidence that there've been two mysterious deaths in less than a month, and McFall's return is completely unrelated. After all, there's no proof of any wrongdoing.

Unfortunately, McFall was all the proof the sheriff needed. He headed up the woods along a trail that opened up on the side of the yard. Stepford had obviously used the path for hunting. Perhaps the dogs really had broken free and taken off up the mountain. The blood spatters could be another coincidence.

Maybe. Littlefield was killing himself with maybes.

Here and there he saw paw prints, and even a few boot prints that were faint from the rain. No one had used the trail in days, but this was probably the route Cole Buchanan, Sonny Absher, and Stepford had taken the night they'd intended on vandalizing the church.

Littlefield was short of breath after a few minutes, gasping and cursing his age. He pulled out the map he'd photocopied in the deed office and calculated his location based on the highway, Stepford's house, and the distance he'd walked. The McFall property extended to the ridge and included most of this side of the mountain. Stepford's property was a puny twenty acres in comparison, and on the other side of the ridge, the land was divided between the Days, the Abshers, and the Buchanans, bordered by the river and encompassing a mix of pasture and woodlands. A strip of designated national forest ran along the road before opening into a much larger parcel to the west.

While the Absher land had been subdivided among multiple heirs, the Buchanan property was consolidated into one large tract. Apparently the Buchanan heirs worked out their property rights and disputes within the family, with half a dozen residences and a Christmas tree farm tucked into a rocky hollow. David Day's property was thirty-six acres, much of it in pasture that he leased to local cattle producers, but he also had a garden and some forest land. From the map, Littlefield estimated that the ridge was maybe five hundred yards ahead, and he wasn't sure he could make it that far.

Littlefield was just about ready to give up and turn around when he reached the fence. It bisected the path with the clear intention of halting foot traffic. It was constructed of new, pressure-treated wood, a series of four-by-four posts with three wide planks suspended between each. It would be easy enough to clamber over the fence and continue along the path, but the message was unmistakable: Trespassers not welcome.

Back in Littlefield's youth, the land in Pickett County had more or less been open for public hunting, hiking, and camping. Local landowners generally didn't post their property or prohibit access, and those who did were considered "contrary." But with more and more outsiders buying up the land for investment, outdoor recreation was now severely limited. Aside from a few designated hunting grounds and the adjoining national forest, only the undeveloped rural sections still offered places where people could get away from civilization.

And now McFall had walled off a little more of the world.

Littlefield bent for a closer look at one of the posts. It bore the same brown spatters as the one in the dog pen. Littlefield considered taking out his pocket knife and shaving off a section, but he couldn't justify the expense of running a test to determine if the blood was human. The fence had obviously been constructed after the two men's deaths, anyway, so the blood couldn't belong to Cole Buchanan or Darnell Absher. Littlefield contented himself with the thought that Stepford's dogs might have trapped a wild animal here and mauled it before dragging it into the woods.

Littlefield walked the fence line for a while, heading downhill. He caught his second wind by the time he neared Little Church Road. Through the trees, he could see the blackened stone foundation of the red church. A bulldozer on a long trailer was parked beside it, ready for action. Littlefield was reminded of how quickly things could change, even for someone as old as he was. Even for a mountain as old as this one.

When he reached Stepford's cabin, he didn't bother knocking to tell Stepford he hadn't found anything. He climbed into his Isuzu Trooper and drove away, relieved that he hadn't added a third corpse to McFall's ledger.

Not yet, he mentally reprimanded himself. *Not yet.*

CHAPTER SEVENTEEN

"**W**hat about the tree ordinance?" Heather Fowler addressed the planning board that was gathered around the conference table in the courthouse. "And the line-of-sight distances required by the Department of Transportation for entrances and exits? This many homes will generate a lot of traffic."

Heather had the unsettling feeling that she was the only one of the five members of the county planning board who had actually read the permit application for McFall Meadows. Her copy of the twenty-two-page document was covered with yellow highlights, scribbles in the margins, and brown circles from coffee cups, while everyone else's copies were pristine, without even an indentation near the staple to indicate that the first page had been turned.

"It all looks good to me," said Wally Kaufman, who owned a local grading company. His copy of the document was sitting in front of him at the conference table—still in its mailing envelope.

The county commissioners had appointed people who were designed to represent a broad cross-section of the community, but with the exception of Heather, all of them had a hand in land development. Heather was the commissioner representative on the board, which met the third Thursday of every month, and she was pretty sure she'd been dumped here so that her voice would be drowned out by all the men who profited from unchecked growth.

"I've visited the site," she said, catching the eye of Larkin McFall, who sat at the table beside the county attorney, Francisco Baldemar. McFall gave her a smile of encouragement as she continued. "The narrow road around the property isn't even paved, and this projected traffic count of nineteen vehicles per hour would double the load on it."

"Little Church Road is on the state's Transportation Improvement Plan," said committee member Bill Willard, a renowned wildlife photographer who'd parlayed his wealth into several large land holdings. Willard especially irked Heather because his developments were damaging the very wildlife on which he had built his fortune. He was representative of the hypocrisy and corruption of the planning board, and, by extension, the entire local development community.

Heather shuffled through her paperwork until she found the state's list. She scanned it and shook her head. "I don't see it on here."

"Emergency approval," Willard said. "It was a rider on a local bill that was passed two months ago by the state legislature."

Heather didn't recall any discussion of such an action, which would have required a good deal of local support. The Republican representative and the Democratic senator for the region wouldn't waste their limited political capital in the General Assembly unless substantial payback had been promised. "But we hadn't even received an application for the proposed development at that point."

Willard shrugged and glanced over at Francisco. The curly-haired attorney cleared his throat. "The state must have identified the road as a future growth corridor," Francisco said. "Just like my client did. Even if McFall Meadows never became reality, other developments would have popped up soon. Despite the poor economy, the area is still a popular destination for second-home owners and real-estate investors."

"Okay, even if the state grants the line-of-sight variance, the county still doesn't allow lot sizes smaller than half an acre. This plan somehow squeezes five hundred and eighty houses, twelve condominium complexes, and four townhouses onto two hundred acres of land. I don't even see how it would be possible to squeeze enough septic tanks onto the property."

"May I?" McFall said to Logan Extine, the chairman of the board.

"The chair recognizes Mr. McFall," Extine said, going through the formality for the transcription benefit of the county secretary, the only other person in attendance even though all meetings were open to the public.

"Miss Fowler, the first phase of the development will be near the top of the property, where the slopes—as you well know—are pretty steep," McFall said. "We'll need to clear a lot of trees to install the required septic lines, which is why we're asking for a variance on the tree ordinance."

"But those are old-growth hardwoods," Heather said. "And I understand there are some rare high-altitude bogs along the ridge as well."

"'Old' is a relative term, Miss Fowler."

"What about the proximity of national forest lands? I'm sure there are federal laws that protect the viewshed and prevent that kind of drastic clear-cutting."

"We're focusing on local approval, Miss Fowler," Extine said, with barely suppressed exasperation. "This board can barely handle what's within our own borders without worrying about a billion other rules and regulations."

"We're sworn to uphold our own rules, though," Heather said, forcing herself to remain calm even as her blood rose to boiling. The last thing she needed was for the other board members to accuse her of hysteria—not that it would change her reputation any. "Squeezing that many residences onto that mountain will create an eyesore. It will also violate at least half of the Unified Development Ordinance."

For emphasis, Heather slapped her palm on the vinyl notebook that held the almost four-hundred-page document. She was the only board member who regularly brought her UDO to the meetings, although a reference copy stood on a shelf in the corner, beneath the American flag.

"The UDO's just a guideline, not the Gospel," Willard said, as Kaufman yawned and snuck a look at his iPhone. "We can choose to override any or all of the ordinances if the project is in the best interests of Pickett County."

Heather shook her head. "No way. The articles clearly state that variances can only be granted if there is proof that they won't have a negative impact. We haven't been given any proof of that."

McFall gave her the type of smile that a weary, patient father might muster for a wayward child. "You have my word, Miss Fowler."

Heather flung up her hands. "A promise hardly counts as proof."

Kaufman and Willard started talking at the same time. Stu Hartley, a carpenter and usually reticent board member who always voted with Extine no matter the issue, even threw in a comment, saying, "This here project looks like a win-win to me."

Heather raised her voice, horrified at her own shrillness. "But the septic lines—"

"That's only the first phase," McFall said. "Once we raise some revenue on lot sales, we're building a small sewage treatment plant down by the river."

The same river I saved when Titusville wanted to tap it for more drinking water? Over my DEAD BODY.

Heather's lip quivered with rage, and she could have sworn McFall smirked. Kaufman and Willard were still rambling, and Extine employed the unheard-of measure of banging his gavel three times on the walnut surface of the table. The rapping was as dramatic as gunshots in the small conference room.

In the ensuing silence, Extine said, "A treatment plant is the best and cheapest option. I amend our approval to include a provision to allow such a plant, contingent upon any state and federal approval, of course."

The vein in her temple was throbbing so mightily, Heather thought she was going to have a stroke. "We haven't approved *anything* yet!"

"If there are no objections, can I hear a motion?" Extine said.

Willard raised his hand like a grade-school student who was pleased to deliver the correct answer to a math problem. "I move that we—"

"We can't just grant a blanket variance because Mr. McFall gave us his *word*," Heather interrupted.

"Yes, we can," Willard said. "It's in the UDO. Article 7, Section F. The last item."

Even a public servant as dedicated and obsessed as Heather could hardly be expected to read—much less memorize—hundreds of pages of dense legalese. But she was familiar with Article 7 because it was basically a summary of the board's powers and limitations. She flipped through her notebook, eager to show the other board members that they had no authority to allow McFall to do whatever he wanted.

She had a good feel for the spirit of the article, which she'd been planning to use as fodder for her argument against McFall's ambitious—and maliciously greedy—design. While the final article granted the board some leeway in granting variances, she was confident that the board's powers were limited.

What she read at the bottom of the article shocked her:

The planning board may, by a majority vote, grant approval for any project if such a project is deemed in the best interests of Pickett County, regardless of whether the project meets other requirements of the Unified Development Ordinance.

Heather squinted at the words. Was she going mad? She'd never seen that article before, and if she had, she would have immediately brought it before the county commission to have it struck from the document. What was the point of crafting a thick planning document and then essentially rendering it useless if three of the five board members wanted it that way?

She glared at Baldemar Francisco. "When was this UDO amendment passed?"

"It's always been there," he said.

"No. Even the ink looks fresher than the rest of the page. Like it's been typed out today. And this has been in my desk drawer since the last meeting."

"Are you feeling okay, Miss Fowler?" Extine said, although his tone lacked any compassion.

Heather ignored him, still pressing Francisco. "This article would never pass legal muster if someone kicked it to a state civil court. Can the county assume that kind of liability?"

The lawyer cleared his throat. "I'm not here tonight in my capacity as county attorney. I am representing Mr. McFall."

McFall didn't even smile—he just sat there as innocent as a lamb. "That's a conflict of interest," Heather said to the attorney.

"No, it would only be a conflict if I was representing both parties. Tonight I'm only representing Mr. McFall."

Heather couldn't even begin to assail such a willfully ignorant position. Unlike many people, she didn't consider lawyers the equivalent of snakes and cockroaches. Justice was built on the rule of law, and orderly society depended upon a widely accepted standard of behaviors. If those were taken away, well . . . .

Then anyone could do exactly what they wanted. Such as build a development at twice the density the property could reasonably sustain.

"We have a motion on the floor," Extine said. "Approve McFall Meadows as submitted, with an amendment to permit a sewage treatment plant according to the owner's specifications."

"I object," Heather said, pushing away from the table and stomping across the room to check the copy of the UDO sitting on the shelf. As she flipped to the proper section, Kaufman said, "I'm missing 'American Idol' for *this*?"

Heather nearly dropped the bulky notebook when she saw it held the same strange language as her own. She couldn't believe such a passage had slipped through under her watch. She was failing the very constituents she'd promised to protect.

Like Larkin McFall, though, all she had given was her word. And words could apparently be changed without warning

"All in favor?" Extine said.

"Aye," said Willard, Kaufman, and Hartley in unison. Extine echoed his own approval, Heather could have sworn that even Francisco threw in a bonus "Aye."

"Project passes," Extine said.

"Nay," Heather said, still standing, the notebook against her hip. The project would pass anyway, but she wanted her objection noted for the record, because she was pretty sure one of the local environmental groups would challenge the decision at some point.

"Are you sure you won't change your mind?" McFall said. "I'd really prefer the appearance of unanimous support."

"I don't like the precedent this is setting," Heather said. "The next developer to walk into this room is going to expect the same *carte blanche* to do whatever they want."

"I don't know about no cart whatever, but if this is a precedent, I say we need more of it," Hartley said. "This is going to put some good people to work and bring money into this town. Mister McFall deserves a pat on the back, not somebody trying to slap him down for trying to help other folks."

Heather was surprised Hartley had that many words in his vocabulary. She looked at the blank faces around her, from Willard to Extine to Kaufman, then at Francisco, who was already shoveling his papers into a leather satchel.

"Sure you won't change your vote?" Extine asked her.

"I'm sure."

"Motion carries, four-one. Can I hear a motion to adjourn the meeting?"

After formalities, Extine banged the gavel again. As Francisco and the other board members filed out, Larkin McFall sidled over to Heather. "Does the UDO say anything about trespassing?"

"Don't rub it in. This isn't over yet."

"Oh, I know. It's just getting started."

His words unsettled her, although they weren't weighted with any obvious menace. They might even have been a pleasantry, like the gentle volley of two friends warming up for a tennis match. Still, Heather didn't like the look in his eyes. The earlier possessiveness she'd seen on the mountaintop, when he'd accused her of trespassing, had shifted into a gleam that she might have called *hunger*.

She blushed, hoping it was anger and not shame that warmed her cheeks. She shoved the UDO back on the shelf and collected her own notebook, while McFall bent over and whispered in the secretary's ear. It was an intimate moment that made Heather uncomfortable, even more so when the secretary giggled.

"Can I get a copy of the draft minutes when they're ready?" Heather asked the secretary.

"Sure, Miss Fowler," the secretary said. Like many females who worked for the county, the secretary was a traditionalist who accepted a male-dominated power structure without hesitation. That attitude usually marched in lockstep with a resentment of Heather, as if she were trying on trousers while all the other women were wearing pretty skirts.

"Can I escort you to your car?" McFall said to Heather. "The recent deaths in town were accidents, of course, but it never hurts to play it safe."

Yes, it does. It ALWAYS hurts. But I've come to believe it hurts either way.

"No, thank you," she said.

"I wish you'd quit fighting me. We're on the same side. I really do have the county's best interests at heart."

"Making millions and destroying mountains while patting yourself on the back. Color me unimpressed."

"Miss Fowler...." He paused and lowered his voice so the secretary couldn't hear his husky whisper. "Heather."

She looked at his face, then at his wedding ring. "Good night."

But it wasn't. It wasn't a good night at all.

CHAPTER EIGHTEEN

"So, you gonna ask her?" Bobby asked Ronnie.

"Ask who?"

"Don't play dumb. You know what I mean."

"She's probably already going with somebody. You know how girls are." Although Ronnie believed *nobody* knew how girls are, which was the problem.

"The dance is tomorrow night, so if you want to go for it, you'd better jump."

"Last time I jumped, I found a dead guy."

"Well, there won't be any dead guys at the dance," Bobby said. "Unless Melanie suddenly turns into a witch and pulls a 'Carrie.'"

They were loading fence posts and boards into the back of Bobby's pickup in front of Lemly's Building Supply. Larkin McFall had hired Bobby to work after school now that baseball season was over, and Bobby had arranged for Ronnie to get a job, too. Ronnie wasn't sure how he felt about working for a McFall, but since his dad and half the town now seemed to be on the guy's payroll, he figured he might as well sock away a little extra money for college. Besides, it beat the heck out of mowing grass for Dex's dad.

"What about you?" Ronnie asked, eager to change the subject. "Did you hook up with Amy Extine yet?"

"She's going with Brett Summers," Bobby said.

"That sucks. He's a real dickhead."

"Well, his dad's an insurance agent who drives a BMW, so what can you do?"

Bobby had a point, but Ronnie wasn't ready to let his friend go down in flames. Especially since he wanted Bobby to be interested in someone besides Melanie. "What can you *do*? You're a rock-n-roller. Look at all the chicks Dex scores. Heck, even if you got some of his leftovers...."

Bobby slammed a fence post into the bed of the truck so hard that some rust flaked off the bumper. "Don't make a big deal out of it. You think I'm worried about girls? No, I'm worried about delivering a tight gig. I want the band to be solid. We've been practicing a lot, but if Jimmy Dale shows up drunk again, we're screwed."

"I wished I'd learned to play an instrument," Ronnie said. "I wasted my time with the piccolo. Can't really stick it to the man with a little tin whistle."

"Never too old to rock-n-roll, unless you're the Rolling Stones zombie patrol," Bobby said, removing his leather gloves and pushing down on the back of the pickup. "That's about all the weight I want to carry. If we hit a pothole, the shocks will snap."

Bobby accepted the bill of sale after a clerk totaled the order, and Ronnie could see that his friend was proud to have the responsibility. Larkin McFall apparently trusted him to sign for materials and track his own hours. "That's 'McFall,'" Bobby said to the clerk. "Put it on his account. M-C-F-A—"

"I know who McFall is," said the smug clerk, who wasn't much older than they were. He was probably a recent dropout. "He's the only one buying building materials right now."

"Don't forget who signs your paycheck," Bobby said.

As they drove out of Titusville, the pickup grumbling in protest over the heavy load, Bobby said, "So, are you afraid of Melanie or something? Scared she'll shoot you down?"

That was exactly what Ronnie feared. As long as there was uncertainty, he could content himself with dreams, fantasies, and hopes. The unknown still offered luscious possibilities. But her rejection would be final. He couldn't really comprehend life after that. He knew it was goofy, even pathetic, but Ronnie's suppressed adoration of Melanie was one of the most real and reliable foundations of his life.

"She won't shoot me down," Ronnie said. "I just want to be respectful."

"She's nice, but she's no Amy Extine, that's for sure."

"What's that supposed to mean?"

"Have you seen Amy's hooters? I swear—she grew a full cup size this year. Or else she had surgery."

"Considering what an asshole her rich old man is, I wouldn't put it past either of them. Trophy daughter."

"C'mon, now, dawg, you can't rag on the home team," Bobby said, some of the humor falling out of his voice. "Her dad's in league with Larkin McFall. In a way, that means we're working for Extine, too."

"Crap," Ronnie said. "Talk about six degrees of suckage."

"Anyway, I got all summer to chase Amy. She's bound to get bored with Brett sooner or later. So, what do we do about Melanie?"

Ronnie's gut clenched. Was it time for them to finally have "the talk"? The one they'd been avoiding for more than a year?

The fantasy is better than the reality. Besides, she kissed you. Even if it was just your cheek, her lips were warm and "sweet."

"Why do we have to do anything?" Ronnie asked.

"Well, if she's going to go to the dance with you, we need to come up with a plan. Make you look good. Win her over."

Ronnie was confused. Bobby had gone out with Melanie at least four times he knew about, and probably more that he didn't. They hadn't quite become a "thing" in the high school hallways, but there was enough chemistry between them that a few of the jocks taunted Bobby about it, asking how far and how often and how deep and all that other asshole talk. The rumors had made Ronnie's head roar and his chest ache, even though he knew Bobby was a good dude and—unlike the other jocks—wouldn't treat her like a piece of meat.

"Well, part of it is I'm embarrassed about my wheels," Ronnie said.

"*Your* wheels? That's your mom's van. That's worse than if that piece of shit was actually yours."

"You're one to talk," Ronnie said. "Look at the steam coming out from under the hood."

"That's just the radiator," Bobby said. "Overheating a little from dragging this pile of wood up the hill."

"You should charge McFall extra for the wear and tear."

Bobby downshifted as they ascended a steep grade, the engine whining and sputtering. "That's not a bad idea. If you ask Melanie to the dance, I'll ask McFall if we can use one of his new trucks."

"You're serious?"

Bobby looked over at him. "Are you?"

"I've got to get my nerve up."

"Try it out."

"Huh?" The truck had topped the ridge and Highway 321 wound rapidly down toward the river and the bridge, the afternoon sun glinting off the big windows in the Riverview development. Ronnie felt the first tickling sensations of dread.

"Pretend I'm Melanie," Bobby said.

"That's weird, dude. I'm not gay."

"If I were gay, I bet you *would* be." Bobby laughed and punched his arm, and then grew serious. "I know Melanie pretty well. Better than you, for sure...."

The statement was true, and it made Ronnie jealous, and it also made a strange kind of sense. Bobby gave a coaxing, "Come on. Just give it a try."

"Okay." Neither of them had a cell phone, but Ronnie put one hand to his cheek, a pinky to his mouth and a thumb to his ear. "Buh-rinnng. Buh-rinnng."

"Hey, this is Melanie," Bobby said, in a pretty decent imitation of Melanie's high-pitched voice. "Who is it?"

Ronnie couldn't believe he was this nervous just faking it. He couldn't even imagine pulling off the real thing. "Huh-hi, this is Ruh-ronnie."

Bobby shifted back to his usual voice. "Who the hell is Ruh-ronnie?"

Ronnie tried again. "Hi, Melanie. How ya doing? This is Ronnie."

"Ronnie who?" Bobby mocked, now back in Melanie's voice. Ronnie punched him on the arm. The bridge was coming up, and he hoped Bobby wouldn't say anything about Darnell Absher's corpse.

"I was wondering if you wanted to go to the dance with me," Ronnie said, his anxiety over the bridge and the river mixing with his anxiety over Melanie, blooming into a chaotic cascade of thoughts and emotions.

I'm such a weirdo, and I'm NEVER gonna get laid.

"No, no, no," said Bobby. "It's like petting a baby goat. You don't just run up to it with your arm sticking out. You have to let it get used to you first, relax a little. You have to warm up to it."

Of course, Bobby was right. And Ronnie couldn't help imagining Bobby and Melanie out on a date, going home after the movies. Had Bobby pulled over by the bridge in the dark and petted her like a baby goat?

"Okay, I'll make some stupid small talk about math."

"Don't talk about class work, dummy. Talk about *life*."

"Say, Melanie, did you see that big brown stain on the bottom of Mr. Holloway's pants? I think he sat on his science project."

They both howled with laughter, even though the river was rolling beneath them, and Ronnie didn't want to look over the side of the bridge into the water. It was just one of those unavoidable facts of life . . . as long as he lived here, he would be near the river, just as he'd been near that stupid red church before it had burned down.

Ah. Okay. It's only water. Just the past moving on downstream.

Bobby slammed on his brakes, causing the fence posts to jostle in the bed and the tires to squeal on the asphalt. "Holy crap, did you see that?"

Ronnie wanted to close his eyes, but he couldn't. His friend was generously helping him steal away a girlfriend, or *possible* girlfriend, or occasional squeeze, or whatever they were, and Ronnie couldn't let him endure the river's horrors alone. No matter what shape they happened to take.

Bobby was staring out the driver's-side window, looking downstream, and Ronnie scrambled over the gear shift so that he could see, too.

"It's just mist," he whispered. The temperature inside the truck had to be about ninety, but he was shivering.

"Mist that looks like a bunch of people walking?"

That was exactly what it looked like. It was just like the night Ronnie had seen them walk from the red church into the river, led by Archer McFall. Only this time they were walking upstream. Back to where they'd come from.

"It's just mist," Ronnie repeated.

As they watched, the mist broke apart under the sunlight and disappeared. Only the river remained, silver and green and gray, winding over smooth stones toward the distant ocean.

"You're right," Bobby said. "Just mist. But for a second there . . . ."

A car that had come up behind them honked impatiently.

"Yeah, yeah," Bobby said in defiance, using his mock-Melanie voice. "Eat my shorts."

"It'd be a pleasure, ma'am," Ronnie joked to break the tension.

"Humor," Bobby said, popping the clutch and sending the pickup toward McFall Meadows. "That's good. Girls always love that. Just don't be a pervert."

"You got it, Coach."

In a way, Ronnie was no longer so scared of Melanie's rejection. The river ghosts had returned. He had something far worse to worry about now.

CHAPTER NINETEEN

"I ran that card you gave me," Sheriff Frank Littlefield said to Cindy Baumhower. "I told the SBI lab to dust it for a robbery suspect's prints. They didn't ask why a thief would be dumb enough to leave a business card, and it turned out not to matter. There were no prints on it."

"But I saw McFall touch it," Cindy said. "He practically felt it up. It was almost like he knew what I was planning."

"Maybe the paper fibers flaked off," Littlefield said. "Or maybe McFall doesn't secrete."

"Gross. I don't want to think about his secretions."

"So we're right back where we started."

They were at Frank's house, sitting on the couch with the flickering television as their romantic campfire. Wednesday was their "date night," although they rarely engaged in the traditional activities of couples, such as dining out, catching a movie, or getting drunk and embarrassing themselves in public. Because Littlefield wanted to maintain the illusion of a platonic relationship until he retired, dates consisted of a home-cooked dinner, cable TV, and a leisurely coupling before Cindy slipped home.

Lately, though, Littlefield had noticed some subtle but disturbing signs that Cindy meant business. First, she had equipped his kitchen with a few wooden utensils to assist in the creation of "heart-healthy stir-fries." As a lifelong bachelor, Littlefield hadn't even been aware of the existence of wooden spatulas, and now he had a decorative clay canister full of them. Next, Cindy had left a toothbrush in his medicine cabinet, and a week later had swapped out his brand of toothpaste for hers. When he'd mentioned it, Cindy had said, "You need to cut down on your fluoride intake. I want you to still be around thirty years from now." And then, of course, there were the subtle verbal hints she dropped about bringing their relationship to the next level....

Littlefield told her about his visit to Stepford Matheson's place and his search of the woods. He left out the part about the blood. "I kind of expected to find him dead," he concluded.

"You sound almost disappointed," Cindy said, leaning her head on his shoulder. "I think maybe you're getting a little paranoid in your old age."

"Maybe so. I want so much to believe that McFall is up to something that I'm going out of my way to nail him. But when you look at the evidence, he's done nothing wrong."

"Just the opposite," Cindy said, reaching for the TV remote—another recent habit that unsettled Littlefield—and turning down the volume of *Braveheart*. "He's supporting a number of community causes. He even bought a full-page ad announcing the groundbreaking ceremony for McFall Meadows."

"He's spreading the wealth, all right. But I can't help but feel he's spreading the bullshit, too."

"I'm starting to see his good side. You're just a little cranky. You need to release some of that steam."

Cindy put her arm around his waist and he kissed the top of her head. "Yeah, I guess I just want a last hurrah. One more epic showdown so the marshal can ride into the sunset on a win."

"Good gunning down Evil in the street, huh? That's a little melodramatic even for a cop."

"Thirty years, Cindy. Thirty years of my life spent trying to make a difference, believing I was doing the right thing. And what do I have to show for it? I'm supposed to serve and protect, but my career has created a trail of bodies that would make a hired hitman proud."

Cindy hugged him more tightly, gazing up at him with shining eyes. "Nobody can save the world singlehandedly. Shit happens, cowboy. And not everything's about you."

"Well, I'd feel better if Absher and Buchanan had waited another year to kick the bucket. I guess God doesn't work according to my schedule."

"Whoa. Are you getting religion in your old age?"

He laughed. "Maybe it goes hand in hand with paranoia."

Cindy disengaged herself from him to take a sip of wine from the glass on the coffee table. Littlefield, a teetotaler, was annoyed by her vice of choice, but was determined not to make their relationship a prison. He took a sip of iced tea, knowing the caffeine would make his insomnia worse. He didn't care. All sleep did was bring nightmares.

"You can retire early, you know," Cindy offered. "The commissioners could appoint an interim replacement from within the department to serve until the election. You've already got your pension locked in, and you could sure use a slight drop in blood pressure."

SCOTT NICHOLSON

Littlefield rose from the couch and paced. "You think I'm going to leave a mess like this on the table for the next sheriff? I thought you knew me at least a *little* bit."

"Oh, Frank." Cindy set down her wine and went to him, wrapping him in an embrace to stop his pacing. "I know the word 'hero' is cheap these days—hell, even the county maintenance workers are part of Homeland Security—but you're the real deal."

She pressed a palm against the center of his chest, and the warmth and firmness of her touch comforted him. "I know your heart," she said. "You think I'd fall for just any old guy? I'm getting older, too, but I'm not desperate. I've been divorced and I've been alone and I've been around. And you're the best man I've ever met."

Littlefield looked into her brown eyes, where reflections from the television glinted and danced. *Damn, I could really love this woman. If I could trust myself to know what love was.* Maybe she was right. He wasn't going to step down early, but why kill himself over something that would make him crazy? Until Larkin McFall actually did anything provably wrong, the man deserved the same treatment—the same presumption of innocence—as any other citizen. Suspecting him of malice simply because of his last name was as bad as racial profiling.

They kissed, and her lips were sweet with wine. Littlefield pulled her body to his and allowed himself the brief luxury of surrender. Then he pulled away.

"What if McFall doesn't *have* fingerprints?"

She gave him a playful swat on the butt. "Shut up and get in here," she said, sliding her other hand behind his belt buckle and tugging him toward the bedroom.

CHAPTER TWENTY

Bobby was on the back deck, where his dad stored old toilets, lengths of scrap pipe, boxes of fittings, and broken power tools like an air compressor and a pneumatic drill. The trailer park was in its typical state of weeknight activity, with loud televisions and stereos blaring from the aluminum-sided homes, the cacophony punctuated with an occasional domestic quarrel. The bugs had just emerged for the season, and something bit Bobby on the neck, but he ignored the pain and itching. He was seated on the lid of a closed toilet, tapping his drumsticks against the bottom of an upended plastic, five-gallon bucket.

RATTA-TATTA-TAT.

He was playing a snare march, one that might have led soldiers into battle back in the old days. He often played the rhythm as a tribute to his lost friend Vernon Ray, and sometimes—when the moon was low and the trailer park was quiet—Bobby thought he heard the cadence echoing back to him from the top of Mulatto Mountain.

Mostly, though, the beat was just repetitive practice, building up wrist strength and working on his timing. The band was only able to practice twice a week because of everybody's schedules, and Bobby was determined that no matter what happened with The Diggers, he was going to continue honing his chops.

The porch light came on and the back door opened. "What you doing sittin' out here in the dark?" Elmer asked him.

"Practicing," Bobby answered, maintaining the tempo even though he dropped the volume a little.

"That ain't practice. That's beating on a bucket."

"We've got a gig Friday night."

"Huh." Elmer scratched one of his armpits and the smell of sour sweat lingered for a moment before the breeze whisked it away. "What are they paying you for that, anyway?"

"A hundred bucks," Bobby said. "But it goes in the band fund to cover transportation and equipment."

"You can talk and beat a bucket at the same time," Elmer said. "I guess that's what passes for music these days."

Bobby stopped playing and rested his sticks on the bucket. "Dad, I'm sorry I lost the game. I thought I *had* him."

Elmer waved in dismissal, or he might have been swatting a bug. The moths had found the porch light, and they cast coruscating shadows as they circled it madly. "You done your best. I still bet you're going to get drafted."

This man's fantasies are as wild as Ronnie's. But I can't blame him. Like he says, he really doesn't have much else to get excited about besides wallowing in raw sewage until he's old enough for Social Security.

"We'll see," Bobby said. "The draft is still two weeks away. A lot could happen between now and then."

"That coach from App State call back?"

"Yeah. He told me to make sure I throw at least every other day. He doesn't want my arm to tighten up before fall practice, when they can get their trainers working with me."

"See, that's *real* practice," Elmer said, his round face shiny with sweat even though the night was relatively cool. "This here beating on stuff and making a racket don't amount to nothing."

"I'll throw after work every day, just like I told the coach," Bobby promised, mostly to shut him up.

Elmer spat off the porch and looked out at the thin strip of backyard, where the grass was worn and the clothesline sagged with laundry. "We had some good times out there, putting in the hours. I remember when we bought that new catcher's mitt and I dared you to throw the ball as hard as you could."

Bobby grinned at his memory of the percussive *thwack*. His dad had howled in pain and tossed the mitt away, wiggling his hand until the sting in his palm faded. Bobby wished he had a way to work that sound into his drum kit.

The howl, too. Hell, Dad's already as good a wailer as Dex.

Elmer apparently didn't want memory to evolve into actual sentiment. He changed the subject. "So you're working for McFall?"

"Yeah, he's giving me twelve bucks an hour, cash."

"Damn, that's sweet. Nothing beats working under the table. This McFall guy's all right, ain't he?"

"It's hard work, but I like it. Keeps me in shape."

And keeps my mind off of things.

"Did you get the contract to do the plumbing for the development?" Bobby asked. This was an opportunity for reasonable interaction with his dad on a subject other than baseball—which always tended to bring his dad around to rage sooner or later—and Bobby figured such opportunities would soon become rare.

"Sorta," Elmer said. "McFall said the job had gotten so big that he was hiring every contractor that applied, and he's just going to split the work up so everybody gets a piece of the pie. Like I said, he's a square Joe. I wish all these other asshole developers were half as nice."

Thunder rumbled in the distance. Bobby had been so intent on his snare rhythm that he hadn't noticed the bruised clouds sweeping in from the northwest. The sudden drop in temperature heralded a storm, and the breeze erased the aroma of Betty Garrison's fried liver mush emanating from next door.

"Gonna rain," Elmer said. "I better roll up my truck windows and get your mom to bring in the laundry."

Bobby stood, knocking his sticks to the deck, where they clacked and rolled around. "Shit. I was supposed to cover the lumber pile at McFall Meadows. We quit halfway through and I . . . well, there wasn't a cloud in the sky then."

Elmer's benevolent mood died like a match flushed down a toilet. "You better get your ass over there, and fast. You don't want to lose a job that good. And I don't want it coming back to bite me, either. Too much of your shit has been sticking to me lately."

And you should know, because you're the world's biggest expert in shit. Your head is FULL of it.

Bobby hurried to his pickup and was halfway to McFall Meadows when the first raindrops plinked against the windshield. He drove a little faster than usual, not quite trusting the front-end alignment but anxious to beat the worst of the storm. Builders hated working with wet wood. Not only was it heavier to handle, it sometimes warped and buckled. McFall would probably be angry if he had to buy a whole new supply.

As he sped over the bridge, he thought of the weird mist he'd seen earlier in the day. The river was usually only misty at night and under the first rays of dawn, the haze melting away as the sun rose, but he'd imagined the roiling, undulating arms and legs of *people* in that thick white shroud. Luckily, the river was so dark that he couldn't see any mist even if he wanted to look for it, and he sure didn't.

Maybe I should have just called Ronnie. He's right next door to McFall's property, and he could have run over and covered up the pile in a minute.

But this was his responsibility, and he knew it. Bobby was the one who'd hauled the materials and signed the sales receipts; Bobby was the one who'd received direct instructions from Larkin McFall. Ronnie was just a helper.

And it wasn't just his personal responsibility that hurried him down Highway 321 and onto Little Church Road. He didn't want to disappoint McFall. The guy was definitely strange, maybe even a bit spooky—*it's the game within the game that matters*—but he'd been good to Bobby, paying him enough so that Bobby would be in good shape whether he went to college or not. Hell, he could even move out and get his own place.

You don't want to play baseball. That's why you don't care that he made you throw that game. Unless you screwed it up all by yourself, on purpose.

The internal conflict kept him occupied until he found himself wheeling his rusty Toyota onto the gravel access road beside the old cemetery. The fencing material was stacked by the church's foundation, beside a flatbed trailer that held one of Wally Kaufman's bulldozers. Bobby and Ronnie had constructed a section of fence under the supervision of Stu Hartley, who mostly just operated the level and griped about the government.

Bobby parked his truck so the headlights were angled over the construction site and the shell of the old church, then hopped out, grateful the storm was holding off for the moment. He dashed to the flatbed trailer and pulled a wadded-up vinyl tarp from beneath it. His head and shoulders were soaked by the time he unfolded the tarp and spread it over the material. Even though it had been a week since the burning of the church, the smell of ash and charcoal still cloyed in the air.

Bobby looked around for something to hold the tarp in place against the wind. Since the grading hadn't begun, there were no stones lying around, and all the stones in the church's foundation were cemented firmly in place. His choice was to either run all the way down to the river in the dark, or ....

He walked over to the graveyard, his sneakers damp from the wet grass. A fallen grave marker was broken into chunks, from an event so long past that the weeds had filled in the cracks. "Forgive me, dude," Bobby whispered, "but right now I need these more than you do."

He bent and collected four large slabs of old gray concrete, one for each corner of the tarp. When he turned, he saw a figure rising inside the church foundation. "Huh-hello?" he said, wondering if Wally or maybe Ronnie had come out here to cover something up.

The figure was a stark gray silhouette in the truck's headlights, slogging toward him through the bed of ashes. The person looked like he was *made* of ash, some kind of freaky ghostly statue that was still smoldering deep inside, smoke and steam trailing behind.

Bobby dropped the chunks of concrete, one of them bouncing painfully off his foot. He sprinted toward the Toyota, not wanting the person—*the stack of smoke and ash*—to get close enough for him make out the details of its face.

Does it even HAVE a face?

He gunned the engine, nearly slewing the truck into the river before he regained control and sped off into the night.

He didn't dare check his rearview mirror.

CHAPTER TWENTY-ONE

Ronnie held his breath with the phone against his ear, trying to remember everything Bobby had told him.

Melanie picked up on the fourth ring. "Hi, Ronnie. What's going on?"

Ronnie lay on his bed and stared at the darkness outside his bedroom window, glad that Tim was busy doing the dishes since Mom was at her bookkeeping class. "Hi, Melanie. What are you up to?"

"I asked you first."

"Been working. Me and Bobby are putting up a fence over at McFall Meadows." Ronnie didn't realize how proud he was to have a real job. Mowing grass for Mac McAllister had been a nice little side gig, but it was better suited to a kid like Tim. It was time to develop some skills and muscles and make real money. Time to become a man.

"I thought you didn't like Larkin McFall."

This wasn't starting off so well. Ronnie hadn't told Melanie much at all about what had happened five years ago at the red church, although she'd heard rumors just like all the other kids in school. "He's okay," Ronnie said. "There's just some trouble between the McFall and Day families that goes way back. Probably fighting over some woolly mammoth bacon or something."

Melanie laughed, and Ronnie felt a small surge of triumph. Bobby was right: If you made a girl laugh, you were halfway home. "Sorry to be so weird the other day," she said.

"You weren't weird." *Just moody, just a girl. Just Melanie.*

"So, why did you call?"

Bobby had advised him to warm her up before popping the question. But what if his friend was trying to sabotage him? Maybe he knew she was already going to the dance with somebody else. Maybe she was even going with Bobby.

No, Bobby would never do that. You're starting to get paranoid.

And with good reason. There's a McFall in town.

"Well, I just...how did you do on your History final?" he asked, knowing he should have kept things light. Bobby had specifically instructed him not to talk about school.

"Okay, I guess. Ronnie, what's really going on? Now *you're* the one that's acting weird."

Ah, hell with it. "Are you going to the dance tomorrow?"

"Of course. It's the big senior blowout. I wouldn't miss it even if I had to wear glass slippers and turn into a pumpkin at midnight."

"Yeah. The Diggers are playing. I haven't heard them since Donnie's birthday party. I bet they're a lot better now."

"Bobby's a kickass drummer, but Dex can't sing a lick."

Bobby again. Ronnie swallowed but his throat was as dry and rough as sandpaper. "Uh...are you going with anybody?"

"Yeah. Only a lame-o goes to a dance alone."

"Yeah. Heh." *So who's the lucky guy? And why did I put off asking for so long?*

But he knew why. "Better the devil you know," went the old saying, but Ronnie preferred, "What you don't know won't hurt you." Although both sayings were pretty stupid when you thought about it. If you put them together, you got something like, "You know the devil will hurt you."

Why am I always thinking crazy shit like that?

He realized the pause had stretched on for uncomfortably long, so he said, as casually as he could manage, "So, who's the lucky guy?"

"Brett Summers."

"*Brett?* I heard he was going with Amy Extine."

"Well, you heard wrong, unless he's dumb enough to think he can play us both."

"Don't kill the messenger."

"Brett's a nice guy. And his dad's—"

"An insurance agent. I know."

"Well, you can thank Mr. McFall for setting it up. He was having breakfast with Max Summers at the waffle house and McFall mentioned that Max had a son my age. The next thing you know, I've got Brett's phone number. I mean, Brett and I hardly ever talked at school."

"He kind of doesn't run in our circles." *Because he doesn't hang with white trash like us.*

"He's really sweet. Mr. McFall was actually the one who suggested that I go to the dance with him. He said it would be good for my personal growth, but warned me to make sure Brett stayed within proper boundaries." Melanie gave a laugh that was almost a titter. "He's so old-fashioned for a middle-aged man."

Some of Ronnie's jealousy and disappointment had faded a little, partly because he'd already resigned himself to failure long before making the phone call. Besides, now he could stretch his fantasy a little further. She hadn't said "No," had she? Someone had just beaten him to the punch, that's all.

"So you and Larkin McFall are best buds now, huh?" Ronnie said. His left arm was falling asleep, and he rolled over on the bed so he was no longer looking at the window, which was spotted with the first spill of rain.

"Hey, you're the one who's on his payroll."

"I thought we didn't trust grown-ups."

"Mr. McFall is different," she said. "I mean, a lot of men his age flirt with me and stuff, but he's always very polite. And he encourages me to respect myself and plan for the future. I'm sort of like his pet project, I guess. Plus, he sure does tip well."

"So you're on the payroll, too. And he sets you up on dates. Sounds to me like he wants to start an escort service."

The joke fell flat, or maybe McFall had taught her not to acknowledge any comments that were demeaning to women. Ronnie felt like a rat navigating a maze, where the only prize was a lump of poisoned cheese.

"Well, I'd better go. I have to work on my dress for tomorrow. Mom's going to help me raise the hem a little so it will pass for a summer skirt."

"Okay," Ronnie said, reluctant to hang up. He'd left far too much unsaid. "What color is the dress?"

"White with light blue flowers," she said. "The blue matches my eyes."

I'll bet it does. "Can't wait to see it."

"So, who are *you* going with?"

"Where?"

She giggled. "The dance, silly."

It had apparently never occurred to her that Ronnie might ask her. She didn't even sound all that curious, more like she was just making conversation. And in his mind he had already spun her into his little web of fantasy. God, he was such a lame-o.

Only a lame-o goes to a dance alone.

Ronnie flipped through a mental rolodex, trying to come up with the name of some girl from senior class who nobody in their right mind would ask. Some loser like him. But if the person he picked already had a date, and Melanie knew it, he'd look even lamer.

"Haven't decided yet," he said, as coolly as he could. "I've got a couple of options."

"Ooh, a player." She lowered her voice, serious again. "Who's Bobby going with?"

"He's going to be too busy with the band to keep a woman entertained. Maybe he'll pick up somebody once he's there. I'm sure there will be a lot of eager volunteers. Everybody loves a drummer."

Jesus. Did she just sigh?

"Well, I better go. I'll see you at school tomorrow."

"G'night."

He had barely hung up when he heard tires screeching and scuffing on the gravel drive outside. A horn blared frantically, then beeped three more times. It sounded like Dad's truck, but Dad didn't fool around with unnecessary noise. He liked the peace and quiet of the country and felt it should only be violated in extreme circumstances.

Ronnie hopped to the floor and collected his shoes, running barefoot down the hall. Tim was standing in the doorway with soapy hands, squinting outside at the headlights.

"What's going on?" Ronnie asked, not stopping.

"Dad's raising a racket," he said, as Ronnie swept by him and rushed across the driveway, little rocks jabbing the soles of his bare feet.

Dad's window was down. "Get in," he commanded. The passenger door was open by the time Ronnie reached it, and he was barely inside the cab before Dad cut a hard donut in the drive, spinning gravel as he headed back toward Little Church Road.

"What's going on?"

"Your friend Bobby."

Bobby? That didn't make sense. Bobby had said he was heading home straight after work. He wanted to get a good night's rest because of the gig.

"What happened?"

"He wrecked his truck."

"What the hell?"

His dad punched the accelerator of the big F-250 Ford, and the truck shook with the speed. Big drops of water spattered the windshield, and Ronnie noticed it was starting to rain in earnest.

"Is he okay?" Ronnie asked, afraid to ask.

"We don't know. I was one of the first on the scene. We called an ambulance, and it's on the way, but...."

"But what?" Ronnie imagined Bobby pinned in the truck, his legs broken, his wrists so mangled he'd never throw a baseball or twirl a drumstick again. Then he thought about Bobby crushed against the steering wheel, his head sheared off by the broken windshield. His dark imagination kicked into overtime, picturing scenes of carnage that were like sick sculptures of flesh and steel. Then he flashed to a mournful Melanie, in a clingy black dress at Bobby's funeral, bawling and wailing as she hugged his casket.

"Well, he's not there," his dad said. "Not on the scene. We thought he might have been thrown free of the vehicle, but we couldn't find him."

"Are the cops there?"

"Not yet. But there were five people on the scene when I came to get you. I figured you could help us hunt. Plus, he's your friend and all."

Ronnie felt weak and faint, but he was glad his dad had included him. Even if Bobby was . . .

the next McFall victim

. . . dead, Ronnie wanted to be there to do whatever he could.

"We figure he was driving a little too fast, and the road was slick. It's always slicker on the bridge, because of the condensation. Well, he must have just lost control and tumbled off the edge."

"Off the edge?" Ronnie pictured the truck busting through the guardrail and plunging twenty feet down into the river, into the black depths of the diving hole.

Where the misty ghosts were.

Now Ronnie could see half a dozen sets of headlights, needles of rain sliding down inside their yellowish beams. A few smaller lights—flashlights—swept back and forth at both ends of the bridge. His dad parked the Ford in a turnout just before the bridge, and Ronnie quickly slipped on his shoes and sprinted out into the rain.

"Anything new?" Dad asked a man who was shining a flashlight down into the river.

"No sign of him."

Now Ronnie saw the truck, and he had to grip the bridge railing to remain upright as his knees turned to wet sand. The Toyota was still in one piece, but it had hurtled off the far end of the bridge and was halfway down the embankment, wedged between two trees. The cab was ripped open like a can of sardines, a spider web of cracks in the rear window. The bed was twisted like a piece of tinfoil, and the driver's side door was missing. The vehicle was clearly unoccupied, but it was impossible to imagine anybody surviving such a crash.

"Come on," Dad said. "Let's go down and help look for him."

Sirens wailed in the distance. Ronnie looked over the railing, and although he couldn't quite see any details in the dark water, he heard the river's incessant susurration, its lulling whispers, its promise that all would be swept away in time.

Please, Jesus, don't let him be down there under the water.

And if he is dead, please let him STAY dead.

McFALL

EPISODE FOUR

CHAPTER TWENTY-TWO

I'm starting to think this is a bridge to hell.

Sheriff Frank Littlefield played his flashlight along the river's edge, wondering if the Eldreth boy had been thrown into the water by the force of the collision. The truck was about fifty feet up the bank, so the impact should have flung the driver into the locust scrub and wild roses that lined the edge of the bridge. But this mystery was hardly the only physical impossibility offered by the wreck. For one thing, despite all the jagged metal and broken glass, there wasn't a single drop of blood in the cab. It was as if Bobby Eldreth had vanished while the truck was in the air.

"See anything, Sheriff?" Officer Perriotte called down from the bridge. He had been the first officer on scene, and an ambulance, an EMT van, and a fire truck had since joined the proceedings, their red-and-blue strobe lights sending silent pulses across the surrounding mountains. It was after midnight and most of the surrounding houses had gone dark, although some curious spectators had made their way down from Riverview to watch from afar and several others were helping dredge the river.

"Not a damn thing," Littlefield replied. "Why don't you head downstream and check for..."

ghosts

"...check for anything."

The sheriff swept his high-powered flashlight beam over the waist-high weeds, where half a dozen searchers stomped and murmured, their small portable lights like fireflies. Littlefield hoped to God they wouldn't find Bobby's body, because a proper investigation would be impossible at this point. Any evidence would be destroyed by the civilian traffic. So far all he had was a truck that looked like it had been shot across the bridge like a missile. The bridge's wet asphalt sported only a short stretch of skid marks, as if Bobby Eldreth hadn't realized he was out of control until the last instant. The vehicle must have been traveling at least sixty miles an hour when it went off—far too fast for the gravel road.

Littlefield's flashlight settled on the brooding face of Ronnie Day, who squinted back at the sheriff as if accusing him of failing to protect his friend. Then the boy turned and stared down into the rocks where he'd found Darnell Absher's corpse not too long ago.

If another dead body turns up and Ronnie's on the scene, I'm going to start wondering if he's the problem instead of Larkin McFall.

Littlefield climbed a muddy path beside the concrete abutment until he was between the bridge and the wreck. The odor of scorched grass, radiator fluid, and gasoline filled the air, competing with the algae stench of the river. The search party had combed a hundred-yard perimeter around the crash site. If Bobby was lying on the ground, dead or alive, he should have been found sometime in the past hour.

Littlefield was beginning to suspect that Bobby had somehow leaped out of the vehicle as it crossed the bridge and was broken and drowned somewhere in the dark green waters of the Blackburn River.

Just like Detective Storie, who went under and never came back up. History is repeating itself, and it wasn't a happy ending the first time around.

A pick-up truck came rumbling up Highway 321, traveling much too fast given the congestion. It slowed to a screeching stop in the middle of the road, and the driver jumped out, pushing past the officer directing traffic.

"Where's my boy?" the man bellowed.

"Easy, Mr. Eldreth," Littlefield said, heading toward him. Sherry from Dispatch had tried several times to notify the Eldreth family by phone, and had finally needed to send a patrol car to their trailer. "We're doing everything we can."

"Everything? Then where *is* he?" Elmer Eldreth spewed venom and beer mist in his panic. When he saw the extent of the wreckage, he wobbled and nearly collapsed, grabbing the bridge railing to steady himself. "Holy hell."

"We're still hopeful, Mr. Eldreth," Littlefield said, hating the lie even as it left his lips. "I know it looks bad, but—"

"You ain't go no kids, Sheriff," the drunken man said, nearly on the verge of blubbering. "What the hell do you know?"

Littlefield had no answer. He glanced over at Cindy Baumhower, who stood beside the emergency vehicles, maintaining a respectful distance. She'd been with him when he'd received the call, and though she'd accompanied him to the scene, she'd stayed on the sidelines as a journalist without Littlefield even having to make the request.

Littlefield took Elmer's arm to steady him. "I'll do everything in my power—"

Elmer slapped his hand away. "Power? Since when have you ever stopped anybody in this town from dying?"

Elmer stormed past him, heading for the shattered truck. Littlefield let him go. He was thinking about going over to Cindy, soaking up whatever comfort she had to offer, when he heard the shout from below the bridge.

"Bobby!"

It was Ronnie's voice. Littlefield ran to the abutment, adrenaline flaring up like electricity, and even as he shined his flashlight in the direction of the shout, he absorbed the fact that the boy's name hadn't been squealed with anguish or horror, but with surprise and joy.

Under his big yellow spotlight, Ronnie dragged Bobby from a thicket of Touch-Me-Nots and honeysuckle. To Littlefield's disbelief, Bobby was actually awake and on his feet, no rips in his sodden clothing, no streaks of blood or protruding bones.

"Are you okay?" Ronnie yelled, hugging his friend. Littlefield wanted to tell the boy to ease off, that Bobby might have internal injuries, but he didn't have the heart. In truth, he was in a state of shock as profound as Bobby's appeared to be.

"I'm fine," Bobby said as the EMTs tugged him away from his friend and forced him to sit in the mud. "Don't wanna get my jeans dirty."

Members of the search party gathered on the bridge, chattering with a sense of shared triumph, as more EMTs scrambled down the bank, Littlefield fast behind them.

The EMTs gave Bobby a quick check before slapping a blood-pressure cuff on his left arm. As one of the techs flashed a penlight into the boy's pupil, the sheriff bent to make his own examination. He didn't smell alcohol, and there wasn't even a scratch on Bobby's face. It was hard to reconcile the dazed but otherwise whole human being in front of him with the wreck on the opposite site of the bridge. But he remembered how solid Detective Sheila Storie had seemed as a ghost, so he gripped Bobby's shoulder just to make sure the boy was truly among the living.

The EMTs asked Bobby a series of questions, which he answered groggily but with evident awareness. Ronnie broke into the circle of people surrounding Bobby, and Bobby gave his friend a grin and a wave. "I know it's way past your bedtime," he said. "But I'm sure glad you didn't play Deathboy tonight. Thanks for finding me."

Littlefield wondered if the boy had staged some sort of over-the-top practical joke—selecting for the spectacle the very site where he and Ronnie had found a corpse—but that suspicion was overwhelmed by a wave of relief.

Suddenly Elmer burst into the circle, face moist with sweat and blotched red with rage. "What do you think you're doing, you little shit?"

Littlefield put an arm out to restrain the man, but Elmer gave him a shove and hovered over his boy, fists trembling at his sides. "You trying to kill yourself? Trying to throw away your future? After all I done for you?"

The emergency tech treating Bobby said, "Sir, please step back and let us—"

"Is your arm broke? Jesus Christ, boy, you just knocked yourself out of the *draft!*"

Bobby flexed his right arm as if it had only just occurred to him to consider whether he'd suffered any career-ending injuries. "Feels good," he said. "Better than ever."

Littlefield gave Elmer a bear hug, ready to fling him to the ground by force if necessary. But the flabby man relaxed his grip on Bobby, the tension draining out of him. "You better be all right,"

Elmer said, allowing himself to be led a few feet away so the techs could finish their examination.

One of the state troopers had helped a first responder carry a stretcher down the bank, but Bobby waved it off. "Really, guys, I'm fine," he said.

He stood, Ronnie on one side and a tech on the other, and he only swayed for a moment before regaining his balance. He really *did* look fine.

"What happened?" Littlefield asked. He'd be on the scene for hours anyway, collecting what evidence there was left to collect, but he was hoping Bobby could answer some of the unanswerable questions.

"I don't remember," Bobby said. "I was over at the church and...then I was here."

Short-term amnesia was a common symptom of serious accidents, but it might also signal a brain injury. A couple of the techs nodded to each other, and then asked Elmer for permission to transport Bobby to the hospital for further evaluation.

"We ain't got no insurance," Elmer said, wiping at his eyes with his shirt sleeve. He seemed small and deflated, like a balloon the day after a birthday party.

"We'll worry about that later," Littlefield said. "Right now, you want to make sure your boy is all right."

"Is there any way we can keep this out of the paper?" Elmer pleaded. "If word gets out...."

"I'm sorry, Mr. Eldreth," the sheriff said, sympathetic nevertheless. He understood a parent's hopes and fears—over the course of his career, he'd shattered plenty of the former and confirmed just as many of the latter. "A wreck's a matter of public record, and anyway, the press is already here. We'll cooperate with the Highway Patrol's office to find out what happened and keep you informed."

As the techs ushered Bobby up the bank to the waiting ambulance and the search party began heading for their own vehicles, Littlefield saw Ronnie standing at the edge of the river, looking across the water. He appeared to be saying something, and the sheriff edged closer so he could hear the boy over the sound of the lapping and gurgling of the currents.

"You didn't get him!" Ronnie said, almost giddy. "We kicked your ass this time!"

Littlefield almost felt the same way, but part of him sensed that the victory might only last a night. While they measured life from breath to breath, the river had forever.

CHAPTER TWENTY-THREE

"**I**'m sick," Bobby said.

When the nurse gave him a look of alarm, he winked at Ronnie. "Sick of all this poking and prodding," he added.

Bobby felt weird lying in his underwear with Ronnie, his parents, and the nurse in the room, even though he was covered by a sheet that smelled of Lysol and bleach. He'd even had to pee in a plastic cup for the nurse, but at least she was homely and dour, her hair knotted in a bun so severe that it stretched the shiny skin of her forehead. If she'd been cute, he wasn't sure he could have squeezed out even a few drops.

The nurse frowned. "You survived a serious crash, but don't push your luck. We haven't completed all the tests."

"Why doesn't anybody believe that I'm okay? I know you don't like to let people out of the hospital before you've wiped out their life savings, but that only took fifteen seconds with me."

"Give her a break, Bobby," Ronnie said. "She's just doing her job."

"Bobby doesn't care about nobody's job," Elmer said. "He ain't never had to work for a living. But he might find out soon enough."

Elmer and Vernell were perched in chairs beside Bobby's bed, both exhausted and looking washed out, his mom wearing a faded pink house robe and tennis shoes without socks, her veins swollen and blue around her ankles. Vernell had nearly collapsed with worry, but Elmer was back to being his usual asshole self. Bobby couldn't believe it was only three in the morning. It felt like he'd been in the hospital for a week.

"How soon can I get out of here?" Bobby asked, giving the nurse his best smile. "I told you, I feel great."

"Yeah," Elmer said to the nurse. "Some of us got better things to do than wait around for the vultures."

"The doctor wants to keep him admitted for observation," the nurse said, adjusting the pulse oximeter clipped to the end of Bobby's left index finger.

"Do they think something's wrong?" Vernell asked, her voice cracking with a dry sob. "Something serious?"

"Just a precaution," the nurse said. "We want young Mr. Eldreth fit enough to walk across the stage for his diploma."

So the nurse knew he was a senior. She'd probably read about his baseball exploits in the newspaper, or maybe she'd even heard about his band—

Holy crap. The dance is tomorrow night! I can't stay here.

Bobby tried to sit up, but Ronnie held him in place. "Look, B," Ronnie said. "I know you're dying to bust out of this disease hotel, but just play along for a while, okay? You saw the truck. It's a miracle that you're alive."

"But the dance," Bobby said. "I can't let The Diggers down."

"You got bigger worries than that," Elmer said. "If word gets around that you got banged up, no team will touch you. And even if you get a clean bill of health, nobody wants to draft a head case."

Vernell clutched Elmer's forearm, her spidery fingers seeming desperate for something solid to hang onto. "Honey, that's not important right—"

"The hell it ain't." Elmer stood so suddenly that even the taciturn nurse gasped in shock. Shoving his wife's hand away, he glowered at Bobby. "You almost threw it all away. Whatever kind of game you were playing on that bridge, you were betting your future—the one *I* gave to you."

Vernell's lips quivered and she fell on her knees before her husband, as if she'd gladly offer her head to his ax if only he'd shift his anger away from Bobby. Bobby found his mom's pathetic attempt at appeasement even more disgusting than his dad's display, and he was embarrassed to have Ronnie witness this bare reality of his life. He wanted to climb over the stainless steel bed rails and slap both of them. The cardiac monitor beeped as his pulse accelerated with adrenaline.

"Please," the nurse said, stepping in front of the foot of the bed as if to shield her patient. "Rest is the best thing for your son right now."

"He'll get plenty of that when he's riding the bench in the minors," Elmer said, pushing his way to the door. "He ain't the only one who feels sick. I better get out of here before I puke."

Vernell gave her son one pained, forlorn look—*Which one of you needs me more?*—and then hurried into the hall after her husband. Bobby sagged back against the pillows and closed his eyes.

"Whoa," Ronnie whispered.

"I see this sort of thing a lot around here," the nurse said, patting Bobby's shoulder. "Stress and drama. I'll be right back. I'm just going to check on that urine test." To Ronnie, she said, "Don't keep him up. He needs his rest, and visiting hours are over, even for family members."

"That's what you get for pretending to be my brother," Bobby said after she left. "Welcome to the family."

"Who cares about that?" Ronnie said. "What *happened*?"

The sheriff had already stopped by to ask Bobby more questions about the accident, but he'd stuck with his story about not remembering anything besides driving to the McFall property to cover the lumber. It was a story he needed to start believing. The alternative was too impossible, too disturbing.

"Maybe I got struck by lightning out at the work site," Bobby said.

"Don't bullshit me, Bobby. I know there's something you're not saying."

There it was again in his mind's eye—the smoldering figure rising out of the gray foundation of the church ruins. The rest of it was like a drifting fog threatening to assemble into terrifying shapes, and Bobby didn't dare feed the fog with thoughts or words. Still, he had a feeling he'd been *taken* somewhere, to a place he didn't care to revisit. The frenetic beating of the cardiac monitor gave away his disquiet, and he removed the clip from his finger before the nurse returned to check on him.

"Did you wreck on purpose?" Ronnie asked.

"What? Why would I do that?"

"To collect insurance money."

"On that piece of junk?" Bobby said.

"Could be that you have some kind of weird death wish."

"Maybe so. I hang around *you*, don't I?"

"I'm not the one lying in a hospital bed."

"Get the nurse," Bobby said. "There's a sudden pain in my ass."

"Not funny. You know she'd just slap on a latex glove and go digging. Maybe she'd find your head in there."

Even though Ronnie would understand—hell, Deathboy was practically the local expert on bizarre occurrences—telling the truth would make what had happened more real somehow, and he did not want to reveal his weakness to anyone. Even though he knew staying silent might create a rift between him and Ronnie, particularly since their relationship was already strained over the whole Melanie thing, Bobby wasn't quite ready to tell the truth.

The wind kicked up a little skirl of ash and you freaked out, he told himself. *You blew the game within the game.*

"I guess I was driving too fast," he finally said, a confession that was close enough to the truth to allow his conscience to skate. "Lost control. But I didn't do it on purpose, no matter what anyone thinks."

Ronnie yawned. "Well, if you're not going to die, and if you're not going to get real, I got classes tomorrow. I better get some sleep."

Bobby almost asked his friend to stay, but Ronnie was right—final exams were the following day, and while Bobby could get out of them if he wanted, he doubted if Stribling and Gladstone would give Ronnie a free pass.

"How you getting home?" Bobby asked.

"The sheriff said he'd send a deputy around. A patrol's heading out that way anyway."

"Make sure you ride up front. Somebody might think you're getting arrested for one of those murders."

"None of them were murders, dorkface."

Bobby grinned, then grew serious. "Thanks for coming by, Ronnie. And for finding me. Means a lot."

"Yeah. Don't get all goofy on me. I'm just being a bro. G'night."
Ronnie paused when he reached the door. "I called Melanie."

"For real? How did it go?" Bobby was glad he'd removed the clip
or his rapid heartbeat would give him away.

"Fine. Except she's going to the dance with Brett Summers."

"That dickhead? I thought he was going with Amy."

"Maybe he dumped Amy when something better came along.
Or maybe Amy dumped *him*. You know how girls are."

"Sure." Bobby closed his eyes. "See you tomorrow."

After the door whispered to a close, Bobby lay in the bright,
antiseptic room and stared at the blackness beyond the window
shades. He retraced his route after fleeing the church ruins, the tense
skidding on the gravel curves of Little Church Road, the accelera-
tion on the straightaway as he approached the bridge. He hadn't
really been going that fast, maybe ten miles over the speed limit.
And while Sheriff Littlefield might think he had been driving reck-
lessly, Bobby had even slowed down once he'd put a mile between
him and the creepy stack of smoke and ashes.

At first, when he'd arrived at the bridge, he'd thought the rain-
storm had cast a thick mist over the river, because vapor thickened
and swelled over the railings as he approached. He'd hit his brights,
but they'd been instantly swallowed by the effluvium. The mist
had begun to roil and twist all around him, and then a gray palm
of gauze had pressed against the windshield, followed by a white,
screaming face. Bobby had punched the accelerator even though he
could barely see the road.

And just before he'd cleared the bridge, the stack of smoke and
ashes had emerged impossibly from the mist in front of him, only
now with articulated limbs and a great, grinning face whose mouth
looked like the deepest dead ember in the cold hearth of hell. One
of its shimmering arms had waved him forward.

Welcome to the game within the game, it had seemed to say.

The last thing he remembered was waking up in the weeds, Ronnie calling his name from a few feet away. Now, in the hospital bed, he rubbed his hands over his face and chest, surprised to find himself in one piece. He'd dodged a bullet. But maybe that was part of the game, too.

The door to his room whisked open, and at first he thought Ronnie had returned. But those gray-white worms of fingers that clutched the edge of the door—

The Ash Man!

Bobby nearly fell out of bed reaching for the button to summon the nurse.

The door swung fully open.

CHAPTER TWENTY-FOUR

"**B**obby," Larkin McFall said. "I heard you had an accident."

Bobby was pale and trembling, which was understandable. He'd had quite a night, and it was just beginning.

"Huh-how did you get in here?" Bobby asked, pulling the sheet up to his chin.

"Visiting hours are just like those rules on the sign at the bridge," Larkin said. "If you ignore them, they don't exist."

"But *why* are you here?"

Larkin checked out all the expensive monitoring equipment hooked up to Bobby. This little misadventure would cost the Eldreth family at least $8,000, including the ambulance ride. If only they had believed Bobby when he'd told them he was fine. But humans were like that, always going overboard to ensure they were "doing the right thing."

"I'm the kind of boss who likes to take care of my people," Larkin said. "We need you at McFall Meadows, so I have a vested interest in getting you back on your feet as fast as possible. Plus . . . ."

Bobby's eyes flicked first to the summon button, then over to Larkin. "Plus what?"

"The dance. The *gig*. I know how much it means to you."

Bobby gazed at his own hands as if wondering how they'd ever held drumsticks, much less tapped out a steady rhythm. "I guess I'll have to miss it."

Larkin shook his head. "This is the game now. This is your heart and soul. This is where you win."

"I don't understand."

"You'll be out at sunrise. I promise."

"But the doctor said—"

"I have a friend on the hospital board. I'll call in a favor while he's eating his eggs and toast, and you'll get the go-ahead."

Bobby still seemed confused, and Larkin didn't blame him. Drifting through the hospital as smoke had been simple, his passage disguised by green fluorescent lights and the smell of disease, but Larkin should have solidified a moment sooner. Bobby was undergoing the classic struggle of trying to deny what he'd seen with his own eyes. Larkin had long used such willful self-denial to his advantage. It was a fundamental principle of the McFall way of life. And unlife.

After all, if he believes what he's seen, he's insane. And if he's insane, he can't believe what he thinks he's seen.

"This is the biggest moment of your life," Larkin said. "Bigger than the playoffs, bigger than the major league draft, bigger than Amy Extine."

"I just want to play the drums," Bobby said.

"And you will." Larkin approached the bed. The boy drew back a little, but apparently he'd decided that Larkin wasn't a danger, at least for the moment. Larkin fished in his pocket and pulled out a ring with two keys. "Go on, take them."

Bobby held out a tentative hand. "What?" he asked, his voice laced with confusion.

"You crashed your truck. You need to borrow one of mine if we want to get any work done."

Bobby's eyebrows arched, and he almost grinned as he squeezed the keys. "Wheels?"

"Chevy Silverado four-door with a crew cab. Just off the lot. Of course, the gas mileage is atrocious, but there's a BP credit card in the ashtray. It's all on the company's dime."

"Gee, Mr. McFall," Bobby gushed like a kid at Disney World, seemingly forgetting all about his employer's strange entrance. "That's...." Without finishing the sentence, he frowned.

"Don't worry about your dad," Larkin said, picking up on his thoughts. "I'll have a little talk with him. It will be okay."

"The game within the game, right?"

"That's my boy."

They were interrupted by the door sweeping open. A confused and almost guilty expression stole over Bobby's face as the nurse walked into the room. She didn't seem overly alarmed when she noticed McFall's presence, just curious. "You removed your oximeter," she said, moving to the bedside to reattach the device to Bobby's finger. "We need the information it gives us at the desk."

"Well, I'd better be going," Larkin said. "Get some rest, Bobby. Big day tomorrow."

"Yes, sir."

"Good night, Mr. McFall," the nurse said.

Larkin saw no need to etherealize for his return trip through the hospital. The hallway was dead, and the two nurses staffing the floor desk were busy gossiping about a doctor. Larkin took the opportunity to stop by Room 213 to pay a visit to Vivian Gregg. The widow had been feeling poorly, and although she was in remission from stomach cancer, the chemotherapy had worsened her heart arrhythmia.

The room was dark except for the tiny rows of red and green LCDs cast by her life-support machinery. Out of sentimental stubbornness, the woman had dabbed perfume somewhere on her frail body, although its scent stood no chance against the dueling odors of decay and antiseptic. She was sound asleep, or as near to that state as was possible for someone strolling the borderlands between life and death. Larkin regretted disturbing her, but she had a debt to pay. She had once accosted Archer McFall in a grocery store, demanding that he "quit that old red church and come to Barkersville Baptist."

You wanted him to get right with God. And he did. Oh, yes, he certainly did.

He laid hands on her. He had the power to revive and restore her, just as he had done with the ravaged corpse of Stepford Matheson, but he didn't feel like it at the moment. One good deed deserved another, but he was fresh out of benevolence after cheering up Bobby. And the Greggs had been arrogant and holier-than-thou for generations.

"Mrs. Gregg?" he whispered, gently shaking her. "Ma'am?"

"Hmm?" She twisted, weak and groggy under her thin flannel blanket.

"How are you feeling?"

She blinked, her eyes attempting to adjust to the dim room. Larkin knew she couldn't see him, although he could see her just fine. All the way through.

"Are you ... the doctor?" she said, the words crawling out of her throat like gravel sluicing from a broken cement mixer.

"No, ma'am."

"Are you an *angel*?"

"Sure," Larkin said. "What do you want more than anything in the world?"

Her eyes shone with confused hope. "To . . . get better?"

He gave her bony hand a reassuring pat. "We're way past that now, Mrs. Gregg. *Way* past. Anything else?"

She was finally alert enough to realize she wasn't dreaming. Her head shifted from side to side as if trying to shake herself fully awake.

"Don't you want to die peacefully?" he asked, as gently as he could.

Her head shook more vigorously.

"No?" Larkin said, squeezing her hand harder until she gasped. "That's not what you want?"

Her skeletal sack of flesh quivered as she drew in air for a scream.

"Okay," he said. "If you insist, we'll do it the other way."

He showed his true face, and confronted with the flash of fire and smoke and ash and squirming filth, her eyes widened and the scream froze in her chest along with her heart. As her cardiac monitor flatlined, he laid her arm across her abdomen and gave it a soothing stroke. He was down the hall before the alarm beeped at the floor desk.

Outside, the night was brisk and cool, the storm clouds having streamed to the northeast. The fragrance of dogwood and azalea blooms enriched the air, and the whole world felt ripe with the promise of renewal. Larkin had taken up a cheerful whistle, but he stopped when he saw a small figure perched on a concrete wall along the sidewalk.

"Ronnie!" Larkin said. This was an unexpected delight; his night just kept getting better.

Ronnie folded his arms over his chest and drew back in a defensive posture. "Hello."

"What are you doing out here at this time of night?"

"I could ask you the same thing, Mr. McFall. But I have a feeling this is your happy hour."

Larkin laughed. "You must have come to see Bobby. I was worried about him, too, but he's going to be just fine."

"One of the deputies was supposed to give me a ride, but I guess he forgot. And my parents are probably asleep."

"You want a lift?"

Ronnie looked around the hospital's silent parking lot, and then at the bright windows of the drugstore across the street, as if willing some other transportation option into existence. "I can't afford a cab, but it's way out of your way. You live in town, don't you?"

Larkin could hardly wait to drive Ronnie across the bridge and past the old burned church. Maybe they could talk about Melanie Ward along the way. Maybe even—

Headlights swept across them as a vehicle turned onto the adjacent street and rolled into the parking lot. Larkin could see the red emergency lightbar atop its roof. Ronnie hopped off the concrete wall and headed toward it without pausing. "My ride's here. Thanks anyway."

As the patrol car slowed, Larkin said, "Some other time."

Ronnie had thrown the passenger door open and was about to duck into the cab when Larkin called his name.

"What?" Ronnie asked, squinting under the streetlights.

"Smile," Larkin said. "God loves you."

CHAPTER TWENTY-FIVE

Heather Fowler clutched the crumpled envelope in a tightening fist as she stood in the hallway of the Pickett County courthouse.

The draft minutes of the planning board meeting wouldn't be official until they'd been approved by a majority of the board members. But as Heather stared down at the sheet of paper for a second time, the same feelings of frustration and helplessness she'd felt at the meeting consumed her.

Below the listing of those present and the time the meeting was called to order was a single, simple paragraph:

> *The board unanimously approved the McFall Meadows development, to include all requests and variances, in addition to an amendment to allow for a wastewater treatment plant on site pending state and federal permits.*

"I didn't approve this," she whispered.

"Did you say something?" asked a young man who was leaning against the wall outside a courtroom. He was probably waiting for a misdemeanor hearing. "Got a problem?"

"Not as many as you," she said, hurrying over to the county manager's office. She intended to confront the secretary and force her to change the minutes to reflect her opposition to the project. But as she reached the stairs, her eyes landed upon the deed office at the end of the hall. Her vote wouldn't stop the project, but maybe she'd find another way to attack the property if she learned more about it.

"How can we help you, Miss Fowler?" said Rita Cooper, the Register of Deeds, when she walked in the room. Although Cooper's position was an elected one, most county employees deferred to the commissioners who set their budget. Heather was uncomfortable with being treated as small-town royalty, but in this case, she was grateful for the fast track.

"I'm interested in some parcels along Little Church Road," Heather said. "Could you please direct me to the tax maps?"

Instead of foisting the duty onto one of her clerks, Cooper escorted Heather into a storage room in which oversized, leather-bound books were arranged in narrow slots along the walls. Several computers sat on a long table in the center of the room, with a stack of papers piled beside them.

"We're in the middle of digitizing our records," Cooper said. "We're starting with the oldest and working forward. Those old deeds relied on details like oak trees and fence posts to mark boundaries, so the whole thing's a mess. But a few years from now you'll be able to look up deeds online."

"I doubt I'll still be in office then," Heather said.

Cooper checked a database on one of the computers. "Little Church Road stretches for three miles. Do you want to narrow it down a little?"

"The McFall property."

"Ah, that's easy." She pointed to a large book lying out on the table. "We've had a lot of activity there. If he doesn't slow down, we'll wear out the pages."

Cooper showed Heather the handwritten original records that bestowed the property to William McFall in 1772, purchased from the original owner, who had received a land grant from the King of England. "It was originally a thousand acres," Cooper said. "But the family sold off pieces of it over the years."

Heather looked at the list of family names—Buchanan, Potter, Matheson, Gregg, Absher, and Day—that encroached around the property in the newest iteration of the deed map.

Buchanan and Absher. The names of those two men who recently died.

Heather studied the two-hundred-acre parcel where Larkin McFall planned to build his development. She'd seen the property map in the permit application, of course, but it hadn't provided any context. Now she could see where the development would fall in terms of the surrounding properties, the nearby Jefferson National Forest, the main road, and the river. "What's this?" she asked, pointing to a slip of paper clipped to the edge of the map.

"It means there's a new land sale in the area, and we'll have to record it," Cooper said. "It's expensive to print these books, so we update them by hand and log the information into the computer as we go. When we have enough changes, we can justify getting new books printed."

Heather folded the slip back so that she could see the typewritten words: "G. Buchanan property transfer to L. McFall." The note bore yesterday's date.

"That's a fresh one," Cooper said. "Like I said, Mr. McFall's been a busy little beaver out there. Looks like he got another good deal."

"What did he buy?"

Cooper turned the page. "Graham Buchanan had eight acres behind the Days. See, he's listed there as 'Grantor.' Looks like Mr. McFall bought the parcel for twenty thousand."

"Isn't that insanely cheap?"

Cooper shrugged. "We've seen half-acre lots go for six figures, and we've seen steep hillsides sell for five hundred an acre. Like they say about real estate, it's location, location, location."

"How many other parcels has McFall acquired recently?"

"Four," Larkin McFall said, entering the storage room. "Counting the one I'm here to record. Good morning, Miss Fowler, Mrs. Cooper."

"Mr. McFall," Cooper said with an unrestrained delight. "You sure are becoming a regular."

Heather looked up from the book, trying to make sense of the expanding empire expressed on the paper with the calm, cultured, *ordinary* man standing before her. The room suddenly seemed far too small, and his odor—subtle cologne failing to mask an animal masculinity—overpowered the scents of pulp and dust from the books.

"I've persuaded Stepford Matheson to sell me his twenty acres," McFall said. "He drove a hard bargain—you know how stubborn these old mountain families can be—but we finally arrived at a deal we could both live with."

Bill Willard had told Heather once that the Mathesons would never sell their land, even to the point of losing it to tax foreclosure. "You're assembling quite a property," Heather said. "Maybe you can lower the density of your development."

"I'd say that's up to you, Heather," he said.

Rita Cooper flung up her hands. "This is between you guys," she said "I just log records. I don't do politics." Walking between them, she hurried back to her office.

Now that it was just the two of them, the room somehow seemed even smaller, and Heather was suffocating, as if all the air around her had been sucked away. "I told you, we're on the same side," McFall said. "We can both get what we want."

"And what do you think I want?" Though they were in the middle of a public building, Heather felt strangely vulnerable and exposed.

"Your *trail*," McFall said. "You want to preserve the ridge at McFall Meadows."

"Not considering the way your development is planned out."

"I can drop the density to half as many houses if you'd like."

"If *I'd* like?"

"And I can establish a conservation easement on the trail and put a county park up there at the top, in that little glen with the great view that you love so much."

"A county park?" Heather's mind reeled with the possibility. This was all so out of the blue that she couldn't reconcile the offer with the plan that had been approved by the board.

McFall flashed a boyish grin. "Fowler Park. What do you think of that? A lasting testament to your goal of preserving the environment. Anyone who looks up at the mountain from Titusville is going to see nothing but trees, and they're going to remember who to thank."

Fowler Park. That would really piss off the Good Old Boys.

"Why is my support so important to you?"

McFall glanced behind him at the open door, and then eased closer to her, dropping his voice. "Isn't it obvious, Heather?"

She looked into his eyes, not trusting herself to speak. They were a dusky maroon, commanding, the center of the pupils glinting with—*what? Mirth? Lust? The reflection of the table lamps?*

A reflection of herself?

223

She moved past him, heading for the door, but he reached out and grabbed her by the elbow, pulling her close. Unaccustomed to her high heels, she was caught off balance, and she fell against him—*sure, you lost your balance, right*—and her breasts pressed against him as he wrapped a firm arm around her waist.

His face was inches from hers, those eyes piercing and forceful, his muscular body hard beneath the fine wool of his suit. "Fowler Park," he whispered. "You can live forever."

For just a moment, her lips parted, open in anticipation of accepting his, but the strangely corrupt smell of his breath was off-putting enough to bring her to her senses. That was when she noticed something else roiling in his eyes—a reddish glint like the front door opening to hell. She managed to push herself free.

"I don't want to live forever," she said. "I'd rather be alive now."

She fled the room, wondering what she would have seen if that doorway in his eyes had opened completely. She was afraid she would have seen herself naked and sweating, limbs entwined with Larkin McFall's as flames licked all around them.

CHAPTER TWENTY-SIX

"**N**o jokes about us being on a date," Bobby said, wheeling the big Silverado to the back entrance of the Pickett High gymnasium.

"You're not my type," Ronnie said. "I'm not into blondes." Bobby had agreed to give him a ride to the dance in exchange for his help setting up the band's equipment. Ronnie had never pictured himself as a rock-n-roll roadie, but at least it gave him a decent excuse not to have a date. The dance started in two hours, which gave The Diggers plenty of time to set up and run through a sound check.

As Bobby dropped the tailgate, Ronnie said, "Don't you think it's weird?"

"I think lots of things are weird, including the fact that I just walked away from a crash that should have killed me. But what do you mean specifically?"

"You joked about asking Larkin McFall for a company truck. And now you have one."

"Hey, I guess I'm on a roll."

"A roll of Russian roulette, maybe. You dodged a bullet, but there's always another in the chamber."

"You think too much, that's your problem. Now shut up and grab this kick drum."

Ronnie carried the drum through the open back doors of the gym. The room was festooned with the school colors of blue and gold—crepe paper drooping from the metal rafters, bundles of balloons bobbing from the bleachers. The junior marshals were busy setting up snack tables, with Principal Gladstone and Sgt. Morley, the jovial and unintimidating school resource officer, keeping close watch to ensure no one spiked the punch. A raised platform underneath one backboard served as a stage, and Dex was busy setting up the sound system.

When Bobby walked into the gym with an armful of cymbal stands, the excited murmurs stopped and a hushed awe descended. One of the members of the previous night's search party had taken a blurry photo of the wreckage, which had made its inevitable way around the school. In a single day, Bobby had ascended to a legendary status that topped even his athletic and musical exploits. Three girls rushed over to greet him and ask about the accident, and Bobby was grinning like a fool.

Looks like Pickett High has a new Deathboy. Enjoy the bloody crown, my friend.

"Hey, Ronnie, come give me a hand," Dex said after he'd made several trips hauling equipment in from the Silverado while Bobby basked in the girls' attention.

Ronnie hopped onto the stage and followed Dex's instructions, running cables and plugging them into the mixing board. Louise Weyerhouse was up there too, trying to mate a microphone to a cable, clearly out of her element. She might have been good at math and social studies, but she couldn't tell a whammy bar from a trombone.

"You ever run sound?" Dex asked Ronnie.

"I can turn on a radio." He was too ashamed to admit he couldn't afford an iPod, much less a decent stereo.

"Easy breezy," Dex said. "You can be an honorary Digger. I'll turn you into an expert inside of fifteen minutes." He lowered his voice. "If you don't do it, Louise is going to volunteer."

Bobby had joined them, and was busy setting up his high hat and cymbals. Floyd Frady turned on his amp and thumped out a few booming bass notes, making the principal cringe. Ronnie looked over at the senior class officers, who were gathered by the door. They were in charge of decorations, programs, and maintaining the appearance of decorum and civility until the mob mentality took over.

Amy Extine was wearing a loose-knit sweater, a black crop top visible through the mesh. Plenty of leg showed between her short skirt and the tops of her vinyl go-go boots. She waved and Ronnie looked behind him, thinking she'd waved at Bobby, but his friend was kneeling to assemble a drum pedal.

Wow. She's waving at me. Maybe rock-n-roll will make me a chick magnet.

Ronnie gave a tentative wave back. Noticing, Dex said, "You better watch it, or Brett Summers will kick your ass."

"I'm just waving," Ronnie said with a shrug. "Besides, Brett is dating Melanie Ward now."

"Yeah, sure." Dex snorted in derision "Maybe Melanie will kick your ass, too."

Ronnie hid his blush. He'd thought his crush was a well-kept secret. Maybe Bobby had told on him. He tried not to picture his friend yukking it up in the halls, joking about Ronnie's pathetic attempts to get into Melanie's pants. No, that wasn't Bobby's style. Probably Dex had heard about it from one of his air-headed girlfriends, idly gossiping in the mean-spirited way of the insecure.

"Just show me which knobs to turn," Ronnie said. "And I'll try not to make you sound as shitty as usual."

Dex smirked at that one and gave Ronnie a quick primer on the soundboard. His newly acquired role was to keep Dex's vocals cranked to the max, mute Jimmy Dale Massingale's screaming guitar leads as much as possible, and stand ready with a fire extinguisher in case something went up in flames. "Gladstone nixed the pyrotechnics, but we've got a fog machine and a little light show," Dex said. "Louise can run that. If she's smart enough to count to four, she can handle it."

After the equipment was set up, including Jimmy Dale's amp tower and row of effects pedals, the band gathered outside the back door, near the Silverado. Louise kept a nervous watch at the door as Dex fired up a joint. Bobby and Floyd both took deep drags, but Ronnie waved it off when his turn came. He was afraid of the stuff. His thoughts were weird enough; he couldn't imagine where they would go with a little artificial, chemically induced stimulation.

"My first time running sound," Ronnie said to stave off comments. "I don't want to space out."

"Where's Jimmy Dale?" Bobby muttered, holding in a lungful of smoke.

"He's always late," Dex said. "But he better get his ass here pronto or we won't have time for a sound check."

Couples were already arriving in the parking lot beside the football field, the guys moving awkwardly in their stiff new clothes, the girls looking fresh in summer dresses. Ronnie strained to pick out Melanie and Brett, unable to resist even though he knew it would hurt. He didn't see them, and he wondered if they had pulled off at the bridge for a little "chat."

A kiss on the cheek, he thought again. *How sweet.*

As Bobby took a turn with the joint and gave it to Floyd, Dex reached down and unzipped a gym bag. "Our new outfits," he said, passing out folded bundles of cloth.

"What the hell is *this?*" Bobby said, unrolling a sleeveless bowling jacket that featured the McAllister Bowling Alley logo.

"Sponsorship, man," Dex said. "It's sort of like we're making a statement on selling out while sticking it to the man. Plus, my dad wants some payback for all the gear he bought us."

Floyd giggled like a stoned idiot and tried on the jacket over his Black Sabbath T-shirt. "Sweet."

Bobby flung his to the ground. "If I wanted to sell out, I wouldn't go this cheap."

"Come on, Bobby," Louise cooed from the doorway. "It'll show off your muscles."

"Yeah," Ronnie said, hoping Melanie would think it was as dorky as he did. "It's cool."

Though he still seemed less than thrilled about the bowling swag, Bobby peeled off his T-shirt, taking obvious delight in Louise's attention and Dex's jealousy. He wriggled into the jacket and flexed his biceps, looking like a caveman Adonis with his ripped chest—just perfect for a rock drummer.

Just then, Jimmy Dale rumbled up on his Kawasaki motorcycle, guitar slung across his back in a soft case. He killed the engine, booted down the kickstand, and stepped off the bike like a Wild West marshal riding into town to clear out the black hats, or maybe to rape and pillage and rob the stagecoach himself. Plucking the joint from Floyd's lips, he said, "Having all the fun without me? I thought we were a *band*, man."

"The early bird gets the buzz," Dex said, laughing at his own ridiculous nonsense.

Jimmy Dale made up for lost time, finishing off the joint and flipping the roach into the weeds. "Killer. Let's rock, boys."

Before heading off with the others, Dex slipped Ronnie a set list, a grouping of straightforward rock standards with a few penciled-in titles he didn't recognize. He assumed they were originals, since Bobby said The Diggers had been working on some tunes that would debut tonight. He wondered if Gladstone had approved the list ahead of time. While "Day Tripper" and "Sympathy for the Devil" were pretty inoffensive, "Californication" and "Gonna Do Ya" didn't promise a whole lot of subtlety.

"No Katy Perry or Lady Gaga, but no 'Hell's Bells' either," Dex said by way of explanation. "And we gave up on 'Stairway to Heaven.' Jimmy Dale only had time to learn the first section."

"Sure, dude, blame it on me," Jimmy Dale said. "We both know your balls would have popped out when you tried to hit those high notes."

As the band filed into the gym and took the stage, Ronnie hauled a chair over to the mixing board. Because he needed to face the speakers, he'd have his back to the crowd for the entire night. Once the lights went low, he'd practically be invisible. So much for netting some groupies.

The band members tuned their instruments as Bobby rolled the sticks around his kit. Principal Gladstone made a big show of covering his ears, and Sgt. Morley actually left the building, shaking his head. Many of the volunteers had left after finishing their service work, and no one would be admitted until the doors opened at nine, so The Diggers' atonal cacophony mostly played to an empty gym. By the time they broke into "Twist and Shout," they were in a groove, Ronnie had mastered the basics of the soundboard, and even old Gladstone was involuntarily tapping a toe.

CHAPTER TWENTY-SEVEN

"**M**cFall's return has been pretty good to you," Sheriff Littlefield said, leaning over the bridge railing to gaze west, where the sun was sliding toward the mountaintops. A distant scar of red marked the road bed McFall had cut for his development, the beginning of a change that would leave the slopes covered with houses. Paired with the sprawling opulence of Riverview, the development would transform this end of the county, making it as crowded as a big city. Gas stations and support services would no doubt follow the houses.

"How do you figure?" Cindy knelt in the dirt at the end of the bridge, examining the tire tracks from last night's crash.

"You're getting a lot of carnage and death for your readers. Plus we get to see him mug for the camera once a week after he performs some magnanimous civic duty or other."

"I thought we'd agreed that Larkin McFall was innocent until proven guilty. Besides, this was just a wreck. There's no connection to McFall besides the fact that Bobby works for him."

Littlefield shook his head, even though he knew Cindy wasn't looking at him. He spoke to the lapping water below as much as to her. "A kid drives over the bridge fast enough to go airborne and walks away without a scratch. And he conveniently can't remember anything. Let's not forget that this is the same spot where he and his friends found Darnell Absher's body."

The demolished Toyota had been removed by a tow truck. Littlefield hadn't bothered to mark off the location with yellow tape—the churned mud and ruined trees showed the trajectory well enough. Littlefield had gone through the motions of measuring the skid marks, estimating the vehicle's speed, and noting on his report that there was no indication of drug or alcohol use. No crime, no victim. Just a coincidence. An accident. Just like what had happened to Darnell Absher.

Cindy had already published her crash photographs on the newspaper's Web site, because the next print edition didn't hit the streets until tomorrow. She was here this evening as Littlefield's companion, not in her official capacity as a journalist, but that didn't stop her from studying the area on her own.

"You think he got thrown from the vehicle?" she asked.

"No way. He had to be doing at least sixty. You can't just roll out at that speed without breaking any bones, assuming you're lucky enough to survive. Besides, unless he climbed out the window and dove for the water, which he didn't have time to do, he would've bounced off the railing."

Cindy touched one of the steel I-beams that supported the wooden railings. "And left quite a mess."

"And we know he didn't go down with the ship. There was no blood in the cab—or on him, for that matter. He would have been toast if he stayed in the truck anyway. It was too old to have air bags, and the roof was practically peeled back to the bed."

"It is curious that Ronnie Day found him, isn't it?"

"Yeah. A guy who always seems to be on the scene when things get squirrelly. And Bobby said the last thing he remembered was leaving the work site at McFall Meadows."

"The site of your red church stories."

"Let's focus on now, not five years ago." He didn't mean to snap at her, but she wouldn't leave the past alone—maybe because she was interested in hauling his past into her future.

"So what do you think? Did he somehow rig the accident? Put a rock on the accelerator from the far end of the bridge and send it on its way?"

"It's possible, but I can't make it fit. What would he stand to gain? Bobby only had liability insurance, so he wouldn't make money if he totaled the truck. In fact, he'd be in worse shape."

"You said he was driving a new truck today."

"Yeah, a new, gas-guzzling Chevy that had a 'McFall Meadows' magnetic sign on the door."

"Sounds to me like he's moved up in the world," Cindy said, coming beside him to take his hand and look out over the river. "Maybe he *did* have something to gain."

"Wait a second. I thought it was your job to talk me out of McFall conspiracy theories."

She shrugged and leaned against him. "I have an inquisitive mind. What can I say?"

"Yeah, I kind of noticed." He wrapped an arm around her and wondered if this was how they'd spend their golden years, sitting on a porch somewhere, watching the world flow by as they chronicled their little aches and pains and made observations on life's quirks and inconsistencies. But that future seemed so distant, he couldn't wrap his head around it. "Someday" was too insubstantial, particularly with a McFall in town. The only thing solid enough for Littlefield to believe in was this woman at his side.

"Cindy, I . . . ."

Seeming to sense that he was about to say something important, she turned to face him, raising a hand to his stubbly, creased cheek. She didn't speak but her eyes sparkled with an expectant "Yes?"

"Maybe we should—"

His cell phone buzzed in his uniform pocket and he pulled it out, not noticing that he'd broken into a sweat until the river breeze dried it and chilled his forehead. Cindy frowned, and then stepped away, granting him privacy in case it was official business.

It was Perry Hoyle. "Hope I'm not interrupting anything."

"Nothing serious." *Just me about to make the biggest leap of my life.*

"I haven't heard anything back from the state on Cole Buchanan," Hoyle said. "Best I can tell, though, he's still dead."

"That's comforting."

"My professional advice is to let sleeping dogs lie. I know you got all twisted up about what happened at the red church five years ago, but I'm sticking by my reports. Those people were killed by wild animals. And these new deaths, well, they're just a cluster of coincidences."

"Gee, Perry, if I didn't know better, I'd say you're more ready to retire than I am."

"Speaking of which, I'll be out of town for a few days. I got a new bass boat that I'm going to break in on Watauga Lake."

"Bass? I thought you were a diehard trout fisherman."

"A man's got to change with the times."

Had Littlefield heard that phrase somewhere recently? A car approached, slowing in deference to Littlefield's uniform. He waved the vehicle across the bridge; as it passed, the young man at the wheel of the BMW gave him a wary nod. A pretty girl was in the passenger seat, her wavy auburn hair tucked back with a sky-blue ribbon. He recognized her as a waitress at the waffle house.

Scrubbed-up young folks out on a date. There's hope for the future, after all.

"What's that?" Littlefield said into the phone, realizing he had tuned out Hoyle.

"I'll check in with you when I get back from my trip," Hoyle said. "Leave some room in your freezer for fish."

"Ten-four."

"And Sheriff?"

"Yeah?"

"Try not to let anybody die while I'm gone."

"I'll do my best."

After ringing off, Littlefield walked to the end of the bridge where Cindy waited beside his Isuzu Trooper. "What were you going to say?"

Littlefield didn't dare look into her eyes, because if he did, he knew he'd be lost. In his weakness he would search for salvation in her. He was a coward, and he'd spent his entire adult life dodging responsibility, living in denial, and hiding behind the badge. He'd let the McFalls' shadow darken his days and steal away his soul away as surely as any demons or vampires or malevolent gods.

But he wasn't about to let that final tiny ember of hope that lived inside him snuff itself out, not while he had Cindy. Not while he had people counting on him. Not while McFall slowly turned his community into an unrecognizable place. If—*when*—he fully committed himself to Cindy, he wanted it to be for the right reasons.

He looked at the yellow sign that said "NO SWIMMING JUMPING FISHING FROM BRIDGE." Beneath the words, someone had spray-painted "No fun!!!" in uneven black letters.

He'd been fishing, but nothing was biting. It was time to step things up a notch.

"Want to go to a dance?" Littlefield asked.

CHAPTER TWENTY-EIGHT

The Diggers were nearly through the first set, and Bobby was feeling good. He couldn't make out the crowd in the dark, but he could sense it beyond the rows of colored lights at the foot of the stage. He smelled the nervous sweat and volcanic hormones of the seniors, and although only a few couples had been dancing at first, the vibe was building. And he was at the heart of it—pounding, pounding, pounding its beat.

Sure, they'd had to dumb down their setlist a little so that Gladstone wouldn't blow a fuse and pull the plug on their performance, but The Diggers were rocking. Opening with classics like "Start Me Up" and "I Can See For Miles" had gotten the crowd on their feet early. Then they'd gone contemporary with The Black Keys' "Gold on the Ceiling," and Bobby saw the great bobbing mass of movement as kids poured onto the dance floor. Although Dex couldn't quite pull off a bluesy growl on vocals, Jimmy Dale tore it up on lead guitar, and the result was garage-band magic: raw, ephemeral, and opening up a kind of energetic possibility that scared them all.

The game within the game.

Bobby didn't know where that thought had come from—crisp, clear, and unmistakable—because he usually fell into a trance while drumming. Fortunately, all the songs on the setlist were in basic four-beat, so Bobby's main chore was to carry a steady tempo, add some flourishes at the build-up to choruses, and get splashy on the high hat whenever Jimmy Dale ripped into a solo. He was even digging the stupid mutilated bowling jacket. It was the first time The Diggers had all dressed alike, and although the gimmick was cheesy, it added a weird legitimacy that somehow seemed to work.

Plus the reverberation of the drumheads against his skull helped drive out the image of the pillar of smoke and ash he'd seen on the bridge the night before.

As the three other guys flailed at their guitars to blast out the final dying chord to "Gotta Digg It," Bobby launched into a drumroll and exploded out of it with a massive cymbal crash to end the set.

"We'll be back after a short break," Dex bellowed into the microphone as the crowd hooted and someone shouted out "Free Bird!" Dex grabbed Louise's hand and dragged her over to the refreshment table, where no doubt he'd bribed a friend to smuggle in a bottle. Floyd, the perfectionist of the band, checked the equipment and tuned the instruments while Jimmy Dale sat on the edge of the stage talking to a couple of girls, arms folded nonchalantly over his bowling jacket as if he were a veteran rock god instead of a kid who'd spent way too much of his youth in a basement alone with strings and machinery.

"You guys are tearing it up," Ronnie said as Bobby stepped off the stage, wiping his head with a towel. Now that he was out of the glare of the stage lights, Bobby realized the gym wasn't dark at all. The lights were just dim enough to provide a sense of anonymity while not so dangerous that some spazzo might trip over his shoelaces and sue the school board.

"Sounds good," Bobby agreed, both to reassure himself and to compliment Ronnie's skill at mixing the instruments. "You've got a knack for that."

Ronnie shrugged. "I just leave it alone unless somebody screws up, and then I just turn them down a little."

"Bobby!"

They both turned at the sound of Melanie's voice. She stood by the mixing board in a white dress that took Bobby's breath away, radiant, her hair flowing out from beneath a blue ribbon in wild tangles, her eyes wide and bright with excitement. Behind her, like an unwelcome shadow on a chest X-ray, stood Brett Summers, wearing a skinny black tie and a smirk.

"Hi," Ronnie said, but Melanie gave him nothing more than a perfunctory smile as she zeroed in on Bobby.

Damn, Ronnie's getting stonewalled hard. What kind of game is she playing?

"Hi, Melanie," Bobby said, and then looked past her. "Hi, Brett. Where's Amy?"

"Amy?" Brett looked confused, which seemed to be his perpetual state.

"Yeah. Amy Extine. I heard you were bringing her the dance."

Melanie turned to Brett. "What's all this about Amy?"

Brett waved toward a gaggle of seniors gathered near the stands, little more than silhouettes underneath the dim lighting. "She's over there somewhere. Like I care."

Melanie ignored Brett and grabbed Bobby by the wrist. "Come on. I need to talk to you."

"I don't have time," Bobby said. "We're about to crank up the next set."

"This is important."

"So's the band."

"You better do it, Bobby," Ronnie said, and Bobby wondered what was going on. He *suspected*, but this wasn't the right time for such drama.

"Okay, you got two minutes," Bobby said. "Hey, Brett, why don't you go round us up some Sprites?"

"Bite me," Brett said, nodding toward Ronnie. "Why don't you get your little groupie to do it?"

Bobby's fists balled. He'd never liked Brett, even though they'd played on the football team together. Not only was the guy rich, he had one of those stupid swooping Beiber hairdos that just cried out to be yanked off his skull. But Bobby couldn't get in a showdown here. If Gladstone kicked them both out, The Diggers would have to do an acoustic set, virtually guaranteeing a place on the school's invisible Wall of Shame.

"Say hello to Amy for me," Bobby said to Brett, letting Melanie lead him to one of the dark corners near the restrooms, where the stands offered a little privacy. The gym was cavernous and open, making it difficult for anyone to evade the all-seeing eyes of Gladstone and his administrative goon squad, but as long as they didn't engage in serious making out or smoking, they'd be left alone.

"Why didn't you tell me?" Melanie asked, getting in his face.

"Whoa, whoa. I don't know what you're talking about."

"You almost died in a wreck, and you didn't even bother to call me. Even after I left all those messages with your mom."

"I didn't get any messages," Bobby said. "I've been kind of busy today, in case you haven't noticed."

"That's just like you," Melanie said. "Always thinking of yourself."

"I wasn't thinking about *anybody*," Bobby said.

"Especially not me."

Two girls walked by holding hands, and one of them giggled at Melanie's outburst. The other muttered "Dairy Queen and Drummer Boy, a match made in hell," before they slipped into the restroom together.

"Look, Melanie, I don't know what you're so mad about, but it doesn't have anything to do with me. Looks like you're Brett's problem now."

She pounded on his chest with clenched fists. "Damn you, it's only because you didn't ask me first."

"Whatever. But did it have to be *Brett*?"

"Well, what did you expect? I wasn't going to wait forever. You only get one senior dance."

Bobby wasn't sure he wanted to march into this emotional minefield. Not when he wasn't sure how he felt about Melanie. True, he could have died yesterday, and so much would have gone unsaid, but maybe that would have been for the best. Right now, death seemed like the easy way out.

He asked her anyway. "Do you like him?"

"Brett?"

"No. Ronnie."

Melanie's mouth fell open as if he'd spoken in an alien tongue. "Ronnie?"

"The original Deathboy. He's been crushing on you since grade school."

"Holy crap, Bobby. If you're trying to piss me off, it's working. I can't believe you're using Ronnie to change the subject."

Bobby could barely make out her face in the shadows, but her wavy hair and shapely figure were clear enough. He didn't *need* to see her face. He knew it well enough, even in the dark. "And you're using Brett to make me jealous."

"Mr. McFall set it up," Melanie said. "I didn't want to disappoint him. Besides, you haven't shown much interest lately."

"Do you know that Brett's called you 'Melons' behind your back for years?" It was a low blow, but the cruelty gave Bobby a sick pleasure.

"Melons?" She looked like she'd been hit with a brick.

"Because of your boobs." That's not the term Bobby had used while they were making love, but this wasn't the time or place for fond recollections.

Bobby wondered if McFall knew about his relationship with Melanie. Bobby certainly hadn't mentioned it, but the older man always seemed to know what was going on in his life. He remembered the way McFall had hinted at fueling Bobby's success, whether on the baseball diamond or the stage. Had he somehow pushed Melanie away from Bobby? Why? To use her as a prize?

A group of three kids walked by, and one of them said, "Hey, great jams, Bobby!" giving him a high five. Once they were past, Bobby said, "You're better off with Brett, anyway. I'm going away to App State and Ronnie's going to college, too. You can bet your sweet ass Brett is going to stick around and take over his dad's business. He's a pretty safe bet, as boring dickheads go."

"Why are you being such an asshole?"

"Seeing things in a new light. Slipping out of the Reaper's clutches will do that to a guy."

"You can talk to me, Bobby. You know that, don't you?"

One of Jimmy Dale's power chords shattered the ardent murmuring of the crowd. "Gotta go," he said. "It's showtime."

As he stepped past her, she wrapped her arms tight around him, and he lost himself in her familiar embrace, the feel of her luscious body. He remembered every inch of her, even with clothes separating their flesh. She kissed him and he accepted it, although he was afraid to let her tongue penetrate. He forced himself away before he totally surrendered, or maybe he was afraid someone would see them. Maybe he was just *afraid*.

"Bobby," she whispered, grabbing the zipper of his cropped bowling jacket, the back of her hand rubbing against his sweating belly and the soft hairs above his belt.

"What?"

"This outfit is ridiculous."

"Brett's probably wondering where you are," he said, pulling free and heading back to the stage. He was only faintly aware of the throng as he passed through, catching fleeting glimpses of faces as he went—Joe Otto, Cheyenne Busby, and Dylan Penderland—although he heard a few cheers of encouragement and rowdy shouts of anticipation. Despite Gladstone's continued surveillance, the odor of alcohol and marijuana filled the room, and Bobby wished he'd smuggled some whiskey in with his drum kit.

He scanned the faces clustered around the double doors at the entrance to the gym, where additional light spilled in from the foyer. That's where the grown-ups were gathered—Sheriff Littlefield and that reporter, Cindy Baumhower, as well as Brett's dad and Dex's dad and Ronnie's mom and—

The thing made of smoke and ash.

Its edges were hazy, like dust swirling in a sunlit window, but the center seemed solid, as if it could shove through the crowd and rush the stage at any moment. And it *was* approaching.

Bobby swallowed and looked for Ronnie—*maybe he would see it too?*—but Ronnie was bent over the soundboard with a pen light. The other band members had already strapped on their instruments, and Dex shouted into the microphone. "Are ya'll ready to *rock*?"

The clapping, hooting, and stomping swelled to thunder, and when Bobby glanced back and searched the faces by the door, the walking gray figure was gone.

It was never there. Get your facts straight, stoner.

Then he saw Larkin McFall standing against the wall, applauding calmly, swaying back and forth as if the music were already playing. A middle-aged stranger stood beside him, wearing sunglasses and a black jacket with a turned-up collar like some kind of imported hipster. Maybe it was somebody in the record business.

Bobby couldn't get the image of the smoke phantom out of his mind, and he was barely aware of tapping his sticks together for a count of four to launch into Nirvana's "Come As You Are." He was a quarter-beat out of rhythm until The Diggers reached the chorus, and by then he was able to convince himself he'd been hallucinating.

Bobby didn't even care when Melanie and Brett slow-danced under the big spotlight to "Take It to the Limit," a song the band hated but felt obligated to play.

I took it to the limit last night at the bridge, Bobby thought. *But maybe that phantom of smoke and ash wants me to take it just a little bit farther.*

CHAPTER TWENTY-NINE

The night air was brisk and exhilarating after the stuffy, sweaty confines of the gymnasium. But Ronnie was pretty sure the high he felt was from his connection with the band. Even though he'd been little more than a knob-twiddling babysitter, he still felt like an orchestra conductor might, as if the whole creative enterprise had somehow depended on him. He had wild thoughts of dropping out of college and touring with The Diggers, maybe becoming their manager. Nothing could bring him down, not even Mom congratulating him in front of his friends.

And then he saw Brett and Melanie standing in the landscaped area outside the gym entrance. They were part of a circle of popular seniors, all of them laughing and shoving each other, ignoring the stream of the people heading for their cars.

A cold knife pierced Ronnie's chest. Bobby, who was standing next to him, slapped him on the back. "Let it go, bro. She's playing in a different league now."

"I was too chicken," Ronnie said. "I should have asked her weeks ago."

"Water under the bridge." Bobby nudged him and pointed to the parking lot, where Amy Extine stood under a security light talking to Louise Weyerhouse. "Besides, there's more than one fish in the ocean."

"You're mixing metaphors," Ronnie said.

"Huh, I guess that's why I've got a C in English. At least I'm getting an *A-plus in rock-n-roll*."

Sheriff Littlefield was looking their way—his arms folded, his face like stone. Then Ronnie realized he was actually watching Larkin McFall emerge from the crowd as if out of nowhere.

"You're a man of many gifts," said McFall, giving Bobby a thumbs-up sign. "That was an impressive performance. I can see why you're so devoted to your craft."

"Mr. McFall," Bobby said. "Thanks for the truck. It's a sweet ride."

"Well, I'm glad I can help. And I'm glad you're all right. I don't want to lose you." He smiled at Ronnie. "Either of you."

"Hi, Mr. McFall!" Melanie yelled, giving an exaggerated wave but staying with Brett and her circle. McFall returned the greeting. "Cute couple," he said, his eyes seeming to taunt Ronnie.

"We better roll," Bobby said. "We want to wind down a little after all the thrills. See you tomorrow at the work site?"

"Sure," McFall said with a wink. "Don't stay out too late. And Ronnie?"

Ronnie's mouth was as dry as dust. Littlefield was still watching them. "Yeah?"

"It's yours if you want it. Good night."

As the two boys walked away from the gym, Ronnie said, "Well, that was weird."

"Oh, he's always saying that kind of motivational stuff. Sort of like a success-guru version of Coach Harnett. I've learned to ignore it."

In the parking lot below, Dex emerged from shadows and joined Louise, lifting her off her feet and twirling her around in a circle. He was apparently riding the same post-gig buzz that had infected Ronnie. His must have been even more intense, being the lead singer and front man.

"Come on," Bobby said. "Let's see what's up. We can say hi to Amy."

"But I thought *you* wanted her." Ronnie was wary. He looked back at the circle of seniors again and saw that Brett had draped a possessive arm around Melanie's waist.

He was still thinking about her when they joined Amy, Louise, Dex, and a couple of other seniors in the parking lot. Amy gave Ronnie a big smile and that did the trick. "So, are you an official Digger now?" she asked him.

"Sure he is," Bobby said. "I'm just pissed that I didn't think of it a long time ago. You need a whiz kid to tie the chaos together."

"You did good, Ron-O," Dex said. "We might even have to dig you up a bowling jacket."

"Closing with 'Comfortably Numb' was a stroke of genius," Ronnie said, even though Dex's voice had gone raspy by then, a fact Jimmy Dale had covered up fairly well with his vocal harmony. "Even the kids who didn't know the song had to pretend to jam out to it."

"The only kids who don't know Pink Floyd are the ones who went home early for milk and cookies," Dex said. "And Jimmy Dale absolutely *shredded* it on the lead."

"And you tore up the drums, Bobby," Amy said, batting her eyelashes at him. Ronnie was confused. Amy had been flirting with him, and Bobby seemed to be pitching her as a possible consolation prize for the whole Melanie disaster. He wasn't musical at all, but he always seemed to be playing second fiddle.

Dex cozied up to Louise, and one of Louise's friends, a chubby, affable girl named Wendy Herrera, sidled up to Ronnie, apparently sensing that the group was breaking into couples. "Hey, Ronnie," she said. "How did you do on the chemistry final?"

"Uhh, good, I guess." He'd never really paid her much attention before, but she had nice eyes and a friendly smile. Her fingernail polish matched her turquoise earrings.

"Okay," Dex said, clapping his hands loudly. "Who's ready to par-*tay*?"

The proposal was met with much enthusiasm, although Ronnie kept quiet. It looked like he was just along for the ride. Pretty much the story of his life.

"I got a pint of Old Crow," Bobby offered.

"I ain't drinking that paint thinner tonight," Dex proclaimed. "I scored a fifth of Maker's Mark from the old man's liquor cabinet. We're going to . . . " Dex broke into an impromptu chorus of Kool & the Gang's "Celebration," quickly joined by Louise and Amy, who shimmied their hips and whooped to the "Come on!"

"Sounds awesome, but we're not adding that shit to the playlist," Bobby said.

"You're way too white, that's your problem," Dex said. Ronnie glanced at Wendy, who was half-Hispanic, but she didn't seem to care. In fact, she seemed a little tipsy already.

Damn. If I just lower my standards a little like any normal guy, I might get lucky.

"Hell, yes, I'm in," Ronnie said.

Bobby looked at him in shock. "I thought your mom said you had to be home by midnight."

"I told her I was staying over with you," Ronnie lied. "Besides, what are they going to do? Ground me for the last two days of senior year?"

"Sweet," Dex said, pulling out a set of keys. "Dad hooked me up with an empty rental in Riverview. Said, and I quote, 'Don't ask, don't tell, and don't leave no goddamned stains on the couch.'"

"How in the world did you talk him into that?" Louise asked.

"It was McFall's idea. He told my dad he'd be doing a public service by keeping us off the highways tonight."

"Mr. McFall is so awesome," Amy said. "I wish he was our principal."

"Hell, I wish he was our *president*," Dex said. "Okay, the gear's packed, so we only have room for one in my Jeep."

"Amy and Wendy can ride with us," Bobby said. "We'll follow you. But don't drive too fast, okay?"

Dex pointed at him as if shooting a gun. "Sure, Drummer Boy. You don't want to push your luck. Maybe you're the reason McFall set us up with a party pad."

"I'm fine," Bobby said. "I haven't had a drop to drink."

"You didn't last night, either," Ronnie pointed out.

"Mount up," Bobby said, heading for the McFall Meadows Silverado that held his drum kit in the back.

Ronnie copped a corny phrase from Charlie Sheen, hoping to impress Amy or Wendy or anybody. "Gentlemen, tonight we ride."

Nobody got it, but it didn't matter. Without another word, Amy piled into the front seat beside Bobby and Ronnie got into the back of the extended cab with Wendy. Ronnie wasn't sure how close together they should sit—if he should start working some moves on the way or what—but Bobby ordered them to strap on their seatbelts, which solved the dilemma.

As they pulled out of the parking lot, the truck's headlights swept over Brett and Melanie, walking hand-in-hand toward Brett's BMW. "Look at those two lovebirds," Bobby spat, blowing the horn. "Out of the way, losers."

"Don't be mean to Melanie," Amy said. "Brett's a dick, but Melanie's just doing the best she can."

Ronnie was surprised by Amy's defense of Melanie, because Amy's style was to cut any potential competition off at the knees. Or maybe she was just feeling generous in the glow of victory.

"If that's the best she can do, she should become a nun," Bobby said, gunning the accelerator and shooting past them. Ronnie put his face to the rear window and waved. Brett flipped him the bird. Melanie looked shell-shocked, as if she'd missed the last helicopter out of the embassy in Vietnam.

Soon they were on the highway, Dex's Jeep just ahead of them. Wendy smelled like a beer can that had been used for an ashtray. But Ronnie didn't draw away when she whispered, "I'm glad you're coming" into his ear. In case her remark wasn't clear enough, she squeezed his thigh.

Amy's cell phone rang, and she had a loud conversation with somebody who was apparently a fellow senior. Even hearing only one side of the conversation, Ronnie could tell she was bragging about hanging out with Bobby. "And we're having a big party up in Riverview," she said into the phone. "You guys should come up. I'll text you when I get the address."

After she rang off, Bobby scowled at her. "This is the band's after-gig party. I'm not so sure Dex wants a million folks up there, especially since it's one of his dad's fancy rentals."

"Loosen up, hon," she said, pushing back her hair and flashing her feline eyes, practically purring for him. "That was Alicia. Dex won't mind."

"Didn't they used to date?" Wendy asked.

"Everybody's had a ride on the Dex-go-round," Amy said. "Nobody takes it personally."

"Well, Louise might," Bobby said.

"Okay, *Dad*. Jeez. I didn't know we invited Preacher Staymore and the church choir."

The truck cab was quiet for a second, but then Bobby spoke up. "Here's where it happened," he said, and all eyes shifted to the bridge as they drove past it.

"I want to look," Amy said.

"No way," Bobby said, speeding up. "We'll lose Dex."

Ronnie glanced at the moon-dappled river. *No mist tonight. At least I get to worry about girls instead of ghosts.*

CHAPTER THIRTY

Bobby wasn't sure what time the party got out of hand. Maybe it had *started* out of hand.

He'd been trying to take it easy with the drinking, but Amy kept plying him with gossip, and he couldn't care less about Stribling's hemorrhoids or Whizzer Buchanan's armed robbery charge or the rumors over whether Cheyenne Busby was pregnant. Alcohol helped. In between spouting pointless stories, Amy had been busy texting out invitations to the party until it seemed like half the senior class had found the five-bedroom mansion on the hill. Bobby had thought Dex would be pissed, but apparently he enjoyed playing the big shot. By the time Brett and Melanie showed up, it had been at least an hour since Dex and Louise had locked the door on one of the bedrooms.

Bobby glared at Amy, although her pretty face was swimming a little in his vision. "You invited *her*?"

Amy giggled and fluttered her thick eyelashes. Alcohol seemed to energize her instead of slow her down. "Why punish Melanie just because she's dating that jerk? She's one of us. She belongs here."

Bobby didn't know who the "us" was. A few nerds were sitting on the floor, sharing a joint and watching a Star Trek movie, while some of Bobby's jock friends were manning the refrigerator, which had miraculously filled up with Busch Light and Pabst Blue Ribbon. Five or six kids, dressed only in their underwear—probably just a few drinks away from nudity—were splashing around in the hot tub on the deck. Floyd and Jimmy Dale were boozily debating whether Metallica qualified as a hair-metal band. Wendy had thrown up seconds after their arrival and was now snoring at the far end of the couch where Bobby and Amy were sitting.

Ronnie was across the room in a beanbag chair, still working on the same can of beer he'd been holding for the last hour. It had to be as warm and flat as horse piss by now.

He noticed instantly when Melanie came into the room, almost like he had some invisible antenna that zapped his brain whenever she passed within a hundred yards. Bobby had already put Melanie out of his mind—even with all her yakking, Amy was looking better and better as that crop top slid up her belly—but he wasn't sure he had much of a mind left.

"So are you going to show us now?" Amy asked. Bobby realized that she was talking to him.

"Show you what?"

"Where you wrecked."

Bobby reached for his drink. The ice had melted and the whiskey in the glass was the color of corn syrup.

Damn, I must have zoned out for a minute. Or longer.

"Come on," Brett said, suddenly right beside him. "Don't be a pussy."

McFALL ✿ EPISODE FOUR

Melanie hovered behind Brett, alert and nervous. Bobby could barely stand to look at her. Just like his mom, she didn't have the guts to stand up for what she believed. But then again, maybe Bobby had no idea *what* she believed.

"Leave him alone," Ronnie said from his beanbag. "He's a little wasted."

"Okay, Captain Obvious, but it's not your call."

"We're all too wasted to drive," Ronnie said.

"Melanie's not. But that doesn't matter anyway. We don't *need* to drive. It's a straight shot down to the bridge. We could walk there in, like, five minutes."

Jimmy Dale dropped down beside him on the couch and punched his arm. "Hey, dude, it's part of rock-n-roll lore now. Like when Jim Morrison rolled up on that truckload of dying Indians when he was a kid. Plus you guys found that Absher dude there. When The Diggers are big time, the YouTube crowd will eat this story up. The drummer who came back from the dead. We're talking *a million page views*, yo."

Dex strolled back into the living room, tucking his T-shirt into his jeans, obviously having caught wind of their conversation. "Yeah," Dex said. "Any of you bitches got a cell phone? We can take a band picture at the crash site."

Bobby was lightheaded, but he wasn't sure whether it was from booze or fear. He looked right at Melanie. "What about you? Do you want to see where it all went down?" Somehow it seemed important, *essential* to know what Melanie really thought.

She bit her lip and nodded. Her eyes were dewy, and that stung him a little. Brett didn't even notice the play between the two of them. Ronnie did, though, and he gave a shake of his head as if to say "I don't think this is a good idea."

255

But maybe it didn't matter. Ghosts, pillars of ash, death crashes—he was leaving it all behind soon. All this shit was a *bridge*, a way to get from here to there. And once he was *there*, none of the *here* would matter anymore.

So why not play the game within the game?

He swayed to his feet and everyone in the room broke into applause. Dex said, "Let's fire one up for the road," but Bobby was already heading out into the cool night air. By the time he'd walked down the deck stairs, he was no longer wobbling. The stars veered and wheeled overhead, the moon a fuzzy wedge of hard milk, but he focused on the ground in front of him. Dex moved ahead of him, guiding him to a trail that he called a "natural resource amenity," and the stoned and drunk seniors trailed behind as if he were some kind of Pied Piper leading innocent children into the unknown.

Ronnie pushed through the crowd and caught up with Bobby. Tugging at his arm, he said, "Something weird happened last night, didn't it?"

"Yeah. I think I died."

"Don't joke about crap like that. You should have died, but you didn't. And McFall came to your hospital room."

"Don't start in on that stuff about the red church and the McFalls. We're not kids anymore."

"You don't have to do this. You think any of these people really care about you? They're just out for cheap thrills."

"I can't let Brett win. I can't let *Melanie* win."

Ronnie stopped in his tracks, but Bobby kept going, determined, almost eager now. Something *had* happened at the bridge. He'd undergone some sort of transformation, and maybe visiting the scene would help him fill in the gaps.

The group emerged from underneath the trees, and there it was ahead of them, just across the highway. The river slipped silently over rocks, winding toward the bridge fifty yards ahead. Bobby wondered what they would do if headlights approached, or if the sheriff made one of his increasingly frequent patrols of the area. But he didn't care about consequences anymore. In a way, nearly dying had given him a blank slate.

And then they were at the head of the bridge, staring off into the path of the wreckage. "Here's where it happened," Bobby said, like a celebrity host on a reality show. The moonlight revealed the scarred bark of the damaged trees and bits of broken glass and sheared metal glinted among the weeds.

"Look at these ruts," Floyd said. "You musta gone airborne."

"That's some serious Evel Knievel shit, dude," Jimmy Dale said.

"Where did Ronnie find the dead guy?" Amy asked. Dex pointed down to the water's edge on the other side of the bridge.

Bobby walked away from the group and went to lean over the bridge railing, gazing downstream. Mist hung over the river, but tonight it was just mist. It didn't try to twist into shapes and figures, and no faces coalesced in the gloom. Ronnie came up beside him but didn't say anything, just stared off in the distance, where the mist, the river, and the mountains all merged into diffuse and endless gauze.

Behind them, the other kids were swapping theories on how Bobby had survived, with Jimmy Dale offering "Good karma" and Brett deeming it "Dumbass luck, and he's got the dumbest kind of all." But they soon grew bored, and Floyd asked if anybody had brought beer.

Bobby spit into the water, watching it arc out and down, making a little plop that was instantly swallowed up as if it had never been.

"So, who's going in?" Brett asked.

"Going back, you mean?" Dex said. "I'm ready. Louise will wonder where I went, and we left Wendy passed out with all those psycho jocks around."

"Not back. I mean *in*."

"Into the river? You're crazy."

"You rock jocks think you're hot shit. But let's see whose balls are the biggest. Bobby? You coming in?"

"No way," Bobby said without turning. "Quit showing off."

Brett unbuttoned his Van Heusen shirt and tossed it onto the asphalt as if he didn't give a damn that it cost as much as a working-class guy's salary for a day.

"Cool it, Brett," Melanie said, clutching at his arm. "It's too dangerous."

"Sign says no swimming," Jimmy Dale said with a stoned snicker.

Brett kicked off his shoes, and then fished out his wallet and handed it to Melanie. "If I don't make it, this is yours. It's all you're after anyway."

"Don't be a dick," Bobby said.

Brett clenched his fists and squared off to face him, and Bobby thought, *Here we go, time for me to beat his ass and get it over with,* but instead Brett climbed up on the rail and wobbled drunkenly.

"Get down from there before you fall," Melanie said. "Please."

"Who's coming with me?" Brett said, finally getting the attention he'd been craving all night. Maybe all his life.

"Let's go back and get a cold one," Dex said.

Brett wailed out the chorus of "Comfortably Numb," strutting and strumming in mockery of Dex, and then dove into the darkness with a loud whoop.

Bobby heard Ronnie whisper, "Not again."

"That'll sober him up," Floyd said as the splash erupted against the million gurgles and trickles and the never-ending wet laughter.

CHAPTER THIRTY-ONE

Ronnie knew what he wanted, but he didn't yet want it badly enough.

Larkin McFall needed to have a long talk with that boy. Ronnie's problem was simply a matter of perspective. His head had been scrambled by too much church, and he suffered from a morbid sense of morality. Well, he'd learn soon enough.

McFall was here to give people what they wanted. And was that really so wrong?

Everybody else had figured it out, including Bobby. Well, almost everybody. Heather Fowler was proving to be a stubborn thorn in his side. At least Sheriff Littlefield was drying up like a scarecrow in the sun, gutless and stiff, just waiting for retirement.

Brett Summers's life was insured for two million dollars. Max Summers was a man who liked to cover his bases—after all, it was the family business. So Larkin looked at this as a win-win. Everyone would live happily ever after, except for Brett, who would never know the difference.

Besides, Brett's mother had been a Matheson, so his bloodline carried plenty of blame.

As McFall rose from the hidden, cold depths of the river, down where the ancient springs seeped from deep beneath the granite, he considered grabbing a rock to bash in Brett's skull, as he'd done with Darnell Absher. But that would be duplicating a pattern, and he wasn't ready to show his hand. Not yet.

Maybe, like Ronnie, he took more joy from the tease than the conquest. The game within the game.

But he didn't tease Brett. He just grabbed the boy's ankle and pulled him to the bottom. Brett kicked and squirmed, then flailed, but he might as well have been pounding mud. Bubbles escaped from his lips as he screamed, but the noise would be lost on the churning surface of the river. They'd find his body miles downstream—another tragic death blamed on alcohol and the recklessness of youth.

In death, Brett Summers would live on as a morality tale that parents would tell their children.

Max Summers would have a little extra cash, perfect for investment in local real estate.

Ronnie would be Melanie's comfort in a time of shock and sorrow.

And McFall?

It was a job well done, and sometimes that was enough in itself, even for someone whose work was never finished.

McFALL

EPISODE FIVE

CHAPTER THIRTY-TWO

Ronnie didn't see Brett's ghost until the end of June, but there was plenty to keep the living busy in the meantime.

Pickett High's two hundred and ninety-three seniors graduated in the shadow of their classmate's tragic death, already scattering onto different life paths that would rarely cross again. Two weeks later, forty rounds of the major league baseball draft came and went without Bobby Eldreth's name being called. The Minnesota Twins inquired about a freelance contract, but Bobby wasn't willing to throw away his college eligibility for a mere $20,000 nonguaranteed. Even Elmer supported that decision, grimly holding out hope that Bobby would have a stellar freshman season at Appalachian State, raising his stock for the next draft.

Sheriff Frank Littlefield investigated Brett Summers's drowning, and was relieved to rule his death an accident. He had grounds to charge several of the kids at the party with underage drinking, misdemeanor possession of marijuana, and maybe even reckless endangerment, but he felt the community would best be served by letting the tragedy float downstream as fast and as far as possible. The sheriff shifted his energy to investigating a rash of meth labs in the western end of the county, while dodging Cindy Baumhower's relentless pursuit of a long-term relationship.

Heather Fowler took a sabbatical during the first summer session at Westridge University, using the time to plant a small, organic garden in her backyard. The month opened hot and humid, followed by two weeks of rain that caused her tomatoes to blight. She attended the regular commissioner and planning board meetings, voting with the majority and making no comment at either. She hiked to the top of McFall Meadows twice with Susan Barinowski, discovering the second time that a section of the new fence had been removed.

Larkin McFall, Logan Extine, and Bernard Gunter laid plans to expand the development across an additional four hundred acres that had been purchased by McFall, bordering on Riverview and the Blackburn River. Wally Kaufman's bulldozer pushed the ashen remains of the red church into a small ravine, where it was buried in topsoil planted with fescue and clover. Foundations for the first six houses had been poured, and crews were already pounding the wood framing into place. David Day and Elmer Eldreth were among the men working on the initial house, which would serve as a sales model and office.

And Blackburn River flowed on.

On June 29, Ronnie helped Bobby install a white picket fence around the old graveyard, which would have been a fine time to see a ghost. The work was conducted under high clouds and the azure sky looked like it rose all the way to the edge of the universe and beyond. The boys straightened the grave markers as best they could, and Stu Hartley slapped mortar between the broken wedges to patch headless angels and marble lambs. Ronnie kept turning around to stare at the gouged brown ruts where the church had stood, as if the building's shadow still fell over him, Archer McFall's red eyes watching him from the dark well of the belfry.

Ronnie was driving a galvanized finish nail into a post when Bobby said, "Hey, look at this."

During the downstroke of his hammer, Ronnie shifted his eyes to Bobby, who was pointing at something in the middle of the graveyard. The hammer missed the nail and bounced off his thumb. He grunted, sucking on it to keep blood from pooling in the bruise. "Gee, thanks," he mumbled around his thumb, dropping the hammer.

Stu Hartley croaked out a laugh and slung some leftover mortar around the gate posts. "Frigging rookies," he said. "Don't know why McFall don't hire real carpenters."

"Maybe he needs some workers who are actually sober," Bobby said, shutting Hartley up fast. The man cocked one bloodshot eye and rolled his wheelbarrow over to a water bucket to clean out the cement, muttering under his breath.

Ronnie squeezed his throbbing thumb as he walked over to where Bobby stood in front of a marker. He recognized it before he even got there, because it was near where he'd found Boonie Houck's body. Deathboy's *first* corpse, where it all had begun. With each step, Ronnie was afraid the ground would open up and pull him under.

"Samuel Riley Littlefield," Bobby said, reading the name engraved in the granite slab. "Dude was only eleven. Wonder if he's related to the sheriff."

"He was one of them."

"One of who?"

"The ghosts who went into the river."

Bobby wiped the sweat from his forehead. "Come on, Ronnie. I thought we'd agreed to let sleeping dogs lie. And sleeping dead people."

Ronnie shrugged. "This place doesn't bother me in the daylight. Especially now that the red church is gone."

"Yeah," Bobby said, his voice trailing away as he looked over at the patch of mud where the church had stood. "I know what you mean."

Pointing the handle of his hammer at the gravestone, Ronnie said, "Samuel was the sheriff's little brother. He died at the church. Broke his neck during a Halloween prank. That's why the sheriff gets so paranoid about this place ... about the whole McFall property."

"Well, you can't blame McFall for what happened to Brett after the dance. He was drunk and acting like an idiot. Hell, you could even say he had it coming, and I wouldn't argue with you."

"You're just pissed because he was with Melanie that night." Ronnie hated saying her name, since it hurt both of them. She'd been avoiding everyone since Brett's funeral. Ronnie figured she felt guilty. "Nobody deserves to die young."

"Tell that to little Sammie here."

Hartley scraped his hoe across the bottom of the wheelbarrow, the noise setting Ronnie's teeth on edge. He fought off a sudden urge to smash the gravestone with a hammer, as if one blow could obliterate the past, setting the course of history reeling in a different direction. Maybe the boy's death had fed the legend of the red church, bringing the McFall family back to town again and again.

Except Larkin is nothing like Archer McFall. Larkin is a different kind of strange. He doesn't lurk in the dark—he hides in plain sight.

Ronnie felt a chill pass over him, cooling his sweat. He had figured it for a summer breeze skating over the river on its way to the northeast, but the sky grew dark too. They might have to hurry to beat the coming storm. He didn't want to work in the rain.

"Anyway, the dead are gone," Ronnie said. "And we'd better get this fence finished if we want to get paid."

"I always settle accounts," McFall said from behind them.

Ronnie turned. Larkin McFall hadn't been there a minute ago, and the model home was a hundred yards away. How could he have walked that far across the grassy pasture without Ronnie noticing?

"We were just taking a break," Bobby said.

McFall studied them both, and then surveyed the graves. He nodded his approval. "Mr. Hartley can finish the fence. I have something to show you two."

McFall walked up the road bed without waiting for a response. Ronnie and Bobby exchanged glances. Bobby shrugged and removed his tool belt. "He's the boss."

No. God's the boss.

But Ronnie followed regardless.

CHAPTER THIRTY-THREE

"Office of the chief medical examiner."

"Hello, this is Sheriff Frank Littlefield from Pickett County." He leaned back in his wooden chair, which gave a squeak of dismay. "I'm just calling to check on the autopsy results for a burn victim we sent your way about seven weeks ago."

"Could you please give me the case number?" said the male voice on the phone at the OCME. The voice sounded as weary of death as Littlefield felt.

He recited the case number from Perry Hoyle's report, and heard computer keys clacking as he added, "I understand you're backlogged, and my ME's been hounding you, but I want to stress the importance of this case. I know we're not a big city, but—"

"Buchanan, Cole," the voice coolly stated. "We emailed autopsy and toxicology screenings to Dr. Hoyle on May 17. He acknowledged receipt and said he would forward the results to the appropriate parties."

Littlefield rubbed his temples. "Are you sure?"

"Yes. I'm looking at his return email as we speak. I can forward it to you if you like."

"No, that won't be necessary. But could you fax—uh, I mean email—a copy of the report over to my department? Dr. Hoyle's been away on vacation."

Except Hoyle's vacation had lasted only three days. He'd given Littlefield four pounds of white bass after his fishing trip to Watauga Lake. And he'd returned in time to handle the paperwork for the Summers boy, which had been an open-and-shut case. So why had Hoyle withheld the Buchanan report?

After ringing off, Littlefield punched up his email account and studiously typed in his username and password. Technology had made law enforcement easier in many ways, but he still resented the drudgery of wading through the avalanche of information. Maybe he'd accidentally deleted Hoyle's email or moved it into his labyrinth of message folders. But even as low-tech as he was, any mention of "Buchanan" in the subject line would have immediately drawn his attention. "Crispy critter from the red church" would have worked just as well.

The OCME address popped up on his screen as he watched, and he opened the email. The report was attached as a file, but the text was also copied into the body of the message. Littlefield scanned the data, noting that Buchanan's blood alcohol level had been one-and-a-half times the legal limit, but he couldn't make much sense out of all the scientific terminology. The bottom line summed up the report so succinctly that even Littlefield could comprehend it: "Death occurred due to blunt trauma to the skull resulting in acute subdural hematoma, previous to third-degree burns over 90 percent of the body."

So Hoyle knew it was murder but didn't tell me. What possible motive could he have had?

He thought of Hoyle's call before his trip. Hadn't he said something about breaking in a new bass boat? As a physician Hoyle could have easily socked away thirty or forty grand to buy a toy for his retirement years, but the man had been a hip-waders and fly-tying trout fisherman for more than five decades. It seemed like a too-abrupt turnabout for the old coot.

Still, Littlefield wasn't ready to confront Hoyle. He couldn't believe the oversight was a mere lapse in judgment, but he didn't know what Hoyle had to gain. Who would try to buy off a medical examiner?

McFall.

Littlefield rushed out of his office, nearly forgetting his hat in the process. Sherry asked him where the fire was, being her usual nosy self, but Littlefield waved her off. He broke the speed limit heading over to the offices of *The Titusville Times*, calling Cindy from behind the wheel with the request to meet him behind the building. He didn't think it was a good idea to be seen frequenting an establishment whose staff influenced public opinion.

When he climbed out of his Isuzu, Cindy looked around to make sure the coast was clear before leaning in for a kiss. She stopped six inches from his lips. "What's wrong?"

"McFall."

"I thought you were over that." She looked like she had forgotten all about the kiss.

"Did you ever follow up with him about that list of his businesses in El Paso he promised you?"

"I didn't see any need."

Littlefield glanced around, checking the parking lot for new vehicles. He realized he was wondering what McFall could have bribed *her* with. "Well, I'm back on it. Cole Buchanan was murdered."

"Are you sure?"

"Somebody beat his head in before the red church burned down around him."

"But how did his body get in the church without it being discovered?"

"That's the question. But the bigger question is 'Who killed him?'"

Cindy flexed her fingers as if she couldn't wait to type up the news. "I don't know why you're so fixated on McFall when other suspects are staring you right in the face."

"Who?"

"How about the rest of the Three Redneck Musketeers who were going to burn down the church? Maybe Cole wanted to go back and finish the job and they got into a fight."

"I wouldn't be surprised to learn that either Sonny or Stepford had killed a man, but only if it was over something serious like women or cars. Anyway, if one of them did, why hide his body in the church? And don't tell me you think they're sophisticated enough to make a political statement."

"Okay, try this," she said. "Your vic breaks into the church to conduct a little vandalism, takes a drunken tumble, and cracks his skull open. Somehow the firefighters overlook the body. After all, it's not really the type of thing they'd be looking for."

"Yeah, a dead guy in a little church. Hard to miss that, all right."

"Damn it, Frank, why do you have to be so stubborn? You were just starting to mellow out, and now the vein in your temple looks like a marble is rolling through it."

Littlefield wasn't sure what was worse—her preference for him when he was dull and sedated, or the diminishment of her legendary inquisitiveness. Maybe she just wasn't seeing the gravity of the situation. "I've been letting these slide as accidental deaths. Three in less than two months. Not to mention the Eldreth boy's near-miss. But now I've got an investigation on my hands."

"Fine," she said. "I won't expect you for dinner as often."

"Cindy, you know this means that I need you to get information from McFall and his wife."

Cindy's eyes narrowed, and he noticed the creases around them for the first time. When sleeping, she looked like a teenager, but the years were crawling in. "Do I get to run a story on the autopsy results?"

"Not until I officially open the investigation."

"What if I run it anyway, citing an 'unidentified source close to the sheriff's office'?" Or just file a public record request with the OCME?"

Littlefield shook his head. Now it *felt* like marbles were rolling through his veins. "Get me the info, and you'll get your story."

She waved him away and went through the back door. She didn't lean in for a kiss this time.

CHAPTER THIRTY-FOUR

Heather wasn't overly impressed with the receptionist, although she couldn't help but wonder if the pretty blonde doubled as Larkin's mistress. Then again, maybe she was just sizing up the competition. She liked to think she was too strong to be seduced by Larkin McFall's power, but over the past weeks she had found herself waking up in the middle of the night again and again, trembling from dreams about his touch. And there were other fantasies, about everything the two of them could accomplish if they combined the strength of their personalities. She knew there was something off about him, but she felt powerless to resist his draw. So when he called to ask her to visit his downtown office, it had seemed inevitable.

When Heather first walked into the office, the receptionist was staring at the wall, her expression vacuous, like a balloon waiting for the first puff of helium. Heather initially assumed she was looking at the decorative photograph, a rural landscape taken by Heather's nemesis, Bill Willard. But her gaze was focused dead ahead, directly at the oak paneling. As Heather closed the door behind her, the woman smiled and her eyes grew animated.

"McFall Meadows, how may I help you?" she said, as if she were answering the phone.

"Is Mr. McFall in?"

"Mr. McFall? Do you mean Larkin?" The smile remained firmly in place.

"Yes. I'm Heather Fowler, with the county board of commissioners, and he invited me to drop by and discuss his developments."

"We will have a wide range of units available, from family homes to more modest condominiums. Our first model will be available for walkthroughs in August, but I'm more than happy to show you floor plans and concepts." She tapped a stack of glossy brochures that had been arranged neatly beside the telephone on the otherwise empty desk.

"No, I'm not looking to buy," Heather said. "I'm a commissioner."

The smile was white and stiff. "I'm sorry, we aren't looking for brokers. We won't be doing commission sales."

Heather wondered if the woman was really that dumb, or if her front was designed to ward off potential headaches for her boss. The receptionist's elegant left hand bore a gold band with a diamond big enough for industrial use. Her eyes were blue as a California swimming pool, and deep as a teaspoon. The top button of her blouse had been left tastefully undone so that lesser folks than Heather might wonder about what mysteries lay beneath.

"You understand I am with the county government, right?" Heather asked. "I reviewed Mr. McFall's project with the planning board."

"Ah, yes. So you're *that* woman. My husband told me about you."

Now Heather understood. Or maybe she was suffering a built-in cultural resentment to thin, attractive blondes who seemed to marry far more wisely than their intelligence deserved. Heather put on her campaign face and smiled back. "And what did he say?"

Mrs. McFall rolled her eyes upward as if reading from a cue card stuck to the ceiling. "I believe he called you a refreshing challenge, a champion of the county that he was very much looking forward to partnering with."

So many words for such a tiny mind.

"Pickett County welcomes the opportunity for mutually beneficial growth," Heather said. "Of course, it's important that we do things the right way. That's why I'm here."

"I'm sorry, you missed Larkin. He's been so busy I can barely keep up with him."

"It's okay, I was just driving by on my way to the library."

"Hold on a sec. I think he left something for you." The woman bent down and opened a drawer. She pulled out a folder, stood, straightened her skirt, and circled the desk. Heather couldn't help but compare herself to the blonde. Heather's figure was better, but Mrs. McFall had that cool, icy beauty that drove some men into a senseless frenzy. She would have expected Larkin McFall to go for someone a little more dynamic.

Like me? But do I really want this? Do I want to be his queen because I'd be a benevolent ruler?

Heather took the proffered folder and saw her name written across the top. "Thank you, Mrs. McFall. Tell your husband I'll call to make an appointment."

"Please, call me Cassie. We're part of the same community now." The woman was already back at her desk, patting the immaculate brochures into a neat stack.

Heather peeked through the window after the door had closed. Cassie McFall was once again staring at the wall. Her face had gone slack, and her eyes were as dull as if someone had switched off lamps behind them. As if the plug had been pulled on a robot. A chill shot up Heather's spine, but she shook it off, chalking up the woman's behavior to airheadedness.

In her car, Heather opened the folder and looked upon a survey map of McFall's combined properties, which seemed to have grown substantially since she'd encountered him in the deed office. The cluster of parcels now extended along a half-mile of river frontage and bordered a swath of Jefferson National Forest. A handwritten note in the corner of the page read "Six down, three to go."

She noted the names of the original owners of the new parcels: Absher, Matheson, Gregg, Buchanan Heirs, Potter, Eggers. The remaining parcels adjoining the McFall land were owned by Day, Ward, and Littlefield.

The sheriff?

The next document was a topographic photo of the McFall Meadows project. She was shocked to see how much had already been done. An uneven, red ellipse had been drawn around the peak of the ridge, and the words "Fowler Park" were scribbled in the same handwriting as the note on the first page. A dotted line between the project and the former Matheson property led from the "park" to the highway and was dubbed "Twin Coyote Trail." A little rectangle along the river was labeled "Sewage plant #1?"

Jeez, is he planning more of them?

The final page in the folder was a personal note to her from Larkin McFall.

Dear Heather,

I've been thinking about you a lot. I so admire your passion, strength, and unwavering commitment to what is best for Pickett County. I want my project to be something you and I work on together—something in which we can both take pride.

I believe we share a common vision. And a common future. Let's shape it together.

With warmest regards,
Larkin McFall

Really? You think you can buy me off that cheaply? Or charm me with your "regards"?

She dug in her purse, found a permanent black marker, and flipped back to the topo map. She scrawled a giant X across the sewage plant. Then, grinning, she drew a wider circle around the makeshift perimeter of the park.

She turned to the first page, which featured the company's letterhead. Between Larkin's name and the office address was a line reading "Cassandra McFall, Vice President." Heather raked the tip of the marker through the words.

It wasn't much, but it was a start.

CHAPTER THIRTY-FIVE

Bobby climbed out of the Silverado and waited at the front of the truck for McFall and Ronnie to join him. The gravel road had dwindled to a set of red, muddy ruts before ending in a wooded glen in which were situated several buildings. A couple of the ramshackle structures were animal sheds but the largest might once have been a house. McFall looked out of place in his long sleeves and tie.

"You guys know I've been expanding the project, right?" McFall said. "Well, this is the latest acquisition."

"Cool," Bobby said. "But why did you bring us? It looks to me like a job for Wally's bulldozer."

McFall gave him that distant smile that increasingly resembled the cool equanimity of a reptile. "We have to help the current resident relocate."

Bobby couldn't believe anyone lived in the house—*well, more like an overgrown shack*—that stood before them. This end of

Pickett County was notoriously poor and barely a generation past moonshine and felony charges as its primary exports. But even the rundown Eldreth mobile home was a palace compared to this relic. Warped gray siding boards peeled away from the framing, and several windows were broken. Another window was covered with tarpaper, and the rusty tin roof was pocked with holes. A squirrel scrambled across the crumbling stone chimney as they watched, then slipped into the attic via a crack beneath the eaves.

"What a dump," Ronnie said.

"That's not a very nice way to talk about your neighbors, Ronnie," McFall said.

Ronnie lowered his head. "We never came over here. Dad told us to stay away from the Buchanans."

"Just like he told you to stay away from the red church?"

Bobby didn't know what was going on between them, but he was irritated. *He* was the boss of this crew. Well, not of McFall, but certainly of Ronnie. The way this worked was McFall gave orders to Bobby and Bobby passed them down to Ronnie. That's why Bobby was making two bucks an hour more and drove a new Silverado. And it was why he was McFall's Golden Boy instead of Ronnie.

"So, what do you want us to do?" Bobby said, hiding his impatience.

"Follow me." McFall headed toward the house, stepping carefully in his polished Ralph Lauren wingtips.

Ronnie and Bobby shared a look, and Ronnie shrugged. They trailed after McFall and climbed the rickety steps onto the porch, which was little more than a series of leaning locust posts supporting three sagging sheets of tin. Bobby wondered if the floor would hold their combined weight.

McFall banged on the door. "Sweeney, come on out."

Bobby listened for movement. All he heard was the ticking of the truck's engine and the distant caw of a crow. "Do you know this guy?" Bobby whispered to Ronnie.

"Just some loony. He was a 'special kid' in grade school until they shipped him off to a group home."

"We're all special," McFall said, overhearing. "But Mr. Buchanan needs a little more care than do others. He's misunderstood." McFall banged the door harder. "But he also *misunderstands*."

Bobby tensed. "So, what? Are we trying to evict him?"

Does this mean we're McFall's goon squad now? His enforcers?

McFall stared at the door as if to open it with the sheer force of his will. "We are merely here to explain that he's trespassing. He should have left with his family, but apparently he ran away and holed up inside."

"Maybe this is a job for the sheriff," Ronnie said.

McFall knocked once more. "Sweeney! We won't hurt you!"

Then he turned to Ronnie. "I'm concerned that Sweeney would not react well to the sheriff's arrival, given the Buchanan family history of arrests. He might get confused. Violent. I'd rather handle this privately if possible."

Bobby looked around for a weapon in case Sweeney attacked them. He only hoped the guy didn't have a gun. Ronnie edged behind him, distancing himself from the door.

"Maybe we should try around back," Bobby said.

McFall reached down and tested the door handle, which turned with a corroded creak of protest. He pushed his way inside and vanished into the moldering darkness.

"You going?" Ronnie asked Bobby in an undertone.

Rather than answering, Bobby simply stepped into the decrepit structure. It took a moment for his eyes to adjust, with only a few lines of sunlight leaking through the windows. At first he thought he was in a small foyer, and then he realized it was actually an open room. The entrance was made narrow by tottering stacks of magazines, books, and newspapers. The odor of rotting pulp hanging heavy in the air.

"Sweeney!" McFall called, moving deeper into the house.

A single, naked light bulb hung from a cloth-wrapped wire in the center of the room. Bobby tried the light switch by the door, but nothing happened. He wasn't surprised. The house appeared to have been built before modern electrical infrastructure was commonplace. And it sure smelled liked mastodons and saber-toothed tigers had been taking a crap in the corners.

Bobby pulled a newspaper from a nearby pile and held it near the open door. It was the sports section of *The New York Times*, and a photograph of Mickey Mantle swinging a bat was featured on the front page. The masthead was dated July 17, 1965.

"Ronnie, you got to come see this," Bobby said.

Ronnie whispered "Wow" from the doorway and picked up a *National Geographic*. "It's from 1956. I wonder if these are valuable."

"Nah, you can find boxes of this junk at yard sales. But if you see any comic books, let me know."

McFall was banging around in one of the back rooms, and light suddenly poured into the hallway when he ripped a curtain from its hanger. Dust swirled and cobwebs swayed in the dim illumination and Bobby noticed that the walls of the large room were covered with ragged-edged pages. Rather than pictures and photographs, the pages mostly contained text.

"This is one creepy place," Ronnie said. "No way was Sweeney Buchanan living here."

Bobby whistled in agreement. "He's a nut case, all right."

A sofa with a faded rose pattern stood angled in one corner, piled high with more magazines, catalogs, advertising circulars, and other printed matter. A blackened stone hearth was blocked by boxes of books, and Bobby wondered if somebody had been burning them to stay warm. He remembered a line from Doris Huntington's history class that went something like, "Where books are burned, people are next."

Well, this isn't history class. It's an even bigger waste of time.

Something clattered in the adjoining room, and McFall said in a calm voice, "Easy now, Sweeney. We're not here to hurt you."

"*I know you!*" came a high, panicked voice.

Bobby hurried to the interior doorway, Ronnie right behind him. The two boys stood shoulder to shoulder, afraid to enter. A haggard man—Sweeney, Bobby presumed—was backed into a filthy corner of the bedroom, brandishing a wicked-looking pipe wrench. His eyes were bright with anxiety, but McFall continued to take steady, measured steps toward him, his palm open in front of him.

"Come on, Sweeney, give me the wrench."

Sweeney looked past McFall to Bobby, who felt the man's gaze plunge into his brain like a barbed harpoon.

"You're the coyotes!" Sweeney shouted.

"Jesus," Ronnie said.

"We should have called the sheriff," Bobby said.

"We can handle this," McFall said, but Bobby wasn't sure whether he was talking to them or to Sweeney. "This is my land now and I take care of my own problems."

"Nuh-nuh-not your land," Sweeney said.

"Yes, it is. This was McFall property until you Buchanans tricked us out of it. But I've come to set things right."

McFall took another step forward. Something clacked drily beneath his feet. Bobby glanced around the room. A bare bed with a blanket piled in the middle and a scarred dresser were the only furniture. These walls, too, were plastered with ripped-out pages, only they were arranged in some sort of pattern.

Letters?

Ronnie must have seen them as well, because he began deciphering the uneven lines and spelling out the letters. "S-U-M-M . . . is that—"

"Summers End," Bobby read. *Is this about Brett's death?*

McFall was within ten feet of Sweeney now, and the man raised the wrench in a menacing gesture. The room was crowded with the metallic odor of fear and sour sweat. Something clacked and rattled across the floor again, and Bobby looked down at McFall's feet. Small, thin bones were gathered there like an ivory pile of tiddlywinks.

"Mr. McFall?" Bobby said, but McFall was staring intently at Sweeney and didn't seem to hear him.

"What do you want, Sweeney?" McFall said, as if they were playing a silly game of Truth or Dare.

"Go away," the man said, his lower lip quivering. "Away, away, away."

"I'm here to help *you* go away," McFall said, in an armchair psychologist's tone.

"No, *you* go away," Sweeney said, rushing at McFall.

Bobby wasn't sure what happened next, but he watched as the pipe wrench swung toward McFall's head, bracing himself for a geyser of bones, blood, and brains. McFall ducked deftly beneath the blow and shoved Sweeney to the floor. Instead of staying there, the man skated across the bones, regaining his balance before making a dash for the door.

Straight at Bobby.

Sweeney swung the wrench again, and Bobby pulled back, letting the metal strike against the door jamb. He heard the whistle of air, and splinters peppered his face, but the impact jarred the wrench loose from Sweeney's hand, and it tumbled to the floor. Bobby thought about driving his fist into Sweeney's stomach but he hesitated just long enough for Sweeney to slip past him, shove Ronnie against the wall, and take off running through the open front door and into the woods beyond. As he fled, he shouted, "Away, away, away!"

"Damn," Bobby said.

McFall kicked at the bones. "These look like canine bones. I guess our boy's a genuine hoarder."

"Well, the eviction notice worked," Ronnie said, but his attempt at humor fell flat. "What now?"

Bobby picked up the pipe wrench. Bits of hair stuck to the hook jaw, held there by a gummy brownish substance. He wondered if Sweeney Buchanan had used it to kill the dogs whose bones had been part of the collection. Assuming they *were* dogs' bones.

No, this is fresher. Those bones are old.

"Summers End," Ronnie repeated, looking again at the letters on the wall. "What does that mean?"

"Dude forgot his apostrophe. Stribling would be all over his ass."

"Why don't you back the truck up to the front door, Bobby?' McFall said. "It's time to take out the trash."

"Wouldn't it be easier to burn it if you just want to get it out of the way?"

"That wasn't so easy last time, if you'll remember," McFall said, looking at Ronnie.

Bobby wiped at the clinging bits of hair. "I think this is blood."

"Dog's blood?" Ronnie asked.

"I'm no scientist. Blood is blood."

Ronnie looked at McFall. "*Now* do we call the sheriff?"

"Yes," McFall said, taking the wrench from Bobby. "*Now* we call the sheriff."

CHAPTER THIRTY-SIX

"It's a family decision," said Linda Day, standing over the pressure cooker on the stove. The release valve spat steam, and water leaked from around the rubber ring that ran along the bottom edge of the lid.

Ronnie was busy stringing and snapping green beans, his habitual role in the annual canning ritual. Tim was responsible for washing the Mason jars and setting out the proper number of lids and bands. David Day sat at the table and drank beer, proclaiming his work finished—after all, he'd tilled the garden and planted the beans, even though his two sons had handled the weeding, which Ronnie thought was the hardest part of the job.

"I don't reckon so," David said. "This was Day land long before I married you." He smiled at Ronnie, but Ronnie wasn't sure he was joking about what he said next. "And these two yard monkeys don't get a vote. This ain't a democracy."

"I don't want to move," Tim said. "I'm already at the bottom of the food chain as a freshman, but at least I have some friends at Pickett High."

Ronnie was pretty sure Tim's objection had a lot more to do with Brandi Matheson than any concern over his social standing in school. Ronnie himself was pretty ambivalent. Now Melanie was pretty much off the radar, and he was almost certainly going to gain a whole new group of friends at Westridge in a couple of months. He practically had one foot out the door already. Maybe he could even get a little apartment near the university.

But part of him still treasured his roots here. Despite the recent rash of deaths and that bizarre incident with Sweeney Buchanan, Ronnie had quit obsessing over ghosts and demons and the possible return of Archer McFall. The destruction of the red church had eased his mind on that front, even though he still sometimes saw mysterious shapes moving in the river fog. If the dead were indeed returning, they didn't seem to have much interest in him.

Oh, face it, Deathboy, you're just not ready to give up on Melanie, and you'd risk walking through hell and high water for a chance at her.

"Dad," he said, peeling a string off a particularly long pole bean, "you know that under North Carolina law, a husband and wife share all community property equally. Since you acquired the land from your family after you and Mom were married—"

"I don't want to hear any mumbo jumbo you read in a book somewhere." David sipped his Budweiser as Linda kept her back to all of them, her expression hidden. "The Days scrapped and clawed and bled on this ground, and that counts for more than the papers some lawyer in Raleigh drew up."

Tim came to the table to scoop up handfuls of broken beans, which he placed in a colander for rinsing. "If we don't get a vote, why did you even bring it up?"

David gave him a bleary glare. It was Friday evening and the twelve-pack of beer had been severely depleted, which meant Linda would be making a run into town before long. This was probably the only chance the others had to talk any sense into him. "I'm just thinking out loud, that's all."

"We can do a lot with that money," Linda said, finally turning. With potholders on both hands, she looked like a prizefighter ready to go a few rounds. "We can pay off Ronnie's school and put some away for Tim's college, too. You always said you didn't want your kids to work with their hands if they didn't have to."

"Ronnie's doing a bang-up job for McFall," David said. "He's already making more money than I did as a carpenter, and he's just day labor. If things pick up around here, he might be better off with a hammer than a pencil."

"Nobody uses pencils anymore, Dad," Ronnie said.

"Don't I know it. How much did that goddamned computer cost?"

"You won't worry about a computer once you have four hundred thousand dollars," Linda said, as if such a number were incomprehensible. "That's nearly twice what Logan Extine offered us a couple of years back."

"Offered *me*, you mean. Extine's an asshole. I wouldn't sell to him if I didn't have a pot to piss in or a belt to tighten up while I was holding it in."

"We can pay off the bank, too," Linda said. "As low as interest rates are right now, we can get a cheaper place somewhere and pay cash. We could get out of debt and start setting some aside for retirement."

"Since when did you turn into Rockefeller with boobs?"

Ronnie glanced at Tim. Something deeper was going on than David's stubborn mountain pride of ownership. He suspected it had something to do with Linda's entanglement with Archer McFall. David was pretty stubborn about letting go of a grudge.

"Since when did somebody ever come in and offer you a way out of all your problems?" Linda said. "In case you haven't noticed, we haven't won any lotteries lately."

"Thirty-six acres," David said. "And this house I built with my own hands. And you want it to go to the McFalls."

"Not the McFalls. To *Larkin* McFall. He doesn't have anything to do with whatever bug crawled up your ass and flexed its little tentacles."

David crushed his beer can in one muscular hand. It wasn't completely empty and foam spurted from the top. The pressure cooker whistled and gurgled, expanding to tighten the rubber seal along the lid. Tim turned on the tap to rinse the beans.

"Besides the garden and the barn, most of that land isn't even getting used," Linda said. "You're paying taxes and not getting anything back."

"You ever heard of a little thing called heritage? I was hoping you boys would build your own houses here one day, settle down, raise your families, just like the Days have been doing for generations."

"Then how come your brothers moved away?" Linda said. "You wouldn't even have this place if they didn't want to sell out and move. And we wouldn't be so deep in debt, either."

"Those woods come in handy when you want a fire in the winter to warm that little tush of yours," David said, clearly beyond caring about the boys' embarrassment. "And that pasture land—well, I've been wanting some cows and goats, but this damned economy."

Ronnie was glad the farm was downsized at the moment. They'd had a small herd of cattle in his youth, and the chores were never-ending. The garden took enough time as it was, and unless Ronnie moved out, he was going to be hoeing rows and yanking weeds for a few more years. He needed all his spare time to study, because he was pretty sure this was his one shot at a degree.

"I think you're just too proud to sell," Linda said. "You're happy to rent yourself out, though. You take McFall's dinky little checks for a week of work, but then you turn down a big payoff because you're afraid to be really free."

"Big talk coming from you," David said. "You know all about whoring for a McFall."

Ronnie was afraid for a moment that his mom was going to pick up the simmering pressure cooker and fling it at his dad. Instead, she laughed like a little girl. "Maybe there's a reason the McFalls always get what they want. Look at their competition."

David launched out of his chair, knocking it to the kitchen floor. He swept his arm across the table, scattering the pile of beans Ronnie was preparing. His eyes contained that same cornered brightness that Sweeney Buchanan's had the previous day, and Ronnie wondered for the first time if his father was capable of murder. Tim shrank back toward the hallway, holding the colander before him as if it were a catcher's mitt that might deflect whatever dangerous object David hurled his way.

David tensed, his eyes flitting around as if looking for something to smash. Ronnie met his gaze and held it, hoping David didn't see the butcher knife lying on the counter beside the packed jars of beans.

You're the man of the house, Ronnie's eyes said, although his heart was thundering a completely different message. *Whatever you do will stay with us forever, no matter where we go.*

"Sorry about the beans," David said, sagging a little. Even the pressure cooker was silent as he walked to the refrigerator and pulled out the remnants of the twelve-pack. He left the room with a pathetic attempt to play it cool, pausing only to say, "This is Day land, damn it. Day now and Day later."

After the door slammed closed, Linda shucked her pot holders and tossed them on the counter. "Maybe I should talk to Larkin. Get him to up the price a little."

"Not a good idea, Mom," Ronnie said.

"Neither is letting David Day run our lives into the same shallow grave as the rest of the bunch."

Ronnie couldn't really argue with that. He got on his knees and offered a silent prayer as he collected the spilled beans.

CHAPTER THIRTY-SEVEN

"**W**orking weekends now?" Littlefield asked Cindy.

"News never sleeps."

And neither do we lately, at least not together.

"Don't be getting any big ideas about running a story on Sweeney Buchanan," Littlefield said. With only a few months left in his term, and Cindy insinuating herself ever deeper into his daily routine, he'd given up on keeping their relationship secret. They were seated at 24/7 Waffle, which was surprisingly crowded even for a Saturday morning. The place was at capacity, and several of the booths were filled with unfamiliar faces. Littlefield figured the tourism season must be picking up, and the local Chamber of Commerce would certainly welcome the SUVs full of money rolling into town.

Cindy spread grape jelly on her bagel and then brandished the sticky knife as if preparing for a swordfight. "I'm not counting on you to feed me anything anymore," she said. "From now on,

I'm using public records and official sources who will actually cut through the bullshit."

Littlefield sighed. The end of his term in December couldn't come soon enough. He just wondered if the coming winter would also put this relationship in the deep freeze. The running joke that she'd only been in it for the scoops was now hitting too close to home.

"Sweeney's not officially a suspect. At least, not until I get test results to see if the blood on the pipe wrench is a match for Cole's. I had to go around Perry Hoyle and send it to a private lab."

"So you're suspicious enough to tap your homicide budget, huh?"

"The blood on the wrench might have come from an animal for all I know. Stepford Matheson lost some dogs a while back. He thought it was coyotes, but maybe Sweeney conked them over the head. God knows, their howling was enough to make anybody want to shut them up one way or another."

"I don't have to wait until you open a formal investigation," Cindy said. "Not everyone is bound by your little unwritten rules of secrecy."

"You don't have anything to run with. Not if you're still pretending to be a responsible journalist."

"'Pretending,' huh? Maybe it's time for that little editorial about a sheriff that's coasting through the end of his term and letting someone get away with murder."

Littlefield slammed down his cup so hard that coffee sloshed onto his plate of eggs and grits. He sheepishly dabbed at the mess with a napkin.

Going to have to work on my fits of self-righteous indignation. If I end up marrying this woman, I'm sure as hell going to need a decent repertoire.

At the counter behind the cash register stood Melanie Ward, the young woman who had been Brett Summers's date on the night of his death. Taking her statement had been one of his toughest acts as a law enforcement officer, because she'd kept repeating, "I shouldn't have come." Now she looked pale and listless, ten years older, and even her curls seemed to have wilted in grief. He guessed she was still carrying around some guilt—*join the club, there's plenty for all of us*—so he was relieved she wasn't their waitress.

"Okay," he said to Cindy. "What do you have on the Sweeney case if you don't quote me?"

"How about an eyewitness account?"

"No way."

"Yes way. I've had a very interesting discussion with a certain Mr. Larkin McFall, and he's willing to go on record."

"I can't believe you'd be that reckless, even to sell a few newspapers."

"I'm not going to accuse Sweeney Buchanan of murder. I'm simply going to lay out the lineage of facts, all the way back to Cole Buchnanan's death, and let readers draw their own conclusions. We've got a lying medical examiner, three suspicious deaths over a couple of months in the same area, and a possible deranged killer running wild. I'll admit, I was as suspicious of McFall as you were—partly because I was under your spell and wanted to please you—but he's starting to seem like the only sensible person around here."

"Why would you want to inflame the community like that?"

"Quite frankly, Sheriff, for a person who puts so much stock in 'evidence,' I think you're deathly afraid of the truth."

"And what would that be?" Littlefield wasn't sure he wanted to know, because there were several possible answers, and all of them whispered of truth.

"You have such a hard-on for McFall that you've closed your mind to anything that might indicate he's not some sort of demon sent here from hell to personally torment you."

"You haven't been much help. You never did get that information on his businesses."

"What do you want? For me to seduce him so you can swab his DNA out of me?" She pushed her plate away and stood. "Are you going to eat that bacon?"

He shook his head. It wasn't much of a peace offering, but right now he'd take what he could get. She plucked the two strips from his plate, shook the remaining coffee dregs from the greasy meat, and shoveled them into her mouth, intentionally smacking her lips. "Your turn to pay," she said, tossing a few ones on the table and heading for the door.

At the register, Melanie took his check and totaled the bill, not looking at him. He waited silently, turning his hat in his hands, until she muttered, "That will be $18.76, please."

He gave her a twenty. "How are you doing?"

"Fine."

"I'm sorry about—"

"Everybody's sorry. Well, *I'm* the one who's sorry. I went out with the guy one time, and now I'm getting treated like a widow. I barely knew him."

A man at the counter, sipping coffee and picking at a piece of apple pie, glanced over at them. Melanie lowered her voice. "He acted like a stupid asshole, and he got what stupid assholes deserve. I'd think a cop would know that better than anybody."

She thrust out the change and he waved it away. "Put it in your college fund," he said.

"Jeez, you been talking to Ronnie Day? Figures." But she slipped the money into the front pocket of her apron regardless.

The cook called out an order and Melanie headed for the grill. Littlefield took the opportunity to get the hell out of there.

CHAPTER THIRTY-EIGHT

"**H**ow did *she* get here?" Bobby asked.

"It's an all-ages club," Ronnie said.

Bobby didn't think "club" was the right word for this craphole. The State Line Tavern was just across the Tennessee border, a tin-roofed restaurant that wasn't much of a step up from Sweeney Buchanan's digs. Half of the business was dedicated to fireworks that were much more potent than those legally available in North Carolina, and the clientele appeared to be the type that would happily blow their welfare checks to hell for a few kicks.

Dex had scored the gig for The Diggers, and the tavern's owner had promised them a cut of the door. Bobby had been suspicious from the get-go, because the tavern's owner, a rat-faced man with a stringy mullet named Lou, wouldn't let the band provide its own door check. Even though the place was packed with a Saturday night crowd, the patrons cared more about drinking than dancing, and the second warning sign had come when a vocal portion of the

crowd had begun chanting for "Sweet Home Alabama." The bowling jackets that had been cool at the high school dance now felt
ridiculous among the plaid-and-blue-jeans crowd.

But that was just rock-n-roll on the road. What really threw
Bobby for a loop was when Melanie showed up in her blue summer
dress, edging her way through the tables until she was right next to
the stage. She stood there swaying by herself through a couple of
songs. A middle-aged man in a cowboy hat came up and said something to her while The Diggers were blasting through a makeshift
version of "Johnny B. Goode." She shook her head and the man
scuttled away, and then Amy Extine popped up beside her, holding
a beer bottle.

At the break, Bobby slipped out the backstage door where the
Silverado was parked. He was glad to be out of the lights and noise.
Ronnie had joined him while Dex, Jimmy Dale, and Floyd went to
talk their way into free beer at the bar.

"Amy must have given her a ride," Ronnie said. "Looks like
they're best buds now."

"I guess it's a good sign. About time she rejoined the living."
Bobby glanced up at the sky, hoping for stars, but he couldn't see
past the moths circling the security light. He leaned against the
truck. His shoulder was sore from work, and he hadn't been throwing any baseballs lately. He'd lied to his App State coach and his dad
about his workout schedule.

"Brett's death was hard on all of us." Ronnie hung back in the
shadows, and Bobby couldn't see his face. In a way, it was like a
confessional booth.

What happens in Tennessee stays in Tennessee.

"I saw him," Bobby said.

"Who? Brett?"

"No, the guy they found dead in the church."

300

"For real? You ought to tell the sheriff."

"You don't get it. I saw him *after* he was dead. That night I wrecked my truck at the bridge."

Bobby told him the story about the stack of smoke and ash—as much as he could remember anyway. The events had become hazier and hazier with the passing days. "That's what's so weird about the wreck. I didn't hit my head or anything, but it's like there's a gap of a couple of hours. Like I was *taken* somewhere."

"Oh Jesus, Bobby." Ronnie's voice was guarded. "I was hoping all that ghost stuff was over."

"I've felt weird ever since. It's kind of hard to explain, but it's like I left something behind. Like part of me is missing."

"Dude, maybe you really *did* hit your head. But we've both seen some weird shit. I don't even know what's real anymore."

"Ever since Vernon Ray vanished on Mulatto Mountain—and he *is* dead, I just know it—I've been praying for him to come back. I don't know how to pray like you do, but sometimes I can hear him playing his little snare drum."

Ronnie emerged from the shadows. His eyes were somber with understanding and something Bobby had never seen in them before. Could it be sympathy?

Deathboy's happy to pass on the crown, that's all.

Ronnie opened his mouth to say something, but then the stage door swung open and Dex came out, the club owner behind him.

"We got a problem, Ronnie," Dex said, a sour smirk on his face. "Lou here wants it louder."

"Yeah," Lou said. "And don't you boys know any *good* music? Like Bob Seger and stuff?"

Bobby shook his head and forced a grin. "Go crank it up, Ron-O. I'll be along in a few."

After they were gone, Bobby walked to the corner of the building and looked out at the parking lot. People sat on the hoods of
cars passing 40s of malt liquor, orange dots of burning cigarette
tips making redneck constellations. A couple of men were yelling at each other as if gearing up for a brawl. Bobby wondered if
a music career would encompass hundreds of gigs like this one,
passing through the lives of strangers who would remain utterly
unchanged by whatever bit of your soul you sliced off and dished
out for them.

To hell with it, let's rock.

Before he reached the back door, a stranger stepped from behind
the Silverado, his sunglasses glaringly out of place. "Bobby?" the
man said.

"Do I know you?"

"We have friends in common."

The upturned collar. "You were with Larkin McFall at the high
school dance."

"I've been listening. You're good."

"You're only as good as the people you play with."

The stranger smiled, pushing his sunglasses up his nose. "McFall
told me you'd say that. But it's bullshit, Bobby. You've got some
chops. You can go places."

"We've been working hard this year. Starting to write some of
our own tunes." Bobby nodded toward the club. "Not that we'll get
to play any of them tonight."

The man dug in his pocket. "Your singer is a pile of shit, Bobby.
And the other two guys are a dime a dozen. When you're ready to
get real, I'll be waiting."

The man held out his palm and Bobby expected to find a business card there, the sort of sleazy L.A. move he'd always pictured.
Except he'd always figured it would be a sports agent, some slickster

with too much hair gel who'd be happy to take a ten-percent cut while Bobby trashed his body with steroids in order to reach the top. Instead, the stranger offered him a glass vial.

"What's that?" Bobby asked.

"Kickass powder, kid. Give it a try."

Bobby shook his head. "I don't know. The guys are counting on me."

The stranger's teeth gleamed, seeming far too large for his mouth. He unscrewed the cap and tapped some of the white powder onto the cleft of his thumb. He held it up to Bobby's face. "One little sniff."

Bobby leaned forward and instinctively pinched one nostril closed. He inhaled through the other nostril and the powder burned its way up his nose and into the base of his brain, simultaneously freezing and burning his skull. His shoulder pain vanished and he felt like he could throw a baseball a hundred and ten miles per hour. The stranger lowered his sunglasses and his eyes sparkled. For a second Bobby saw him as the stack of smoke and ashes and his heart stuttered and clenched.

It's the drugs, that's all. That's all.

The stranger pressed the vial into Bobby's hand. "Consider it an advance," he said.

Bobby staggered through the back door and onto the brightly lit stage, and there was Melanie, standing beside Ronnie at the sound board. She lifted one corner of her mouth in a speculative smile, but Bobby ignored her, settling behind the drum kit like a space pilot preparing to guide a faster-than-light machine toward a black hole. Dex launched them into "Take It To The Limit," and even though it was a mellow song, Bobby somehow filled it with flourishes and accents, as if the sticks were moving by themselves. Melanie jiggled her body to his rhythm, the hem of her dress swishing across her thighs, and he couldn't help but remember her writhing and whimpering beneath him.

He wondered if Brett had experienced the same sensation before he'd gone down for a final time.

To hell with it, let's rock.

Bobby might not have fully returned from wherever he'd been taken that night at the bridge, but at least he was better off than Brett and Vernon Ray and Darnell Absher and that Buchanan guy who'd gone to hell in the red church.

At least part of Bobby had come back.

CHAPTER THIRTY-NINE

Bobby toweled the sweat from his hair and tossed Ronnie the truck keys. "Your wheel, bro. I had a few too many PBRs."

Ronnie looked down at them, pleased with the responsibility. "Sweet. Guess I'm officially a roadie now."

"You awake enough to make it?"

"Better than awake. I'm *alive*."

The drums and sound system were packed in the truck and covered by a tarp. It was about two in the morning. Mullethead Lou had paid them eighty-eight bucks for their share of the door, which Ronnie calculated to be at least two hundred dollars short, but Lou had threatened to call the cops on them for underage drinking, loitering, and whatever else the Buford County law could throw at them. He'd made a point of mentioning that his brother-in-law was a deputy.

Since The Diggers had barely made it through the gig without a riot from the drunk, raucous crowd—only a blistering twenty-minute guitar solo during their third run through "Johnny B. Goode" had saved them—they'd decided to get the hell out of Dodge while they still could. Dex and Floyd had taken the Jeep, and Jimmy Dale had roared off on his motorcycle, some scrawny local gal hanging on behind him for dear life. Ronnie had noticed that when the band members finished performing, they seemed to suffer from a bizarre mix of adrenaline high and exhaustion. Given Bobby's confession about seeing a ghost, Ronnie was glad to be in control, especially since Bobby's eyes were bloodshot and foggy. Even worse, his pupils harbored some sort of secretive, mad glint.

What if he sees that stack of smoke and ash while we're booking down Slate Mountain at seventy miles an hour? Or worse, what if I see it myself?

"Warm up the engine while I take a whizz," Bobby said.

Ronnie climbed into the driver's side of the Silverado, enjoying the feel of subdued power. He started the engine and switched on the headlights. There was a silhouette at the edge of the parking lot, just beyond the yellow reach of the beams. Ronnie wondered if it was one of those drunken cowboys, pissed off because the band had failed to play any Toby Keith, thereby revealing themselves to be a bunch of socialist Obama lovers. Ronnie goosed the accelerator, letting the V-8 engine do the talking for him.

The silhouette stepped forward into the pool of light.

Melanie? I thought she left with Amy.

She walked toward him, almost ethereal against the surrounding darkness. She had talked to him a little tonight, but he'd been so busy running sound he hadn't had the chance to say anything important to her. Well, maybe this was his chance.

Ronnie rolled down his window as she came around to his side of the truck. "What are you doing here?"

"Amy's sleeping it off until she sobers up. I don't want to be stuck here all night. Can I catch a ride?"

"Is she safe?"

"Yeah. She drove to that Wilco down the road; it's open all night."

Bobby opened the passenger door, apparently having overheard their conversation. "Hop in."

She hurried around to the other side and got in the middle of the bench seat. Bobby settled in beside her. Ronnie had been looking forward to talking with Bobby about his supernatural encounter, but with Melanie beside him, he couldn't really focus on anything other than the warmth of her body and the clean lavender smell that cut through the lingering stench of cigarettes and beer.

Ronnie's hand brushed Melanie's bare thigh as he reached for the gear shift, but she didn't flinch. As he put the truck into first, he couldn't help but feel the heat rising from her lap. He didn't have much experience driving a straight, but he sure wasn't going to ask Bobbie for tips. He popped the clutch and the Silverado lurched forward, jackrabbiting a few times before he steadied out the RPMs as they rolled across the mostly empty parking lot toward the two-lane highway.

"Well, isn't this cozy?" Melanie said.

"You could have got in the back," Bobby said.

"No, I want to see your faces."

"Faces?" That's plural. Ronnie concentrated on the blacktop and the double yellow lines, glad that there was no traffic as he mastered the shifting of gears. The Silverado's cab was enormous, but now it felt cramped, claustrophobic with expectation.

Bobby's beer intake had apparently washed away any impulse for discretion. "I was surprised to see you here."

"What can I say? I dig The Diggers."

"So much that you'd ride an hour to see us?" Bobby said. "We're not *that* good."

"Amy's hot for you. I just came along for the ride."

Ronnie wished they would save this conversation until he was out of the picture, but a sad, sick part of him clung to every word.

"I haven't talked to Amy since that night." Bobby sniffed and wiped at his nose. "Come to think of it, I haven't talked to *you*, either."

"Been busy."

"You okay, Bobby?" Ronnie asked. "Sounds like you're coming down with a cold."

"I'm just wiped out. That was an intense gig."

They swapped stories about the night's experience, mostly making fun of Lou and the guy who'd tried to pick up Melanie, but Bobby soon lapsed into sullen silence. Melanie prodded him, trying to keep him alert. Like Ronnie, she hadn't been drinking, and Ronnie hoped she would stay awake.

Plus, every time he downshifted to slow the truck's descent of Slate Mountain, his wrist rubbed against her soft skin. And he realized his crush had not been buried these past weeks, it had been sleeping beneath the surface, waiting to crawl out and make him miserable all over again.

When Bobby started snoring, Melanie muttered "Lame" and turned on the radio, although she left it low enough for them to talk over it. Ronnie asked her about work and college—the stuff Bobby had warned him against mentioning—but she opened up a little and soon he found himself telling her about Sweeney Buchanan and McFall's offer to buy the Day property.

"If Dad sells, then I'll probably be staying in a dorm next year," Ronnie said. "I might never come back to Barkersville."

She didn't pick up on his wistful tone. "Good for you," she said. "You can leave all these bad memories behind. The rest of us are stuck here."

Ronnie wanted her to ask what a potential move might mean for "us," even though he knew there was no "us," not with the two of them. The only "us" was in his head, and he knew he'd say something stupid if he didn't change the subject. So he talked about other things, and she shared some stories from the waffle shop.

"You'd better drop Bobby off first," Melanie said. "He needs his beauty sleep. Lots and lots of it."

Bobby was groggy when they pulled up to his trailer, and together they wrestled him out of the cab and to his feet. Elmer Eldreth came out red-eyed and cussing, telling Ronnie, "Keep that damned racket down before you wake the whole trailer park."

"Tell Bobby I'll bring the truck back over tomorrow," Ronnie said.

"Damn straight you will. McFall will ream his ass out if you put so much as a dent in it."

"Goodnight, Mr. Eldreth," Melanie called cheerfully as they loaded back into the Silverado.

As they hit Highway 321, Melanie said, "No wonder Bobby wants to blow this popcorn stand. His dad sure is an asshole."

"Bobby can take care of himself." Melanie was sitting farther away now, and Ronnie could no longer brush against her to change gears. Even though it was the middle of the night, he felt more confident operating the big pickup now, and he welcomed the chance to show Melanie that he wasn't a total wimp.

Then he felt her hand on his arm, and he nearly drove off the edge of the road. "I'm glad we're alone," she said. "I wanted to tell you something."

Ronnie's mouth went dry. He focused on the yellow lines in the highway, which seemed to waver in his vision. "Tell me what?"

Melanie switched off the radio so that the only sound was the subtle rumble of the engine and the whirring of rubber on asphalt. "You know Mr. McFall set me up with Brett Summers," she said.

"Yeah, you mentioned," Ronnie said. Even though he had longed for Melanie to talk about personal, intimate, *real* stuff with him, this wasn't happening the way he'd envisioned. For one, in his imagination they were sitting on a blanket in some meadow, under the summer sky with honeybees buzzing around the wildflowers. For another, they were talking about "us," not some dead guy.

But what did you expect? Everything you touch turns dead sooner or later.

"Mr. McFall told me that anyone who acted so foolishly was not a good partner," she said, her hand still on his arm, her fingers warm and firm. "He apologized for making a mistake and told me I deserved better."

"Great. So you let McFall run your life now?"

Her fingers squeezed hard enough to hurt. "He's the only grown-up that ever cared about me. That ever helped me out. Looks like he's helping you, too. I don't know why you're trying to knock him down."

"Sorry," Ronnie said. "That shit at the red church screwed me up when I was a kid."

"Archer McFall and those animal attacks? Yeah, that was a mess. But that was five years ago. We're different people now. And Larkin's not Archer."

And I'm growing away from you. I'm going to Westridge and you'll still be a waitress in that greasy spoon. You'll probably be pregnant within a year.

"I hope you marry Bobby," he said, having no idea where that came from. "He's a good guy."

She punched his arm. "Shut up. Me and Bobby had a thing once, but McFall said he's no good for me. He told me Bobby has other plans."

"Yeah, right. I'll bet it's McFall who has other plans for Bobby."

Melanie unhooked her seatbelt and slid over until she was leaning against him. Ronnie held himself very still, clenching the steering wheel with both hands, afraid to breathe.

"You know what I want?" she whispered.

"No," Ronnie said. They were coming up on the bridge, which seemed like horrible timing, the kind of coincidence that would never occur in a random, chaotic universe, and certainly wouldn't happen by divine plan.

"Yes, you do," she whispered. Her lips were on his cheek, and this time he turned his face and their lips met. Even as he slowed the truck, he knew what was going to happen next, what she couldn't help but say.

"Pull over at the bridge."

CHAPTER FORTY

What do I do with my hands? She smells good behind the tavern smoke and sweat. Is this seat big enough for this? Damn, what if somebody drives up? Thank God it's three in the morning.

Ronnie didn't resist as she pulled him down, and he just knew he was going to say something stupid. Luckily, she kept her lips on his and he couldn't escape. Not that he wanted to. Ever.

He'd kissed girls before, several times—Cheyenne Busby in particular had given him a workout when she'd discovered he was a virgin, but she'd quickly lost patience with him when he didn't press the issue. But those encounters had been uniformly awkward, more like he was kissing the girls because he was supposed to than because it's what he wanted.

You were saving yourself for Melanie. You and your stupid imaginary morality.

But none of that mattered now, because it was finally happening, and he faded into her yielding curves. He wondered if he was crushing her, and he tried to lift himself up, but she wrapped her arms and legs around him and pulled him closer. Her dress was riding up her thighs and moist heat rose from between her legs. Despite his nervousness, his groin pulsed.

She pulled her lips away. "I don't know why we waited so long," she whispered.

"Doesn't matter why. Here we are."

This was too easy, too *natural.* Even the river seemed normal tonight, the wedge of moon casting just enough light to simultaneously sparkle and shadow their eyes.

He nibbled at her neck, keeping his teeth covered like he'd read in a book somewhere. She guided his hands to her breasts, and they were heaven. He dreaded the moment when he'd fumble with her bra strap, but that was okay, that was a rite of passage, just one of those things you got through. But Melanie must have been more impatient—or more experienced—than him, because she arched one arm over her shoulder and freed the elastic.

"Melanie," he said, his voice husky and strange. No wonder. He was on the verge of becoming a man. But he wanted to do it right.

"Hmm?" she murmured, dreamily, as if she were floating far away on a distant breeze. He glimpsed her white panties in the dark crevasse beneath the hem of her dress. His hand slid up against the cotton fabric and paused against the mystery behind it.

"I love you."

She tensed beneath him, then pushed him away, sitting up as she held her bra in place with one hand. Then he looked at her face, and her expression was icy, her lips no longer swollen and inviting.

"Why did you say that?" she said.

"I thought . . . I thought that's what you wanted."

"Don't worry about what I want. Don't make this weird."

"Weird? Melanie, I've wanted this for a long time. Ever since sixth grade, when we had kickball in gym and you wore those little purple shorts and socks up to your knees."

"I don't remember that," she said, glancing out at the river as if she couldn't bear to meet his eyes. "It's burning up in here. Why don't you crack the window?"

The mood had subtly shifted, but Ronnie was still aroused. He had to turn the key to let down the power windows, and the fecund odor of river mud rolled in on the fog. Melanie hadn't pulled away completely, and one leg was still tangled between his. The memory of her soft, damp panties was still fresh on his fingers. Her freckled cheeks were alabaster in the moonlight, and her eyes were wide and imploring.

Ronnie put a trembling hand on her thigh. "Do you love me?"

"That's not fair. Don't make me answer that."

"Fine. Do you love Bobby, then?"

"Quit all this and lay down with me," she said. "Why do you have to make everything so complicated?"

Birth control. And what if she's a virgin, too? Should I ask her? Will we make a mess on the seat? God, why don't I carry a condom in my wallet like every other red-blooded American teen male? And DOES SHE LOVE ME?

"I want you," Ronnie said. "But I want *all* of you."

"Jesus, Ronnie. McFall warned me that you'd be like this."

Ronnie's heart clenched in his chest and took a staccato hiccup. His heart was the very thing he'd been willing to offer, but now it was throbbing and gasping and searing around the icy dagger she'd just driven into it.

"McFall told you to do this?"

"Ease up, Deathboy. It's not like he *paid* me."

Ronnie hung his head out the truck window, sure he was going to vomit.

And that was when he saw Brett Summers standing there on the bridge, wrapped in fog, water dripping from his nearly naked body, smiling like all was fine in the world beyond.

"Ronnie?" Melanie's voice came from the bottom of some dark well, and she tugged on his shoulder until he finally turned to face her. She'd climbed against him and her luscious body was pinning him to the door, but he was cold inside, the volcano doused, his head running wild. When he looked out at the bridge again, all he could see was fog and the softly lapping river.

"Come on, honey." Melanie kissed him and slid her hand down to his groin, but he stared ahead and let the cold sink deep into his bones. So he really had been deluding himself. Everything Bobby had said was true. The ghosts had never left.

"Okay," she said. "I love you. Better?"

He took his hand from her thigh and reached for the ignition, hoping the headlights would help disperse the fog. "I'd better get you home."

CHAPTER FORTY-ONE

Larkin McFall normally took Sundays off, not from any religious impulse but simply because it was expected. Today was an exception. The sun was high and bright, the sky free of impending storms, and Cassandra McFall had a new belted pantsuit she'd been dying to wear. It was even worth sitting through Preacher Staymore's impassioned call for his flock to stay on the path of righteousness, making oblique references to a television show, professional football, and a political issue that had more to do with patriotic fervor than grace. But McFall could certainly agree with the central message of the sermon: "Therefore keep watch, because no one knows the day or the hour."

McFall put a hundred dollars in the plate, careful to slide the folded bill under the ones and fives lest someone think he was grandstanding. After the closing hymn, he stood in the vestibule and greeted those he knew. Logan Extine, his wife, and his charming daughter Amy made such an attractive family that McFall almost yearned for children. But Cassie wouldn't be much help there. And besides, fatherhood required sacrifice, something best left to others.

"Hello, Larkin," Extine said, shaking his hand so that others could see they were friends. "A pleasure to see you both here."

McFall draped a casual arm around Cassie's waist. It seemed to be the thing to do. "I regret it's taken us so long to drop in."

Max Summers and his wife came down the aisle and the congregation grew quieter as they passed. Max appeared to have aged twenty years since his son's funeral. While McFall had expected the payoff from the boy's life insurance would dull the sharp edges of loss and pain, Max still wore the same suit and drove the same car as he had when his son was alive. What was the point of insurance if you let death stand in the way of a better life?

But McFall quickly forgot all about them when he saw the Day family. Well, not the entire Day family—David was probably sleeping off a bender. Linda was fresh and tidy, Tim was scruffy but clean, and Ronnie looked like he hadn't gotten a wink of sleep. The skin around his eyes was puffy, his complexion gray.

"Mr. McFall!" Linda said, with a delighted enthusiasm that seemed wholly out of place in Barkersville Baptist Church. Tim hung back, but Ronnie stepped in front of his mother as if to protect her.

"Hello, Linda." McFall nodded at the boys. "Ronnie. Tim."

He introduced his wife and was about to invite the Days to join them for lunch when Linda said, "David doesn't want to sell."

"I understand. I don't blame him. But I had to try."

"But *we* do," Linda said over her son's shoulder.

Ronnie stared at McFall with hate in his bloodshot eyes. His lower lip trembled.

He's coming around. McFall hid his self-satisfied grin. "What about you, Ronnie? What do *you* want?"

"I thought you knew."

"Ronnie," Linda admonished. "Be polite."

"It's okay," McFall said. "He's on the doorway to manhood, and it's never an easy path."

"Because no one knows the day or the hour, right?" Ronnie said.

"I'm sure David will be willing to listen," Linda said. "Give him a little time. He's just a little stubborn."

"Pride isn't necessarily a sin," McFall said. "Your husband is an excellent carpenter, and I'm *proud* to have him working for McFall Meadows. Ronnie, too. I can see where he learned to put in a hard day's work."

"I quit," Ronnie said, raising his voice, causing Linda to gasp loudly.

McFall had figured mere money wouldn't be enough to buy Ronnie, so he wasn't overly upset. As long as David was on the payroll, Ronnie would stay within range, especially since he had Melanie as bait. Although McFall was beginning to understand why Archer McFall had failed here. Ronnie was a formidable foe, even if the boy was only scarcely aware he was engaged in battle.

"He got in late last night," Linda said by way of apology, but Ronnie was already heading outside to the parking lot, not even stopping to shake Preacher Staymore's hand. "He's been spending time with Bobby's rock band, and I swear it's bad news."

"Patience, Mrs. Day," McFall said. "It's a difficult path, but it's his. All we can do is walk beside him."

"I guess so," Linda said. "Come on, Tim."

"So those are the Days," Cassie said after they had left. "I don't see why you waste so much time on them."

"We're all family here, in one way or another," McFall guided her toward their Lexus, waving to those he recognized, most of whom worked for McFall Meadows in some capacity or another.

Once they were in the car, McFall punched a number into his cell phone.

"Who are you calling?" Cassie asked.

"Your replacement."

"Oh." She flipped down the sun visor and checked her eye shadow in the little mirror clipped there.

"Hello, Miss Fowler?" McFall said into the phone.

"Is this Larkin?" came the response.

"Have you ever considered higher office? I hear the state congressional race is wide open."

The line was silent for a moment. "Democrat or Republican ticket?" Heather asked, wary.

"Does it matter?"

CHAPTER FORTY-TWO

Sheriff Littlefield wasn't yet willing to organize a manhunt for Sweeney Buchanan, especially since he wasn't convinced the man had done anything wrong. He'd quietly let his department know that Buchanan was a "person of interest," but he wasn't going to open an official investigation because he didn't trust Cindy to keep it quiet. Her spunk was one of the things he liked best about her, but sometimes it was a pure pain in the ass.

None of that prevented him from conducting a personal search of the former Buchanan property. Especially because the prints on the wrench had matched Sweeney's records from Wendover Home, one of his stops on the merry-go-round of the state's mental health system. But what was more notable was that Sweeney's finger-prints were the only ones besides Bobby Eldreth's on the wrench, even though Larkin McFall had personally handed the evidence to Littlefield.

He exited Little Church Road and drove his Trooper toward Stepford Matheson's place, intending to use the hiking trail to cross the mountain. Even though Stepford had sold his land to McFall just like the others, he must have negotiated some sort of use agreement, because he was sitting on his porch when Littlefield pulled up.

"Howdy, Sheriff," Stepford said. He looked hungover, and Littlefield wondered if the man had drifted into harder drugs like meth or Oxycontin. He cradled his stomach as if he had a bellyache, and Littlefield could have sworn his shirt was bulging as if wads of wet fabric had been shoved inside. The man smelled like rancid sausage.

"Hello, Stepford. I see nobody's come out to fix that broken window yet."

"Been real busy." Stepford nodded to the raised hood of his Plymouth Duster. "I gotta keep it all tied together if I want to keep motoring."

"Do you mind if I take a walk through the woods yonder?"

"Ain't my woods no more."

"I know, but it's the neighborly thing to ask."

Stepford lifted a hand to wave him on, and his shirt bulged even more grotesquely. "If you come across my hounds, send 'em home for supper."

"I'll do that. You haven't seen Sweeney Buchanan around, have you?"

"Not since his brother died. You ever figure out why he burned up in the church?"

"Afraid not."

"You ain't figured out much of nothing, have you?"

Littlefield held the man's gaze, but he wasn't sure anybody was home behind those dead, dark eyes. The old Stepford had been fueled by cunning and defiance, but the man in front of him didn't seem to give a damn one way or another. Maybe McFall's buyout had changed him. Maybe he'd contemplated a world beyond Barkersville and found it just as pointless, only with higher taxes and gas prices.

Littlefield headed up the trail, feeling Stepford's gaze on him as he climbed to the edge of the forest. He glanced back at him. For just a moment, he saw a torn heap of raw meat piled high on the porch, glistening red with bits of white bone showing here and there.

The sheriff fumbled with the holster strap on his sidearm, his knees nearly buckling, but then the vision reassembled and it was only Stepford.

The sun ... in my eyes.

"Something eating you, Sheriff?" Stepford called out to him, putting a cigarette in his mouth.

"Did Cole Buchanan say anything about going back to the church and finishing the job?"

"Last time I saw Cole, he was knocking on my door in the middle of the night."

"Oh, yeah? When was that?"

"Last night." Stepford lit his cigarette and exhaled a long gray stream of smoke. "No way in hell was I gonna let him in, though. What kind of manners is that?"

For one horrible moment, Littlefield pictured Cole's charred corpse rapping on the door, flecks of scorched flesh falling from him in the dark.

He heard Cindy's voice in his head, telling him he was making excuses, selectively winnowing evidence to reach his own desired conclusions regardless of the truth. He was willing to accept a supernatural explanation for the recent deaths—in fact, that had been his first instinct—but such a case could never be tried in a court of law.

But he was helpless in the realm of the dead. He'd failed repeatedly there. At least with Sweeney, he could bring a murder charge and deliver a small measure of justice. It was one thing he could control in a world that was rapidly vanishing beneath his feet and opening onto a bottomless black pit.

The cool forest was a welcome reprieve from the humid June air. In the weeks since Littlefield had last walked this trail, the canopy had filled out more, and sumac and Virginia Creeper had extended their grip along the loam and humus of the leafy floor. Littlefield reached the fence and headed toward the summit, using the satellite imaging map to guide him to the intersection where McFall's land bordered the parcels he'd purchased from Stepford and the Buchanan heirs. Sweeney didn't have a car and had never learned to drive, and he didn't have the mental capacity to plot a sophisticated escape, so Littlefield was betting the suspect was hiding out in the woods where he'd grown up. Just like crooks usually robbed the store where they bought their beer instead of a store outside the neighborhood. But he also figured that Sweeney wouldn't have a gun—otherwise he would have used it instead of the pipe wrench to murder Cole.

After a hike of twenty minutes, during which the terrain grew rockier and steeper, Littlefield veered off the trail and followed the ridgeline. He had maybe three hours of daylight left, and he wasn't sure his trembling legs would hold out that long. He leaned against a tree to catch his breath, taking off his hat and slinging sweat from the band. The birds had fallen silent with his passage. He'd been scuffing up leaves as he walked, making too much noise, but stealth would have hindered the amount of ground he was able to cover. He hadn't thought about what he'd do if he found Sweeney, but he'd probably take him into custody on a charge of criminal trespassing until he got back the results of the blood test. It was risky because the ACLU would have an army of lawyers crawling up his backside, but he could likely hold Sweeney in the county jail for a least a week. That would be enough time to—

A shadow moved at the periphery of his vision, among a copse of poplar and silver birch.

Littlefield planted his hat on his head and crouched low, jogging toward it, trying to keep his boots lighter than the fifty-pound boulders they seemed.

He saw the shadow again, and then a glimpse of gray fabric. He broke into a sprint, his lungs burning. The figure was now about thirty yards ahead, but Littlefield was gaining.

Looks too short to be Sweeney.

"Stop," Littlefield shouted. He dug at his holster, pulling his revolver. But it wasn't like he was going to shoot. He slid the gun back onto his hip and dashed between the trees, low limbs slapping at his face.

The person giggled, and the sound was high-pitched.

A girl? Or a murderous lunatic?

Littlefield stumbled over a root and fell to his knees. By the time he scrambled up from the mud, the figure had vanished into the thick foliage. Littlefield listened for a moment, but he heard no footfalls. Then the giggle came again.

From behind him.

He turned, and the boy in gray stood twenty feet away, his soiled cap sitting askew on his tousled head. The Confederate Army uniform he'd been wearing when he'd disappeared was filthy and ragged, the toe of one leather boot yawning open.

"Vernon Ray?" Littlefield whispered.

Had the boy been hiding out here since he'd vanished on Mulatto Mountain all those years ago? Had he been kidnapped? But that didn't make sense. He would be older now, probably eighteen. This boy—

Vernon Ray's eyes faded to empty black wells as the skin of his face stretched tightly around his skull. The uniform grew limp, as if hanging on a rack of bones, and one skeletal hand flipped to the bill of the cap in a salute. The giggle came again and the boy turned and ran.

Littlefield was frozen in place, afraid he was cracking up. He accepted ghosts as a reality of his turf, something endemic and even natural to these ancient mountains. But why did he seem to have such an intimate relationship to them? Was madness somehow contagious?

He recalled something he'd once heard: *No matter where you go, you carry your demons with you.*

But the boy had looked solid enough—at least, the uniform had. And if he could grab a piece of that fabric, he'd have tangible proof of the encounter.

He willed his legs into motion, flailing awkwardly after the boy. He stuck up his arm to ward off a low-hanging branch and the movement caused him to slip. As he tumbled down the ravine, that mirthless laughter came again.

Littlefield picked himself up, mud caked on his hands and feet, a leaf sticking to one cheek, and tracked the laughter as best he could as the sound moved between the trees. He drew his gun again. Even though it would be useless against a ghost, it gave him a little courage.

He climbed back up the bank, crawled over rotted and moss-covered deadfall, and squinted into the gloom. Whatever sun had leaked through the canopy had now faded with the onset of evening. Soon it would be too dark to see.

And Littlefield would be alone in the dark.

But maybe not alone enough.

Squatting to peer beneath the branches, he saw a figure in the dusk. Except this time it wasn't Vernon Ray.

Samuel?

His heart squeezed with the sight of his little brother standing there, eyes bulging and hollow, limbs scrawny, looking the same as he had on the night he'd broken his neck at the red church.

Littlefield stepped forward, wanting to scream, wanting to apologize, wanting to die, too, but then the shadows shifted and it was no longer Samuel.

It was Larkin McFall.

"May I help you?" McFall said. He was dressed in a green T-shirt, khaki shoes, and hiking boots, a canteen slung over his shoulder.

Littlefield licked his lips, wheezing for breath. "The boy . . . did you see him?"

McFall looked around. "Looks like it's just you and me."

"What are you doing here?"

"Walking around my land. Is that legal, or are you going to shoot me?"

Littlefield looked down at the revolver in his hand. He lowered the weapon but didn't holster it. "I'm looking for Sweeney Buchanan."

"I assume you have a search warrant?"

"Damn it, McFall, you're the one that put me onto him. With that little story about the bloody wrench."

"Believe me, I want you to find Sweeney Buchanan more than anyone. He's a danger to my project and my reputation. Who would buy a lot in a development where hillbilly lunatic killers are running wild in the woods?"

"Help me find him, then. You know this land better than I do."

"Sure, Sheriff. I can help you out. But I'll have to ask a favor in return." McFall seemed to merge with the shadows as the forest grew darker, as if he was part of the untamed landscape.

"I'm not in a position to negotiate when it comes to murder charges." Littlefield's breathing had returned to normal, but his heart was galloping.

"I'll give you Sweeney if you stay on as sheriff," McFall said. "*My* sheriff."

"What are you talking about?" Littlefield didn't like the way the man's eyes grew brighter against the darkness, as if they were generating their own light from within.

"What are you going to do without your badge? Who *are* you, Sheriff, if you're not sheriff? Take away your gun, and you're nothing but a long list of failures. But I can bring them back. Your sergeant Sheila Storie. Darnell Absher. Vernon Ray Davis. Your brother Samuel. *All* of your dead."

Littlefield lifted his revolver and pointed it at McFall.

One bullet. Out here in the middle of nowhere. Everybody would blame Sweeney. And even if they didn't, even if I got caught, to hell with it. At least it would be over.

"I want you out of my jurisdiction," Littlefield said. "Out of my life."

"You don't have a life, Sheriff." McFall held out his arms. "And this jurisdiction is now mine."

Littlefield ached to pull the trigger, to commit one final failure, but he had just enough doubt remaining that he couldn't do it. *Innocent until proven guilty.*

Or maybe he was just a coward, fleeing the ghosts of his past.

He shoved his revolver into its holster and headed back toward where he thought the trail lay. Tomorrow he would resume his search for Sweeney—on his own—but tonight he craved the sanity and safety of civilization.

The giggle followed him home.

McFALL
EPISODE SIX

CHAPTER FORTY-THREE

"**M**cFall ought to just burn this place down," Bobby said.

"That didn't work out so hot the last time, remember?" Ronnie said. The old Buchanan place was sweltering, even with the boards ripped from the windows and the door standing open. It was the first of July, and humid air had seeped into the moldering contents of the building. Amid the musty piles of newspapers and books they'd found the dried-out husks of opossums and rats, nothing left but leathery skins over brittle bones.

Bobby shoved a stack of magazines into a cardboard box. "I don't know why McFall asked us to go through all this junk anyway."

Ronnie was working a little more slowly, taking time to examine all the oddities and read from the old newspapers. The ancient copies of *Life, Time,* and *The Saturday Evening Post* were shot through with silverfish and crumbling with water damage. "Maybe he thinks we'll find something valuable," Ronnie said. "You've heard those stories about people finding copies of letters from Abraham Lincoln or shoeboxes full of old baseball cards."

"No way." Bobby sniffed and wiped his nose. "There's nothing in this dump but allergies."

"I'm surprised the sheriff didn't declare it a crime scene." Ronnie rubbed his hands on the legs of his jeans, but the mildew and dust seemed to have seeped into his pores.

"McFall isn't going to press assault charges. And the sheriff said it was probably animal blood. Sweeney's crazy, but he doesn't seem like the killing kind." Bobby heaved the box of magazines onto his shoulder. "Well, this ought to fill up the truck. I'm taking a break. Come on and get some sunshine."

"Be out in a minute."

Ronnie hadn't told Bobby about trying to quit his job. Reality had set in shortly after he'd confronted McFall at Barkersville Baptist Church. As his mom had pointed out, not only would his dad be pissed but nobody else in town would hire him because almost everyone worked for McFall or his business partners. Ronnie wouldn't be able to afford college without the summer income. Even losing a few weeks of pay would be a disaster. When he went to work the next day as if nothing had happened, McFall didn't say a word—he merely smiled and nodded.

As if he never doubted I'd show.

The house seemed preternaturally quiet to Ronnie, like a library of the forgotten past. McFall's bulldozers would soon erase all signs of Sweeney Buchanan's obsessions. The thought made Ronnie sad. Even though most of the artifacts were damaged, at least Sweeney had found some purpose in life.

Like leaving weird messages on the walls.

As if his thoughts had summoned the sound, something clattered to the floor on the other side of the wall. Inside the bedroom.

"Bobby?"

His friend was probably playing a joke. He must have snuck around the side of the house and crawled in through the window. Bobby's sense of humor had grown morbid since his accident. He'd get a kick out of spooking Ronnie.

But two could play that game. Ronnie plucked a loose sheet of newsprint from the wall and used it to pick up one of the desiccated opossum corpses by the tail. It swung back and forth between his fingers like a pendulum. He could already picture it: When he opened the door and Bobby jumped him, he'd fling the dead animal right into his face.

Even though the doors and windows were all open, the building's interior was somehow still dim. When Ronnie left the living room a chill settled upon him, as if he'd walked into a cave. The imagined prank felt silly now, but he was determined to carry it through. He couldn't let Bobby think he was chicken.

The clatter came again, and Ronnie wondered if Bobby was messing with Sweeney's bizarre bone collection. Ronnie paused at the door, which was already cracked open. He couldn't see any shadows of movement, so he waited for a moment, breathing softly through his nose. When the clatter came again, he kneed the door wide and stepped inside, the animal corpse raised.

A man crouched in the dark corner of the filthy room, his identity concealed at first glance. It definitely wasn't Bobby. The man was too small and thin, and he was wearing hardly any clothes. Ronnie's first thought was that Sweeney had returned, but Sweeney had been jittery and wild, and this person was just huddled there, his head down, unmoving.

"Hello?" Ronnie's throat was clogged with dust and fear.

Brett Summers unfolded himself and emerged into the light by the bed, his dead eyes—as black as the bottom of the Blackburn

River—staring at the pages arranged on the wall that spelled out "Summers End." He was far more solid than he'd been on the bridge that foggy night. He was pale, his translucent flesh speckled with drops of water, and he was wearing only his socks and underwear, just as he'd been found when his cold corpse was fished out of the water. Ronnie dropped the dead opossum and took a step back.

The bedroom door slammed shut behind him, and Bobby's laugh echoed in the hallway. Ronnie tried the antique handle, but his hand was slick with sweat and he couldn't get a grip. He pounded on the door. "Bobby! Lemme out!"

When he looked back over his shoulder, he saw Brett approaching him—not walking but *gliding*, as if he were surfing on a few inches of air. Dark spots of water collected on the floor beneath him, the only sound in the room the soft *plop plop plop* of the drops. Ronnie twisted the handle but it didn't budge. Bobby had to be holding it.

"Lemme out!" Ronnie repeated. His friend just laughed on the other side of the door.

Brett was only a few feet away now. He seemed to glimmer the closer he got, as if his body was refracting the sunlight from the window. He looked like milk turning into cheese, and Ronnie wondered what would happen if he slammed into him and made a run for the window. But the frigid gaze of those eyes kept his muscles locked in place.

The most horrible thing was Brett's expression. He was smirking, just like when he'd dared Bobby to jump off the bridge, only now his lips were swollen and purple. The odor that rose off of him—corruption and mud and stagnant water and an ancient, reptilian stench—was so repellent that Ronnie flinched.

Gliding closer still, Brett reached for Ronnie's face with one grub-white arm. Closing his eyes, Ronnie started to pray, but his mind was racing too much to string together anything more coherent than *Pleeeeeeease God, save me.* He felt the cold radiating off the ghostly limb as it passed within inches of his cheek, and then there was a moist, squeaking sound against the wood of the door.

Ronnie blinked his eyes open once, only to shut them just as quickly when Brett's hollow gaze stared back at him from mere inches away. Then he submitted to prayer until the squeaking noises had subsided. After the permeating cold eased he opened his eyes. Brett—or the thing that had been Brett—was gone. Ronnie's legs were cotton by then; he felt like he was about to fold like a rag doll.

When he wrestled with the doorknob again, it turned easily in his hand with a rusty *skree.* But before he opened it, he saw the dark letters that had been smeared onto the wood by Brett's waterlogged fingers.

Days End.

Ronnie fled outside to find Bobby sitting on the Silverado's bumper, fiddling with a little glass vial. The truck bed was piled with rotten paper and garbage.

Bobby looked up at him with bored indifference. "What were you yelling about? Why did you lock me in?"

"Dude, what are you talking about?" Bobby slipped the vial in his pocket and wiped his nose. "I been out here soaking up the sun. I'm done in there."

"I saw Brett Summers."

Bobby squinted at him for a few seconds, as if trying to make up his mind whether Ronnie was bullshitting. Then he said, "I guess you're done, too."

CHAPTER FORTY-FOUR

Littlefield had barely slept, and the few scraps he remembered from his nightmares featured Samuel's milk-white face, eyes imploring as a skinny arm reached out to his brother for help. Behind Samuel had stretched the growing shadow of Larkin McFall, rising from the ashes of the red church and his family's homestead to spread across the forest, the river, and the towns of Barkersville and Titusville. The sheriff gave up fighting insomnia at 6:00 A.M. and crawled out of bed for coffee.

When he walked into the office two hours later, Sherry studied him as if he had a contagious leprosy. "What?" he asked.

She shoved the fresh edition of *The Titusville Times* across her desk. The banner read "McFall expands plans, adds jobs," and McFall's mug smiled out at the newspaper's readership with benevolent compassion.

"So?" he said. "Just another slobber job. What's new?"

"Page two is what's new."

Littlefield flipped to the editorial page and Cindy Baumhower's column, "Outside the Law." While not mentioning Littlefield by name, Cindy claimed that the sheriff's office had been failing the public through secrecy and the suppression of public records. She listed the deaths from earlier in the year and hinted at negligence on the part of the local law enforcement. She even revealed the bungling of Cole Buchanan's autopsy results, quoting Perry Hoyle as saying, "I delivered the case file to the sheriff as requested and never heard another word about it. That was a little unusual, since we always discuss any suspicious deaths."

Cindy went on to excoriate the sheriff for any number of lapses, digging up crime statistics and a solve rate that made it look like the county was teetering on the edge of anarchy. She also used skewed statistics to suggest that the office was soft on drugs because only one methamphetamine lab had been closed down that year, when in reality a series of busts the previous year had driven most meth cooks to other counties—something Cindy well knew.

He crumpled the paper and flung it to the floor. "She's just bitchy because the Internet is killing her career."

Sherry did Littlefield the favor of pretending to check her email as he stormed into his office to call Cindy. He'd tried her several times the night before without success, and now he waited through ten rings before clicking off his phone without leaving a message. A similar call to her line at the *Times* likewise went unanswered.

How could she stab me in the back like that? Was I not moving fast enough for her? Hell, she keeps pink shampoo bottles in my shower.

On his way out, he passed Perriotte, who was about to walk through the front door. The deputy stepped aside, evidently recognizing his boss's dark, sour mood. "Uh, Sheriff?"

"What?"

"We got a call from the Ward girl's mom. She's missing."

"Shit. How long?"

"Could have been anytime during the night. The mom woke up at seven and didn't see her, but she didn't think anything of it until the girl didn't show up for work. And it looks like she took some personal effects with her, purse and cell phone, anyway."

Littlefield glanced at his watch. "Technically, we need to wait twenty-four hours to file a missing persons report."

"That's what I told her. But she was worried about . . . you know, copycat stuff."

"Like we ought to look for her in the river?" Littlefield glowered. "She's a recent high school graduate stuck in a small town. I wouldn't be surprised if she hightailed it for California. Hell, I would if I were her."

Perriotte shook his head. "You don't buy that, do you? You're just taking the company line."

Littlefield pressed forward and stuck a finger under Perriotte's nose. "I'm not covering up anything. I might be incompetent, but it sure as hell isn't on purpose."

Perriotte looked at the finger as if it were a gun barrel. "So, do you want me to check the river or not?"

Littlefield sighed. "Yeah. Spread the word, but tell the department to keep it quiet for now. Especially Sherry. I know how she likes to gossip."

"Yes, sir."

Littlefield stepped outdoors, then turned. "You ready?"

Perriotte was perplexed. "For what?"

"To take over." Littlefield removed his hat and rubbed the brim as he looked down the street. Few pedestrians were out before noon, and businesses were just now opening. Stella Potter was sliding handcrafted rockers into a row in front of her antique shop. Jim Graham was smoking a cigarette near the ATM outside the BB&T branch. A car horn blew at someone in a Honda SUV who was having trouble parallel parking. Some shops were already flying the American flag for the upcoming Fourth of July. A normal day in a normal town. Or so it appeared.

"Take over?" Perriotte said, although it was clear to both of them what they were discussing.

"It won't be my decision, but I'll put in a good word for you with the county commissioners," Littlefield said. "That is, if my word carries weight anymore. You'd make a good sheriff, and maybe the interim deal will give you enough momentum to win the election."

Perriotte gave a brief smile. "That's real noble of you, Sheriff."

"I'll clean up my messes as best I can before I throw in my hat," Littlefield said. "Keep me up to date on the Ward girl. I'll join you at the bridge soon, but I have a stop to make first."

As he walked away, Littlefield nearly bumped into Skeeter Aldridge, who was emerging from the drugstore carrying a prescription bag. Normally Littlefield would stop and chat with Skeeter about the man's views on the Middle East, the rich assholes who'd siphoned off the American dream, and the government spying program—often at the same time, because Skeeter saw them all as ingredients in a doomsday gumbo. But today Skeeter barely met his eye, curling his lip and flaring his nostrils as if Littlefield hadn't changed his underwear in a month. Littlefield muttered a quick "Howdy, Skeeter," and kept on walking.

As he walked to the courthouse to retrieve his Isuzu, he found himself wondering if the town would look different to him as a civilian. Maybe he could finally pull the nails out of his hands and climb down from the secular cross he'd built from the timbers of his ego. He could interact with the townsfolk without feeling like their self-selected shepherd.

Littlefield drove to the hospital. When he shoved through the door to the morgue, Dr. Perry Hoyle was sitting at his metal desk, scrawling on a piece of paper.

"Hello, Sheriff," Hoyle said, looking up and adjusting his bifocals. "I was just about to leave for the day."

"Altering some more paperwork?" Littlefield asked, circling the stainless-steel autopsy table to loom over the desk.

"What do you mean?"

Littlefield looked down at his old friend. Hoyle was probably approaching sixty-five, and the deep wrinkles around his eyes made him look tired. Maybe a bass boat would be just what the doctor ordered.

"You buried the report on Cole Buchanan and lied to the newspaper about it." Littlefield watched as Hoyle's rheumy eyes flitted to the corners of the room as if he were seeking escape.

"Oh, that. Didn't you get my email?" Hoyle's face contorted into an impassive mask. "I bet you accidentally deleted it. Maybe I should have dug up some stamps instead."

"And how about Brett Summers? That was a straight drowning, right? But I remember you saying there were bruises around one of his ankles."

"Sure, sure," Hoyle said, talking faster. "Could have caught his leg between some rocks and got banged around in the current."

"Current's not that fast around the bridge. Plus, when I pulled the report—the one that's in the case file—I noticed that there's no mention of those bruises. Something like that should have been officially recorded."

Hoyle pushed away from the desk, putting a little distance between himself and the sheriff. "Why sweat the small stuff? Life's too short, Frank."

"The 'small stuff' is at the heart of what we do," Littlefield said. "The devil's in the details."

Hoyle studied the various organs and specimens that floated in jars of formaldehyde on a shelf over Littlefield's shoulder. "Maybe we've been doing it too long."

"What does McFall have on you?"

Hoyle's cheeks grew red. "How many dead people have we laid out on that table there?" He hitched a thumb over his shoulder toward the refrigerated drawers where bodies were stored. "How many have we piled into the meat locker over the years? Maybe you like to stick your face in it, but you get to walk away and play the hero. Well, I've always been stuck down here with the stink."

Littlefield clenched his fists and ground his knuckles into the desktop. "I thought you were on *my* side."

"It's not my war. I'm not part of the old families." Hoyle was still avoiding Littlefield's gaze, but he wasn't even bothering to hide his betrayal. "Besides, it's not your town anymore. It's his. I know which way the wind blows."

The sheriff took a closer glance at the refrigerated drawers. Judging from the tags inserted into the little slots beneath the handles, there were six dead people waiting for their moment in the spotlight.

"Two Mathesons, a Gregg, a Potter, and three of their in-laws," Hoyle said with a smirk. "All from natural causes. But every death is natural, when you get right down to it. It's what we do here in Pickett County."

Littlefield rushed forward and grabbed the man's throat with one hand, shaking him so hard his bifocals flew off and cracked on the tiled floor. As Hoyle's foggy eyes bulged and his lips turned blue, Littlefield whispered, "Is this natural enough for you?"

The frail man batted ineffectually at Littlefield's wrist, trying to loosen his death grip. Littlefield heard laughter and looked wildly around, releasing Hoyle's neck. Hoyle flopped forward and banged his face against the desk, a raspy whimper leaking from his lungs.

One of the morgue drawers began to slide open, giving a glimpse of the darkness within.

Littlefield backed toward the door to the morgue. Hoyle raised his head, dark blood oozing from one nostril, his bald head sweating. He croaked a mixture of a cough and laugh. "It's what we do here."

The drawer slid open another two feet, releasing a slightly sweet stench. A marbled hand ascended from the sheath of darkness, fingers testing the air.

Littlefield didn't wait around to see what more the drawer contained.

CHAPTER FORTY-FIVE

Larkin McFall watched her for a minute from the edge of the picket fence.

She was attractive, yes, but what really appealed to him was her innocent humility and lack of self-consciousness as she knelt before her squash plants and dug with her trowel. Heather Fowler didn't mind getting her hands dirty, and she wasn't afraid of hard work. From such clay McFall could mold quite a woman.

Cassandra had been a mistake; he'd known that for a while now. He'd picked her up in rural East Tennessee without much thought. At the time, he'd figured her beauty would be enough, but even with careful guidance she had proven to be a poor investment. She was vulgar and dull. Insipid.

As the great matriarch Mama Bet McFall used to say, "You can put lipstick on a pig, but it's still just a pig."

Heather's face was hidden by a cute sunhat with a floppy brim, so he was able to observe her a moment longer before she sensed his presence. Finally she glanced towards the edge of the garden.

"What are you doing here?" she said, looking around to make sure the neighbors weren't watching. No worries there. Unlike university professors, the rest of the fine folk in her section of town had day jobs that stretched through the summer.

"Just passing through," he said. "Mind if I look at your peas?"

She pointed her trowel at the gate, waving him in. He could have stepped over the fence, but the inside perimeter was lined with marigolds, peonies, and rose bushes. The layout reflected an organized and ambitious mind. McFall's every instinct about Heather was proving more correct by the day.

By the time he'd maneuvered between the rows of squash and cabbage seedlings, she was standing, brushing dirt from the knees of her jeans. She had on a sleeveless cotton top that revealed freckled shoulders. Her dark hair was tied back in a ponytail, and she looked more like a college student than a professor.

"Cassandra's gone," he said.

She wiped her sweaty forehead with the back of her wrist. "Where?"

"Back to El Paso."

"You don't seem too torn up about it."

He tested the tension of the strings providing scaffolding for the pea vines. "I want people to have everything they want. And it's what she wanted."

"Very unselfish of you."

"It helps me get what I want, too. As we say in the Chamber of Commerce, it's a 'win-win-win.'"

"You and she make two wins. Who gets the third?"

He could smell her sweat, and beneath it a faint, floral scent, as if she'd absorbed some of the sweetness of her garden. He didn't experience physical desire in its purest form, but he could appreciate the subtle signals of his borrowed human senses. He hoped he was dressed appropriately; he'd left his jacket in the seat of his car, his sleeves were rolled to the elbows, and the top button of his shirt was undone. The breeze was even tousling his hair, as if eager to help him with his seduction.

"You do, Heather," he said.

His instincts in such matters were unrefined, as the lifestyle he had to offer had been far more important to his former wife than any fairy-tale romance. Perhaps with Heather things would be different. He smiled, just the way he'd practiced.

The suspicion in her eyes melted away. "People will talk."

"Only for a while, and only the little people. The ones who don't matter. Most will feel sympathetic once they learn that she was a gold-digger who married me for my money and then extorted me for a hefty divorce settlement. You'll be seen as the woman who reawakened my heart and restored my faith in love. And soon people will realize how good we are for the community."

She sighed. "You make it sound so *practical.*"

McFall had planned to step forward after saying those words, taking her into his arms, but now he was confused. He was pretty sure he understood her. After all, she'd responded to all the bait he'd laid out. She wasn't the type to lose her head—or her soul—based on physical attraction alone. He'd offered her a kingdom, and a king to rule by her side. Wasn't that enough?

Ah, you fool. You forgot the most important thing.

He let his face grow solemn and vulnerable. He'd expected her to surrender, but she would only feel that she'd achieved victory through *his* surrender.

He moved closer, close enough to hear her breath coming in small gasps through parted lips. Looking into her eyes he could see doubt, vulnerability, and a glimmer of defiance. But beyond those emotions was something vague and indefinable—that thing these humans called a "soul."

"I love you," he whispered, and those walls in her eyes broke down.

He didn't even have to lunge, because this time she did the falling, and all he had to do was put his arms around her. Her body was much more feminine and pleasing than Cassandra's, and he realized he liked a little give in the hips and chest. Yes, this one was an upgrade.

He pushed back the brim of her sunhat and moved his lips to hers. Her mouth was warmer than Cassandra's, and while Cassandra's tongue had flopped like a cold fish, Heather's was active and ardent. He was caught off guard, but he echoed her movements as best he could. He was so intent on the action that he had to remind himself to breathe before she noticed he wasn't.

She broke away, looked around again, and clutched his hand. "We should go inside."

"I'm not ready for that."

Her eyes narrowed with passion. "Not ready? It's been two damn years for me. I've practically been revirginized."

He couldn't tell her that he truly was a virgin. After all, he had been married to Cassandra, so such an admission would mark him as peculiar. He gave a shrug and a charming grin. "I'm old-fashioned. What can I say?"

She kissed him again, and he let it go further. Maybe he wouldn't make her wait too long. After all, flesh was flesh, and you could make it do whatever you wanted. He listened to the drone of the bees in the garden, a distant lawnmower, and the heavy pounding of her heart beneath her generous breasts. When they paused she said, "I'm going to figure you out sooner or later."

"I'd like that," he said. "I'd like that very much."

He excused himself, claiming he had an appointment with electricians at McFall Meadows but would call her later. At the gate he looked back at her, which he'd seen humans do in such situations. She was sweating and panting, a little dazed, and her grip was tight on the trowel in her right hand.

Maybe he'd use that trowel tonight. He'd take Cassandra out of his car trunk and plant her in Heather's garden, right there in the potato hill. If Heather ended up disappointing him, he'd have a way to take her out of the game. A very *practical* way. Even someone as inept and washed-up as Frank Littlefield could build a murder case based on that kind of evidence.

McFall hoped it wouldn't come to that, though. He really did like her. But his time in Barkersville, as both a husband and as a mockery of a human, had taught him the importance of a back-up plan.

CHAPTER FORTY-SIX

"**Y**ou ain't hanging out with them dopeheads until after you finish your workout." Elmer Eldreth was slouched on the couch in a wifebeater, rubbing his belly. The middle of his shirt was blotched dark with sweat.

"I told you, I threw yesterday with Coach Harnett." Bobby was fidgety and didn't feel like enduring another lecture. The trailer seemed to be closing in around him, and the box fan in the window wasn't making a dent in the heat.

"Bullshit. I called him this morning and he said he ain't seen you in two weeks. If you show up in the fall with a rubber arm, App State will park your ass on the far end of the bench."

"He's in good shape," Vernell said. She was sitting across the room from her husband with an old *Reader's Digest* in her lap. "All the work he's been doing this summer has been making him strong."

"Bulking up don't make you no better of a pitcher," Elmer said. "Hell, we might as well put him on steroids. Juice him up."

"I'm surprised you haven't already injected him in his sleep," Vernell said. "You do know he'll still be your boy even if he doesn't ever become a star, don't you?"

Bobby was impressed by her resistance, but wary, too. Elmer's upper lip curled into a sneer as he sipped his beer. After stewing over his response for another moment, he said, "I've sacrificed for years so he could have a shot. Least he could do is give me a little respect."

"I'm standing right here," Bobby said. "Maybe you could look at me when you talk about me."

Elmer let his bleary eyes roam up and down his son, as if surprised that the Little Leaguer he'd played pepper with was nearly a grown man. He'd had three beers since arriving home from work, and the couch looked like it was going to swallow him whole. "I told Harnett you'd be there in an hour. He's got a couple of juniors ready to go through drills with you."

He wondered what Elmer would say if he told him about the walking pillar of smoke and ash at the church site. Or Sweeney Buchanan's bloody wrench. Or Ronnie's tale of seeing Brett Summers's ghost. There was a whole world out there of which Elmer had no knowledge, a river flowing by. What if Bobby had told him he'd been approached by an agent, only it was someone who wanted to represent his music and not his golden arm?

"I can't," Bobby said.

Elmer sat forward as if he couldn't believe what he'd heard. "You *can't*? Did what I said sound like a question?"

"You don't get to order me around anymore," Bobby said as Vernell twisted her fingers nervously in her lap.

"As long as you're under my roof, I sure as shit do. For years, I worked so you could . . . ."

"Yeah, yeah," Bobby said, waving him off, sick to death of the old refrain. "You're a real role model."

Elmer struggled to sit up, then roared to his feet, knocking over his beer. "You little shit, I ought to—"

Bobby stood his ground, daring Elmer with his eyes, but then made the mistake of looking at his mom, who was quivering in her chair like a bird on a frosted February fencepost. He glanced back at Elmer, and his old man suddenly looked nervous, like he wasn't quite so sure what he "ought" to do.

"Okay," Bobby said. "You win. I'll head over to the diamond."

He went to his bedroom and packed his baseball gear, putting his bats, cleats, and glove in a sports bag and collecting a nylon satchel full of baseballs from the closet. Stopping at his desk he put on his Pickett High Pioneers cap, adjusting the brim as if he were heading out to the mound for the first inning of a big game. Before leaving the room he retrieved his drumsticks from his desk drawer and slipped them in with the two bats.

By the time he passed through the living room, Elmer had resumed drinking and Vernell was mopping up the spill. "See you tonight," he said to his mom.

"Stay away from them dopeheads, like I said," Elmer yelled just before Bobby shut the door.

Bobby climbed into the Silverado and pulled out the little glass vial the man had given him at the State Line Tavern. Even though he'd been sniffing the stuff for days, there was just as much white powder in it now as there had been that night behind the club. Maybe even more. He inhaled some as he sat behind the wheel. The drug burned his nostrils going down, and it felt like his brains were running down the back of his throat.

Kickass powder is right. I could sure get used to this.

He'd heard about coke and meth, of course, and had seen them used at parties before, but coke was for rich kids and meth was for rednecks. And neither drug seemed to compare to the "Special K," as he'd come to call it. He kept expecting the agent dude to show up again and sweet talk him some more, maybe even make him an offer. But so far, nothing.

Bobby hadn't told the other Diggers about the encounter. Jealousy screwed up so many bands, whether it was over chicks, song credits, or whose instrument stood out the most in a recording. He hadn't even told Ronnie.

Maybe he should, though. After all, he and Ronnie had both seen ghosts, and now that Bobby had decided to stay away from Melanie for good the tension between them was gone. It was a relief, because if anybody could make sense out of whatever weird shit was going down around here, it was Ronnie. Besides McFall, Ronnie was just about the only guy he could trust.

As the buzz kicked in, simultaneously relaxing him and sending fire through his veins, he started up the Silverado. Bobby had no intention of driving to the high school to play silly games with Harnett and his boys. He was going to pick up Ronnie and then head over to Dex's place for band practice.

When he came to the bridge, he eased the truck to a stop near the scene of his accident. He took his baseball gear out of the cab and carried it to the middle of the bridge and stood gazing into the water where Brett Summers had disappeared more than a month ago. The red-orange sun was dipping into evening; it was that quiet hour before the night shift came alive in the forest.

Bobby unzipped the gym bag full of baseballs and pulled one out. Curving his fingers around the seams as if preparing to throw a rising fastball over the plate, he reared back and tucked his body into a windup, hurling the baseball as far downriver as he could. It landed with a wet, smacking sound, sank for a moment, then bobbed back to the surface, spinning as it was swept downstream.

He threw the baseballs one by one, sometimes a curve, sometimes a heater, until only one remained.

A car approached from the far side of the bridge, moving slowing until Bobby waved it past. *Everybody's a tourist out here.*

Bobby didn't recognize the driver, but he hoped his red-eyed stare would encourage him to speed up. The man looked like a weasel-eyed accountant or banker, some asshole who sat in an air-conditioned office all day making money off the sweat of other people. Sure enough, the car accelerated toward the highway, stirring up a haze of dust.

"Take this, Brett, you asshole," Bobby said to the water. "And don't come back no more to bother Ronnie. You're dead."

Bobby launched a fastball that might have been the best of his career—he wished that scout at the championship game could have locked his radar gun on it—and as the ball launched, he felt something tear in his arm, up near the shoulder. The ball struck with a *sper-dunkkk* and then it, too, bobbed to the surface and was carried away by the current.

What did you expect? Brett to jump out of the water with a catcher's mitt and make a grab for it?

Bobby opened his sports bag and tossed his cleats over the bridge, followed by the glove—*"I wallowed in shit for three weeks to buy this, so it damn well better catch everything you can reach!"*—and his aluminum bat. He pulled out the wooden bat his dad had insisted he use for practice, because aluminum bats weren't allowed in the majors and, of course, Bobby had to plan for the future.

He felt a sudden urge to slam the bat into splinters against the bridge railing, but instead he squeezed the handle until his fingers ached, and then rested it on his shoulder. He plucked the Pioneers hat off his head by its brim and flung into the water like a Frisbee.

As he watched it float downstream, a strange mist coalesced above the wet stones, and the splashing of hundreds of ripples rose up like laughter. The surface of the water glimmered in the dying light. Blackburn River seemed alive, like a green-backed reptile slithering its way into primordial mud. And it seemed as though that monster was intent on spitting up its secrets.

Shit, no. Bobby backed up but couldn't tear his eyes away as the mist coalesced into a figure drifting toward him twenty feet below.

Stay down there, Brett. You don't belong here anymore.

But it wasn't Brett. It was he himself, *Bobby.*

He ran to the truck, hurled the bat onto the floor of the passenger side, and spun gravel as he barreled across the bridge. When he hit Little Church Road, he fought for traction, wondering if the part of him he'd lost that night of the crash was finally coming back.

He wondered where it had been and what it had seen.

And why it had returned.

CHAPTER FORTY-SEVEN

Ronnie heard the phone ringing, but he didn't want to get off the bed. He was planning on studying physics at Westridge, so he was reading a book on Nikola Tesla. Ronnie wasn't particularly brilliant at math, but working as sound engineer for The Diggers had expanded his worldview a little. Besides, fields like that led to a real job. Poets and English majors had better hope they knew how to play guitar or rob banks.

Tesla could probably have invented the first electric guitar if he'd seen any practical use for it. Most intriguing of all, he'd remained a virgin his entire life, apparently choosing to invest all his mental energy in dreaming up some of the greatest technological advancements of the Twentieth Century rather than trying to figure out women. That insight alone marked him as a genius. Too bad he'd left it to rich assholes like Edison and J. P. Morgan to exploit his best ideas.

Tim opened the bedroom door without knocking. "Hey, fiddle fart, it's for you."

Ronnie reluctantly closed the book, his thumb marking his place. "What is?"

"Telephone."

Ronnie climbed down, noticing that dusk was settling outside the window. He wondered if Bobby had called to tell him that band practice had been cancelled. He wouldn't mind too much. He was still shaken from seeing Brett's ghost again, and that cryptic message *"Days End"* played across his mind every time he closed his eyes.

The family only had one phone besides his dad's cell, and Ronnie made his way to the kitchen, where it hung on the wall. The location of the phone, and the fact that it wasn't cordless, made it almost impossible to have a private conversation.

"Hello?" he said into the receiver, glancing into the living room to see his dad snoring on the couch, the Weather Channel flickering on the television with the sound turned down. Mom was off at her pottery class, so tonight was a rare cease-fire in the war over selling the Day land.

"Ronnie," McFall said. "How are you?"

Ronnie tensed. "Fine."

"Good, good. Did you and Bobby finish with the old Buchanan place?"

Ronnie wondered if McFall knew. *Of course he does.* It was probably the whole reason he'd put the two of them on the job. "Mostly. We couldn't get it all in one truckload, though."

"Find anything unusual?"

"Like what?"

"Anything Sweeney might have left. If he truly committed a crime, he might have left some clues."

"The sheriff went over the place last week."

"Yes, but he might have missed something. People are starting to question his competency."

Ronnie felt as if he were being tested. But he always felt that way around McFall, as if every sentence contained a double meaning or hidden threat. "He's a good guy. He saved us—"

"Saved you from Archer McFall, yes, I've heard the stories about my cousin. All I can say is that I'm glad he's gone."

"I have to go, Mr. McFall. Somebody's picking me up."

"The Diggers have band practice."

How does he know? How does he always know EVERYTHING?

McFall didn't wait for his answer. "I've got a job for you later."

"I'll be in tomorrow morning."

"Tonight. After practice." It sounded like a command, not a request.

"Is it important?"

"I need people I can trust."

Trust? That didn't seem like the kind of relationship Ronnie wanted to nurture with McFall.

"I can't."

"You *can*. Bobby will give you a ride."

"I have to ask my dad."

David Day rolled over on the couch and stopped snoring. He'd been working ten-hour days lately. It meant he wasn't around much, but the extra income had helped him regain confidence, which made him less of a jerk. Or maybe he just drank more and slept more these days.

"He already knows," McFall said. "By the way, have you heard from Melanie lately?"

Ronnie didn't think his bowels could twist themselves any tighter, but they contorted into fresh, burning knots. "No."

"She wasn't at the waffle shop today."

Ask him. Ask him about how he manipulated her. Ask him if he turned her into his whore.

"I haven't talked to her in a while."

"Really. I thought you two were having a 'thing.'"

"We're just friends."

"Okay. If you hear from her, please let her know I was asking about her."

I wouldn't be surprised if she's sitting there beside you. Or LYING there beside you.

"I gotta go. Bye."

Ronnie banged the phone down so hard that his dad blinked awake and sat up. "What the hell, Ronnie?"

"Sorry. Wrong number."

"McFall said he had a job for you and Bobby tonight. Probably a late shipment, some toilets or plywood. Maybe he'll pay you a little overtime."

Ronnie almost told his dad he was quitting—for good this time—but he didn't want to wreck one of David's rare good moods. "You're going to need a little money to spend on all those hot college girls," his father added with a wink.

"I won't have time for stuff like that."

"Maybe you will. I've been thinking more about McFall's offer. If we sell out, you won't have to work when you start college. You can study and make good grades. Plus, I'd have another hundred houses to build, and that would pretty much keep me busy until retirement."

Ronnie wanted to clamp his hands over his ears. "But this is Day land! You said it yourself. It's like we belong to it instead of it belonging to us."

"A man's got to change with the times."

Tim walked out of the hall and opened the refrigerator, pulling out a carton of milk. "You're selling out?" he said to their dad. "My life will be ruined, but nobody cares. I'm just a kid."

Ronnie heard the Silverado in the driveway and headed for the door without another word. As he left, his dad called out, "Be sure to do a good job. We got a lot riding on McFall."

When Ronnie climbed into the truck, he was shocked by how ghastly Bobby looked under the dome light, like a mutant, alien junkie. "What happened? Did you see Brett again?" he asked, shifting the baseball bat on the floorboards so that his feet had room.

"I don't know what I saw. Something—*somebody*—in the river, coming toward me."

"Great. And we have to cross the bridge again."

"Maybe I could just drive real fast?"

"That didn't work out so well for you last time, remember? Maybe you should let me drive."

"No," Bobby said, squeezing the steering wheel. "I got this."

As his friend shifted the truck into first gear and let out the clutch, Ronnie said, "Okay, just go easy."

They rode in silence down Little Church Road, Ronnie glancing back and forth from the woods on one side to the river below the bank on the other, half expecting a ghost to drift in front of the headlights and cause Bobby to lose control. But ghosts couldn't really hurt you, could they?

Brett left water marks on the door. He interacted with the physical world.

He needed to think about something else, *anything* else. "Have you heard from Melanie lately?" he heard himself asking.

"Not since the State Line gig. She left a message saying she had something important to tell me, but I'm staying away."

"McFall told me she didn't show up for work. She'd never do that without calling in first."

Bobby shook his head. "Women. One day you'll learn, Ronnie." He slowed down even more as they passed McFall Meadows. The sales model was nearly complete, and three other houses were well underway. The fenced-in cemetery no longer looked a hundred years old, and grass was already growing over the site of the red church.

"I don't see your dude of smoke and ash anyway," Ronnie said.

"Maybe he's waiting for us at the bridge."

"Mr. Optimistic." Ronnie grabbed the baseball bat and held it upright. "If I see anything that doesn't belong, I'm going to knock it back to hell."

"Maybe *we're* the ones who don't belong," Bobby said. "Vernon Ray used to say that some people just came into the world at the wrong time. Like their souls didn't ever quite catch up with their bodies."

"You been smoking something?"

"Like you've never had weird thoughts. Sounds like the kind of stuff that runs through your head all the time."

Ronnie didn't answer because the bridge was just ahead of them, the trees yielding to a great expanse of black, hoary air that hung over the river. Even though he couldn't see the water, he felt its presence, oozing up and out from an antediluvian darkness whose secrets were so old and poisonous that even God had forgotten them.

But you haven't forgotten me, have you, God? You did place my soul in the right body, didn't you?

Bobby slowed to a stop at the entrance to the bridge. "See anything?"

The mist was thickening into an ominous, funereal veil that could harbor anything, including Brett, Darnell Absher, the sheriff's little brother, even Archer McFall and his flock. Plenty of room for all the restless dead who had been rejected by both heaven and hell.

A vehicle approached from the other side of the bridge, cutting through the fog and emerging next to them, the driver blinking his high beams on to thank Bobby for letting him pass first. The fog parted in the wake of the car and then swirled back into a dense, tangible mass.

"I wouldn't go in there," Ronnie said, palms sweating around the handle of the bat. "Screw band practice. Even rock 'n' roll isn't worth dying for."

"I'm not worried about the band. But Mr. McFall's counting on us."

"He mentioned a job on the phone. No way in hell am I getting in any deeper."

"You can back out, but I'm not going to let him down."

"You don't owe him anything."

"Bullshit. I owe him *everything*."

The mist was moving now, silken threads insinuating themselves into suggestions of knotty sinew and bone.

"I'm out," Ronnie said, opening the passenger door. "If you think this is a test of your manhood, then go for it. You're my best friend, but I won't go in there even for you."

"It's not a test. It's the game within the game. If you can't compete, get out of the batter's box."

"Fine, dude, but I'm taking the bat with me."

Ronnie climbed out of the pickup, wooden bat in hand, and the chill instantly wrapped around him. He was almost as afraid to be outside of the truck as he was to venture onto the bridge. Almost.

Ronnie headed up the road, waiting for Bobby to turn around and come after him. But Bobby's eyes had been so wild and bloodshot, Ronnie wasn't even sure his friend had heard him. The truck was still idling in place as the river chuckled and gurgled with hidden movement and the forest sighed in anticipation. Ronnie sped up, not looking back until he reached McFall Meadows. The truck's brake lights were like dim, red eyes in an animal's den.

He glanced at the cemetery.

The red church stood there, whole, healed, alive, the crippled cross on its steeple stabbing defiantly toward the ceiling of night.

Ronnie broke into a frantic sprint, and he wasn't sure he took a single breath until he reached his front door.

CHAPTER FORTY-EIGHT

*G*o.

Bobby's hand rested on the knob of the gear shift, the vibration of the engine working its way up his arm and rattling his rib cage. The Special K jumped from his head to his heart, which was pumping faster than it ever had from any drum solo or two-out showdown with a batter.

This is the game within the game. This is where you win or lose.

He eased forward, barely aware that Ronnie had ditched him. After all, you don't need a co-pilot when you're taking the Big Ride. Ronnie had Jesus and God and all that, but when the rubber met the road, you had to go it alone. No scout or agent or girlfriend or mentor could escort you through your baptism of fear.

The Silverado was a third of the way across the bridge when Bobby felt the structure lift from its moorings and turn, like a massive luxury liner steering to starboard on a stormy sea. He couldn't see either shore, and his stomach gave a queasy lurch as the bridge descended into an even thicker layer of fog. The surface of the river couldn't be more than a few feet beneath him, but he had lost all sense of physics and geometry. If the bridge bottomed out, he'd be trapped in the truck by the weight of the water.

But then the mist knitted itself into a figure that stood before the truck's headlines, a soft silhouette that was too short to be Brett Summers. Next came a gentle RATTA-TATTA-TAT and he noticed that the figure was wearing a blunt Civil War cap.

Vernon Ray?

Bobby got out of the truck, his mouth dry. He nearly lost his balance, and he desperately wanted a snort of the Special K, but he steadied himself. "It's you," he whispered to the original Drummer Boy.

Two small tunnels of empty eye sockets appeared beneath the brim of the cap. Hands slid from the larger shroud and rattled the snare harder, the forlorn cadence moving in rhythm with the splashing current below. Bobby wasn't sure whether the next words were spoken—if indeed it was Vernon Ray, the boy had certainly *changed*—or only in his head:

"None of us belong."

Then the figure merged back into the mist as if rejoining a parade of the lost, the drumbeats fading with him.

"No, wait!" Bobby shouted, moving into the stage lights of the truck's high beams. "Come back!"

As if in answer to his summons, the figure reformed, the drumsticks still rising and falling in its hands. But the apparition was larger now, as big as a grown man. Had Vernon Ray somehow aged while he was in the land of the dead?

Then the figure marched toward him from the mist. When it emerged into the glow of the headlights, Bobby found himself looking at—and through—himself. He wanted to flee, but the bridge bucked and swayed beneath his feet, nearly tossing him into the railing and perhaps over the side into nothingness. He saw his own pale, ethereal face frowning at him in disappointment.

You blew the game within the game.

The transparent version of himself slipped inside of him. He closed his eyes as bracing cold slid down his spine like fingers of ice. He staggered for a moment, almost marching in place, and when he opened his eyes his empty hands were flailing up and down in a soundless drumming motion. He clenched his fists and stilled them before wiping the clammy sweat from his face.

Bobby climbed back behind the wheel of the truck. The bridge seemed to settle into place once again, with a great trembling of ancient bedrock. Bobby was positive that the bridge had turned completely around so that he was facing McFall Meadows and Little Church Road once more.

Whatever part of him he'd lost the night of the crash had returned and reintegrated itself. Or maybe the dead Bobby was the real one, not the hunk of flesh he'd been hauling to work, band practice, and the Eldreth mobile home for the last few weeks.

The fog cleared a little, and he drove the truck forward. Highway 321 was just in front of him. He glanced at the dented sign that said "No Swimming Jumping Fishing From Bridge." He wondered if ghostly encounters were also against the law. Or being kidnapped and held hostage by your own soul. No wonder he'd felt so out of it lately. He may well have *been* out of it.

Bobby pulled the vial of powder from his shirt pocket and dumped some onto the back of one trembling hand. He sniffed a small mound into his nose. His hand steadied. He wheeled the Silverado onto the asphalt and stomped on the accelerator.

Larkin McFall was waiting.

CHAPTER FORTY-NINE

Sheriff Littlefield banged on the apartment door. "Cindy!"

He could see through the curtains that her lights were on. The apartment complex was just outside Titusville, within range of the traffic noise and streetlights from the main commercial strip. A country boy, Littlefield had never been comfortable in Cindy's place, which was part of the reason they'd spent most of their time at his house. Now it looked like it was going to stay *his* house, instead of theirs.

He pounded once more and raised his voice again, not caring if the neighbors heard. He was soon going to be the ex-sheriff, so their votes no longer mattered.

The door opened a crack, the safety chain stretched taut. One brown eye peeked out at him. "Hush it or I'll call the cops."

She'd do it too, he had no doubts about that—and she'd snap photographs while they cuffed him and put him in the back seat of the squad car. The only question left was whether they'd throw him behind bars or in a rubber room.

"We need to talk," he said.

"Oh, *now* we need to talk. When there's nothing left to say."

"Look, I don't care about your column. Hell, I even agree with half of what you said. But all hell's breaking loose out here, and I can't duct-tape it back together with lies and denials. I need you. I need your help."

The eye narrowed, speculating. "Can I get column inches out of it?"

"Whatever you want. All access. But nobody's going to believe it."

"They didn't believe it when little Vernon Ray Davis got lost in that cave, or when some of those guns in the last Civil War re-enactment started firing real bullets. They didn't believe it when your detective drowned right outside the church on the same night Archer McFall mysteriously left town. Under your leadership, I think they've gotten real good at not believing."

"That's not fair, Cindy."

"Remember Heather Fowler's slogan during her campaign for county commissioner? 'Use whatever you got.' It worked for her, so I've decided to adopt it too."

"Sounds good to me. I'll use my fear. Because it's all I got left."

She sighed, released the chain, and opened the door. It had only been two weeks since Littlefield's last visit, but the bookshelves had undergone a massive change. Most people's bookshelves just sat there and collected dust, but hers were like a living organism in a constant state of flux. Some books were open and spread out on top of a row, while others had their spines facing up instead of out. It reminded him of Sweeney Buchanan's squatter hovel in the woods.

She swept a stack of national daily newspapers from the couch to the floor. She had a cat named Clemens around somewhere, and although the animal was reclusive its odor was not. Littlefield sat, already feeling a little itchy from the tufts of hair floating around.

"Put down your hat," Cindy said.

Littlefield realized he'd been rapidly turning it by the brim. He perched it on his knee for a moment, then used it to cover a copy of *Newsweek* that featured the president's jug-eared mug on the cover. "The ghosts are back."

Cindy nodded. As a paranormal enthusiast she accepted such things as a given.

"Except it's not just dead people. It's everybody. And somehow Larkin McFall is turning them all against me."

"Against *you*? So this is all about spooking Frankie Littlefield. Or, as they say in the cop movies, 'This time it's personal.'"

"Don't look at me like that. Hoyle sold me out on the Cole Buchanan report, and now he's holding corpses I wasn't even informed about." He wasn't sure he wanted to tell her about seeing the morgue drawer slide open and that blue-veined hand reach out, but he did anyway. He also told her about his encounter with McFall in the woods, and his sightings of Vernon Ray and Samuel.

He'd covered up his county's secrets for far too long, which was why he felt so isolated and disconnected from the people he served. And from the woman he probably loved.

"I'm pretty sure something's going on with those kids who were partying at the bridge the night Brett Summers drowned," he said. "When you connect all the dots, Ronnie Day and Bobby Eldreth are there every single time. And so is McFall, except most of the time he's standing somewhere just off stage, back behind the curtain."

He expected Cindy to jump up with her renowned passion and curiosity, demanding that they pay McFall a visit at his condominium. Or maybe get a search warrant and check out the morgue. But she sat on the far end of the couch, her expression bored, as if she were wondering what was on television.

"You know why I became a sheriff?" he asked.

"Because you like wearing a hat on the job?"

"Because of my little brother. After he died in that prank at the red church, I didn't want anything as terrible as that to happen ever again. I promised Samuel I'd devote my life to protecting the innocent."

"And then you finally realized that nobody's innocent."

"A girl's missing, Cindy. You know Melanie Ward, that young waitress down at the waffle house with the bleached streak in her hair? We searched a little, checked out the river, called some of her friends. She's not official yet, but if she hasn't turned up by morning . . . ."

"You'll actually follow protocol and open an investigation? Color me impressed."

"I'm quitting. I keep thinking I should wait to retire until I tie up all my loose ends, but more ends come loose every minute. I've got nothing *but* ends."

Littlefield thought she'd welcome the news, seeing as she was the one who'd suggested his retirement in the first place. "And you've got fear," she said. "Don't forget that."

"So, are you going to help?"

"I'm a journalist. I don't take sides."

He snatched his hat from the coffee table and stormed over to the door. "I thought we were in this together." Then he looked back at her and he knew. "What did McFall offer *you*?"

"What do you think? A good story."

374

CHAPTER FIFTY

The third of July in Pickett County, North Carolina, was born with heavy dew that soon gave way to humidity so thick the tiger lilies would sag until noon. The Blue Ridge Mountains were ribbed with skeins of haze that had more to do with Midwestern coal-fired power plants than the natural smoke of morning. The corn had reached its desired, knee-high state, and farmers checked the signs and went ahead with their first cutting of hay. Blackburn River ran low and quiet and a little thirsty.

Ronnie Day awoke to find he'd slept with the baseball bat tucked next to him under his blanket.

Bobby Eldreth jerked awake in the cab of the Silverado, parked behind the high school football stadium, his clothes dirty and his head aching, as if someone had rapped drumsticks against his skull all night.

Heather Fowler sipped black coffee with stevia while contemplating life in a condominium, never noticing the freshly turned dirt in her potato patch.

Sheriff Littlefield finished the pint of whiskey he'd been saving for an emergency, wondering if he should take a nap before checking on the situation with the Ward girl.

Meanwhile, work continued at McFall Meadows. David Day and his crew hung hardwood cabinets in a kitchen. Elmer Eldreth soldered copper water pipes while wondering if Bobby had ruined his future by partying with dopeheads. Wally Kaufman's bulldozer blazed the trail for another hundred feet of gravel, steel treads grinding ever closer to the ridge line.

Sweeney Buchanan and Melanie Ward were holed up in a sagging barn on the Gregg farm, one of Larkin McFall's recent property purchases.

McFall emerged from the woods, crusted blood on his lips, the world at his fingertips.

Ronnie was late for work, but he didn't care. And he was glad he'd skipped the secret, "little" job last night. Let McFall fire him. If David Day was selling out, Ronnie really didn't need the money, and he couldn't bear the thought of being around the sinister son of a bitch all day. But he was worried about Bobby, who hadn't been returning his calls all morning. So he'd told his dad to go ahead, and he later walked back to McFall Meadows, following the same route he'd scurried over hours before.

If he didn't know better, he would have thought it was all a bad nightmare fueled by his mom's spicy lasagna. But those ghostly shapes in the mist had been there—Bobby had seen them, too—and the red church had seemed just as solid as when he'd attended services there with his mother. He was positive that if he'd opened that creaking, wooden door, Archer McFall would have been standing at the lectern, arms spread in welcome, his smile full of sharp teeth.

But today the church site was just a bare stretch of pasture, the newly planted grass like green tufts of baby hair. Hammers echoed across the job site. A delivery truck was unloading stacks of Sheetrock. Kaufman's bulldozer sent diesel exhaust boiling into the sky, the engine growling as it plunged ever deeper into the ancient mud. Bobby's Silverado was nowhere in sight, but McFall's Lexus was parked by the model home, which would soon be open for real-estate sales.

Ronnie climbed the steps, appreciating the craft of his dad and the other workers. But he wondered if they really understood what they were building. This development was just a new kind of church, one that would feed McFall's corrupt empire.

When Ronnie entered the living room, which had been out-fitted as an office, McFall was sitting in a high-backed, leather chair behind a polished, maple desk. The room itself was amber from the morning light streaming through the bay window. The view was magnificent, with the river winding away to the bridge in the distance. Even the fenced cemetery looked almost charming.

"Ronnie. I've been expecting you."

No surprise there.

"Where is he?"

McFall's innocent expression would have fooled almost anyone— except for someone who knew the McFall family and what they were. "Where is who?"

"Bobby."

"I'm looking for him myself. We worked late last night, and he must have slept in. We could have used your help, you know."

I'll bet. Well, there are still a few of us left who haven't given up their souls to you. But the day is young.

"What about Melanie?"

McFall motioned for Ronnie to sit in one of the Queen Anne-style chairs in front of his desk, but Ronnie shook his head. "I didn't think you cared," McFall said. "She said you rejected her."

"I rejected *you*," Ronnie said, his voice bouncing off the wooden floor and bare walls. "I don't want anything bad enough to let you win. That's the game within the game, right? Everybody thinks they're going to get what they want, but they're really just giving you what *you* want."

McFall tapped his fingers. The cell phone on his desk buzzed and he flipped it open. "Excuse me," he said, shoving his chair back and heading for the door.

Ronnie watched through the window as McFall walked down to the entrance of the development, where a car awaited him. The man—*he's not really a man, he's a McFALL*—had left his cell phone open on his desk.

Bait. No way would he leave it there otherwise.

Ronnie couldn't resist, any more than his mother could resist Archer McFall, any more than countless generations of Days, Potters, Mathesons, and Abshers had been able to resist other McFalls.

Ronnie recognized her number. She'd been so proud of her new cell phone, the first thing she'd bought with her waitress tips. It had been proof to her that she was an adult.

The text said: "*help. sweeny. greg he*"

Sweeney? The guy was a little out there, but not even the sheriff had taken him seriously as a murder suspect. Everybody thought he was long gone, that he'd hitchhiked to Charlotte or Atlanta, where he'd huddle under pedestrian bridges and scavenge fast food from dumpsters. Besides, his last name was Buchanan, not Gregg.

She'd obviously typed the message in a hurry. Melanie wasn't an A student, but she took pride in her spelling. She said language separated the trailer parks from the gated subdivisions. Was she in danger? If so, why had she texted McFall instead of her mother or the sheriff's office?

McFall was coming back, accompanied by a woman dressed in a suit jacket and professional skirt who was carefully maintaining her balance as her high heels probed the gravel road. Ronnie recognized her from the newspaper; she was that county commissioner who'd made a big deal about the water plant the town wanted to build. A real friend of the river. Obviously, she didn't *know* the river.

Ronnie retreated to where he'd been standing when McFall had left the room.

McFall made a big show of introducing the woman. "Ronnie, this is Heather Fowler," he said. "She's going to be helping us out around here."

As he nodded a greeting, Ronnie noticed that her eyes were hidden by the same type of sunglasses McFall's wife always wore. "Well, I better get going."

McFall circled his desk, glanced at his phone, and clicked the screen to black. Ronnie waited for him to say something about the cryptic message.

"Don't go far," McFall said. "I need you to clear some brush at the Gregg farm. After we level the Buchanan place, we'll be starting over there."

The Gregg property was about a quarter-mile from the Day farm, separated by a strip of Absher land. McFall had pretty much gained control of all the valleys surrounding the ridge of his family homestead. His dad was the remaining holdout, and it didn't sound like the hold was very strong. As Ronnie left the office, Heather Fowler was settling into the leather chair as if she were trying out a throne.

He went to the house where Elmer was working and asked him where Bobby was.

"Hell if I know," the pudgy man said, as he worked beneath a kitchen sink with a pipe wrench balanced on his belly. "Didn't come in last night."

"Is he okay?"

Elmer shoved aside the water lines he'd been connecting, wriggled awkwardly out from under the sink, and sat up wheezing. "Guys your age, you know it all. Well, let me tell you, real life will slap you in the face soon enough. You think it's all about honeys and music and freedom, but then the bills pile up, the doctor puts you on four different kinds of pills, and the government shits all over the economy. So you put your hope in your kids, the next generation, and damned if they don't turn out the same as you."

"Can you tell him I'm looking for him if you see him?"

"We're like a river, Ronnie," Elmer said, reaching for his thermos. When Elmer twisted the thermos lid free, the odor of whiskey filled the kitchen. "It's not new water rolling by, it's the same old water coming back in a million different ways, over and over again until one day it dries up."

The river. Ronnie knew one more place to look. Maybe after meeting with McFall, Bobby had finished what he'd started that night he ran off the road. Maybe the Silverado was ten feet beneath the surface, Bobby's bloated corpse bobbing against the roof of the cab. Without bothering to reply to Elmer, he jogged outside and veered around the lower end of the property so that McFall couldn't see him.

He was sweaty and exhausted by the time he reached the bridge. The sign upon which someone had spray painted "No fun" had been replaced, but a new graffiti artist had already been at work sometime during the night. Beneath "No Swimming Jumping Fishing From Bridge" was a wiggly "No dying."

Ronnie climbed down the bank, ending up near to where he'd found Darnell Absher's corpse. That discovery seemed years in the past now, from a time when Ronnie had still possessed a bit of optimism and courage. Or maybe at the time he'd just been burying his memories deep enough to start believing his own fairy tale: That Archer McFall was just a spooky story grandmas told to keep their bratty grandkids in line, that Ronnie could pull a magic sword from a stone and win the heart of his princess Melanie Ward.

He walked the shoreline, stepping from mossy rocks to mud, careful not to let the current lap onto his sneakers, as if the water might reach up like a hand and drag him under. Even though the water level was lower than usual because of the heat he couldn't see the bottom. But he didn't see the pearlescent finish of the truck, either.

He climbed back to the highway and was considering plan C when he heard the powerful rumble of an engine. The Silverado was driving toward him, its turn signal on. Bobby stopped the truck and rolled down the window. Ronnie welcomed the blast of air-conditioning but was shocked by his friend's wan complexion. Bobby's face looked as if it had been drained of blood, his veins filled with milk instead.

"Shit, Bobby. What happened last night? You look like hell warmed over."

"Get in. We got work to do."

Ronnie wondered if McFall could see the truck from his window. Probably. Anyway, it didn't seem to matter whether McFall saw things. He *knew* things.

Once inside the cab, Ronnie said, "Sorry I bailed on you last night. I was freaking out big time."

"It's okay," Bobby said as he drove across the bridge, his stare fixed dead ahead. "I realized it was like a drum solo—something I had to play alone."

"Real life slapping you in the face?"

"Don't know how real it was, but it's done."

"What did you and McFall do?"

"If it was any of your business you would have been there."

Fine. So you didn't get much sleep.

Ronnie told him about the text message Melanie had sent McFall. He didn't share his suspicion that McFall had deliberately allowed him to see the message. Bobby was McFall's Golden Boy, and Ronnie realized he could no longer fully trust his best friend.

"Sounds like we better get to the Gregg farm."

"Yeah, that word 'help' freaks me out," Ronnie added. "What if our special friend Sweeney did something to her?"

Instead of turning into McFall Meadows, Bobby drove past the entrance, where Heather Fowler's car was parked in the grass by the cemetery. "We're going to stop at your house first to get my bat. I've had that thing since Little League. Dad always said I'd make my first hit in the majors with it."

When Ronnie ran in to grab the bat, his mom asked him why he was home in the middle of the day. Ronnie said, "Lunch," and headed straight for his room. Tim was busy doodling some cartoon monsters, so he did little more than grunt at Ronnie. He didn't seem to notice when Ronnie pulled the bat out from underneath his blankets. His mom saw it when he headed into the kitchen, though, and he came up with some story about how Bobby had let him borrow it—thankfully, she didn't ask why—then grabbed the sandwiches and fled.

Back in the truck, Ronnie saw Bobby wiping his runny nose. He'd had that same cold for days now. So much for the health of a superior athlete. But Ronnie wasn't his mother or his girlfriend, so it was none of his business.

The last few houses were soon behind them, and pasture gave way to raw forest. "I don't know what Melanie would be doing way out here," Ronnie said.

"Maybe this is where she hooks up with McFall for . . . you know, *recreational* activities," Bobby said.

Ronnie kept silent. He'd been thinking the same thing.

The road soon narrowed to a set of rocky ruts that wound between saplings whose young, green branches slapped at the Silverado's flanks. Even though it was barely afternoon, the forest grew perceptibly darker, as if a night was approaching that had no regard for hours and borders and the stubborn futility of light. They soon had to give up on the truck and walk the last bit, Bobby carrying the bat over his shoulder and occasionally swiping it at weeds and branches in their path.

They had nearly reached the farm when they saw Sweeney sneak out of the woods and enter the barn.

CHAPTER FIFTY-ONE

"**S**o it's official?" Deputy Perriotte asked.

"Missing persons case," Littlefield said. "Put it out on the police wire. She doesn't qualify for an AMBER Alert because she's eighteen. This could still be a runaway case, but I'm going to play it by the book."

Perriotte fingered the photograph he'd scanned with the report that would be sent to surrounding law enforcement agencies and posted to the state website. "Pretty. I recognize her from the waffle shop."

"Yeah, I wouldn't be surprised if some horny guy took her to Vegas, but nobody's stepping up with any information. I talked to her friends and family. Her mom said nothing was missing but her purse. She usually catches a ride to work, but nobody picked her up yesterday morning. She was just *gone*."

"I'm pretty sure she wasn't hitchhiking, unless she was lucky enough—or unlucky enough—to get out of town without anyone noticing."

"You're sheriff material, all right," Littlefield said. "She's a looker, though, and her looks might have made the first guy stop. The *wrong* guy." Littlefield had a hunch that McFall was that wrong guy but, as always, he had no proof. He wasn't sure what he could do about it even if he did have proof.

"Want me to send this out to the radio and the newspaper's website, too?"

"We need all the help we can get, even if it causes public panic."

"Gossip, more likely."

"You sure know your constituents. I can hardly wait to turn this badge over to you." Littlefield gave him a weary smile. "But I'm keeping the hat."

"Your head's way too big anyway, Sheriff."

"Why don't you stay here and run the command center, and I'll hit the road? Might as well get used to the office politics."

"Sure thing." Perriotte looked around the room as if he were already mentally redecorating.

"I'm taking Little Church Road. A couple of Melanie's friends work at McFall Meadows, so I'll check with them to see if they've heard anything new."

Driving out of Titusville, Littlefield saw that the sky had dawned clear and was the color of old robin's eggs, menacing, wispy clouds rising from the western horizon. A thunderstorm would cool things off, but it would also dampen the search effort.

Come on, Frank. How much searching are you really planning to do?

He didn't really have to search. Many of his fellow officers acted on hunches or "gut feels"; they tended to remember when past hunches had panned out, developing amnesia about the million other times. His certainty that McFall was involved was stronger than a hunch. It was where his whole career had been heading, his whole life. The winged monster of the red church had brought him here. Sometimes he wondered if the McFalls were demons he had intentionally summoned just so he could wage war.

His cell phone rang and he wrestled it from his pocket as the Isuzu rolled along Highway 321. It was Cindy.

"I've got a tip," she said.

"So we're still on speaking terms?"

"This isn't about us. This is about the news. The truth."

He swallowed his sigh. "What, then?"

"The old Gregg farm. On the backside of the McFall development."

"Yeah, I know it. Our family land is near it."

"Sweeney Buchanan kidnapped Melanie Ward and is holding her there."

Littlefield involuntarily pressed the accelerator harder. "Where did you get a tip like that?"

"I have my sources."

"Did you call it in to my office?"

"No. I figured you'd want this one for yourself. A hundred bubble lights and sirens out there in the woods and your hostage situation will go south real fast."

Littlefield tried to remember the layout of the place, but it had been over a decade since he'd been out there, so his memories were hazy. In his mind's eye, he could see several tumbledown outbuildings and barns, the house site nothing but a circle of charred embers with a stone chimney. It had been wildly overgrown even back then. By now it might have fully returned to forest.

"I guess you wouldn't consider sitting this one out?" he asked. "As one last favor?"

"Not on your life." She said it as if she wouldn't mind using those words in a headline.

He set the phone on the seat and approached the bridge. He'd begun to think of the bridge as a metaphor. The bridge carried you from the present into the past, and not everyone made it all the way across. And on *that* side of Blackburn River, McFall was judge, jury, and executioner.

He didn't slow as he passed McFall Meadows. Cindy's tip could have come from only one source, so McFall would be along in due time. He'd worry about that later. First he was going to do what he could to save Melanie Ward.

If you had been serious about bagging Sweeney before now, it wouldn't have come to this.

Or maybe it would.

When Little Church Road got too rough for his vehicle, he pulled into a little glen where an animal shed stood draped with honeysuckle and Virginia creeper. It was a short but steep walk to the farmstead, and he took a trail he'd used for deer hunting in his youth. When he topped the rise the trees began to thin, and he could see a slew of rusty roofs below, the color of dried blood.

He waited and listened, one hand on the butt of his revolver. What if Cindy had sidetracked him with a false alarm, and McFall was off performing an atrocity somewhere else?

No, that wasn't McFall's style.

Littlefield descended the slope, stepping carefully as the soil grew rockier and muddier. The Greggs had once grown all manner of cash crops like buckwheat, cabbage, sugar cane, and corn, but like many mountain families, they eventually found that hard work didn't pay when you were competing against corporations and their machines. Most of the family now lived in trailers and manufactured homes along the gravel road, leaving a hundred acres of their heritage fallow.

McFALL ❧ EPISODE SIX

He didn't see or hear any movement as he came to the edge of the woods. The barn was the most likely place to hold a captive, because it had retained the most structural integrity.

And there are plenty of pens to keep someone prisoner.

He planned to make a slow orbit around the barn before moving closer, but then he saw someone kneeling behind the stone chimney.

Ronnie. Shit.

Maybe Ronnie had gotten the same tip as Littlefield. McFall was spreading his bait, setting them all up.

This was the kind of complication that could lead to an accidental death. Littlefield was pretty confident that Sweeney's life was most in danger. The poor guy didn't have enough sense to tell "surrender" from *Saturday Night Fever*. He'd probably just stumbled upon the pretty young thing and gathered her up. Maybe he didn't even know he was breaking the law.

Littlefield changed his plan, intending now to send Ronnie away from the crime scene. And where Ronnie was, his friend Bobby was likely not far behind. They were the Tweedledum and Tweedledee of the epic fantasy known as haunted Barkersville. And, just like Littlefield, both boys had endured tragedy from supernatural sources. It made sense that they were in McFall's web.

Yes, we're all a part of the same local legend. Cut from the same bloody cloth.

Littlefield took cover behind a steeply canted outhouse, looking for Bobby now. The barn had two stories, and the upper loft was beset with several open windows that looked down into darkness. Sweeney could be in there watching. Perhaps he had a gun.

Or a bloody farm tool.

The sky had grown darker, a herd of roiling black clouds stampeding in. Littlefield hadn't even brought a flashlight. If this situation dragged on for a few more hours, he'd have to walk back to the Isuzu and call for backup. But he wanted to wrap this up alone, and fast, before it became an event.

He took a step forward and stumbled like an old fool. Ronnie swiveled his head around and their eyes met. Ronnie held up two fingers, mouthed a silent "Melanie," and then pointed at the barn.

So Melanie and Sweeney *were* in there.

And then Littlefield spied Bobby.

The son of a bitch was at the rear of the barn, crouched against the weathered, gray siding, clutching a baseball bat as if preparing to play hero.

CHAPTER FIFTY-TWO

It was dark inside the barn, but Bobby could still see Melanie.

She was trapped inside a corn crib, half hidden in shadows. Chicken wire ran along the plank walls of the crib, effectively creating a cage. Melanie didn't appear to be tied up, and she was fully dressed, but she looked scared and exhausted, slumped in a sitting position on the hard-packed dirt.

What's that little creep done to her?

Bobby hadn't seen Sweeney since they'd followed him to the barn. He'd sent Ronnie to watch the front entrance, more to get him out of the way than because he thought Sweeney would leave again. In a physical confrontation, Ronnie would just slow him down. They hadn't hatched any kind of plan, but Bobby felt confident enough with the baseball bat. Unless Sweeney had a machine gun, he liked his odds.

He still felt strange after last night, though. He remembered driving across the bridge and seeing Vernon Ray and what he now believed to be his own ghost, but he couldn't remember what had happened afterwards. He had flashes of digging under the moonlight with McFall, and moving something heavy out of the man's trunk, but he couldn't tell memory from dream anymore. He took one hand from the bat and patted his shirt pocket, comforted by the feeling of the glass vial. It seemed to be just about the most solid thing in his life lately.

He imagined bursting through the barn door, whacking Sweeney, and rescuing Melanie. She'd probably kiss him. He wanted to whisper her name, to let her know she'd be safe soon, but she might inadvertently alert Sweeney. Something thumped on the warped boards above him.

Sweeney's footsteps scuffed across the loft floor as the man muttered a repetitive phrase. The mantra sounded like, "Coyotes are coming, coyotes are coming."

This guy really is off his rocker. No telling what he'll do next.

But because Sweeney was upstairs, Bobby could slip inside, free Melanie, and get out before the maniac even knew what had happened. If he went in through the door, though, it would make a loud squeak and probably trigger vibrations that Sweeney could feel. Bobby looked around for a gap in the siding and spotted a section that had rotted away at the bottom. He pushed the bat through, then lay on his back and wriggled inside after it.

Dust stung his eyes, and it took a moment for his vision to adjust to the dimness. He rolled to his knees, collected the bat, and studied the layout of the barn. He was inside a pen, but its planks and rails had collapsed and he could step through them into the main part of the barn. An uneven set of wooden stairs climbed the wall at the far end of the room, and here and there square holes were cut into the loft floor, probably so that hay could be tossed down to the animals. Sweeney was somewhere in the middle, walking back and forth as if he were looking out the windows first on one side of the barn and then another.

Bobby moved quietly over to the corn crib, examining the stick and twist of baling wire that had been used to fasten it shut. Melanie looked up at him, her eyes large and gray. She opened her mouth to speak, but he made a shushing motion with his finger against his lips.

Then he began to loosen the makeshift latch.

Sweeney's footsteps came to an abrupt stop overhead. "The coyotes are *heeeeere!*"

CHAPTER FIFTY-THREE

When Ronnie heard Sweeney's demented howl he burst from his hiding place and ran for the barn.

Littlefield hissed the command "Stop!" but Ronnie wasn't about to sit around and watch while two of the people he cared about most were in danger. Ronnie remembered Sweeney's surprising speed and strength from their confrontation with him in the old Buchanan place. Who knew what kind of drugs he was on, or if the voices in his head had fueled him into a superhuman frenzy? Even somebody as muscular as Bobby might not stand a chance on his own.

And maybe Sweeney's not on drugs. Maybe he's on McFall.

But Ronnie didn't believe McFall was controlling the man. McFall had looked worried when he'd cornered Sweeney at the Buchanan place, almost scared. It was the only time Ronnie had ever seen him lose his cool.

When Ronnie reached the barn door, he paused to press his ear against the wood for a moment. Then he threw the rusty hasp and wrestled the door open. It sagged, unable to support its own weight, so Ronnie dragged it until he could slip through the opening, boards rattling loudly as he forced his way between them.

Sweeney, who'd fallen quiet, broke into a gallop overhead. "Coyotes are *here*!"

Ronnie saw the silhouettes of Bobby and Melanie hugging on the far side of the barn. "He's coming," he hissed at them.

A shadow dropped from above, landing with a thud in the middle of the barn floor. Sweeney lifted himself, staggering from the impact of his leap, and held up the wicked curve of a sickle. "Coyotes get cut."

To punctuate his words, Sweeney stroked the air with the antique tool. It looked rusty but plenty sharp. Bobby stepped in front of Melanie and raised his baseball bat.

Sweeney gave Ronnie only a glance—clearly he was the less threatening coyote—and approached Bobby, waving the sickle back and forth. Ronnie debated rushing Sweeney, but before he could make a decision, the barn door parted wider.

"Hold it or I'll shoot!" the sheriff yelled.

CHAPTER FIFTY-FOUR

Littlefield only had a moment to make a choice.

He'd lost any chance to gain control of the situation and conclude it peacefully. Just another failure—one of many, but he still had his gun.

Sweeney was right beside Melanie, wielding some sort of weapon. She screamed, the sound ringing through the barn.

"Hold it," the sheriff repeated, but even as he spoke he knew it was useless. Things were already in motion. No time to try for a disabling shot. Sweeney needed to be taken down, and fast.

Littlefield aimed for the chest and fired twice.

"No!" Ronnie cried, diving for the gun, nearly taking the bullets himself as he slammed into the sheriff.

Melanie screamed again as the silhouette staggered and dropped its weapon.

Littlefield regained his balance and lifted his weapon again, stepping over Ronnie's fallen form, the sound of the shots ringing in his ears. He shifted his aim to the other figure in the middle of the barn—the one he'd assumed was Bobby.

Sweeney dropped his sickle and smiled. "Coyotes duh-duh-dead!"

A cold sweat broke out across Littlefield's skin. Melanie was still screaming, and Ronnie had crawled over to her.

And to Bobby, who lay on his back in the dirt, his baseball bat beside him.

But I shot Sweeney, not Bobby!

Littlefield had a feeling he'd be repeating those words at a deposition someday, and no one would believe him—just as he barely believed himself now.

"One coyote not dead," Sweeney said, but as he bent to retrieve the sickle Littlefield took three steps forward and kicked him in the chest. He fought the urge to stick the barrel of his revolver against Sweeney's skull and blow his brains into soup. But another death wouldn't erase his mistake.

Instead, he spun the man face down onto the barn floor, jammed a knee into his spine, and wrestled him into a pair of handcuffs. A bright orb of light settled on him, and he squinted into it.

"Shit." Deputy Perriotte said from behind the flashlight. The beam bounced over to Bobby's still form. Melanie wailed in anguish as she knelt beside Bobby's damaged body, Ronnie by her side.

"Call an ambulance," Littlefield croaked, although he knew it was far too late.

CHAPTER FIFTY-FIVE

As Bobby lay on the floor, blood oozing from the gap in his chest, his eyelids fluttered open and he flailed his arms. To Ronnie, it looked for all the world as if Bobby was playing a final drumroll, riding the crash cymbal into the afterlife.

Ronnie blinked away his tears, his ears still ringing from the shots, his nose twitching from the bitter odor of gunpowder. He fell to his knees beside Melanie just as Bobby's lips started moving, a bubble of blood welling up and popping.

Melanie wailed Bobby's name over and over like a siren as she rocked back and forth. Perriotte said something Ronnie couldn't understand, because his focus was on one thing: Bobby was dying, and fast. He wished everything would just stop so he could hear what his friend was trying to say.

Ronnie put his hand on Bobby's shoulder in a pathetic attempt at comfort. "Hang in there, bro. You . . . you'll be okay."

Bobby's mouth worked again, and his dimming eyes implored Ronnie to come closer. Ronnie leaned in toward him even as Perriotte pulled Melanie away so that he could check on Bobby.

"Game . . . within the game," Bobby whispered, and died.

Ronnie went limp as Perriotte pulled him away, then stood, looking at a dazed Littlefield, who was holding Sweeney in hand-cuffs. For the first time, he noticed the faint pulsing of emergency lights down the road. It had grown even darker outside, and thunder rumbled menacingly.

He turned to look at Melanie. She would, for the rest of her life, think Bobby had sacrificed himself for her. Ronnie suspected he'd been sacrificed for a different cause, but he'd never be coldhearted enough to say that to her.

Eyes wild, Melanie turned to him and took him in her arms. He tensed and resisted. His best friend's blood was all over her.

"It's over," Ronnie said, not even believing his own soothing bullshit.

She shook her head and pressed harder against him, her tears hot on his shoulder. The feeling of her against him caused something inside him to weaken, and he asked Jesus to make him strong for her. They'd both suffered a devastating loss.

And, damn it, I still love her, despite it all. I'm the biggest idiot on the planet.

Most pathetic of all, he felt a little thrill in the fact that Bobby was out of the way and Melanie was all his. And he knew only one source of such a horrible thought: McFall.

Maybe Sweeney had killed the wrong coyote.

"It's not over," she whispered at last. "Not for me. I'm pregnant."

His chest froze, and the rain finally broke, drumming the tin roof above them. *Oh, God, did that creepy bastard put a little McFall in her?*

He would do just about anything to help Melanie, but nurturing and loving and raising a little McFall was beyond contemplation. He'd sooner grab Sweeney's sickle and perform a spontaneous abortion.

Melanie lifted her head from his shoulder and searched his face. Her eyes were the bluest he'd ever seen them, almost dusky. Maybe she did—or at least *could*—love him. But he couldn't be weak. Then she looked over at Bobby's body. "His."

Ronnie could handle that: for Bobby. For Melanie. For himself.

Deathboy ends up with the Girl Whose Lovers Keep Dying. A match made in heaven.

The thing that bothered him was that it sounded exactly like the kind of outcome McFall would want.

He hugged her as the heavens poured forth and Blackburn River replenished itself.

CHAPTER FIFTY-SIX

Both Barkersville and Titusville held their annual Fourth of July parades, using scarce taxpayer dollars to roll their fire engines and police cars down the street. The spectators waved little flags and imagined that they were free. Later, there were fireworks at the high school baseball field, an event that doubled as a public memorial service for Bobby Eldreth.

Cindy Baumhower's story was picked up by Associated Press and United Press International, with versions of it appearing in many major dailies. Bobby Eldreth was hailed as a hero, Sheriff Littlefield as a hero who had made a tragic mistake, and Sweeney Buchanan as a madman who would surely have gone on to commit ever greater atrocities if not for the fatal confrontation. Melanie Ward was mentioned as a minor character, suggesting a possible romantic angle for readers without crossing the line into maudlin.

Ronnie Day was not mentioned, nor were coyotes, nor was Larkin McFall.

Elmer Eldreth took a week off work, and scouts from three major league teams sent their condolences in the form of guest tickets to games. The rest of the workers at McFall Meadows kept on with their work, although McFall generously gave people time off with pay if they chose to attend Bobby's funeral. Most took him up on the offer. The crowd at Barkersville Baptist Church that day was bigger than any that had ever attended a baseball game Bobby had pitched or a performance by The Diggers.

Melanie Ward never found the phone she'd dropped when Sweeney abducted her. A week after the incident, Heather Fowler stood on the bridge and flung it into the Blackburn River. Her potatoes were prolific that summer.

Those who weren't dead kept living.

Ronnie climbed out of the Silverado and walked into the new sales office in the model home at McFall Meadows. Heather Fowler had redecorated, and the walls featured a number of scenic photographs. He'd seen some of them before on magazine covers taken by local celebrity Bill Willard. Ronnie had to admit that the region's natural beauty made for one kickass selling point.

Heather sat behind the desk, perched in her leather chair. She was staring at the opposite wall, and her face was lax, as if she were dozing with her eyes open.

"Is Mr. McFall in?" Ronnie asked.

She jerked erect and her eyes lit up. She seemed younger somehow, prettier. Something about her face had changed, or maybe it had to do with her eyebrows and the wrinkles around her eyes and on her forehead. Before, she'd had a slightly pinched, severe aspect to her appearance. Now she seemed relaxed.

She's softened, Ronnie thought. *She got what she wanted. Just like the rest of us.*

"Hi, Ronnie," she said. "I hope you are well today. How's it going?"

"Good. Dex and Floyd are finishing up the fence at the Matheson place. You should be able to start selling lots over there by October, once Wally finishes the grading."

"We're lucky to have river access on that side. It's a valuable resource. We can screen the sewage treatment plant enough so that no one sees it from the canoe landing. We don't want to interfere with anyone's enjoyment of nature."

McFall emerged from the room he was now using for his personal office. "Ronnie!" He ambled cheerfully across the room. He squeezed Ronnie's arm. "You're really filling out. A good summer of hard work is making a man out of you."

"I appreciate the promotion. College is going to cost a lot more than I figured. Plus, with Melanie . . . ."

McFall put a fatherly arm across Ronnie's shoulders. "If your dad sells his land, I'll bet things will ease up for you a little."

"Days are stubborn, you know that."

"Yes, I do."

"Well, I better get back to the job site. If you don't nudge them along . . . well, you know how musicians are. They think everything's about sex, drugs, and rock 'n' roll."

Heather looked vaguely offended, but McFall laughed. He walked Ronnie to the door, still embracing him. "No big hurry. There's something I want to show you first."

Though McFall's arm felt cool and limp, like a dead snake, Ronnie endured it. Melanie was counting on him.

And so is Bobby, Jr.

Besides, he had to admit, that Silverado was one bad ride. He was proud to drive Melanie around town in it, and she had expanded her wardrobe, buying dresses and Bohemian outfits from the little shops on Main Street. They were already being accepted as a couple, although of course the gossip mill had ground plenty of rumors between the stones of jealousy and self-righteousness.

"Whatever you say, boss," Ronnie said.

"Tell Gunter and Extine I'll be back soon," McFall said to Heather, but she was already staring dully at the wall again. Ronnie followed him out of the building and across the lush, closely mown grass where the red church had once stood. The walking trail that followed the fence line to the ridge began at a picnic pavilion by the cemetery. Ronnie had helped build it; he'd even suggested that they use the modern-rustic style of construction to match the log-home appearance of the development.

"How is Melanie?" McFall asked. "I haven't eaten at the waffle shop in some time."

"She's doing well. Not showing yet or anything, but her body's changing a little. It's pretty freaky."

McFall gave him a friendly punch on the arm, much the way Bobby would have done if he were still alive. "Sweet stuff, isn't it?"

Ronnie blushed a little despite himself. It was everything he'd always fantasized about, and then some. And he enjoyed being with her so much more now that he was sure she was willing—now that she loved him.

"I'm so glad they stopped Sweeney before he could hurt her," McFall said. "That man was dangerous. He didn't play by the rules."

"Too bad about the sheriff," Ronnie said. "It sounds like he won't get jail time, but his reputation has been destroyed."

"The sheriff got what he wanted. He never really cared whether justice prevailed. All he wanted was a showdown. Like most nihilists, he's both lazy and simple. All failure did was confirm his worldview, so now he can live happily ever after, believing he was right all along. But I suspect he prefers unhappiness."

McFall walked briskly for a middle-aged man, and Ronnie struggled to keep pace. They came to a rocky ledge where the trees were stunted by the wind. Blackburn River lay below them, constantly new but always drawing from the same well. Ronnie found himself scanning the surface for misty shapes. One in particular.

"When am I going to stop seeing ghosts?" Ronnie asked.

"I hope they don't bother you anymore. I'd say they're a 'necessary evil,' but evil is never necessary."

"What about Bobby? Was *he* necessary?"

McFall looked genuinely saddened. "I loved Bobby like a son. But sometimes you have to make sacrifices for the greater good. Unless Good is just as unnecessary as Evil."

I know the difference between Good and Evil, but I believe you have them confused.

They continued on. The steepest stretch of terrain lay ahead, and it would be months yet before the main road reached here. Besides the fence and the trail, this part of the ridge was primitive and wild, the trees as twisted as witches, the boulders like jagged fangs.

"The real problem, Ronnie, is that people look for explanations," McFall said. "They look for reasons. Like why children get cancer or why cruel people succeed. I'm not religious like you are, but I can understand the appeal. It would be easier for everyone if the world was black and white."

Ronnie had to admit that it was a problem. He'd prayed about it for weeks. *Why? Why? Why?*

In the end, he hadn't received a satisfactory answer.

But maybe he hadn't asked the right person. "Why?"

McFall spread his arms to indicate the forest and sky. "These are the oldest mountains in the world, Ronnie." He stomped the dark dirt beneath his feet. "The world's oldest river starts down here, squeezing out from the bedrock. Science says two other rivers are older, but science doesn't know everything. Science doesn't believe I exist. This is where it all started. And it always comes back here, so this is where it has to end. But until then, here we are."

"So this is where Good and Evil meet?" Ronnie asked.

"This is where we do battle. As you told me the first time we met: The river's never new. It's different every second. It never repeats itself. The same goes for us through the generations. Wendell McFall—the one you know as 'The Hung Preacher'— couldn't win here. Archer McFall wanted you so badly, but he still lost. I'm the one who did it." McFall grinned with wolfish satisfaction. "I won."

"Why me?"

"Why you? Because we *can't have you*. Because, despite all evidence to the contrary, you still cling to faith. Because there's always a Day who screws things up, just when everything is almost perfect. Our family has a saying: 'I just can't wait for the final Day.' Cute, huh?"

Ronnie was breathing heavily now. McFall was right; he was much stronger from all the physical labor, but he still wanted to improve. This was going to take everything he had. He needed to strengthen his mind, and his soul, too; there was plenty of metaphysical labor left for him to endure. "If Good and Evil are indifferent, why should they do battle?"

For once, McFall seemed out of his depth, in uncharted territory. He shrugged, still walking. "It's what we do."

They were at the top of the ridge now, and McFall climbed onto a moss-dappled boulder and knelt, admiring the view.

Ronnie joined him. He hadn't been up here since they'd finished the fence. The valleys were veiled in a thin haze, the Blue Ridge Mountains rising above it all like great beasts swimming in an ocean of lost time.

"I wanted to turn this into a public park so that everyone could enjoy it, but Heather talked me out of it," McFall said. "She wants to build our home up here. With lots of glass."

"I don't blame her."

McFall gave him a gentle smile. That of a father, a brother, a lover, a savior—all rolled into one.

"This will all be yours someday," McFall said.

"I'd like that," Ronnie said. Tears filled his eyes. "Thank you."

Keep your friends close and your enemies closer.

You surrendered to them, you let them trust you, you even let them love you. You gave them what they wanted. And when your enemies grew content, they eventually grew vulnerable. And that's when you struck.

It was the game within the game.

And one day or another, one way or another, Ronnie was going to win.

ABOUT THE AUTHOR

Marie Freeman

Scott Nicholson, the bestselling author of 20 thrillers including *The Home*, *After: The Shock, Liquid Fear*, and *Disintegration*, has sold more than 500,000 eBooks worldwide in the last three years. Nicholson has been in the Kindle Top 100 with five different books in the United States, two in the United Kingdom, four in Germany, and two in France. Amazon's Thomas & Mercer thriller imprint has released his *Fear* series, and *The Home* is in development as a feature film.

His website is www.AuthorScottNicholson.com.

Kindle Serials

This book was originally released in Episodes as a Kindle Serial. Kindle Serials launched in 2012 as a new way to experience serialized books. Kindle Serials allow readers to enjoy the story as the author creates it, purchasing once and receiving all existing Episodes immediately, followed by future Episodes as they are published. To find out more about Kindle Serials and to see the current selection of Serials titles, visit www.amazon.com/kindleserials.

Made in the USA
Middletown, DE
04 August 2017